ZAGREB COWBOY

ZAGREB
COWBOY

A MARKO DELLA TORRE NOVEL

ALEN MATTICH

SPIDERLINE

This edition published in 2012 by
House of Anansi Press Inc.
110 Spadina Avenue, Suite 801
Toronto, ON, M5V 2K4
Tel. 416-363-4343
Fax 416-363-1017
www.houseofanansi.com

Distributed in Canada by
HarperCollins Canada Ltd.
1995 Markham Road
Scarborough, ON, M1B 5M8
Toll free tel. 1-800-387-0117

House of Anansi Press is committed to protecting our natural environment. As part of our efforts, the interior of this book is printed
on paper that contains 100% post-consumer recycled fibres, is acid-free,
and is processed chlorine-free.

16 15 14 13 12   1 2 3 4 5

Library and Archives Canada Cataloguing in Publication

Mattich, Alen, 1965–
Zagreb cowboy : a Marko della Torre novel / Alen Mattich.

Issued also in an electronic format.
ISBN 978-1-77089-108-1

I. Title.

PS8626.A874Z32 2012   C813'.6   C2012-902171-7

Jacket design: Alysia Shewchuk
Text design and typesetting: Alysia Shewchuk

 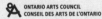

We acknowledge for their financial support of our publishing program the
Canada Council for the Arts, the Ontario Arts Council, and the Government
of Canada through the Canada Book Fund.

Printed and bound in Canada

For Lucy, with love

THE MERCEDES SALOON ran a red light, barely slowing as it turned into King Tomislav Square. The medieval warrior-king's bronze statue stood in the middle of the manicured public garden, silhouetted against a lowering purple sky. He sat high on his horse, spear raised in memory of the country's brief flowering of independence. A millennium ago. Tomislav had been somewhere in his mid-thirties, roughly Marko della Torre's age, when he'd vanished from history.

Maybe Bosnians had carted him off into the night too.

Della Torre didn't find his own joke very funny.

Apart from the big Mercedes and an occasional tram grinding its way through the still evening, Zagreb's streets were largely empty. It was the spring of 1991 and civil war was in the air. Croatia was struggling to become a separate country as Yugoslavia fragmented. Money was short, and besides, there was nowhere for anyone to go; shops and cafés shut early if they opened at all. So people stayed at home, watching the news on television and waiting. Pensioners were reminded of what it had felt like waiting for the Germans in 1940.

The atmosphere in the car was close. One of the Bosnians was driving, while della Torre was wedged between the two others in the narrow half-seat in the back. The Bosnians smelled of acrid sweat and farmyard. Wailing pop, influenced as much by the Ottomans as by ABBA, pumped out of the car's countless speakers.

Once they'd driven through the city's centre, with its long rows of elegant five- and six-storey Austro-Hungarian offices and apartment houses, they crossed the Sava on a characterless bridge where the river had been made canal-straight between high, grassed embankments.

They'd taken a funny route, heading out of town in the wrong direction and now doubling back through the new town. Zagreb's drab southern suburbs blurred past in an artificially lit, nicotine-tinted wash of concrete tower blocks.

"You sure you wouldn't like help with the navigation?" della Torre asked.

The driver muttered something incomprehensible.

"We want suggestions, we'll ask for them," said the skinny, doleful Bosnian to his left. "I didn't hear anybody asking anything."

"Maybe you could turn off the wailing and I'll spare you the advice," della Torre said. The music set his nerves on edge.

"No," said the skinny one, the only one who'd done any talking.

"Customer's always wrong, eh? In that case, you fellows wouldn't happen to have a spare cigarette?"

"Besim doesn't like smoking in the car. Says it gets into the upholstery. Cuts the value."

Besim, the driver, grunted his agreement.

"Oh." Della Torre didn't know what to say. The thought of not smoking in a car for any reason short of a leaking fuel line was astonishing enough. But for Bosnians not to smoke, Bosnians who as a rule breathed tobacco from the moment they were born? Della Torre would have been less surprised to discover Karl Marx had, in fact, been a bearded lady in a French circus.

He tried to cover his annoyance.

"So, have you guys worked with Strumbić much?"

"First time," said the tall, skinny one.

"Is that right? How'd you find each other? D'you advertise?"

"We've got friends in common."

"Like?"

"Like it's none of your business."

"Ah, don't tell me, he once arrested you for soliciting, and since then you became the best of friends," della Torre said.

"Nope."

"You do know he's a cop?"

"Course we know. Doesn't matter, does it, boys?" the skinny one said to his companions. "We handle them all the same way, cops or wiseguys like this one."

The offhand rudeness surprised della Torre. He was having a hard time figuring out what Strumbić, a detective on the Zagreb police force, was doing with these guys. But then again, Strumbić was involved in all sorts of unorthodox sidelines.

"So what sort of stuff are you doing for Strumbić?" della Torre asked. "Besides your very fine taxi service. Singalongs?" He couldn't get over how much they looked like Elvis impersonators.

"Are you being smart?" The skinny one turned to della Torre, his face for once animated.

"Take it easy," della Torre said. "It was just a joke."

"Watch what you say."

"Never mind, you're best off sticking to what you do. Whatever that is," della Torre said. "What is that, by the way?"

"We do odd jobs."

"Yes? How odd are these jobs? Any I might have heard about?"

"Maybe the one down in Slavonski Brod. Probably the one in Karlovac last month—"

"Shut up." The talkative Bosnian was cut off by the hitherto silent one to della Torre's right, a stocky, square-headed type.

Slavonski Brod didn't ring bells, but Karlovac made della Torre squirm.

There'd been a hit on a local businessman who had crossed one too many people in power. Nobody would have known anything about the killers had they not made a mess of the job the first time round. The victim had four holes in him but still managed to stay conscious till the ambulance got him away.

Two days later, witnesses described how three Bosnians had shown up at the hospital. The receptionist could tell they were Bosnians by the accent of the guy asking directions. And because they wore black pointed shoes with white socks and trousers that ended a couple of centimetres above the ankle. For some reason the local police hadn't bothered to put a guard on the businessman. Della Torre could guess why.

The Bosnians shot the businessman dead this time. And his mistress, who by a stroke of bad luck had come to make a surprise visit while the businessman's wife also happened to be at his bedside. It hadn't been a happy scene when the Bosnians got there, but it was downright ugly by the time they left. They'd emptied more than two magazines into the room.

Even so, they got away with at least a quarter of an hour to spare before the police bothered turning up. Witnesses spotted them driving off in a Zastava. Della Torre suspected their payoff might have involved an upgrade.

Come to think of it, he remembered something about a grenade thrown into a café in Slavonski Brod around the turn of the year...

"Shut up? Why do I have to shut up?" the tall one to the left said, patting della Torre's chest. "What's this?" he asked, pulling a notebook out of della Torre's inside coat pocket.

"My notebook," della Torre said, wincing. He didn't like anyone handling the book. He'd taken too many risks taking the notes he had, even if they were largely indecipherable to anyone else. "Mind if I have it back?"

The Bosnian ignored him, dropping the little black book into his own pocket.

"See, he's not tooled up. And he's not going to be telling anyone much of anything after tonight. Neither's that cop. Maybe we should charge extra, eh, boys?"

"I said shut up," said the one to della Torre's right.

"Besim, I thought you said your cousin had manners," the skinny Bosnian muttered to the driver. Besim didn't say anything.

Della Torre smiled rigidly, as though he hadn't understood. In truth he felt like he'd been slapped by a corpse. There wasn't much doubt about what the Bosnians were there for.

A sliver of rising moon flashed in and out between the highrises. Wherever they were planning on killing him, it seemed they were first going to Strumbić's, or at least they were heading in that direction.

Reflexively, della Torre reached for the side pocket of his jacket, twisting a little to free his shoulder. The Bosnian to his right jabbed his arm back. It didn't matter. Della Torre didn't have any cigarettes on him anyway. He was sure there was a last packet of Camels somewhere in the apartment. He'd looked for it under the piles of papers on his kitchen table. But maybe it was skulking in the laundry basket. Keeping his gun company.

What he would have done for a smoke right then. And the Beretta.

He ran his hand over his top lip, smoothing his moustache, as he did when he was feeling tense. His thoughts flitted around, trying to stitch together what was going on.

It was hard to credit now, but he'd almost laughed when he first saw the Bosnians. They'd arrived early. They pressed the buzzer and then kept pressing it. Della Torre's intercom no longer worked; it hadn't done for a long time. He'd been tempted to throw a window open and shout down to the street to tell them to knock it off, but the catch stuck and he didn't want to risk not being able to shut it again. It was a mild spring day, but mild spring days in Zagreb had a habit of turning sullen. As it was he could only afford to heat a couple of rooms in the flat. A window blown open would have meant sleeping in his overcoat.

So he hurried out, taking two stairs at a time. The maddening bell was still echoing down the high stone stairwell when he got to the entrance hall. Glass shards crunched underfoot. The window in the heavy wooden front door had been smashed again. He was starting to think it wasn't accidental. Luckily the ironwork grille had held.

His irritation had melted into bemusement when he stepped onto the pavement. The Bosnians were caricatures of country boys come to the big city from the deep black valleys a long drive to the south. Their suit trousers were too short, exposing lengths of white sock ending in brothel creepers at least thirty years out of fashion. Their vinyl jackets were the roadkill equivalent of imitation cowhide. He was sure they Brylcreemed their hair.

But the bulges under their arms had made him bite his tongue. It seldom paid to laugh at people with guns. Even ones who looked like an Elvis tribute band.

Am I the only secret policeman in the world stupid enough to forget his own service pistol when every yokel in the country's armed these days? della Torre thought.

Not that it would have helped. They'd quickly frisked him as he got into the car. It was a clue he wasn't dealing with an ordinary taxi service. Though it took the conversation for him to figure out what they were really there for.

Della Torre shook his head imperceptibly. *He hired farm boys to butcher me like some smallholder's hog.*

He couldn't understand it. What did Strumbić have against him? Why had Strumbić set him up, especially if he was going to come out of this just as badly? It sounded like he was being double-crossed. But you could never take anything for granted with Strumbić. It took some skill to be as corrupt as he was and to grow as rich without ever having met a bullet or a jail cell.

Maybe if I'd smoked less. If della Torre hadn't been paid in nearly worthless currency, he wouldn't have had to spend most of his salary on American cigarettes. If he hadn't needed the money, he wouldn't have taken the risk of becoming involved in one of Strumbić's little sidelines. If he hadn't grown used to doing deals with Strumbić, he wouldn't have so readily accepted the ride with the Bosnians. If he hadn't got into the car with the Bosnians, he wouldn't now be on a fast road to a shallow grave. If...

Della Torre's wife — ex-wife — used to tell him he wouldn't make it past middle age the way he carried on, that he'd be spending his late forties or early fifties watching paint peel off the walls in some chronic hospital ward. She was wrong. The way things were working out, he'd never even make it to lung cancer.

Cigarettes. American cigarettes and amateur killers.

Funny to think he'd liked Strumbić. They'd almost been friends. He'd liked Strumbić's roguishness and conviviality. In retrospect, he'd probably liked Strumbić's money too much.

Once through the suburbs, Besim the driver took the motorway west. He turned off where the Zagreb river plain rucked into the steep Zagore hills, and wound his way through a small town called Samobor.

Della Torre had always been fond of the place, with its Baroque church and late medieval wooden houses jutting over a small river. It was close enough for short excursions out of the city, but still had plenty of provincial charm. In spring and summer it was vibrant with flower boxes and pretty country girls. In the winter, snow clung to Samobor's narrow streets and broad square long after it had turned into sludge in Zagreb.

But on a Sunday evening in March, the town didn't hold many attractions for a condemned man. Della Torre felt an unfamiliar jab of compassion as they passed a heroic statue of a soldier toting a machine gun. It reminded him of the German sympathizers the partisans had hung in Samobor's main square at the end of the Second World War.

Besim managed to get through the narrow streets after four wrong turns and two near misses. He even reversed out of a dead end at rally speeds. And the pace didn't slacken once they'd climbed the hill that rose like the back of a chair behind the town.

Once beyond Samobor's faint night glow, the Bosnian followed a narrow, roughly made road along a wooded ridge, neither nightfall nor tight bends convincing him to slow down. At the pace they were going, they'd be at Strumbić's in little more than ten minutes.

The atmosphere in the car was choking. Della Torre moved to unknot his tie. Force of habit made him dress professionally whenever work called, but he figured he didn't need to be wearing one to get shot.

The Bosnian to his right glowered and dug him in the ribs with his elbow.

"Just taking my tie off. I'm getting a bit hot. It's not a formal occasion we're going to, is it?"

The Bosnian shrugged.

Della Torre felt the silk. A nice tie. It had been given to him on a job in Rome. The Italian police had kept him locked up for four days on suspicion of... they'd never said, not in so many words. It all sorted itself out in the end, and the arresting officer, in contrition, had given him the tie. A spare, he'd said. The Italian cop had probably been glad to be rid of it, but it was della Torre's favourite — dark blue silk with a pattern of even darker blue foliage. All his others were a shiny socialist polyester. He slipped the tie through his fingers like worry beads.

The Mercedes's headlights swept across fields and small vineyards carved out of the hillside forest. The beams bounced around as the car twisted along the bumpy road. The reflection of a village boundary sign flashed up. In a few hundred metres they'd round sharply to the right as the road followed a gully carved out by a little stream, and then just beyond that was the turning to Strumbić's weekend house.

It was dark in the car, except for the blue, red, and green glows coming off the dashboard indicators.

Tension had been building in della Torre's muscles. The Bosnians next to him could feel it. They shifted away from him. They watched him. The blood had drained from his face and the insouciant air he tried to put on just made him look like he'd swallowed his own sick. He felt the sweat rolling down his chest. His shirt was sodden. His nerves resonated like the strings of a piano dropped down the stairs.

Later della Torre couldn't remember making any conscious decision or forming a plan. It could have been that stress had switched on his long-forgotten military training. But he couldn't be sure.

Some unconscious reflex made him jerk forward, loop the tie over the Bosnian driver's head, and pull back. But if della Torre had intended to garrotte him, he'd missed. He only just managed to get the dark blue Italian silk under the driver's nose.

DELLA TORRE FELT the car grind over loose gravel and hit a little ramp or ridge, maybe a narrow verge of grass. For an instant he felt weightless.

The car was airborne. It had come off the edge of the road and was heading into the gully. A tree stopped it, just short of the stream. Somehow the tree remained upright, though the rending crack of a rupture deep through its heart echoed the explosion of crushed metal.

The two Bosnians sitting next to della Torre reacted a fraction too slowly.

It was a spacious car, but even so, three grown men didn't leave a lot of wiggle room in the back. Della Torre was taller than either of the Bosnians and his shoulders pressed against theirs so that when he sprang forward, they naturally twisted away and had to turn again to face him. The one to his right, Besim's cousin, reached for his gun while the skinny, talkative one tried to knock into della Torre's arms. But della Torre kept a tight grip on the tie, and the struggle merely whipped the driver's head around.

Della Torre felt the talkative Bosnian slam into his side with the impact of the crash. His ribs felt like they'd been tapped by a sledgehammer. His left knee pounded painfully into the back of the driver's seat. For a moment he felt as if the seat belt, a proper three-pointer, was quartering him in some modern approximation of a medieval instrument of death.

The Bosnians had looked at him with suspicion when he'd buckled up. Wearing seat belts was an idiosyncrasy left over from his American childhood. No proper Yugoslav ever used them.

"Those things are for fairies," the skinny one to his left had said.

"What?"

"Seat belts. Besim's the best driver. Could be professional. He's better than Senna even. See that, Besim? He's going to wet himself. Drive carefully. We don't want our guest to ruin the seats."

They probably thought differently now. Assuming they could still think.

Besim's cousin had gone clear over the front seat, through the windscreen, and was now in the stream, picked out by the Merc's sole working headlight. He might have been swimming, but unless he was competing for an underwater endurance record, there was a fair chance he was dead. The skinny Bosnian was no longer so talkative; in fact, he wasn't saying anything at all. He was crushed up against the back of the driver's seat, wedged against the doorpost. He didn't so much moan as let out a series of staccato grunts. An airbag, a real novelty for della Torre and probably for the driver too, had prevented Besim from joining his cousin in the water or impaling himself in the trunk of the tree. He didn't seem to be moving, but della Torre wasn't sure he was dead either. He didn't really care.

He unbuckled the belt and took a moment to get a sense of whether he'd crushed his liver or burst his spleen or had suffered any of the other myriad of ugly wounds car wrecks routinely inflicted. But other than a generalized soreness, della Torre felt that whatever ailed him was survivable.

He fished his notebook out of the talkative Bosnian's pocket and then reached inside the man's coat. He was still breathing, but della Torre wasn't checking his vitals. He found a Beretta, nine millimetre. Just like the one della Torre had left at home. He popped it into his coat pocket along with the precious silk tie and tugged on the door handle on the side where Besim's cousin had sat. It wouldn't open. He struggled with it for a while and then remembered the automatic lock. Randomly pressing buttons and knobs by the driver, he started up the rear wipers, rotated a wing mirror, and switched off the radio. He'd resigned himself to crawling out through the missing windscreen when he heard the clunk of four bolts.

He turned the key in the ignition to stop the engine whining, switched off the headlight, and then gingerly opened the door. It was a drop getting out of the car, and his knee complained. It complained again as he scrambled up the ravine's steep slope.

The front of the car was completely smashed. Even in his dazed state he marvelled at the German craftsmanship. They must have gone from eighty kilometres an hour to zero in the space of the tree, and yet the Merc's electronics still functioned. The only things that worked as they were supposed to when the Yugo he owned had rolled off the assembly line were the wheels. And that, della Torre figured, was down to pure chance.

Della Torre let the relief of being alive wash over him; he'd always had luck in his misfortune. The Benz was wedged between the tree and the rocky incline. They could have crashed the car a hundred times, and ninety-nine would have resulted in an end-over-end roll or some other metallic gymnastics that would have left them all looking like off-cuts in an abattoir. Never mind avoiding a bullet in the back of the neck.

He sat on a lonely stone bollard marking the edge of the road and considered what to do. He could walk back to Samobor. But his knee hurt, and hobbling back would take most of the night, by which time Strumbić might well find him and finish the job. He could wait for a passing car and get a lift. But there wasn't much traffic up here. The village beyond Strumbić's couldn't have more than thirty houses. He didn't feel like knocking on doors, and people in the countryside were wary of strangers appearing out of nowhere at night. If he told them about the accident, they'd call the police, and police meant being in Strumbić's hands before long.

So della Torre was left with just one other option. An amble into the lion's den. At least Strumbić's wasn't far, no more than five hundred metres along the road and then another hundred or so down a track through the woods.

The going wasn't bad to start with; there was just enough moonlight to navigate by. But before long it was as miserable and painful a walk as he could remember since his army days. His knee was swollen tight in his trousers and breathing made his ribs hurt. The occasional stumble over exposed roots didn't make him feel any better either. By the time he got to the gate where the forest track opened out onto a clearing, he was doing a geriatric shuffle.

The moonlight etched the scene like a woodcut. The meadow was carved out of the steep forest hillside, though halfway up it flattened like a step, just wide enough to give Strumbić's cottage a level base. The people who lived in the villages in these hills were still poor. There were plenty of families of della Torre's generation with a dozen or more children who'd grown up in two-room houses, hovels really, in much the same way Tito had at the turn of the previous century. But now rich people from the city were coming in and buying up property and building cottages in the hills, weekend retreats not much more than an hour's drive from their town-centre apartments. Some were newcomers, but many had roots in these impoverished and beautiful valleys, coming back for rural nostalgia after they'd made good in Zagreb through intelligence or hard work or crooked deals. Or all three. Like Strumbić.

Strumbić was a senior detective in Zagreb's regular police force who set new standards for venal dishonesty in an organization notorious for being on the take. Not that he'd ever been caught.

Della Torre worked for Department VI, the UDBA's internal investigative service. He was a lawyer, primarily responsible for investigating extrajudicial killings the intelligence service might have been involved in. The special unit had been set up five years previously when the country's parliamentarians started to realize that the secret police weren't always acting on behalf of the State. Sometimes, it did so for the private interests of the most powerful members of the country's cumbersome rotating presidency—a particularly complicated Yugoslav compromise to ensure that each of the country's six republics and two autonomous regions felt they had equal say in its running. What this really did was create a coterie of shadowy politicians with considerable power.

It was how della Torre justified working for the UDBA. To himself at least. He'd say to himself Department VI wasn't really UDBA. Sure, it sat under the umbrella of the organization, but Department VI people were the good guys. They were the only internal check on the organization's concentration camp guards, on its torturers, its killers, because in truth the UDBA was Yugoslavia's equivalent of the KGB. The Stasi. The Gestapo.

For much of the time della Torre had worked for the organization, Strumbić had been his instrument. He'd used Strumbić to help him hook crooked UDBA officers. In exchange, Strumbić got a measure of protection from the law for his sidelines and also received the occasional whisper about a leading politician, judge, or businessman. Their relative positions were clear. Della Torre held the power. Strumbić did the legwork.

But then Yugoslavia started falling apart. While the UDBA continued to be feared, its strength waned in Croatia and Slovenia, the two republics seeking independence. The UDBA's main seat of power had always been Belgrade, capital of both the country and its biggest republic, Serbia. Department VI was headquartered in Zagreb as a way of silencing complaints within Croatia of the UDBA's heavily Serb identity. Which meant della Torre's authority quickly evaporated.

So the relative roles of the secret policeman and the Zagreb detective had changed, subtly but inexorably. Strumbić was no longer della Torre's supplicant; rather it was the other way round. Now, instead of swapping crumbs of information and doing della Torre's digging, Strumbić was paying money for more valuable nuggets than ever before. Not just the rumour of a judge's mistress, but photographs of them in bed. Not a whisper that a prosecutor was suspected of shady deals, but photocopies of foreign bank statements. Not the hint that a businessman had been compromised by taking drugs with prostitutes, but the times and dates and names. And more besides.

Strumbić never mentioned what he did with the information della Torre passed on, and della Torre never asked. All he knew was that Strumbić paid in cash. Deutschmarks.

And he needed the cash. In the space of little more than a year della Torre and his colleagues had gone from being among the country's best-paid civil servants to making less than ditch-diggers. Della Torre's official monthly salary now barely covered the cost of a carton of cigarettes as rampant inflation destroyed his paycheque while Belgrade and Zagreb squabbled about whose responsibility it was to fund Department VI.

Strumbić was never one to let a golden commercial opportunity pass him by. He had money. A lot. And most of it in Deutschmarks or dollars.

He knew della Torre had access to secret files, interesting and lucrative ones. And so della Torre would make the trip out to Strumbić's weekend place every couple of months to trade.

Strumbić had around twenty rows of vines, along with fruit trees, mostly plums and pears, which he picked in the summer, fermented, and then cooked into a potent spirit alcohol. And then there was the ancient cherry tree that turned the ground purple with its juice in August.

The house itself was built on top of an old wine hut. The thick and roughly made concrete-and-stone walls now formed a self-contained ground-level cellar, where Strumbić matured the wine he made from his own grapes, distilled his spirits, and hung cured hams and salamis that he bought from the local villagers. Above the cellar was the house he'd built, one full storey under a steeply pitched roof. In all there was a large sitting room and balcony that looked out over the valley, a kitchen, a bathroom, and two bedrooms, one of which Strumbić used as an office.

But mostly when he was there, Strumbić sat in the cellar or at a rickety table by the side of the house under the huge cherry tree's canopy. It was an idyll. Della Torre always looked forward to his invitations. Strumbić was liberal with the booze and American cigarettes and was a fount of amusing stories.

Mornings after Strumbić's were another thing entirely. More than once della Torre had woken in his car by the side of the little road to Samobor, the early sun converting him to Christianity with the force of a seventh-century bishop. Never had he prayed harder than when begging God to save him from those hangovers.

The gate was open. Della Torre could see Strumbić's BMW coupe parked in its little barn. There was enough space in front for a couple more vehicles, but Strumbić didn't seem to have company. Della Torre picked his way along a stony path gently traversing the hillside. There were some lights on in the main part of the house, but the glow in front of the wine cellar told him Strumbić would be down there.

Della Torre approached carefully. A radio played europop and he could smell Strumbić's cigarette. His footsteps crunched on loose stones.

Strumbić was inside, sitting on a folding lawn chair. Gun on his lap.

3

THE CIGARETTE IN one hand and a tumbler of wine in the other made Strumbić slow to reach for the gun.

Della Torre shook his head.

Strumbić cocked an eyebrow and then gave him a broad smile. "Ah, Gringo, what a nice surprise."

"Do me a favour, Julius, and knock that paperweight off your lap and then nudge it away with your foot," della Torre said. Strumbić let the gun slide onto the floor and gently lowered his drink so that his hands were free and visible to della Torre.

"I'm guessing that's not sausage for me in your pocket."

"You'd be guessing right."

"Not usually a man for carrying his gun. World must be changing."

"Oh, not that much. I borrowed this one," della Torre said.

"You look like you've been in the wars. Like you could do with a glass of something."

"Thanks. I'll help myself."

"I didn't hear the car. What happened to the other fellows?"

"They decided they'd rather drop me off. They seemed a little distracted when I left them. Something about the Merc's engine being in the back seat and a tree growing out of the bonnet."

"I see. Well, can't be helped. Shame about the motor, though. Rather nice piece of Germany." Strumbić moved to get out of his chair.

"Listen, Strumbić, I know you won't take it the wrong way, but would you mind terribly if you just sat there for a while? In fact, I'll tell you what. My nerves are a bit on edge. Probably comes from spending too much time with Bosnians who want to kill me. Would you be a sport and put the wine down and stick the cigarette in your mouth and pop your hands on top of your head. Only for as long as it takes me to find those handcuffs you always keep around."

"You want to make it interesting, let me get my girlfriend to come over. The things she does with handcuffs." Strumbić gave him one of those winking leers he always used when telling dirty stories.

"Or Mrs. Strumbić."

"You know how to hit a man where it hurts."

"You're hard on the poor woman," della Torre said, not really meaning it. She was a shrew with a cat's ass of a mouth. He'd met her only a couple of times, but that was enough.

"What I have to put up with, Christ, you don't know the half of it."

"So where are the cuffs?"

"In the jacket, on the table. Don't worry, you can come in. I won't jump a man with a gun in his pocket," Strumbić said.

Della Torre was getting chilly standing by the door. He sidled into the cellar, kicking Strumbić's gun across the floor, the movement making him wince with pain as he put his weight on his sore knee. He reached into the cop's jacket, where he found the cuffs. He threw them onto Strumbić's lap.

"It's been a while since I last had occasion to use any of these. Would you mind slowly getting them with your left hand, popping a cuff onto your right wrist, and then putting your hands back on your head."

"Sure, what are friends for?" With a practised hand, Strumbić clicked the cuff onto his wrist.

Della Torre edged around Strumbić, pulled the cuffed right arm behind his back, and then the left, and then tightened the cuffs to his satisfaction, pocketing the key.

"You couldn't get the cig out of my mouth, could you? I don't want it dropping on my lap. New American jeans."

Della Torre took the cigarette out of Strumbić's mouth and took a long drag. Lucky Strike.

Now that he had Strumbić secured, he relaxed a bit, sitting on a wooden stool by the little table. The table was covered in a blue gingham waxed cotton cloth that spoke of a history of spilled drinks, dripped wax, dropped cigarettes, and bread and ham cut a little too hard. The cellar was more than five metres wide on each side. It had a packed dirt floor and the sour smell of old wine, blended with tobacco and cured meat. The walls were rough, with horizontal stripes where the concrete had bulged between the planked frame when it was poured. There were three big wooden barrels on their sides, the newest one yellow, the other two blackened with age, all raised off the ground on wooden cradles. A Pirelli calendar hung on one wall, showing an exotic topless girl leaning back against an exotic topless car, but otherwise it was undecorated. A single unshaded bulb hung towards the front of the room.

Della Torre kept his eyes on Strumbić. They were around the same age. Maybe Strumbić was a couple of years older. He couldn't have been more than forty, but it was hard to tell from just looking at him. He looked old enough to be della Torre's own father. Strumbić had the flabby, doughy face of a man who lived hard. He smoked heavily and drank constantly. He enjoyed his work, thriving on the adrenaline of both the legal and illicit stuff he did on the side. But you could see it also wore away at him. And then there were the women.

He'd been married for twenty years to a fierce, hard, un-yielding harpy. She could never have been remotely attractive. But she'd also been the only daughter of Zagreb's chief of po-lice when her eye settled on Strumbić, a young cadet straight out of military service with a streak of primitive but cavalier charm and an instinct for his own best advantage.

Her father, himself a self-made peasant and Partizan during the war, was opposed to the match. He thought she could do better and made every effort to frighten Strumbić off. It might have worked had his daughter not had twice the will of both men put together. Whatever either man thought of the matter, she got her way.

Strumbić may not have had a university education, but he was canny enough to marry well. For her part, his wife drove him relentlessly through the police hierarchy. Maybe she'd seen something of her father in him.

Her saving grace, as far as Strumbić was concerned, was that she understood what it meant to be a cop—the strange hours and frequent silences—which allowed Strumbić plenty of op-portunity to indulge his sybaritic tastes. He was discreet. But she wasn't all bad. She made delicious cherry strudels.

Strumbić's girlfriends, on the other hand…Della Torre couldn't think of them without shaking his head. Pneumatic, lewd, tacky, and dumb. And undoubtedly damn good at what-ever Strumbić wanted from them.

"So…?" Strumbić asked.

"I'm thinking. I don't suppose you'd be wanting to answer any questions?"

"Sure, why not?"

"And incriminate yourself?"

"Incriminate? You're starting to sound like a lawyer, Gringo. Trust me, this is not a case that's going to court."

Della Torre knew he had a point. Strumbić's cash had pull with prosecutors and judges and plenty of his bosses besides.

What's more, if he brought Strumbić in, della Torre would also have to explain his little document-selling sideline. Bad as it might be for Strumbić to have been buying the files, it would have been worse for della Torre. Yugoslav courts took a dim view of UDBA agents selling secrets, especially when they included foreign bank records of leading prosecutors. Or surveillance photographs of minor politicians snorting drugs. Or judges in bed with their mistresses.

"It's not just about the files, Julius. It's about those men you hired to kill me."

"Don't be ridiculous."

"You set me up to have those Bosnian hicks kill me."

"Don't be so dramatic. I merely facilitated them offering you a ride. Which is all they said they wanted to do with you."

"That doesn't wash," della Torre said.

"Calm down. What are you going to do? Shoot me? You're not the kind," Strumbić said, giving della Torre his Cheshire cat's grin. He was a cool one.

"Julius, who were those guys?"

"How the hell do I know? Farmers who think they're Elvis."

"You're the one who sent them to pick me up, to bring me here. Remember?"

Strumbić shrugged.

Della Torre had been finishing a bite of supper in his narrow kitchen when the phone rang. He was on his last cigarette. Somewhere, he had a packet left from the stack of imported cartons he'd bought off a friend coming back from Austria, but hadn't been able to find it. *It'll be back to the local lung-rot tomorrow.*

"Hey, Gringo, it's Julius." The only people who called him Marko were his family and his ex-wife. Otherwise it was della Torre or Gringo, a nickname he'd always loathed but couldn't shed.

"Yes?" Della Torre was wary on the phone.

Life in Communist Yugoslavia was full of awkward compromises and hedged conversations. Especially when someone else could be listening in.

"Listen, Gringo, I've got a job that might interest you. It shouldn't take much time. And I'll make it worth your while."

"I'm listening."

"Not really something I can talk to you about over the phone, if you know what I mean," Strumbić had said.

"When do you want to meet up, then?"

"Well, if you don't mind, I've sent round a couple of boys to pick you up. They'll bring you over to my weekend house. We can discuss it here."

"At this time of evening?"

"Like I said, I'll make it worth your while. We'll be able to finish up tonight, and there's the small matter of four thousand Deutschmarks." He was being indiscreet, but the bait worked.

Della Torre whistled.

"Nice, eh? Only I need you here. I sent the boys off already; they'll arrive to pick you up in half an hour, tops." Strumbić wasn't asking any longer. He was telling.

"Your people?"

"Cops, you mean?" asked Strumbić.

"Yes."

"No. These guys are just muscle, they don't have anything to do with anyone. Best that way."

"Muscle? What do we need muscle for?" The only extra-curricular work that interested Della Torre was trading information.

"We don't. They happen to be around. I'm using them for some other stuff. And right now I'm using them to get you here."

"A delivery service."

"Something like that. I told them to buzz and you'll be down straight away. Don't disappoint me."

"Do I need to bring anything?"

"No, just your happy, smiling face," Strumbić said. "I'll see you in around an hour and a half and they'll bring you back home before midnight, so you don't have to worry about turning into a pumpkin. I promise."

Those alarm bells that people living in Communist countries spent their lives cultivating, plus the bigger ones lawyers and secret policemen got with their diplomas and their badges, should have been sounding for della Torre—if they hadn't been muffled by money.

4

"**YOU WEREN'T REALLY** expecting me to come back here, were you?" della Torre asked. "That's why you looked surprised when you saw me. What'd you think? That those guys would take me to Belgrade, where somebody would rip my toenails out or break my knees? Or did you think they'd just pop me one on the street when I came down?"

"Gringo, you take these things too personally. How the hell do I know what they wanted to do with you?"

"Maybe because you set me up."

"I didn't set you up. What happened was these guys wanted to talk to you and I . . . I arranged an introduction. That's it."

"Is that why you were sitting here with a gun on your lap? You knew they'd be back for you."

"Thought crossed my mind."

"D'you really think you'd be able to fight them off with that?" Della Torre pointed at Strumbić's handgun with the toe of his shoe.

"Gringo —"

"Julius, please just answer my questions."

"Okay. Look, I thought they might be a little crooked so I was playing it safe. It's one of my failings. To be suspicious. So

I figured if they came back I might take a little walk in the woods and then call some of my colleagues from the village."

It wouldn't have taken Strumbić long to disappear in the forest. He could have made it to the village on the valley floor in a quarter of an hour with the aid of a small flashlight. Any stranger following him ran the risk of missing the path and falling into one of the hill's steep gullies, breaking a leg or a neck.

"So you'd have had the terrorist squad bottle them up here on the hill and then pick them off."

"You've got to have contingencies," Strumbić said apologetically.

"Nice. You'd figured out how to double-cross them just as they were double-crossing you."

"Only if they came back to bother me." Strumbić shrugged. "It came to me that those Bosnian boys might have wanted to tidy things up a little. It'd have saved them some money, and what could be neater than making it look like you and I had shot each other? I mean, if that's what they were looking to do. Which I doubt. Like I say, I'm sure they only wanted to talk to you. But if they didn't, well, Zagreb cops and the UDBA have never been the best of friends." He paused, giving della Torre a cringe-making smile. "Us excepted."

"Makes me well up to think of what a good friend you've been," della Torre said, deadpan. "So why'd you do it?"

Strumbić looked pained.

"Why'd you set me up? What was in it for you?" della Torre pressed.

"Why do you think I did it? To gain personal advantage? Why do you always think the worst of people?" Strumbić said, his expression showing deep hurt.

"Because that's what you're like, Julius. How much did you sell me for?"

"Gringo, really, it was never about the money. I swear on my grandmother's grave."

"Your grandmother was alive last I heard, and if I remember

right you don't care much for her. How much?"

"I can honestly say that I did not do it for money. I did it because I had no choice. It was me or you. Probably would have been both me and you. I figured this way at least one of us would have been okay. Just by accident that happened to be me."

"Spill."

"The money was incidental."

"Julius, will you just give me a straight answer before I decide to shoot you out of frustration and malice?"

"Fifteen thou, give or take."

"Dinars?" Della Torre was puzzled. Like most people he still thought in terms of the old dinars, before they knocked four zeros off the bank notes to pretend the currency wasn't becoming worthless by the day. Fifteen thousand wouldn't have bought a loaf of bread. On the other hand, fifteen thousand new ones — well, that was real money. For at least a week or two, anyway.

"Dinars? Who talks dinars these days unless you're buying a newspaper or a packet of sweets? Deutschmarks."

Della Torre nodded. That was a decent-sized price on his head. He worked it into dollars — about ten thousand as near as he could make it.

"Who wants to pay fifteen thou to kill me? Put a bum in an old Yugo and they could have run me over for the price of a bottle of booze."

"Gringo, don't sell yourself so cheaply. I wouldn't have taken a penny less. I value you too much."

"Thanks."

Della Torre picked up the pack of Strumbić's Luckys and lit himself another cigarette.

"Help yourself," Strumbić said. Della Torre ignored him.

"So what happened? Why'd those yokels want me dead? And what I don't want to hear from you is 'I don't know' or 'Because your name came up on a list.'"

"Like I'm going to be smart with a man who's got a gun in his pocket. It is a gun, isn't it?"

"No. It's an Italian silk tie."

"I've got a dozen of those. Can't wear them around the office, though. People start asking where the hell I can afford silk ties from. Which is also why I've got to drive that VW of mine around town." Strumbić, in fact, had two VW Golfs, exactly the same colour blue and with sequential licence plates. One was always hidden in his Zagreb garage so that his neighbours wouldn't snitch. The amount of effort Strumbić devoted to hiding his wealth kept della Torre entertained.

"Nice Golf. I can't afford one."

"Course you can't. Still, I'd rather get more use out of the Beemer. Now that's class. Problem is, too many people get jealous when they see you with nice things—cars, watches, girls. Then they start making trouble. And that's just the wife." Strumbić laughed at his own joke.

"Julius—"

"Okay. Okay. I know you're tense; I'm just trying to lighten the atmosphere a little. It's like this. I'm up here for the weekend minding my own business, and these three Bosnians come driving up in this big brand-new Mercedes with fifteen thousand little storm troopers in an envelope wanting to set up a surprise meeting with you. Who am I to say no?"

"Julius. I'm not playing this game. I'm too tired to play this game. I'm going to shoot you in the kneecaps. First one and then the other if you don't tell me what's going on."

"Fine. That's fine, Gringo. But let's just establish the ground rules first."

"Ground rules? You're sitting in a chair with a pair of handcuffs behind your back. I've got a gun that wants to be used. You've just set a bunch of killers on me. What the hell sort of ground rules do you have in mind?" Della Torre was finding it hard to keep control of himself.

"I understand your unhappiness with the situation, Gringo, really."

"Unhappiness? What the hell —"

"Yelling won't do either of us any good."

Della Torre hung his head for a moment, holding it with his right hand.

"Julius —"

"All I want to say is if you want honest answers you have to promise me something."

"What?" della Torre asked through gritted teeth.

"That at the end of this inquisition you do not seek to exact revenge. That we part company with fond memories of a long friendship, for the most part a mutually advantageous friendship."

"I'll tell you what, Julius. If you give me an honest account, I won't shoot you. I may just lock you in this cellar for a little while, until I can make sure you're not lying. When the time comes, I will call your wife and get her to get you out."

"That's harsh, Gringo. I don't deserve that."

"I'm petty that way."

"Okay. Doesn't matter anyway. My girlfriend will probably come looking for me first. I hope. But if I'm really lucky I'll get to wait until the end of the week, when the guy comes to check the vines. He's got a key. Hey, I've got at least four hundred litres of wine and about three pigs hanging off the ceiling. If you bring down a carton of smokes and a loaf of bread from the house, I'll be all set. There's some cushions back there for the benches. I've had worse beds. I've got a couple of westerns down here and the radio. What more could a man want? Be a proper holiday, it will. I've been needing some time off."

Della Torre marvelled at how Strumbić could keep his cool. Yet there was an edge to his insouciance, della Torre could feel it.

"So we've got a deal? No revenge?"

"We've got a deal, Julius. Now, for the love of God, spill."

5

JULIUS STRUMBIĆ WAS supposed to have gone home for lunch on the Wednesday afternoon, but he couldn't face his wife. The day before, she'd found a packet of condoms in the pocket of his uniform trousers and had given him grief all night.

Mr. and Mrs. Strumbić had no need for them. They'd never been able to conceive, and they'd long since given up trying. So on finding the condoms she'd immediately thought the worst of her husband. He'd been put on the spot. He'd come home too soon after a bottle of wine and wasn't thinking clearly. He'd told her it was for some undercover work. He should have said they used them to keep their gun barrels dry when working in the field. She'd have understood that.

No, he should have told her the truth. That they belonged to a prostitute. He could have left it at that. Implied he'd arrested her and merely pocketed the rubbers as evidence or something. It wasn't like he ever used the things.

So he went out for lunch on his own, tired from a long night of being harassed. Even when he went to sleep on the sofa, she followed him to make sure he got an earful. She was there when he woke, sitting and staring with those slitted Slavic eyes that made her look like a wolf, starting up again

30

from the exact point when she'd finally let him fall asleep.

He went to a place around the corner from the railway station. It was one of the few remaining restaurants in this part of town that didn't just serve meat on a stick. He was halfway through his boiled potatoes and schnitzel, tough grey meat under greasy breadcrumbs, when the two men came in. They ignored the waiter and the empty tables and headed straight for him.

"There's somebody who'd like a word with you," said the taller, skinny one. He had a Bosnian accent. The other one was shorter, square-built, once muscular but now with some extra weight on his frame. They both had slicked-back hair and pointy shoes. The look might have been retro, except Strumbić had a feeling their style was a hangover from the first time round. Whoever they were, they looked the sort who made sure the opposition limped off the pitch when they played a friendly game of football.

"He can make an appointment with my booking sergeant. I might be free next month. Of course, if you two were to start sucking each other off in here, I'd make sure you had an interview a lot quicker than that. I'm working vice this month." He had to put some effort into cutting the veal. Maybe it was just the blunt knife.

"Heh. Hear that, Besim. The man made a joke," said the skinny one to his companion. He turned back to Strumbić. "You probably don't understand. This is a friendly invitation. We do unfriendly ones too." The man smiled as if it cost him money.

Strumbić put his cutlery down and looked at them. They might have been regular hoods. Or they could have belonged to one of the security services. The UDBA often employed criminals, though sometimes it was hard to tell them apart from the secret policemen.

They didn't show any ID, though that could have meant something or nothing. The secret police didn't always feel the need to introduce themselves formally. On the other hand, they weren't dragging him out of bed at three o'clock in the morning, so it probably wasn't official and might not have been unfriendly.

"I guess you know what the proper channels are if you want a formal conversation."

"Just a chat. And not with us. There's somebody else who wants a word with you. It's not far. It won't take you long."

Strumbić thought about it. These guys were too much like hicks to be secret police. But you could never be certain. If it was the security services and he made their lives difficult, they'd just try to kick his ass that much harder with their steel-capped boots. But that depended. The Croatian government might not allow them to kick his ass. On the other hand, if they were coming from Belgrade, they might not be inclined to ask the Croatian government if they could speak with him. After all, there wasn't a lot of love or co-operation between the federal institutions and the Croatian government these days.

Still, whoever they were, they'd found him. Not that it would have been hard. They could have followed him from the police headquarters. They could have had an informant. This was Yugoslavia, after all. There were always snitches.

Strumbić weighed the probabilities. Criminal or operating on behalf of Belgrade? Maybe it was a setup. No. If it was a setup, they'd have pulled up next to him and bundled a rug over his head and thrown him into the boot. If they didn't shoot him instead. Or they'd have taped a grenade to his car's chassis, tying the pin to the wheel so that it went off when he drove away.

Things were uncertain enough in those days that it was worth cultivating friends everywhere. And if these guys weren't the friendliest, at least they were polite. Who knew what would happen in the coming months. Favours granted now could be called in during more difficult times.

"If I was to go talk to this friend of yours, I'd be making life easier for you and less pleasant for myself. For instance, it would mean not finishing this very fine meal or this excellent beer." Strumbić lay on a doleful expression, ignoring the piece of gristle in the middle of his plate.

"I'm sure our friend will make it worth your while."

"I'd like to think so," Strumbić said. Curiosity was getting the better of him. He figured he didn't have much to lose other than the rest of the schnitzel. And it hadn't been much of a schnitzel in the first place.

They didn't drive far in the big Mercedes limousine, a model so recent he'd never seen one before. They stopped in the old town, near the cathedral. What few good restaurants and bars Zagreb still had were concentrated there. Had he been less lazy, Strumbić would have gone to one of them for lunch. But the weather was grim; it couldn't decide whether to rain or snow.

They parked on a mostly pedestrianized street and went into one of the eighteenth-century village-style houses that remained in this corner of town. The driver, Besim, held the door open for him, but neither Bosnian followed him in.

The Metusalem Restaurant was empty and gloomy in the late winter light. A dim yellow lamp cast shaded light in a corner of the room, which was furnished largely in dark-stained wood, and showed a small old man sitting alone with his back to the wall. A waiter appeared from nowhere and led Strumbić to the table, where he pulled a chair out for him.

"Please, order yourself a drink," said the old man. His voice was light and friendly. Strumbić asked for a Karlovačka beer.

"Thank you for allowing yourself to be dragged away from your lunch," said the old man. "I think you'll agree that an informal conversation right now is so much more pleasant and rewarding than having to do this another way."

The waiter brought Strumbić's beer in a glass and then left.

The old man was drinking Coca-Cola. He looked oddly familiar, though Strumbić couldn't tell why.

"If you don't mind, I won't introduce myself. It doesn't really matter who I am; I'm just an intermediary. In fact, I'm retired. You can say I'm doing a favour for some friends."

"Some friends in Belgrade?" Strumbić asked.

"Friends whose interest is to ensure the stability of the Yugoslav state, the homeland for which we fought so bitterly during the war against the fascists and for which we have struggled in the decades since."

An old Communist, Strumbić thought. *An old, well-connected Communist.* He knew the face, just couldn't place it.

"God bless the proletariat," said Strumbić, raising his glass. He took a long drink of beer while the man watched him coolly. His face was expressionless, oddly frozen.

At long last the old man spoke again. "My friends have noticed that certain sensitive files have been leaking from the organs of state security."

"How terrible," Strumbić said. "So you'd like the Zagreb police to investigate? I'm sure if your friends made a formal complaint, my superiors would do whatever they could to track down any thefts of official secrets from sources within this city. Not something I could help with, I'm afraid. I'm on vice for the next month. Helping them out." He gave the old man a theatrical wink. "I'm sure your friends will be looking to do similar investigations in Belgrade and Ljubljana and Skopje and Sarajevo and everywhere else one might find leaky organs," Strumbić added blandly.

"No. That's not necessary. We know the files are leaking from the UDBA's Zagreb offices."

"Oh?" Strumbić said.

"Yes. And we know that they're leaking through you."

"That's a serious allegation," Strumbić said, mustering as much shock as he could.

"Yes, very serious."

"It needs a considerable burden of proof."

"No. I don't think so. You see, my friends are not interested in a conventional prosecution. They know enough to be confident in their suspicions."

Strumbić shifted uncomfortably.

"What they would like from you is the name of the person who has been passing to you official state secrets."

"Mr. . . ." Strumbić paused meaningfully.

"My name is irrelevant."

"In these difficult times a great deal of information is finding its way into the wrong hands. I may have seen one or two things and passed them on to interested parties—though this is not an admission of anything—but to pick me out is like a fisherman casting a hook for a particular sardine."

"My friends are interested in one specific file. A file they traced to you. Now they want to know who gave it to you."

Strumbić raised his hands as if in supplication to some god of memory, but the old man was having none of it.

"The file concerns Pilgrim."

"What?" The name meant nothing to Strumbić.

"Pilgrim. Who gave it to you?"

"Much as I'd like to help . . ." Whatever the file was about, there'd have been only one source, della Torre was the only person Strumbić had got anything from.

"Detective, I don't think you understand the position you find yourself in. All that hard-earned money of yours—my friends think that you are fully deserving of it. Fully. Yugoslavia's third way has always left open scope for smaller-scale capitalism within the embrace of a wider socialist ideal. You are a small businessman and a valued technocrat. Perhaps you could benefit from closer ties to Belgrade in the future. Belgrade can be a very good friend, if you know the right people there. It would mean not having to run away to, where is it? Šipan. Or Varaždin.

Or Opatija. Though I understand it might be very tempting to go with one of your lady friends. Renata, is it? Or perhaps you are reconciled to a long, happy retirement with your wife. But I'm afraid not everyone sees things as my friends do. Many, many people in senior positions in the Yugoslav government would wish to take away what you have earned through your industry. And to punish you for your presumption."

Strumbić smiled, but his blood froze at how much this man seemed to know about him.

"That's all hearsay, malicious gossip."

"Detective, our burden of proof is different from a court of law's. Belgrade and Zagreb may have their differences, but the organs of the State still have some sway here. And even if the State were challenged now, would you bet against martial law being imposed were things to degenerate further? Do you think that if the Yugoslav army took control you would still feel the same sense of immunity?"

Strumbić nodded in appreciation. He'd always been a deft chess player. When he was young, members of his chess club, the undergraduates and professionals, would patronize him as an uneducated boor, a lowly traffic cop. That was until they found their queens pinned by a merciless knight, forked and defeated from nowhere. And if they'd really offended Strumbić during the course of the game, there would be another beating to follow in a dark alley. He was starting to feel like one of those undergraduates. But he wasn't giving up the game altogether.

"Information has a price. So far, all I've had in return for my time is a beer to replace the one I had to abandon at lunch," he said.

"Very good. It is admirable that you see sense. Of course we would look to come to some agreeable arrangement. But I suggest we negotiate along Anglo-Saxon rather than Balkan lines."

"Oh?" Strumbić wasn't quite sure what the man meant.

"I give you a proposal and you accept it."

"That's not the way I usually work. These things have to be carefully considered..."

"Fifteen thousand."

"Marks?"

"What else?"

"You are a shrewd businessman. That was exactly the number I had in mind," Strumbić said.

"That's not all. We wish help in arranging our interview with the source of your information."

"But of course. I'll give him a call now and get him up here. Assuming you have the money?"

"No, I think it can wait for the weekend. Make yourself available. Tell the gentlemen outside where you can be found. They will come to you and pay you once you've fulfilled your part of the agreement."

Strumbić rose and held his hand out, but the old man ignored it. So instead he turned to leave.

"Nice doing business with you. And thanks for the beer."

"Detective, please don't do anything to make us think you are being duplicitous. My friends are very generous, but they can be vengeful when their generosity is abused."

6

"**SO YOU SOLD** me for fifteen thousand pieces of German silver?" della Torre said.

"Don't get stuck on the number. He could have offered fifteen marks or a hundred and fifty thousand. Whatever it was, I had to take it. It's hard negotiating with a stranger who's slapping your nuts with a stick."

"No idea who he was?"

"No. He looked familiar, like one of the old Communists you saw in the background of Tito's photographs. I swear he was probably dug up out of Mirogoj," Strumbić said, referring to the beautiful and imposing Zagreb cemetery under whose long arcades many of Croatia's great and good were buried.

"It was at the Metusalem?"

"Yes. I don't know much about the place. Looked it up when I got back to the office but it was red-lined. So the people who run the restaurant are close friends of the State. Or its enemies."

"I'll look it up," said della Torre. "By the way, the Bosnians did the Karlovac job."

"I know. Idiots told me. It's not like they didn't know I was a cop."

"Maybe they thought you were corrupt."

Strumbić's instant and genuine hurt expression made della Torre backpedal, despite himself.

"I mean like the Karlovac cops." He couldn't believe he was offering a roundabout apology to Strumbić for calling him crooked.

"Called a mate in Karlovac. They'd made a real mess there. The amount of covering up the cops did should have won them an Oscar. I think next time when they've got a job, they'll just do it themselves."

"So why didn't they shoot me in Zagreb? Or drop a grenade in my soup?"

"Maybe you've got the wrong end of the stick. Maybe all they really wanted to do was take you for a nice Sunday evening drive."

"Trust me, it was a hit. I wasn't going to be coming home," della Torre said. "And they made it pretty clear you were next."

Della Torre pulled the little notebook out of his breast pocket and flipped through the pages, looking back through months of tight, small-handed notes that filled about two-thirds of it. It was unlined so that he could condense as much information as was humanly visible onto a page in his immaculately neat, almost technical writing. He used the finest draftsman's pen he could find.

"Did he say anything more about Pilgrim? I never gave you a file about Pilgrim." He'd kept a record of everything he'd passed on to Strumbić.

"Sold."

"I never sold you a file about Pilgrim."

"Gringo, we have a deal, right?"

"What deal?"

"I'm honest with you and you accept the truth in an honourable and noble way."

"What are you telling me, Julius?"

"We have a deal?"

"Julius."

"Do we?"

"We have a deal. I promise not to shoot you."

"Okay. Okay. You remember when I came round to your office with that attestation from the ex-UDBA guy who'd drowned his wife?"

"The one I wasn't interested in."

"That's it. Remember you poured me a shot of Bell's?"

"How could I forget? You asked for it the second you got into the office, reminding me you'd bought it for me in the first place."

"And you got it out of your locked filing cabinet?"

"Because that's where I keep it."

"And then you got called away."

"Yes."

"Well, I'd arranged to have your secretary give you a buzz to tell you Anzulović wanted you."

"Anzulović didn't want me. He wasn't in."

"That's right."

"It was a mix-up, she said."

"It was a bottle of French perfume, she meant."

"I see. So you corrupted the office secretary. I'm not liking where this is going, by the way."

"Gringo, listen. The files you kept bringing for me, they were crap. I won't beat around the bush, but they were crap. Don't get me wrong. I mean, some of the stuff was amusing. Good for a laugh. A few helped me drag some favours out of people. But frankly, most of it wouldn't have made it onto page twelve of the evening paper."

Della Torre figured Strumbić was exaggerating. But not much.

"So why'd you buy them?"

"Because, Gringo, I didn't want to see you starve. It was my Christian duty."

"You're telling me you bought files from me, that you knew were useless, as an act of charity?"

"That sort of thing," Strumbić said. He gave della Torre what he thought was a beneficent look, the sort a kind priest might give. But it just made him look like a hungry scavenger.

"So you never managed to sell any of the stuff I gave you."

"Sold me."

"Sold you."

"There is this guy at the Italian consulate who was in the market for any old dross. But I'm telling you, Gringo, I barely broke even. I mean, once you factor in my costs, I was taking a loss on that rubbish. Once you gave me something worthwhile and I overpaid for it, thinking I'd encourage you. But you just didn't get it." Strumbić ignored the non-pecuniary advantages of having something on prosecutors and judges.

"And?"

"And, well, I felt that you owed me maybe a little more. Okay, maybe I was wrong, maybe I overstepped the bounds a little. Just a little. But can you blame me? Really?"

"Julius." Della Torre looked at the cop coldly, tempted to hit him. Just the once.

"Don't tell me you wouldn't have done the same."

"You stole files from my office. You created a ruse to steal from me. Those were my private papers."

"I wouldn't say steal. I'd say borrow. I borrowed the documents with every intention of returning them. I promise. And I was going to cut you in. Share and share alike, right?" Strumbić kept up a pleasant expression but he was pale in the light of the naked bulb and sweat beaded his brow despite the evening's chill.

"You know Anzulović hates it when you come round the office? Calls you a snake. He's right."

"Anzulović. He and that Messar think they're whiter than white," said Strumbić. Anzulović was the head of Department VI and

Messar was one of della Torre's colleagues. "I'll tell you something about Anzulović. He may have clean hands, but what about his wife, eh? She's a manager at Nama," Strumbić said, referring to a department store chain. "Never short a dinar, those people. They've got their scams running. Hiding stock, marking it sold on the inventory sheets, and then putting it back on the shelves when the prices have gone up, pocketing the difference. Why do you think that most of the time there's no coffee or toilet paper to be found for love or money, and then suddenly that's all you can find? And his daughter works for them now too." Strumbić sounded wounded.

"Julius, right now the issue isn't Anzulović's wife. Right now it's about me trying not to shoot you."

"We had an agreement, Gringo."

"Oh?"

"Gringo, you're not the violent sort. You're a lawyer. You're the sort of lawyer who'd be working for the Citizen's Advice Bureau if you weren't doing what you're doing now. You don't want to shoot people. You're an honest man" — the words were stumbling over each other — "trying to do the right thing, doing an impossible job in impossible circumstances when the world's against you."

Della Torre knew Strumbić was playing on his sense of martyrdom. As a young prosecuting lawyer he'd been roped into Department VI soon after its formation. Anzulović, a senior detective himself hired from the regular Zagreb police force to run it, had tapped della Torre because of his knowledge of Italian and English and because he'd trained in international law, all useful for investigating the UDBA's activities abroad. It had paid well, and ironically it was — had been — a mostly honest job. One of the few truly honest jobs in a country rotten through with corruption and compromise.

But the UDBA was widely hated. It didn't matter that his job was to keep it as clean as possible. To most people the UDBA was poison. It may not have pervaded society as deeply as East Germany's Stasi, but its long reach meant that no one was comfortable expressing honest political opinions, even to their spouses. Its penal colony, the Adriatic island Goli Otok, was a frozen hell in winter and a burning hell in summer from which few came back to join the living. But what the UDBA did better than any of those other hated organs of state viciousness was the murder of its dissidents. The organization and its predecessors had liquidated more than ten thousand souls during internal purges over the decades. It did so without compunction and with naked brutality, and there was no country in which an enemy of the Yugoslav state could feel safe from the reach of its long and crimson arm.

"So what do I do now? Go back to Zagreb and wait for the next hitman to show up?"

"Look, Gringo. If it makes you any happier, I'm in it at least as far up my neck as you are. You sure those Bosnians are fixed?"

"Like a row of cabbages," della Torre said wearily. "Mind if I pour myself a drink and help myself to another of your cigarettes?"

"Don't insult me. We're informal here. You know you don't have to ask," Strumbić said extravagantly.

Della Torre poured a tin mug of wine straight from the tap in the barrel, thinning it with a finger of bottled mineral water that tasted of soap, and lit one of Strumbić's Lucky Strikes. A moth batted itself against the light bulb.

"They should have pumped an anti-tank rocket into my apartment," della Torre said.

"Maybe next time. Or maybe they'll find some people who can drive."

"So what do you do now that these people from Belgrade think you shafted them?" della Torre asked.

"I'll have to go somewhere else for a while. Just like you," Strumbić said, chewing on the inside of his lip.

"The place on Šipan?"

"Problem with the island is all the locals know when you're there. If somebody who doesn't like you knows one of the islanders, you're stuffed. Opatija is out of season. You end up looking like a priest in a whorehouse."

"So, not unusual, in other words."

"Hah. You know, you're almost funny sometimes. But the people in Belgrade know about all those places anyway."

"What about your little bolthole in London?" della Torre asked.

Strumbić grimaced. London was his ultimate sanctuary, the place he had lined up for when he finally disappeared with his money. Ditch the wife. Ditch the jobs, official and otherwise. Ditch the aggro. Live it large in a proper city where he wouldn't be afraid somebody would snitch on him about the car he drove or how fat his wallet was when he pulled it out to pay the restaurant bill. The action was better. And if he wanted sun, he could get to anywhere from London. Not just to Croatia, but to places that had proper hotels and did food other than just meat on a stick.

Nobody else knew about the London apartment. Only della Torre.

He'd been at Strumbić's weekend place on a sunny afternoon the previous summer, eating cherries right off the tree and drinking wine, shirtless and sweating. Strumbić hadn't owned the apartment long and was dead pleased about it. Bravado and the long-bottled-up urge to tell somebody made him talk. Ironically, della Torre was probably the safest person to say anything to. He was selling files to Strumbić and had no desire to get on the cop's bad side. Besides, secret policemen knew how to keep their mouths shut. Better than priests. Better than lawyers, even. So a secret policeman lawyer was the best of all.

"I've done the smartest thing you've ever heard," he'd said, savouring the wine.

"What's that? Turned honest?"

"What sort of cretin do you take me for? I've lined up my retirement plan."

"I thought you were going to work till you keeled over.
Which must be sometime next week, the way you're going."

"Naw. Bought myself a place."

"Another one? How many have you got? Two flats in Zagreb
I know about, that villa on Šipan, this place, and haven't you
got some farm outside of Varaždin? How much do you need?"

"They're all in this country. I've bought something abroad,
for when the shit really hits the fan."

"Oh yeah? Where? Albania?"

"That's not even humour. London."

"London?"

"Yeah, a place called Hampstead. Big apartment right in the
middle of the park."

"The Heath?"

"That's right, you were a student there for a while, weren't
you?"

"I try to forget," della Torre said. He'd spent the gloomiest
eight months of his life in London, doing a course on international law paid for by his then employer, the Zagreb prosecutor's office. It was where he'd had his first dealings with the
UDBA. Dealings that had compromised him, eroded his prin-
ciples. Back when he still had them.

But he shifted his thoughts back to Hampstead. He'd had
some nice walks in the big park there, wandered around John
Keats's house back when he'd still read poetry. A decent place
to escape London's relentless urbanity if you couldn't afford
the plane fare out.

"The building's right in the middle of the Heath. I mean, not
in the middle middle. It's on the edge. But the park surrounds
it on three sides. Up near the top of the hill. Big brick building with these white, what are they called? Dormers. White

dormers. I've got this fourth-floor apartment, just below the penthouse, windows on two sides. Look out my living room and London's spread out like a whore on her back. A good-looking, expensive one, covered in jewels. I tell you, it's fantastic. Too bad you'll never see the place. Two hundred square metres, even bigger than my Zagreb apartment, in one of the classiest parts of town."

"Sounds nice. I guess London's a good enough place if you can afford it."

"Great town. Clubs, restaurants, girls. What girls! Every colour you can think of. Green, probably, if you looked hard enough. They got a real spark. Not like the ones in Zagreb, who look like they've come out of a morgue, except if you wanted to you could always get a corpse to smile."

"So what does Mrs. Strumbić think about retiring to London?"

"Mrs. Strumbić doesn't know Mr. Strumbić is going to spend his golden years where he won't have to worry about bumping into Mrs. Strumbić again."

"So that's how it is. Well, lucky you. Though I'd have preferred somewhere like Rome or Barcelona." Della Torre popped another fat black cherry into his mouth.

"I'd just sweat like a pig and develop another ulcer over how corrupt it is."

Della Torre choked. For a moment he felt the cherry stone rising through his nose.

"London works properly, like a proper city," Strumbić said.

"If you say so," della Torre said, spitting out the stone.

Della Torre had sensed that after the initial smugness and braggadocio, Strumbić rather wished he hadn't mentioned London. So that summer afternoon della Torre had dropped the subject.

But not now. Now he wanted to remind Strumbić he had something on him.

"So you'll be heading to London, then, will you?"

"Listen, you make your plans and I'll make mine."

"You owe me some money, Strumbić. Remember?"

"Do I?"

"Our phone call earlier this evening."

"Oh yeah. There's an envelope in a soup pot under the kitch-en sink. Take out four thousand Deutschmarks. No, take out five thousand and buy yourself a new suit. Least I can do after your inconvenience."

"Gee, thanks."

"Don't mention it. Just don't rip me off."

"Rip you off?" Strumbić's brass neck forever amazed him. "Listen, Julius, I'm inclined to believe what you told me. But I don't trust you not to stitch me up again. So I'm afraid I am going to lock you in the cellar. I'll leave you a key for the cuffs, though."

"Always a considerate friend."

"Don't mention it."

"When you go upstairs, come back down and bring some cigarettes. Alright? And when you've disappeared, to Italy or America or wherever you're going, don't bother to send me a postcard. I won't be around to read it."

Della Torre stood up. He ached and was tired and was only just starting to think about how he'd get home. He rubbed his fingers on the silk tie. Distractedly, he started to pull it out of his pocket. That was a mistake.

The gunshot was deafening in the cellar's hard-walled space. The noise rang like the inside of a church bell. Della Torre must have flipped the safety off somehow without noticing it. And obviously the Bosnian had kept it primed with a round in the barrel. The tie had snagged the trigger.

Any other time that bullet would have planted itself harm-lessly into the dirt floor, or maybe flattened itself against a wall. But that night chance played funny games with della Torre. The bullet hit something it shouldn't have. Like Strumbić.

7

DELLA TORRE WAS momentarily deafened. All he could hear was the blood pounding in his head. The surprise, the noise of the explosion, and the shock of the car wreck earlier in the evening caused his vision to narrow into two small tunnels of light. He thought he was passing out.

A shriek snapped him back into alertness. At first he couldn't make any of it out, but then Strumbić's bellowing formed itself back into language of sorts.

"You fucking fuck, you fucking shot me, you fuck, I'm fucking going to fucking kill you! Gringo, you are dead. Dead. I can't believe you fucking shot me. Fuck it hurts. Fuck, fuck, fuck…"

Strumbić's chair tilted back at an alarming angle, balancing on a single leg so that della Torre thought it was going to drop him on his back. With his arms cuffed behind him, the fall would probably dislocate Strumbić's shoulders. Maybe break a wrist as well.

But Strumbić's right leg had gone rigid straight in front of him, and that little bit of offsetting weight ensured that the chair righted itself rather than making the shot cop's night that little bit worse. It settled heavily, threatening for a moment to overbalance.

"Calm down. Where'd it hit you? You'll be fine. Just calm down."

"In my leg, in my goddam leg. My shin."

"Oh, is that all? The way you're going on about it I thought I'd shot your balls off."

Della Torre looked at the rigid leg; it was shaking uncontrollably. There was a hole in the new jeans about a hand's span below the knee, directly in the front.

"Here, I'm going to have to cut your jeans off around the bullet hole to have a look."

"Like buggery you are. Do you know how much these things cost? God, my leg hurts. Get these cuffs off me so I can blow your brains out, you moron."

"They've already got a hole in them. Making it slightly bigger isn't going to make much difference."

Della Torre found a hooked knife, used for trimming vines, hanging off a nail in the wall and sliced a patch off the front of Strumbić's trouser leg. The first thing he noticed was that there was hardly any blood, just a red, roundish hole with a black rim right on the shin. In fact, he thought he could see the bullet mashed up against the bone just under the skin.

"Christ, this is a crappy gun with crappy ammo. The bullet barely broke the skin. Might have cracked the bone, though."

Gingerly, della Torre pulled the automatic out of his jacket pocket, which had a hole matching the one he'd just cut out of Strumbić's jeans. He flipped the safety on and had a closer look at the gun.

"Well, that figures. It's some Bulgarian knock-off. Either it goes off on its own or doesn't do anything at all. Whatever's most inconvenient. The ammo's probably Bulgarian too. Bet they were filling only half the casing with powder and then making up the rest with sawdust or something. No wonder your assassins took two goes and fifty rounds to kill that crook down in Karlovac. That mistress of his must have had some bad luck to have died as well."

"Heart attack. Superficial bullet wound but died of a heart attack," Strumbić said through shallow panted breaths.

"What were they going to do, club me with this thing until I passed out and then run me over? Somebody should have given them on-the-job advice."

"Just shut up and get me a doctor."

"Listen, Strumbić. If I take you to a doctor now, your cops will be all over Zagreb looking for me ten minutes later. Because you'll tell them who shot you, forgetting to mention both that it was an accident and that it was the least you deserved. And when they find me, they'll park me in a holding cell where half of Zagreb's squaddies will stand in line patiently waiting to knock out whatever teeth I have left. And the other half won't be so patient and'll just kick me into the next world. You are not going to die. In fact I hurt myself more shaving this morning. So quit squealing or I'll tell everyone you wear your girlfriend's suspenders and bra. Whether it's true or not."

"Bastard."

"Where's the slivovitz?"

"There's a jerry can beside the barrel."

Della Torre poured the rest of his wine onto the dirt floor and filled the tin cup with the potent alcohol. And then he took a long swig.

"Hey, I thought you were getting it for me. What about me?" whined Strumbić.

"Oh, sorry, you're right," della Torre said, and splashed the rest of the cup on Strumbić's open wound. He was pretty sure they'd have been able to hear Strumbić on the other side of the valley. Some farmer on a trip to the privy was probably wondering why anybody would be slaughtering a pig at this time of night and this time of year.

"What the fuck did you do that for? That hurt even more than getting shot!"

"Don't want you to get an infection, seeing as you're not going to be able to make it to the doctor tonight."

"Jesus. You do know I'm going to kill you when I see you next, Gringo. For free. I'm going to get one of those Bulgarian guns and I'm going to put fifty holes in you and then make you eat the goddamn thing with the safety off. And then kick you in the stomach. Give me some of that stuff to drink rather than just baptising me."

"Sorry, can't. You're in shock. Never give someone in shock alcohol. Shouldn't really smoke either."

"Bastard."

Della Torre stepped out of the cellar, pulled down the iron shutter on the cellar's only window, padlocked it from the outside, and then came back into the room.

"Now, I'm going to put the key to the cuffs on the table here, just here on the edge. It might take you a little while to get here, what with the state your leg's in, but you've got all night. I'm afraid I'm going to have to lock up the cellar and you're just going to have to lump it until somebody rescues you. But the longest you'll have to wait is until Tuesday, because even if your wife or your girlfriend doesn't come looking for you, or your guy doesn't come to do the vines, I'll make sure somebody else does. On the other hand, look on the bright side. It'll be a great time to stop smoking," della Torre said, pocketing the packet of Lucky Strikes. He almost left without picking up Strumbić's gun, but then he spotted it and heaved it into the darkness of the vineyard below the cottage.

He locked the heavy wooden door behind him with an oversized key that he found hanging off the knob and then hung the key on a nail half-driven into the front of the door frame. He didn't want to make it too difficult for Strumbić's eventual rescuers. He then put the big iron bar across the door and padlocked that too.

"Della Torre, you're dead. You hear that, Gringo? Next time

you see me will be the last time you see anything at all. Dead, Gringo."

Della Torre went up into the main house.

The door was open and the lights were on. In daylight the kitchen had a beautiful view of the deep, wooded valley, which curved away from Strumbić's hillside towards a peak that loomed like a forested incisor. But he wasn't there for the sights. He opened up the cupboard under the sink and found the envelope in the soup pot. It was full of Strumbić's little storm troopers. Della Torre ran his thumb along them. The whole fifteen thousand, it seemed. He took a deep breath. At first, his intention had been to take the four thousand promised him. Plus the extra thousand. But, thinking about it, Strumbić had never intended to pay him anything at all. Why should he play square with a man who'd helped in a conspiracy to kill him? So he pocketed the lot.

On the way out, he passed a nice leather coat. His own suit jacket was distinctly the worse for wear, not least from the bullet hole in the pocket. Strumbić's coat was shorter in the arms and looser around the body than della Torre expected, and it wasn't really the sort of thing he'd ever wear. It looked too — well, too secret police. Or it would have done had it fit properly. As it was he looked like a country bumpkin. But the leather was top quality. Italian probably. So he decided to take it anyway, especially because he knew it'd piss Strumbić off.

Della Torre transferred the gun, the tie, and the little notebook from the one coat to the other. He found the key to the BMW on a ring with half a dozen others hanging off a hook. A couple of small ones might have been for simple padlocks or maybe letter boxes. But the rest were unfamiliar. He shrugged and pocketed them all.

He was about to leave when he spotted the three cartons of Lucky Strikes on the sitting room coffee table. Della Torre couldn't really see any reason not to take them, now that Strumbić was quitting.

As della Torre stumbled up the stony path in darkness, the moon having already passed behind the hillside, all he could hear was the sound of barking dogs in the village far below and the crunch of loose rocks underfoot. He unlocked the car by feel.

It took him a while to figure out all the buttons and levers on the BMW, but when he did the engine purred to life and he pulled away. His left knee hurt as he pressed the clutch, making for rough gear changes. But otherwise it was a pleasure to drive the car. He'd always wanted to.

He came off Strumbić's track onto the Samobor road and was starting to accelerate around the bend when a shape loomed out of the dark at him. Della Torre pounded the brake and clutch at the same time, cursing at the pain that shot up through his leg. The seatbelt tugged in on him with the sudden deceleration, causing him to feel the agony in his ribs as well.

He sat there for a long moment, taking deep breaths, reminding himself not to drink so much when stealing an unfamiliar car, before he finally registered what he was seeing in the stark light of the car's lamps. It was a man, standing hunched, half swaying, more or less in the middle of the road. Della Torre got out of the car. As he got closer he could see it was the tall Bosnian. At least it wasn't the drowned one.

Gingerly, della Torre put the man's arm round his shoulder to give him support and straighten him out. But the Bosnian, the one who'd done all the talking, was bent sideways like a banana. He groaned.

"Bad accident, eh?" della Torre asked in the soothing voice he put on for difficult interrogations.

"Ummm," the Bosnian replied. Della Torre wasn't sure if the injured man recognized him.

"Here, I'll lend you a hand. Can you walk a bit?"

The Bosnian moved his legs like a marionette, but mostly in the same direction, and slowly the two men edged out of the glare of the headlights to the side of the car, where they stopped. Della Torre slipped his hand into the pocket of his new leather coat and took out the Beretta. He replaced the gun in the Bosnian's shoulder holster and clipped the holster down so the gun wouldn't fall out. And then, turning him slightly, della Torre ducked out from under the Bosnian's arm and leaned back against the car. For a long moment the tall Bosnian swayed there unsupported, almost upright, in the dusting of the car's headlights, wavering like an erratic pendulum. Blackness spread behind him. His eyes blinked hard, as if he were having difficulty focusing, his high, hard cheekbones and sunken cheeks making the effect all the more ghoulish. He growled unintelligible sounds, saliva bubbling in the corner of his mouth until it became a thin line of drool.

Della Torre stepped forward and gently pressed his fingers against the man's chest, as if to steady him. And then he gave a sharp push. Flesh hit stone as the Bosnian fell back into the ravine, and then there was the sound of sliding scree. Apart from an initial surprised grunt, he remained quiet.

"Must have hurt," della Torre said, standing at the edge of the road. It was like looking into a bottomless well. "But it's better than getting run over."

Della Torre sidled back into the car, trying not to bend his sore knee too much. He didn't feel the smallest grain of remorse. If the Bosnian had survived the car wreck, clearly he wasn't made of icing sugar and baked custard. Chances were he'd survive the fall too. If he didn't, too bad. The man was a cold-hearted killer, and not a very good one at that. Worse still, he'd had his sights on della Torre.

If by some freak of nature Strumbić died from his wound, or more likely from a heart attack as he tried to dig his way out of the cellar, the cops would find the Bosnian in the ravine, match the gun with Strumbić's bullet wound, and solve a five-star cop-killer crime. Strumbić was a senior detective. The gun was probably one that had made such a mess in Karlovac. So unless the investigating officer was even dimmer than a September firefly, he'd have a brace of solved premier-league crimes under his belt. Who cared that the Mercedes married to the tree was facing the wrong direction from Strumbić's? The Zagreb cops had never been good on details. And if Strumbić lived? Maybe they'd pin the attempted murder on the Bosnian anyway.

Della Torre was tired. It was nice driving this car, but it didn't make up for the evening he'd had. His knee and his ribs kept reminding him they weren't happy. He was tempted to go straight home and into bed. But he knew that whoever had hired the Bosnians would probably be keeping an eye on his place too. Just in case.

He really couldn't think offhand what he knew that would make somebody want to get rid of him. No, that wasn't right. He knew lots about a lot of people in high-up places. Ugly things. But most of those people had other, more pressing problems. Having been deeply involved in the grubby parts of the Communist machine, they were exposed to all sorts of flying shrapnel now that the machine was flying apart. What della Torre knew may not have been the least of their worries. But it wasn't top of the list either.

It wasn't time to think about these things. Luckily traffic going into Zagreb was light, and he mostly let the car drive itself. If he couldn't go home, he'd just have to go to Irena's. Yes, that'd do the trick. He'd just have to hope his ex-wife didn't have company.

8

AT FIRST HE knocked lightly on the glass door to the kitchen. Then he tossed pebbles at her bedroom window. No sign of anyone. He started to worry she might not be in. Where else could she be at this time on a Sunday night? He knew she wasn't at work. She wasn't on call. A thought occurred to him, but he pushed it out of his mind. Surely she wasn't seeing anyone else. After all, he wasn't. It'd be too unfair if she started first.

He hammered on the door that little bit louder, until the lights in a neighbouring apartment came on.

He was on the balcony of a building that was up a small hill overlooking the city. It had four flats, one on each storey. Hers was on the third.

He looked across at Zagreb's illuminated streets, sparkling like necklaces. They reminded him of the first evening he'd spent with her. It had been a particularly warm evening late in the spring. Or maybe that was only how he remembered it. What he was sure of was that he'd spent much of the time trying not to look down the front of her dress. And failing. He'd recited odd lines from a not particularly appropriate poem, though he forgot what it was. Even now he cringed, hoping it hadn't been the one comparing pretty girls to hitting tractor production figures.

"You seem to be enjoying yourself," she'd said. They were standing at the top of the cannon tower in the old town, the medieval part of Zagreb built on its central hill.

"Aren't you? It's a beautiful view."

"Hmm," she said, looking into the distance. "The French have a word for it; it's called décolletage."

"Ah, yes, décolletage." He repeated it a couple of times, burning it into his memory, pretending to know what it meant. If it didn't work out with this girl, it'd be useful to have a bit of French to use on the next one who came along.

But he hadn't wanted the next girl. He wanted this one. As soon as he looked the word up the following day, he realized he loved the strikingly pretty medical student friend of a friend.

Funny to think of it. The view of Zagreb that night had been a full frontal, with all the ugly industrial chimneys and distant tower blocks included. But the view from her balcony was a discreet look at the city's prettiest, most seductive aspect. Zagreb's décolletage.

At the base of the apartment building, a big communal garden made a steady descent to where the hill flattened. It ended at a high, blank brick wall—the back of a row of nineteenth-century stables and storage sheds. The sort of fences that surrounded tennis courts separated their building's garden from the neighbouring ones, making it one of the most secure around.

But there was a secret path from the main road, along the side of the shop, through a stable yard, and into a shed that led into the neighbour's garden, where there was a broken bit of fencing behind some big shrubs. Della Torre was pretty sure he was still the only person who knew about it.

He'd discovered it as a kid, when he'd lived in the apartment with his father and needed a way to get in and out at night without the old man noticing. No one had ever bothered to fix the fence or the bit of broken wall at the back of the shed. His father still owned the apartment, though he'd moved out to his old farmhouse in Istria, near the coast, after della Torre and Irena married. When della Torre left the marriage, Irena had stayed on in the flat. So now he thought of it as hers.

Della Torre had climbed up the back of the building as he had done in his youth, not realizing quite how difficult it would be with a busted knee and a cracked rib. Just as well there was little risk in stopping at each balcony. One of the apartments he passed on the way up was almost always empty; it was the home of a banker who mostly lived in New York. The other was occupied by a deaf old lady, the widow of a member of the Yugoslav politburo.

"The least Irena could have done was to leave the balcony door unlocked," he grumbled.

Finally, a light came on in the kitchen.

"Oh, it's you. Should have known," she said, having first peered through the glass. She suppressed any enthusiasm she might have felt on seeing him.

"Who'd you think it was? Burglars?"

"I was hoping for a Romeo."

"What? An Alfa Romeo? You want another car already?"

"I have no idea what you're talking about," she said. "Why didn't you just let yourself in through the front door? You've got keys."

"I do. But they're at home," he said, closing the door behind him.

"And you're locked out and you need my spare set, but— don't tell me—it was too much trouble to press the buzzer."

"I didn't want anyone to see me. And to tell the truth, I wouldn't mind staying for the night." He eased himself onto a wooden chair with a padded cushion, one of two in the small kitchen.

"You didn't want anyone to know because it's illegal to visit your wife?"

"Ex-wife."

"Oh, so you signed the papers and sent them to the lawyers, then, did you?" She crossed her arms and frowned.

"Um, no. I don't remember you giving me any papers. Have they got lost in the post?"

"No. I haven't bothered doing anything about it," she said.

"So it's still wife, then."

"It's still wife." It was a conversation they'd had more than once.

"Well, anyway, aren't you going to offer to make me a cup of herbal tea or something?" He helpfully waved his hand towards the cupboard.

"Would you like a cup of herbal tea?"

"Yes, please."

"The kettle's there and you know where the tea's kept."

"Look, I'm sorry I'm so late. Um . . . you haven't got company, by the way, have you?"

"Who'd be keeping me company this time of night? I just got back from work. I was in the shower."

"Oh, I don't know. I mean it's been, what? Nearly two years?"

"More like three." Irena remained standing.

"Three years? I thought doctors from the hospital would have been all over you now that you're free."

"Hmm. With a husband in the secret police I'd be a real catch for a middle-aged adrenaline junkie. Anyway, it's really none of your business. You know very well I'm never going to lock you out of this place. And if I start seeing somebody, it won't be here. So what's the big deal that it means you have to climb in and out of your own apartment like a thief? Some scorned woman? Or her husband?"

"Maybe. Though I haven't the foggiest which. All I know is whoever it is that doesn't like me had a bunch of Bosnians sent around to have me killed. Wasn't you, was it?"

"Were they doctors?"

"No. But when I left them, they looked like they could have used one."

"Then it couldn't have been me. I spend my whole life with other medics. And patients too sick to be wandering around killing people," she said.

"Well, that's a relief, then." Della Torre winced. He'd made the mistake of trying to bend his knee.

"Is that why you're dressed like a Gestapo scarecrow?"

"Friend gave me the jacket. Would have been rude to turn him down. Mind?" he asked as he pulled a Lucky Strike out of Strumbić's packet.

"Let me shut the kitchen door and open the one onto the balcony." Irena had never liked the smell of cigarette smoke, which for someone living in Yugoslavia was a permanent cross to bear.

He smiled at her. Her hair was tousled; grey was beginning to streak the black, though she was three years younger than him. It made her look even more elegant. She'd never been one for fashionable clothes. Even so, her striking features, her carriage always turned heads, men's and women's. Her skin absorbed sun so that she looked tanned year-round. Most people assumed she had Gypsy blood. But that was only because there were so few Jews left in Zagreb.

One lot of Irena's grandparents hadn't survived the wartime transportation. But her mother and her mother's parents had been kept hidden deep in a forest village for the duration, the locals glad to have an eminent physician at their disposal, mostly because they thought he was a vet. The villagers didn't know they were Jews, only that they needed to be hidden. So they were treated well, though they lived in the same primitive conditions as their hosts. Her mother couldn't remember much about it; she'd been too young.

Irena's father never spoke about how he'd survived the war, though whenever someone offered him food he didn't like, he'd say he'd already eaten enough roast rat to last a lifetime. Not everyone took it as a joke. He never meant it as one.

Della Torre still loved her. He was pretty sure she returned the feelings. They got on well and had dinner together once every week or two. But the arguments had become too frequent for the relationship to survive. For five years they'd managed, but it got ever worse. Always about the same thing. When eventually she'd got pregnant, by accident, she was euphoric. He'd never felt such panic in his life. Or such elation as when she miscarried.

He shouldn't have made it so obvious. For a time her loathing of him was unbearable. She suspected he'd poisoned her. It was an unfair accusation, but his job made it an easy one. The dam finally burst at a summer party a fellow doctor from her hospital had thrown at his country place.

Neither della Torre nor Irena had ever spoken honestly to anyone else about his job. Besides being secret, it tended to put people off. When they had to, they said he was a criminal lawyer at the prosecutor's office, working on cases where it was suspected that personal vendettas on the part of officials had caused miscarriages of justice. Which was more or less what he did. An honourable job. And the answer always sufficed.

Except that at this party, after he'd finished giving the stock answer to a doctor who'd just come up for training from Macedonia, Irena interjected with deep sarcasm, "Yes, he's a real humanitarian. For the UDBA."

The man had only just made an indiscreet witticism about how if della Torre were sorting out all the country's politically motivated cases, he'd have enough work for two lifetimes. He'd need two because he'd be spending one of them in prison. So at first the medic treated Irena's comment as an uncomfortable joke and laughed nervously. Della Torre gave him the biggest, most sincere smile he could manage, trying to defuse the situation. But Irena's stony look gave the game away. She was telling the truth.

The man's face took on the sort of rigid terror della Torre had once seen in a teenage criminal he and Strumbić were interviewing. Strumbić, fed up with the boy's posturing and refusal to be polite, had hung him by the ankles from a tower-block window until the boy fainted. Later they could see his sick streaked down the side of the building.

All conversation across the whole of the party more or less stopped right then. People who'd lost their inhibitions to strong wine and a lovely summer's evening grew instantly sober. Irena and della Torre were the first to leave, staying only just long enough to thank the shell-shocked host. No one would have wanted to go before them, for fear of being noticed. It didn't do to make a member of the UDBA think you were offended by his company. But by the same token, Irena knew the party was dead, crushed by the cold, hard hand of fear, everyone trying desperately to think of everything they'd ever said to Irena's husband that had been political or might be construed as such. Or, indeed, to Irena.

It was probably the most unkind thing Irena had ever done in her life, and she regretted it instantly — but only on account of the people at the party, especially that poor little man. She didn't care what della Torre thought.

"I suppose I'm in the small bedroom," della Torre said, while sipping on his tea in the sitting room.

"Unless you prefer the sofa," she said.

"Nope, small bedroom will do. What time are you getting up?"

"The usual."

"Can you wake me just after, around six-thirty? I've got a few things that need doing."

"Okay," she said. Then, giving him a long look, she added, "Take off your trousers."

"Thought you'd never ask. I see my charm still works."

"Don't be stupid. Take them off."

He did as he was told. She brought a lamp towards him and squatted down to look at his knee. It was livid, a blackish purple, and looked like it'd had a run-in with a bicycle pump.

"How far can you bend it?"

"Enough to push in a clutch and climb three storeys up an apartment building on the outside."

"Show me."

He winced as he flexed his leg. She prodded it, though not nearly as gently as she might have done a patient's. But remembering how undignified Strumbić had been, he kept the whining to a minimum.

"I'd need an X-ray to be sure, but I'm guessing a bit of ligament damage. Nothing catastrophic, but it's not going to feel very nice. Do you want some codeine for tonight?"

"It might be nice."

She noticed that he was favouring his left arm.

"Off with the coat and shirt."

"Regular floor show you're wanting. I charge by the dance."

"I charge by the wound. And if you're not careful you'll be developing a few more tonight."

She had to help him take his undershirt off, and then gave a knowing nod when she saw the Rorschach of bruises across his chest.

"If I didn't know any better I'd say you'd been in a car accident but that, very sensibly, you were wearing a seatbelt."

"Right in one."

She palpitated his tender belly and under his right ribs and seemed content with the results, but when she reached around to his left side, he yelped.

"Cracked rib maybe? Is that what it feels like?"

"I don't know, never cracked a rib before. Though breathing's a bit uncomfortable."

"So don't breathe, see if that makes you feel better."

"Haw," he said, but that just made him cough, which he regretted.

"Sure you don't want to come in with me tomorrow? I can arrange a discreet X-ray."

"And what's an X-ray going to tell me that you haven't?"

"Not much, I suspect."

"And what exactly am I meant to do with a ligament-damaged knee and a cracked rib?"

"Well, if the damage is bad enough, you might need an operation from a top knee surgeon. I can recommend one in Zurich, a former colleague."

"Gee, thanks. You think he'll take an old Yugo as a trade-in?"

"No. As for the rib, best we can do is put your arm in a sling. But that's just to stop it hurting. Otherwise the prescription is just a bit of tender loving care. Which you're not going to get here."

"What about a warm hug?"

"Sure, that might do you some good. Don't know where you're going to find one this time of night, though. And it's only a single bed in the small bedroom, in case you start thinking of ordering in. Goodnight."

9

HE **JUMPED OUT** of bed, startled. He instantly regretted the sudden movement. It felt like some small, vicious animal was trying to kick its way out of his head.

He'd slept badly. Despite his tiredness, anxiety and sore ribs made worse by an overly hard mattress had given him a restless night. He'd lost consciousness only in the small hours. But his nerves remained taut. So when Irena came into his room to see if he was still sleeping, her presence triggered a sudden panic that he'd be too late to catch Anzulović.

"Ow," he said, the pain migrating to his knee and then to his chest. "You didn't spend last night braining me with a frying pan by any chance, did you?"

"Nope. The thought barely crossed my mind."

"Oh. Then it must have been something I ate."

"Liquid supper, was it?"

"Barely a snifter."

"Remember, it's not only the quantity, it's also the quality."

"Gee, thanks. I'll pop that little gem of insight in my mental drinks cabinet," he said sarcastically, though she had a point. Strumbić's slivovitz always left him feeling like there was no mercy left in heaven or earth. "What time is it?" He noticed she was fully dressed and wearing her outdoor shoes.

"Don't worry, it's only six."

"Six? How long have you been up?"

"A while. I woke up early and then couldn't get back to sleep, so I ran a couple of errands. Got some bread for breakfast."

"You're going to be dead beat. Take the day off."

"Gee, thanks, boss. But I can't. I've got a list of appointments that if I miss, people might die."

Zagreb's doctors were busy. Croats were leaving the parts of the republic where large communities of Serbs had created mini-republics, carving out a third of the province. They had grown belligerent in their desire for an independent Croatia. And the Yugoslav army was backing the Serbs. Some of those displaced Croats found shelter with relatives. Many had made their way to Zagreb. It wasn't a big migration. Yet. But it had started to put pressure on local services, not least the hospitals.

So far in Zagreb there was only the smell of war, the general glumness and worry. The streets were full of more uniforms than he could ever remember, ill-fitting surplus, including ridiculous baseball caps they'd copied badly from the Americans, with the ubiquitous chequerboard crest. Reserve police they were called, though nobody was fooled.

But there were incidents in the regions, small but ugly skirmishes and sieges. Mostly it was the two sides trying to decide who they were before squaring up.

"And don't worry about my sleep. I can survive on a lot less than you think. You know, it's the woman thing. We're designed for babies crying all night and then waking before dawn," she added.

"Touché," he said.

"I also went to your flat."

"You're kidding. See anything? Has anyone been around?"

His place was, strictly speaking, an UDBA flat given to him not long after he'd joined. He and Irena had been married for a

year or so and living with his father when they'd been offered
the apartment. It had come up suddenly, and della Torre leapt
at it.

It had been occupied by a senior UDBA operative who had
come under suspicion for reactionary views and anti-socialist
leanings. And taking bribes. The file had been passed through
the anti-corruption unit, where della Torre helped to check on
legal details, though largely for form's sake. People arrested by
the UDBA didn't get off on technicalities.

He should have felt bad about scavenging the place, because
that's what he felt like, a scavenger. Here was a man in late
middle age who was now going to spend the rest of his days
chipping stones on Goli Otok, blistering in the heat of the summer, cut by the northeast bora in the winter, and whose family
would be left with at most some modest savings and a severely
curtailed pension, homeless and almost entirely cut off from
human sympathy. On the other hand, he'd been a crook and
had himself stolen the flat from its rightful owners, using his
UDBA authority to do so.

The flat was situated on a big road, so the front windows
were never opened. Worse still, it was largely unchanged since
the late 1930s. The paint was new, the bath had been replaced,
and a gas water heater had been installed, but little else. It was
one of those large Austro-Hungarian apartments with enormously high ceilings, hugely thick walls, interconnecting
rooms, and large ceramic stoves to heat each of the four main
rooms. But there was something oppressive about it, gloomy
and haunted.

Irena had always refused to live there. So he rented the place
out to students and pocketed the money. After the split, della
Torre moved in.

"The flat was fine," Irena said. "If anyone's been round, they
certainly did a poor job of cleaning it. There wasn't any obvious
evidence someone had been through your stuff. I couldn't tell

if anyone was watching it. Not really my line of business. But I brought this back for you anyway."

Irena pulled from her straw shopping basket a leather case about the size and thickness of a hardback novel.

"And before you ask, nobody'd moved it. It was where it always is, in the dirty laundry."

Della Torre kept it there because that was the last place an ordinary burglar would look. Secret police, on the other hand, knew where people who knew where to hide things hid things. So either the place had been searched by amateurs or it hadn't been searched at all. He plumped for the latter. This was a good sign. It suggested that whoever had hired the Bosnians didn't know they'd failed. This happy ignorance wouldn't last long, though. The crashed Mercedes would be found soon. And he'd have to arrange to have someone release Strumbić within a day or two.

He unwound the elasticized string that kept the case shut and checked that everything was where it should be. His Yugoslav passport was there. Fat lot of good that was, though. The rest of Europe was already terrified that refugees would flood out of the country when the shooting started. More useful was the Italian passport. A fake, but a real fake, so good and built on such solid documentation that the Italian government was happy to keep renewing it. When he'd been jailed in Rome, the Questura had spent four days trying to decide whether it had somehow been forged. They'd been through all the official records but couldn't come up with anything. They were sure he and his papers were as fishy as week-old mackerel and told him as much. But they couldn't figure out what was wrong. So they gave the passport back to him when they let him out of jail. Together with the blue silk tie.

And then there was the precious U.S. passport. That was real, a hundred percent bona fide, from when he was a kid and had been naturalized alongside his mother. As far as he knew, the UDBA were unaware of it, and he'd always been careful to get it renewed abroad. It was his version of Strumbić's London flat. His ultimate safe haven. The magic key. He pulled it out and kissed it.

"You know, Marko, you're probably the only person in this country with one of those who isn't either underage, retired, working for the U.S. government, or in some mental institution. Anyone with the smallest grain of sense and one of those would have left this wretched place and taken his wife back to America long ago."

"Ohio's overrated."

"So you say. It'd have been nice to find out for myself."

"I'll go back one day. We'll get you a green card."

"Too late. I've got my own plans."

"To go to America?"

"No. Remember Vesana, the one who used to work in the radiology department?"

"Cute, but a bit short and fat?"

"That sort of thing."

"What about her? She went abroad somewhere, didn't she?"

"She did. She went to London. We keep in touch. Anyway, she was back for a visit over Christmas and we met up. She said there were some good jobs to be had, X-ray technicians. So I applied for one at her hospital and they're interested. If I bring my diplomas and show I can speak English well enough, they'll give me a job. The pay's about three times what I earn here."

"An X-ray technician? You're a consultant and a damn fine one. Why are you taking a job as a technician? They train illiterate teenagers to do that."

"Because I can do it. I'm qualified for it, there's a job on offer, because I feel like going abroad and starting over before I turn completely grey and lose my looks and the will to have children, and because if I work there for a while and then take some exams, they'll eventually recognize my qualifications and I'll be able to work as a specialist again."

"Yeah. But London? Why would you want to go to London? It's the most miserable city in the world. It makes Belgrade look good. Hell, Skopje's bearable by comparison. Why couldn't you go somewhere civilized, like Rome or Barcelona or somewhere nice in France? Even anything in Germany's better than London."

"Because my Italian and French aren't good enough, I don't speak Spanish, and I'd rather work in England than Germany."

"London, eh?"

"London."

"Oh well, I suppose you'll be coming back to see me occasionally."

"You can count on that. When it comes time to get you to sign those papers."

"You can be so cruel. So when are you going?"

"In a couple of weeks."

Della Torre gawped like a beached fish.

"A couple of weeks? You were going in a couple of weeks? Without telling me? How could you do that? Up and go without telling me?"

"I just told you."

"But surely you ought to have discussed it with your husband first."

"Ex-husband."

Della Torre sat heavily back down on the bed. It was bad enough to have people wanting to kill him. But to also have his ex-wife abandon him . . .

"Where are you going to live?"

"Vesana has a spare bedroom. She's happy to put me up until I get sorted with the job. It's not far from a hospital called the Royal Free. Sounds nice, doesn't it? Better than the Socialist Worker's Medical Institute or the Bloody Partizan Who Slaughtered Wounded Germans for the Glory of the Yugoslav Industrial Proletariat Pediatric Clinic. Anyway, she's in a place called Golders Green. Do you know anything about it? You used to live in London."

"Never heard of it. Or the hospital either. The pediatric clinic rings bells, though. It's in Pazin, isn't it? Anyway, where in London are these Green Royals and Free Golders?"

"She said north of the river. That's supposed to mean something."

"Well, that narrows it down to around seventy percent of the city. I mean, the place is only around fifty kilometres across."

"It's easy to get into the centre, she says. It's a short ride on the underground."

He shrugged. They'd already spent more time talking about London than he cared for. Besides, he had to get dressed.

"You didn't by any chance think to pick up any clothes for me?"

"You've got some of your father's underwear here and I'm sure he won't mind your borrowing a shirt. I brought you a pair of clean trousers. Oh, I also thought you might need these." She pulled his service Beretta out of the straw bag, together with a box of ammunition.

"Shit. You carried that around Zagreb in a straw bag? Had a cop stopped you, you'd have been in for some serious fun."

"I thought you needed it. And a policeman's never stopped me for anything except to tell me how pretty my eyes are or how well my summer dress fits me."

"Modest, aren't you."

"I am, rather. Which is why I never believe them."

"Anyway, thanks. You're right. I could certainly use these … You didn't happen to find a pack of Camels while you were at it?" he asked hopefully.

"In your laundry basket?" He wasn't sure whether the look she gave him was one of disgust or mere disapproval.

"Never mind."

He dressed as he talked, getting Irena to help him put his undershirt on. She even tied his laces for him. He should have had a bath but didn't really have the time. He didn't want to miss Anzulović.

"Are you taking your scarecrow coat?"

"No, I'll stick to the old cardigan I left here."

"You mean the one with paint on the sleeve?"

He shrugged. "I'll go shopping later. Listen, I might be back or I might not. So I'll probably say goodbye now. There could be a bit of excitement over the next few days. If anyone asks, you haven't seen me. If anyone saw you go to my place, it's because you're worried that the U-bend in the kitchen is cracked and the tap is leaking and you're afraid I'm too incompetent to sort it out myself, so you're dealing with it to make sure the place doesn't flood. That's all true, by the way. You wouldn't mind lending me your Golf from tomorrow, would you? My car's useless and the one I borrowed is going to attract a lot of attention pretty soon."

"How long do you want it for?" she asked.

"Well, I need to disappear for a while. Call it five, maybe six years."

"Oh, is that all? I thought it might be a long time. No, you can't borrow my Golf. I need it to go to London."

"You do realize that the steering wheel is on the wrong side for England."

"I'll manage."

He shrugged. He reached into the leather coat and pulled out his tie, which he put on, his little notebook, and the envelope of money, both of which he slid into the leather wallet Irena had brought back from his flat. But first he took out four thousand Deutschmarks and handed them over to her.

"Here, this might be useful."

"Where'd you get all these Deutschmarks?" she asked as she counted the money.

"I've been taking bottles back for their deposits. I'm fortunate to know so many alcoholics."

"Fortunate is not a word I'd use about you very often. I won't refuse. But I will pay you back. Thanks."

"Don't thank me, just give me a kiss." She did. And she meant it.

"Give me a call later, let me know what you're doing. I should be back for lunch and then after around eight. I'll leave my contact details with your father."

10

STRUMBIĆ GROUND HIS teeth. The throbbing stretched from his ankle to his prick; the whole of his shin blazed with it, as if della Torre had set light to the slivovitz he'd poured on him. Bastard. Strumbić could smell the slight oiliness in the almost neat alcohol.

After shouting until he thought he'd strip his vocal cords, he shut up. Della Torre wasn't going to change his mind and nobody else was going to hear. So he sat as still as he could for the first hour, until the pain died down enough to let him think that his legs might not buckle if he tried to stand.

Getting up out of the low-slung lawn chair was harder than he thought. At first he'd got stuck tilted forward, the chair folding itself in on him. His ass had pushed through the gap between the fabric on the chair seat and the back, and for a while he was wedged and couldn't get back into a normal sitting position. It was a strain on his good thigh, not to mention his gut, where his belt started to dig into his flesh.

"Goddamn it."

But by leaning forward he managed to lift the chair off the ground, getting most of his weight on his left leg. There was the constant risk he'd overbalance and end up on his face, but by wiggling carefully and pulling on the back of the chair with his cuffed hands he finally managed to unwedge himself. The effort threw him forward so that he bent double over the rickety table. He could feel its legs tremble under his weight. When he straightened himself he saw that the keys had fallen.

There was nothing for it. He tried to lower himself as gingerly as he could, but his good leg finally gave out from supporting more weight than it was used to, landing him heavily on the packed dirt floor. On the way down his wounded shin hit a table leg, making him shriek. He'd landed on the keys.

For a long while he lay there breathing hard, until he thought he might hyperventilate. Some concerted floundering got him to where he could reach the keys. He struggled to unlock the cuffs behind his back but eventually triumphed. By the time his hands were free, he'd worked himself into a cold sweat and had to sit down in the lawn chair again. He poured himself a tin mug of slivovitz, but as he went to drink it, the smell made him gag, so he put it back down. So instead he focused on how he was going to get out of the cellar.

The walls were more than half a metre of stone and poured concrete, and the ceiling was concrete reinforced with steel rods. He had only two options. The cellar's foundations weren't particularly deep, but trying to tunnel out through the packed dirt floor would be a day's work at least. The tools he needed were in a neighbouring shed. He didn't like the idea of pounding away with an iron bar and then scraping dirt out with his hands or a tin plate. Besides, it was stony ground up there on that hill. That left the door and the window.

The door was heavy wood bound in riveted metal. A pair of big padlocked iron bars on the outside made it more secure than some banks. It needed to be — these wine huts in the hills were ripe for pillaging by thirsty peasants. The window didn't have any glass; instead there was the shutter, a solid, heavy sheet of iron, also padlocked on the outside. The window frame, like the one for the door, was wood, but it too was solid and well seasoned and bound into the concrete walls with thick iron bolts.

The window it had to be; it was the weakest point in the structure.

At first Strumbić hammered at the shutter with the iron bar. But this didn't make the least impression and only succeeded in deafening him.

He sat back down and stared at it. The shutter was secured at the bottom by an iron flange set into the concrete. To release it there, he'd either have to use enough force to break the padlock, which was as big as his fist, or work the flange loose from the wall. He'd have more joy just digging his way through the concrete. It would have to be the shutter's hinges, which were set into the wood at the top of the frame and bolted on. He didn't have the tools to work them loose, but if he could weaken the wood he might be able to break the hinges off. He'd still have to force the shutter outward.

The only way to weaken the wood around the hinges was to burn it. At least della Torre had left him his matches. And the slivovitz was an excellent accelerant. There was a stack of paperback black-and-white comic-strip westerns, mostly *Zagor* translated from the Italian, that would burn. It was a shame; they were Strumbić's favourites. Still, if he could avoid dying of smoke inhalation, they'd help him get out.

Strumbić filled a tin bucket with wine to douse any fire that burned out of control. Then he dabbed slivovitz on and around the hinges. He pulled his shirt off and wrapped it around his face and then lit the frame. It burned fast, the paint bubbling and letting off black fumes. But once the slivovitz had burnt off, the fire went out. Strumbić found himself a candle stump. It was going to be a long night, and he didn't have enough matches to waste them.

11

DELLA TORRE WENT down the building's stairwell, his limp making an awkward echo against the hard terrazzo surfaces. He chewed on a slice of bread Irena had pressed on him. He ignored the main entrance and walked down a further storey to the garden level, where he unbolted the secured back door and then retraced his steps from the previous night back to the BMW, parked a few blocks away. He was relieved no one had broken in to steal the three cartons of Luckys he'd negligently left in plain sight on the back seat.

Even worse than opportunist thieves were the cops. Had one spotted the cigarettes, they'd have been long gone by now. Together with the car. Della Torre wouldn't have put it past a Zagreb flatfoot to call out a municipal tow for some make-believe parking violation. Things often went missing in the pound.

Just as bad were the vandals. Croats had been smashing up cars with Serb licence plates. So Serbs had taken to removing Croat plates on expensive cars and replacing them with fake Serb ones.

Della Torre drove through the lower town. It had been neatly laid out during the Austro-Hungarian imperial reign

on flat land north of the river, at the foot of the medieval and
Baroque old town on the hill above. He passed block after silent block of once-elegant buildings like the one he lived in.
But now they were a forlorn parade of impoverished dowagers.
In many places, the detailing on their façades had crumbled,
great flakes of filter-yellow paint chipped to reveal their drab
grey rendering underneath.

Decades of Communist neglect together with the recent
fear and uncertainty gave Zagreb a cold, hard look. Even the
lower town's grand squares — big, formal spaces — offered no
relief.

He passed King Tomislav's statue. At least Tomislav kept
his spear high. A cavalryman from the Wild West of Croatia's
collective imagination, ready to ride to the rescue. They were
crazy about westerns in this country. When della Torre was
a kid, over from America to visit relatives, he'd never failed
to be amazed by the stacks of comic books bought by grown
men, cowboy adventures full of six-shooters and Indians, piled
high at every news kiosk. No wonder he found it impossible to
shake off his unwanted nickname. Gringo. He couldn't even
remember who'd given it to him.

Della Torre followed the route the Bosnians had taken to
Zagreb's southern suburbs. Traffic was light; working people
usually started early, but not quite this early.

He parked the BMW in front of Anzulović's modern apartment block, another of an endless series of late-1960s concrete eyesores. He didn't have more than three cigarettes'
worth of a wait before he saw Anzulović take his wife's decrepit piss-yellow poodle for its morning walk. Anzulović
stopped in the building's shadow, on a weedy, overgrown
patch of lawn, while the creature strained. Della Torre went
over to him.

"Gringo. What brings you here, other than the sights?"

"Guess."

"You wanted to pay me back for that cigarette I gave you on Friday, because you knew I'd left mine upstairs."

"Right in one." Della Torre handed Anzulović the now nearly empty pack of Strumbić's Luckys and then gave him a light. "I also wanted to buy you breakfast, if you can bear to get into the office a little late."

"As long as we're having a work-related conversation about movies or broads, that shouldn't be a problem."

"Great. I'll wait for you in the car. It's the BMW over there." Della Torre pointed a thumb over his shoulder. Anzulović appraised the car and glanced at della Torre from the corner of his eye. He looked back at the car and nodded but didn't say anything.

"On your way, do you mind helping the mutt out with its crap. Just give it a little kick. Don't worry if it keels over. I'll buy you a nice bottle of Bell's to help you get over the trauma," Anzulović said, eyeing the dog with contempt.

Della Torre hadn't been waiting in the car long when Anzulović came back down, more than happy to get away from his wife and three adult daughters, every last one of them a nag.

"Nice motor. Yours?" Anzulović asked.

"No."

"Didn't think so."

"Borrowed?"

"Stolen."

Anzulović nodded sagely. "Legally?"

Della Torre thought about this for a little while and then said, "Nope."

"I see. So it's a piece of crucial evidence in one of your cases, then."

"Something like that."

Anzulović looked around the car, keeping his counsel, taking in the glossy wooden panelling and the grain of the leather-covered dashboard.

"Nice motor," he repeated meaningfully.

Della Torre could tell he was clipping facts together. The car. The early visit. Della Torre was notorious for not liking mornings. And New Zagreb was well outside of his normal orbit. It had to be serious.

Anzulović ran Department VI, but he was more like an avuncular colleague to della Torre than a boss. Maybe because he'd worked his way up from traffic cop through the regular Zagreb police's hierarchy before leaving to set up the new UDBA unit, while della Torre had been the international law expert at the prosecutor's office, good enough to take an academic post had he wanted one.

Della Torre had been one of Anzulović's first appointments.

Years before, they'd worked together on a tricky cross-border fraud investigation that, ironically, had involved an UDBA agent. Anzulović came to appreciate della Torre's intelligence and clarity.

At first della Torre had underestimated the older man, as a lot of people did, dismissed him as a bland bureaucratic time-server. But his prejudgment had been overturned by Anzulović's political skills, ironic cast, and, despite all appearances, ability to get things done.

So when offered a move from the politically suffocating Zagreb prosecutor's office to Anzulović's new UDBA unit, della Torre gave it serious consideration. And the more he considered, the more he was swayed. Department VI would give him unusual freedom. He'd have a boss he liked, who would insulate him from political crap rather than exacerbate it. And he would be able to look into files that would otherwise have forever remained mysteries.

During the good times, Anzulović ran the department efficiently, making sure his staff were protected from Belgrade's often baleful attention. What's more, he allowed his people some of the UDBA's perks. Like revoking tickets for minor traffic violations. And a certain flexibility with their expenses. Not to mention allowing private use of cars, equipment, and "safe houses" on the Adriatic coast.

But anyone using their UDBA status as leverage in ordinary neighbourly disputes or to force discounts from shopkeepers was fired. It happened a few times in the early days, and then people learned.

Anzulović had risen in standing from a good boss to a great one during bad times. As the Croat government put the screws on the department, he moved heaven and earth to make sure his people had enough money to live in something more than outright poverty. Those of his staff who were Serbs he protected from the Croat government's increasing hostility, refusing to fire any of them.

The UDBA brass had never wanted Department VI, but when it became inevitable, they insisted on appointing an ineffectual, supine bureaucrat to lead the charge. And they were conned into thinking Anzulović fit the bill. In time, the UDBA leadership realized their mistake, but he wore away at them too. What Department VI's UDBA colleagues wouldn't provide willingly, he'd use other means to get. He wasn't above skulduggery. Or, when necessary, threats.

But it was a careful balancing act. As a Croat, Anzulović lived under the permanent threat that he'd be accused of having an anti-Yugoslav nationalist agenda, which meant he had to be exceptionally deft in dealing with Belgrade—obsequious and friendly on the outside, but in reality calculating, with an extraordinary sang-froid. Department VI, encouraged by Anzulović, learned patience and improvisation. And cunning.

He was the one who'd arranged for Strumbić to do the occasional bit of intelligence work for della Torre.

"You didn't drive all this way in an almost new car, two hours before you normally get up, to give me an American cigarette."

"Have another one."

"Thanks, I don't mind if I do. You can develop a taste for these."

He lit the cigarette and smoked in silence for a while.

"Somebody wants me dead," della Torre finally said.

"We work for the UDBA. Plenty of people would happily dance on our graves."

"No. It's not like that. Somebody put a hit on me."

"Oh? How do you know?"

"Because last night I was in a car with the guys who were going to do the job and on my way to a very unpleasant end."

"You're sure they wanted you dead? I mean, you seem a bit stiff, but you're not what I'd call a corpse."

"They weren't very good. Remember those guys who did the really messy hit in Karlovac on that businessman who wouldn't play with the local protection racket? That's the story, anyway — had a factory and wouldn't pay his insurance."

"I remember. Bosnians, wasn't it? The Karlovac cops were surprisingly reluctant to investigate."

"That's the one."

"And? You got in the car with them because...?"

"I was set up," della Torre said.

"I see. Set up by...?"

"A friend. I'll tell you about him later."

"So your friend wants you dead. Sure it wasn't your wife? Couldn't say I'd blame her."

Anzulović had always had a soft spot for Irena, whom he inevitably compared favourably to his own women.

"I had a word with my friend. He says he was put up to it. Had no choice. That sort of thing. It was a help-or-else proposition."

"So if your friend doesn't want you dead, who does?"

"Belgrade."

"Oh? Anyone in particular? Or has the federal government decided it doesn't like you?"

"I don't know. Somebody took offence at something I had."

"This is starting to feel like twenty questions. I think I'm just going to have a little shut-eye on the way into the office and enjoy my luxurious surroundings, and if you decide to start talking sensibly, maybe I'll listen."

Della Torre drove in silence for a while.

"Nice leather. Should fetch a bit," Anzulović said in his slow, ruminating way. "Shame it's stolen. Though it'd be hard to keep, even if you got yourself new plates. Expensive to run. Still, if you could flog it there'd be a few pennies in it. Lord knows we could all use the money. I think Belgrade and Zagreb are competing to see who can starve us out of our jobs first."

"Okay. You've got me. I was selling stuff. Selling some files to this friend. Nothing sensitive. Just some of the lowest-classified stuff that was kicking around."

Anzulović nodded.

"Really. No state secrets. I promise. Nothing to compromise anyone or any investigation. Just the sort of dross they're not even bothering to burn." Files were being destroyed wholesale at the UDBA's various archives.

"Alright. I get it. So these files you flogged got you into trouble?"

"See, that's the thing. They didn't. Not the ones I sold."

"I'm afraid I'm a little slow. Probably has to do with age. When I was a younger man, I could watch those Russian films that never made any sense except as some sort of puzzle. You know, Tarkovsky," Anzulović said. But della Torre didn't know. Anzulović was always going on about films that della Torre hadn't a clue about. "But these days it's Hollywood straight down the line. Give it to me Hollywood."

"The person I was selling files to didn't find them very useful. So he stole some. From me."

"And just what sort of files did he happen to steal?"

Della Torre squirmed as he took a corner, slowed down, and then drove over the curb to park on one of Zagreb's wide cobbled pavements, the car pointed towards the door of the little café just far enough from their offices that there was little chance of bumping into colleagues, but close enough for Anzulović to walk into work.

The older man turned towards him but della Torre sat facing forward. "Hobby files," he said. "Background stuff."

"Oh? You mean the sort of things you're strictly forbidden from keeping?"

"It makes life easier."

"What, keeping dead investigations around just in case they come in handy? Notes on things you might find useful sometime in the future? I'm afraid, my boy, what's logical for a normal cop is very bad form for the UDBA. What do you think would happen if there was an internal investigation and they found you with a filing cabinet full of stuff you weren't meant to have?"

"I kept it locked..."

"So how did this person get your files?"

"I unlocked it."

Anzulović sighed. "Let's get some breakfast, and I'll see if I can dig any more out of you before I die of old age."

They sat in a booth and ordered coffees and rolls that looked vaguely like French croissants. Della Torre studied his boss. He was in his early fifties, lugubrious, with a long face and a pot belly on an otherwise thin frame. He had permanent black bags under his eyes. A thatch of black and grey hairs grew out of his potato nose, matching the ones sprouting from his ears.

"So do you know what was in the stuff that was stolen?"

"Something about Pilgrim." Della Torre had his notebook out and was going through the back pages, where he kept brief descriptions of cases that struck his curiosity.

"You know, that notebook is just as bad as keeping illegal files. What happens if it gets stolen?" Anzulović said.

"Good luck to anyone trying to decipher it."

"If it's the UDBA they won't have to. They'll just beat you until you tell them, and then they'll use it as evidence that you're a spy and hang you. Unless they shoot you. No wonder somebody lined you up for the nine-millimetre solution."

"Thanks for cheering me up."

"So what is this Pilgrim file about?"

"I don't know. I mean, I've got a little in here, and I'll tell you what I can remember, but I have no idea why anyone would be touchy about it."

"Give me a go."

"The reason I took an interest is because one of the Montenegrin's files mentioned Pilgrim. So when I ran across the Pilgrim file, I... well, I thought it might come in handy one day."

The Montenegrin had been a thread running through della Torre's professional life. He'd been a senior agent, on the liquidation teams. And then, around the time Department VI had been formed, he'd been promoted to be the head of the UDBA's wetworks. Its killers. The people della Torre was charged with investigating.

It was the Montenegrin who'd approached della Torre that first time in London — back when the UDBA was still some mysterious, malign, distant force — and demanded co-operation from the student lawyer.

"And?"

"And nothing. It was a real curiosity. It had something to do with centrifuges the Swedes were selling that went through Belgrade sometime in the mid-1980s."

"To Belgrade?"

"No, they moved on. I don't know where to."

"So?"

"It was strange, that's all. They were centrifuges made in Sweden by some German company based in Cologne that for some reason was connected to the Montenegrin."

"Centrifuges? You mean the things hospitals use to do stuff to blood?"

"I guess so. My notes don't say what they're for. But there were a lot of them. Thousands."

"Sounds like a lot of blood," Anzulović said.

"Who knows, maybe it has something to do with AIDS?"

"Horrible disease. Killed Rock Hudson. Not the greatest actor, but God's a pretty harsh critic if that's what it came down to." Anzulović looked hard at della Torre. "Something you're not telling me about? Who stole the file?"

Della Torre sat back in his seat and exhaled a long breath of smoke.

"Strumbić."

"Strumbić, eh? Figured it must have been something like that. He's got more tendrils than a . . ." — Anzulović looked around for inspiration — ". . . than we do. So who wants you dead?"

"You mean other than a bunch of Bosnians who did the Karlovac job? I don't know. Strumbić says they were hired by some old Communist who happens to know the management at the Metusalem. It's a restaurant up in the old town."

"I know it."

"Can you do me a favour? Can you look up who he runs with? Maybe find out who the old man is so I have a better idea of who hates me enough to have me dead."

"I take it you don't want to come into the office because you're worried these people in Belgrade might have some connections to the UDBA."

"Something like that."

"And what are you proposing to do, then?" Anzulović asked.

"I was wondering what you might think about my taking a little time off. A couple of months. I've got some holiday built up. I don't feel great about being in Zagreb when there are people who want to kill me and they're being helped by the cops."

"Cops? Or a single cop? Are you saying Strumbić is in this with somebody else from the Zagreb force?"

"No. Just Strumbić. I think."

"Okay. It's important to be clear about these things. Some people want to kill you, possibly ordered by somebody in Belgrade, though we don't know this for sure, and Strumbić was coerced into helping. Is that working for you?"

"Yes," della Torre admitted.

"I'll tell you what, Gringo. I'll go back to the office and do some digging and come back with what I get. You just stay nice and cosy here. I agree with you that you'll be better off going away for a little while. Nobody's getting much of anything done here these days anyway. I'll put it down that you're on extended leave. I'll make sure your salary is still paid, whatever good that does. We'll investigate from this end. It'll give us something to do now that we've been put on ice. Keep the troops motivated. I have no idea what we'll do if we find out Belgrade's behind this thing. You'd better hope for Croat independence in that case. Anyway, I'll be back in a little while. Cool your heels until then."

"Sorry, boss."

"You should be. And for the record, we never talked about you selling information. Right? Or about how you keep records of things you shouldn't," Anzulović said, helping himself to one of della Torre's cigarettes. "Nice, these."

"Want a carton?" della Torre asked.

"That a bribe?"

"No."

"Shame, because if it was, I wouldn't feel that I had to pay you back, and I can't afford American cigarettes," Anzulović said.

"It's a present."

"In that case, thank you very much."

Della Torre walked to the car with Anzulović and pulled out a carton of Strumbić's cigarettes. Anzulović held it close.

Della Torre went back to the café, ordered another coffee, and lit a cigarette. He bored into his little black book, wishing his notes had been more expansive. Centrifuges? They didn't even seem to have much to do with Yugoslavia. From what he could remember of it, the file looked like an analysis of foreign industry. Okay, so there were a lot of centrifuges, a couple of thousand, and they'd been transhipped through Belgrade, but it was hard to see how a bunch of machines designed to spin blood, as Anzulović had pointed out, would be of interest to anyone. He'd made reference to a couple of oddities about the file in his notebook. The machines appeared to be quite large. They were described as long tubes, and—if the shipping dimensions were anything to go by—more than two cubic metres per unit. And they'd been re-exported, but if the original files had mentioned where, he hadn't written it down. He didn't know anything about centrifuges. He'd ask Irena.

What could they have had to do with the Montenegrin? Other than that the UDBA's wetworks spilled a lot of blood. The document dated from the mid-1980s. That's when the spread of the AIDS plague had become clear and terrifying. By then people knew it had something to do with bodily fluids. Maybe that's where the centrifuges came in. For a moment he had a ridiculous thought, that the UDBA's wetworks were using AIDS as a means of killing dissidents. But he dismissed it just as quickly. When the UDBA killed, it liked to spread terror around the community of dissidents about their political activities, not about whom they shared needles with.

By the time Anzulović got back to the café, della Torre had been there the best part of two hours. Anzulović handed him a thin file.

"Just the highlights. It cost me four packs of Luckys to get the archivist to piss off long enough to copy them. They were in the restricted section, but he's being friendlier these days now that the Communists are looking shaky." There was a long and meaningful pause, which della Torre chose to ignore.

"I'm afraid it doesn't say much. The people associated with

the Metusalem are Belgrade through and through. Owned by a retired Communist who spends most of his time in Crkvenica," Anzulović said, referring to the Adriatic holiday resort. "But he has plenty of old friends. One of them is the Dispatcher."

"Who?" The name rang a bell for della Torre, but he wasn't sure why.

"One of Tito's men. Disappeared into quiet retirement after Tito's death. Watchers have seen him at the Metusalem recently."

"Yes, of course. Spent a time on Goli Otok and then did Tito's dirty work during the Croatian Spring."

"That's the fellow."

"Have you got anything on him? I mean, why he might be interested in me?"

"Not much. I'm sure there's stuff in the archives if I dug around. I'll have to get the archivist in a better mood, though. Leave it to me and I'll have a look while you're on holiday. I'm always curious about people who want to kill my staff. By the way, is there anything else you might want to tell me?"

Della Torre looked thoughtful and then shook his head.

"No?"

Anzulović's beeper went off. He looked at the number.

"Office calling. Like they couldn't tell me what they wanted when I was there. I hate these bloody things. You can never get away from them. Probably some overdue bill or cretin politician," he said. "So what are you planning on doing with the car? I'm assuming Strumbić will want it back. He'll have his friends on the Zagreb force looking for it if you borrowed it without asking nicely."

"He's okay for a little while."

"What'd you do, tie him up?"

"Something like that."

"Well, I didn't tell you this, but there's a garage just this side of the tram station at Černomerac. The owner knows me. He'll do you a deal for the Beemer. Just don't go around telling everyone. And I'll make sure you can disappear for a while. Bereavement. Death in the family ought to do. But keep your head down. I'll think about how maybe to keep you alive until we can arrange to get you killed off by the coming war. Oh, and I'd wait until lunchtime to go to Černomerac. They can be busy in the morning."

"Gee, thanks."

"Who knows where the cards are going to fall? Not just for you but for all of us… hmm, sounds like something out of *Casablanca*," he added to himself as the beeper went off again. "I've got to go. Good luck, and let me know where you pitch up. And remember, this is just a holiday while we try to figure out who the hell wants you in a cosy two-cubic-metre place of your own in Mirogoj. Don't be thinking about making it permanent or anything."

12

FOR A LONG time, Besim the driver thought he was blind. He
knew he was alive, but he couldn't see anything. His face hurt.
He could taste blood, his face was sticky with it. His tongue
was enormously fat, and he could feel something digging into
it. His lips were swollen, and he had to breathe through his
mouth because his nose didn't seem to work. There was a ringing in his ear as if he was sitting in a church bell.

He tried to speak but he could form little more than grunts
and snuffles. He was holding something. Yes, he knew what it
was. A pistol. He remembered pulling it out of his holster as
his head was being pulled back by that rope. Caught him right
under the nose. He'd tried to keep control of the car with his
left hand and bring the gun around with his right but it had all
happened too quickly. He'd only just pulled the gun out and
was drawing it in front of himself when there was the explosion of noise. And then he couldn't remember anything.

He felt the fresh air on his face but he knew he was still
in the car seat. Ingrained habit made him reach forward and
feel for the key in the ignition. It was there and he turned it.
A headlight blazed forward, the radio came on, and a windscreen wiper flapped in the air. The bonnet was crumpled in

front of him but he could see past the car on the passenger side. Slowly the scene in front of him assembled itself into something he could understand. The headlight pointed downward. He could see a stream and some shapes, and he could hear someone shouting his name in a hoarse, guttural tone. He bellowed in return, sounding like a wounded cow.

The shape below made its way to the side of the headlight. As it drew up alongside the car, he realized there was something familiar about it, though it seemed to twist to one side.

"Besim, Besim, are you alive? Put the gun down before you shoot me. Point it down. That's better. Think you can get out of the car?"

Besim nodded uncertainly. With some effort, he managed to wrench the door open. But he underestimated how much of a drop there was. He fell heavily to the ground and then slid headfirst down the slope until a protruding root stopped him. He hadn't thought his face could hurt any more than it did. He was wrong.

"Besim. Besim, what are you doing?"

Besim got up and grunted.

"Come here, over to the light, let's have a look at you. Allah, you look like somebody hit you in the face with a shovel. Did you shoot yourself in the head?"

Besim rocked slightly, trying to shake his head.

"Can you talk?"

Besim did his little snuffle-grunt but then gave up. It hurt his mouth too much. A big, hard object pressed between his palate and tongue. He spat it out and then realized it was probably a tooth.

"Your cousin isn't doing too well. He's dead. I think he drowned. Maybe he couldn't swim. Could he swim?" The banana-shaped Bosnian had found Besim's cousin face-down in the bottom of the stream, looking like something he once saw in a nature documentary. Or was it a war movie? He couldn't remember.

Besim shook his head. At least it hadn't been one of the cousins he'd been fond of. Or one who had a lot of brothers. This one was older and liked to run things, even though he was pig ignorant. He was the one who'd got their dodgy guns from some fly-by-night dealer in Banja Luka.

"Here, give me a hand. Let's get him up to the road. Maybe we can flag a car down or something."

They went to the stream and dragged the corpse back up the hill as best they could. Twice they lost their grip and it started to roll back down the slope. When they got up to the road, they couldn't see a thing. There was a weak glow from the car's surviving headlight reflected back up the gully, but that was all. The moon had disappeared and clouds covered the stars, but they could see a faint smudge of grey where a gap in the trees offered them a view east along the broad Sava River valley. Dawn would be breaking before long.

In the distance they heard a car.

"Besim, here, let's get your cousin into the road."

"Wha?" Besim seemed to say, though the banana-shaped Bosnian wasn't sure.

"Here, like this."

They dragged the corpse by its feet so that it stretched across the middle of the road.

"Don't worry. If he gets run over it won't hurt too much. He was never too polite anyway," the skinny, crooked Bosnian said. He grabbed hold of Besim and pulled him out of view to the side of the road.

The farmer in the green Zastava swerved when its feeble headlamps picked out the body ahead. His brakes squealed and he got out quickly.

"Fucking drunks," he said aloud. "Lying around all over the roads these days. No wonder they're always getting killed."

He prodded the body in front of him with his boot.

"You—get up, you, and get out of the fucking road before

somebody squashes you flat. Couldn't blame them if they did."

Behind him he heard a door slam. The farmer turned in surprise as Besim revved the engine and popped the clutch. The car leapt forward, dropping the man hard to the ground. Besim braked before he ran him over.

"Mary, mother of God. You hit me with my own car. You could have killed me." The farmer was flat on the ground, voice trembling, his face the length of a nose away from Besim's cousin. "Shit. This man is dead. This is a dead man. Sweet God, don't kill me."

"Get up, mister," said the banana-shaped Bosnian.

The middle-aged farmer struggled to his feet. He could make out an oddly twisted man pointing a gun at him.

"I've got nothing, sir. Nothing. I was just going to Zagreb. I've got an appointment with a specialist early this morning. But I've got nothing to steal."

He was about to reach into his pocket when the Bosnian said, "Keep your hands in front of you." The Bosnian thought for a moment. "Now here's what you're going to do. You're going to take your trousers off very slowly. And when you've taken them off, you're going to go down into that gully, down to where that stream is, where it's lit up by the car. Then you're going to get into that stream and squat down and put those trousers over your head. And if you move I'm going to shoot you. My friend is going to take your car, and I'm going to stand here and watch you, and if you move, you're dead."

The farmer trembled out a "Yes sir, yes sir" and did as he was told.

"Okay, Besim. Let's get your cousin in the back seat. We'll have to get him back home to bury him. And you're going to have to get your face looked after. I don't feel none too hot either. Then we're going to come back and find that della Torre and that Strumbić and I'm going to shoot them and you're going to run them over. After we've got our money."

13

CAUGHT IN A convoy of Yugoslav army vehicles heading towards
Slovenia, Anzulović took longer than he'd expected to drive
out to the hospital. Having to take one of the old Zastavas
made it all the less pleasant. There were a couple of official
Mercs left, but one was in the garage for servicing while somebody else was using the other one. Maybe Messar.

Setting off, he'd had a little fantasy about making a quick
stop in the centre of the little town. Under the ornate verdigris
steeple of the yellow Baroque church, in sight of the ruins of
an old castle built for the tax collectors of the Magyar nobles
who'd once ruled those forested valleys, was a pastry shop.

It wasn't just any pastry shop but a pastry shop that specialized in one specific sort of cake, an improbably fluffy custard
cream on a delicate filo base topped with yet more filo and a
dusting of powdered sugar. The pastries had the absurdly ugly
German name of *kremšnita*. There were cake shops that sold
versions in Zagreb, but nothing to compare with the ones in
Samobor. The mere mention of a Samobor *kremšnita* made
Anzulović blush with joy and anticipation like a teenage girl.
Even the smallest pretence would spur him to take the round
trip to Samobor if he could make it coincide with the shop's

criminally short opening hours—confined to when the pastry was freshly baked and still at blood temperature.

Except now that he had a reason to be in Samobor, he didn't have time to make a detour into the centre of town from the provincial hospital on its fringes. Maybe on the way back, though he'd have to hurry. The shop shut for lunch.

Messar was waiting for him at the front reception, where he gave Anzulović a quick rundown. Messar was tall and blond; he looked the way movie people thought jackboot-wearing Germans ought to look. But his ethnic Germanness went deeper than looks. He operated on German notions of efficiency and was a stickler for rules, though when the two conflicted, he preferred efficiency. Efficiency meant that he had one of his junior officers monitoring the Zagreb police frequency at all times, as well as the ticker of telephone traffic to and from the police headquarters produced by the UDBA's communications team.

Which was how Messar had come to know that a Zagreb cop had been shot by an UDBA officer. That was the entirety of the message he'd left for Anzulović, along with instructions for Anzulović to meet him at the Samobor community hospital. And because Anzulović trusted Messar, as he did all his staff, and because there was the prospect of *kremšnita* at the end of it, he went when called.

"So what's the emergency, then? An UDBA agent shooting a Zagreb cop ought to be cause for celebration," Anzulović said with forced levity.

"We're not clear on who the shooter was just yet. But the complaint is that one of our people's involved. And the cop's a detective. The head of internal investigations from the Zagreb force, Lieutenant Colonel Kakav, is wetting himself over the prospect of getting an UDBA scalp. He's here, by the way."

"Kakav, eh? At least they didn't send anybody competent. By 'our people' I assume you mean Department VI?" Anzulović was developing an uneasy feeling that he knew what was coming.

"Yup, della Torre."

"Gringo, eh? As far as I know, he's never carried his service pistol. Uses it as a paperweight, doesn't he? What'd he shoot the cop with, a staple gun?" Anzulović kept the tone light, but there was a note of irritation in his voice. Irritation with della Torre for not having told him the whole truth.

"A popgun. A nine millimetre with all the force of an air pellet," Messar said, their steps echoing up the stairwell.

"So not so much wounding with intent as scratching without a chance. Who's the lucky flatfoot with an extended holiday?" he asked.

"Detective Strumbić. Heard of him?"

"Oh yes..." he said.

"Anyway, he says he was minding his own business at his weekend house when della Torre — our della Torre —"

"Naturally, who else's?"

"When della Torre dropped in on him uninvited, along with some Bosnian hoods. They threatened Strumbić, wanted him to do something for them—Strumbić isn't very clear on this point. Suffice it to say he refused on grounds that it was corrupt and illegal. They got angry and shot him, and then locked him in the cellar of his weekend house."

"Della Torre shot him?"

"Something else he's not clear on. He got shot. Della Torre was with the Bosnians. They all had guns. Strumbić says he's not sure who pulled the trigger. I think his memory will improve when he sees where his advantage lies."

"I think you're right."

"He strikes me as a pretty crooked cop."

"Messar, your perceptiveness never fails to astound me. But right now we're not the ones to be making any accusations. We're just going to listen and offer suggestions. By we, I mean me. The Zagreb cops will take every opportunity they possibly can to give us a good kicking, and these days they're the ones in favour. We might have to bend over for this one."

"I got his statement from the Zagreb homicide dick who's been put on the case."

"Homicide?"

"The most senior staffer Kakav could round up on such short notice. They were here first thing. The detective has gone back to Zagreb to start pushing paper."

"Smart of you to get here so quickly," Anzulović said.

"Nothing else going on. Most of my people take turns waiting in line at the bread shop. Either that or they're moonlighting, if they can find another job."

Anzulović nodded. Not only had Department VI been starved of funds, but for the past six months its workload had been shrunk. Belgrade had pulled its investigations, worried about how sympathetic Department VI might be to the new Croatian administration. And the Croats, well, they'd hated the UDBA ever since the early 1970s, when the service had crushed the republic's independence movement and set about kidnapping or killing dissidents.

Two police officers were on guard outside of the hospital room. Anzulović showed them his ID, and they demanded the same of Messar. Instead, Messar gave them a look of withering contempt and then turned to Anzulović.

"Did you know that at the bottom of both sides of the page of a Zagreb police exam it says, 'Please turn over'? That's the test. Anyone who keeps flipping the page is considered prime cop material. Memories of goldfish," Messar said. The cops backed down, bristling, but nonetheless fearful of the UDBA man.

Messar was still talking when they walked into the room. Strumbić was in bed, his face china white. Kakav took up the only chair in the room.

"Detective," said Anzulović to Strumbić, and then stretched

his hand out to Kakav, a fat, middle-aged man in a too-tight, shiny suit. "Colonel, thank you so much for waiting for me to arrive."

Kakav wore a serious expression, but Anzulović could see from the man's eyes that he was feasting on something at least as delicious as a fresh custard cream cake: the prospect of revenge on the intelligence service, an enemy the whole of his professional life.

"Major," Kakav said to Anzulović. Like most Department VI staff, Anzulović rarely used his official rank. "This is a regrettably serious matter, as we explained to your officer here," he said with pompous gravity.

"It must be, for someone of such seniority as you to have given up his morning," Anzulović said.

"Of course, our primary concern is the health and well-being of our comrade, Detective Strumbić. But his accusation against one of your people is shocking. Shocking that a wanton attack should be made on an unimpeachable member of the Zagreb force."

"I've heard the outlines of the accusation from Captain Messar here, one of our finest officers," Anzulović countered. "As you know, because the complaint has been made against one of our people, the rules say that the investigation falls under the remit of the security services of the Ministry of the Interior."

"Major —" Kakav started to protest, but Anzulović held up his hand.

"Colonel, we all know that times are changing. Rules are being adapted and amended to fit the new reality. I don't know if you've met Captain Messar before, but you'll know him by reputation." Anzulović wasn't flattering Messar. He had an astonishingly high reputation even among the civilian forces. Few Department VI people had nailed more UDBA agents on corruption charges. Or Zagreb cops along the way.

Kakav nodded.

"You will know that he's probably the best investigating officer in the intelligence services, if not the whole of Yugoslav law enforcement."

Kakav raised his eyebrows slightly, wrinkled up his face, and shrugged.

"My suggestion is," Anzulović went on, "that Messar takes charge of the investigation, but otherwise that it is handled by the Zagreb police. That way we can say we followed the rules, in case some authority raises questions about procedures. We can always say that since Messar led it, it was an UDBA-directed operation. But it will be entirely transparent to the civilian service." Anzulović's warning to Kakav that the Zagreb police's new-found authority could well prove temporary if the Yugoslav state asserted its will in Croatia again was not lost on the senior Zagreb policeman. "But we can also show the new spirit of co-operation between the agencies of the new Croatian state."

"There aren't many precedents for these arrangements. We'd have to come up with a protocol and get our senior people to agree to it," Kakav sputtered.

"Colonel, this is a matter of great and immediate urgency. By delaying, by insisting that all the details be nailed down, you do realize you run the risk of losing sight of what needs to be done in the name of justice? Of appraising this very serious complaint and finding the perpetrator? If you wanted to be... legally precise, you would have to leave it to the intelligence service and then revert to the courts for permission to take over the case. We could be arguing about who has what powers in this case for the next three years. All I'm suggesting is that the Zagreb police carry out the investigation, but with Messar supervising efforts. If your detectives think he's doing a bad job, they can take it to you and you can take it to me and we'll replace Messar with me and your choice of appointee as co-heads of the investigation. Does that sound reasonable?"

Kakav nodded, knowing that everything Anzulović had said was reasonable, but at the same time understanding he'd somehow had his trousers pulled down and a bull's eye painted on his ass.

"And now, Colonel, I have no doubt that you have pressing concerns in Zagreb. Captain Messar will go back as well and start proceedings, if I understand correctly that a statement has already been taken from Detective Strumbić."

Anzulović shook Kakav's hand and the colonel found himself being ushered out of the hospital room by Messar.

"Messar," Anzulović said when it was just the two of them and Strumbić, "do you mind giving me and the detective here five minutes? We know each other from way back, and I think a man who's suffered such a shock as he has might find it less overwhelming to talk to an old friend. If you've got a car, you might as well go back to Zagreb and start organizing things. But try to keep the cops from getting too far ahead of themselves. Wait for me."

"I'll have to track down della Torre."

Anzulović nodded. It was out of his hands. Della Torre would have to be brought in. Unless he'd had the wit to leave already. Stupid boy. If only he'd admitted to shooting Strumbić. No. Anzulović would have had to take him in and launch formal proceedings. It just wasn't done to shoot Zagreb cops. Especially not these days, however much they might deserve it.

Messar walked over to Strumbić's bed. "Detective, we'll catch your man. You can rest assured. You're in good hands," he said, giving Strumbić's leg a hearty slap.

Strumbić howled with pain. "You stupid—" He bit his tongue as Messar walked out, smirking to himself.

Anzulović said nothing. Messar had his methods.

"Anzulović, where'd you get Messar from? Left over from the Nazis? What'd he do before? Torture children and maim puppies?"

Anzulović shrugged. "He was just trying to reassure you he'll be on top of this case."

"Yeah? Well, tell him della Torre's the guy to be kicking around, not me."

"I'm surprised Kakav came out. He must love you."

"We're like this," Strumbić said, crossing his fingers. "Except he's this one" — Strumbić wagged one of the fingers — "the one I wipe my ass with. My luck to have the village idiot fighting in my corner. You guys don't fool me for a second. You're going to be batting for Gringo and screwing me."

"Listen, Julius," Anzulović said, sitting down on the edge of the bed, "I haven't got a lot of time to talk crap." He paused almost apologetically. "We don't need to mince words, do we? You tell me what really happened and I'll listen sympathetically. You bullshit me and you will, I guarantee you, regret it."

"Just don't touch the fucking leg. They're being stingy with the painkillers. A bit of local, and that's mostly worn off," Strumbić said, feeling sorry for himself. He rubbed his leg. "It was like I said. Gringo and these three hicks came down and made me an offer. I said no thanks and one of them shot me."

"Not della Torre?"

"Might have done. Couldn't tell. Gun went off, bullet hit me, and suddenly I had other things on my mind."

"Julius, I won't fool around with you here. We haven't got a huge amount of time. You see, I actually know what happened. You set Gringo up with those Bosnians. For some reason they screwed up and Gringo decided to take a bit of revenge on you." Anzulović was guessing, but figured it was probably close to the truth. "What happened to the Bosnians?"

"Who knows? They disappeared. Their car's wrapped around a tree, but they went, *puff*, into thin air," Strumbić said, not bothering to deny Anzulović 's accusations.

"Now, Julius, you're right. I've got Gringo's interests in mind. He shouldn't have shot you, but he did. When it comes up in front of the judge, he'll get plenty of sympathy. Nobody thinks it's a bad thing to wound somebody who conspired in trying to kill you. Except between here and there, Gringo might end up in a lot of trouble. If your Zagreb cops get hold of him, whoever is trying to get rid of him will have a free ride. So we'll do our best to get him into UDBA custody. But that's not an optimal solution either. Not for you, anyway. You see, Julius, life for you will be very tricky if Messar happens to get hold of Gringo or the Bosnians. Sure, Gringo will be in trouble for selling you crap files, but not as much trouble as you'll be in for having stolen good ones off him. Or for being party to a hit on him. I may not be able to bury this, because your bosses want to give me as much grief as possible. I don't know what advantage you thought you'd have in fingering Gringo. Did you think it would make you a hero with the Zagreb force? Or did you think that if you blamed the Bosnians they'd think it was a fight between a bunch of crooks and a corrupt cop? No, don't answer me. I'll put it down to shock. Normally you're not that stupid. I suggest you start writing another version of what happened, one that puts Gringo in a better light. And then maybe, just maybe, we can make this whole thing go away, find the Bosnians, and figure out who wants to kill one of my employees."

Strumbić stared sullenly at Anzulović. Before he joined the UDBA, Anzulović had a reputation for being able to cut through seven degrees of bullshit, and Strumbić knew that Anzulović was at least Messar's equal in solving a case.

"Messar is as good an investigator as we're likely to find," continued Anzulović, "so there's a very, very good chance we'll have Gringo in by this afternoon. Which means you'll have to pull your quill out and make Shakespeare look like an Albanian ditchdigger pretty damn quick. Do I make myself clear?"

"Crystal."

"Good. How bad's the wound?"

"I'll live."

"How long they likely to keep you in here?"

"They say they're sending me home today." Strumbić didn't sound too happy about the prospect.

"Even better. Tomorrow morning I want you in my office with that affidavit. I'll have a lawyer in to witness it. Make it believable. And make it good. My motto is that what makes movies bad is bad scripts. Write me a script that wins Academy Awards. Explain exactly what happened, exactly the way it happened, so long as Gringo's one of the good guys. Got that? I've got an urgent appointment right now. But you be sure you're at that office at nine a.m. sharp. Understand?"

"Like you said it in Greek and I was born in Athens," said Strumbić.

"Goodbye, Detective," Anzulović said.

"I'd like to say it was a pleasure," Strumbić said to Anzulović's retreating back.

Anzulović looked at his watch as he was walking to the parking lot. *Della Torre.* He shook his head. The situation had certainly become complicated.

The young lawyer... No, he wasn't young anymore. Della Torre was seeing the tail end of his thirties. Yet to Anzulović he was the same young prosecutor he'd first met when Anzulović was with the Zagreb detectives, what was it, a decade before? There'd been something joyfully boyish about him. Not quite naive but maybe an underlying optimism. Growing up in America must have rubbed off on della Torre. It was an attractive but strange quality for someone to have in Yugoslavia, a country where if people weren't complaining they weren't conversing.

The air felt crisp after the hospital's oppressive heat. Anzulović quickened his step to the car, which he'd parked over the middle of two spaces. It felt colder in the car than it had outside. He'd heard the newest Mercedes had heated seats. He could have used them right then. Though he might as well wish he were Cary Grant.

His thoughts drifted back to della Torre. There was something Hollywood about his looks, though Anzulović could never pin down who it was that the lawyer reminded him of. None of the recent actors. None from the previous generation either—not Newman or McQueen or Eastwood. Though there were shades of Kristofferson playing Billy the Kid.

He couldn't figure it out.

Anzulović wouldn't have minded della Torre as a son-in-law, if he weren't already married to Irena. They made a nice couple. Clever. Attractive. With a genuine streak of goodness. Though anything Gringo had, Irena had more of. Shame they were on the rocks.

There was something innately lucky about the lawyer.

No, that wasn't quite right. Della Torre's mother had died when he was a boy. He'd been dragged back from America, back from the land of unlimited promise to . . . to this.

Anzulović checked his watch and pressed down on the car's accelerator. Right now, the only thing that mattered was that if he hurried he might just be able to make it to the pastry shop before it shut for midday.

14

DELLA TORRE WALKED back through Zagreb's main square, Trg Republike. There had been talk about changing its name back to the old one from before the Communists, Trg Ban Jelačić. It was named after Duke Jelačić, a bald man with a big moustache who'd run the country for the Austrians at one time. His statue had been taken down by the Communists when they'd changed the name. Apparently someone had kept it hidden since the war. *No doubt another cavalryman on a prancing horse,* thought della Torre. *Another Zagreb cowboy.*

The sound of an explosion made della Torre flinch. Pigeons, scrawnier than he remembered, wheeled into the air. It was the midday cannon booming out from the old watchtower on the hill. It aimed south towards the Bosnian border, where Croatia's Serbs were getting restless. *Maybe they should start loading it with shot,* della Torre thought.

The drizzle had lifted slightly, but it was the sort of day that had all the colour wrung out of it. Trams trundled into the square. People hurried to wherever they were going. Few ambled these days.

Della Torre's stomach churned with uncounted cups of strong, sweet coffee. He'd sat in the café after Anzulović left, but then finally went for a walk. He thought better that way.

Somebody wanted him dead. Somebody high up in Belgrade, if Strumbić was to be believed. They'd still want him dead now. An old Communist based in Zagreb had been dug up out of whatever hole he'd been in to make the arrangements. So either the people in Belgrade were no longer in a position of power or they didn't want official involvement.

Serbia was changing too, just like Croatia was. The nationalists were also running the show there. The old cadre who'd helped Tito build a Communist Yugoslavia from the ashes of the Second World War had been sidelined everywhere. Even the Yugoslav army barely clung to the Yugoslav ideal. Every day it became more and more an instrument of Serb nationalism.

What had he done to nettle the old Yugoslav Communists?

Della Torre figured they'd used the Bosnians because the UDBA had made a fine art of integrating criminals into the secret service, hiring them as assassins and agents. Old habits...

Pilgrim. Swedish centrifuges. The Montenegrin. That's all he had in his little notebook. The centrifuges were cylinders like big pipes, two metres or so in length, shipped to Belgrade in their thousands during the mid-1980s. From Belgrade, they'd been sent on abroad, only he couldn't recall where to, if the files had even mentioned it. It was only because the file had been connected to the Montenegrin that he'd noted it, collected it, added it to his curiosities. What the Montenegrin had to do with it wasn't clear, just that he'd been involved with something called Pilgrim and Pilgrim had something to do with centrifuges.

He was a strange curiosity, the Montenegrin. A thorough, utterly ruthless professional killer. Sometimes he was subtle, slowly reeling in his quarry with the right bait, placed perfectly on the right hook.

Della Torre had been the hook when, more than a decade earlier, they'd first met in London.

What had the Montenegrin said? "You work for the prosecutor's department. As an officer of the Yugoslav state, you
have some responsibilities. I have one for you to discharge.
There is a man called Svjet who goes to the Croatian Mass at
the Brompton Oratory on Sunday mornings. Go to the service.
Get to know him. You don't need to record anything; just make
sure he gets to know you and trust you."

He dared not ignore the UDBA man.

So he met Svjet. Got to know him and his family. The
old man had married late because of the interruption to his
life — seven years on Goli Otok. He could be tedious about
politics, but drag the conversation away from the Church and
Croatia and he changed. He was full of humour and insight
into film and art and books. He played the viola and performed
duets with his daughter on the violin.

When, at the end of the academic year, della Torre had to go
back to Zagreb, the Montenegrin came to see him again, handing him a package. Papers, he'd said, about Bušić's killing. Give
them to Svjet.

Della Torre hastily arranged a meeting with the old man.
Nothing could have kept Svjet from coming. Ante Bušić had
been a close friend, another dissident writer and also part of the
Croatian Spring movement. He'd been killed in Paris by the
UDBA a couple of years before. Svjet had more than once told
della Torre how he reminded him of a younger Bušić. Maybe
his fondness for della Torre had really just been nostalgia.

Years later, when he left the prosecutor's office and joined
Department VI, della Torre became reacquainted with the
Montenegrin. Though now the Montenegrin wasn't just an
UDBA agent but also the head of the wetworks operation.

With the job came the opportunity for della Torre to look
into the UDBA file on Svjet, though he'd long suspected what
had happened. He'd been coaxed to Trieste by the package della
Torre had given him about Bušić. He'd been picked up there by

UDBA agents, people who worked for the Montenegrin. Svjet had been taken back to Belgrade. And then he'd disappeared. The file said nothing more. But it didn't need to. It had been the story of many other dissidents. Kidnapped and disappeared.

As far as he knew, Svjet's wife and daughter still lived in London. As far as he knew, they'd spend their lives wondering. He'd never spoken to the Montenegrin about it. It was never one of della Torre's cases.

There was a certain irony to his present circumstances. He'd spent years hunting down the UDBA's killers. Now he was the hunter hunted. His big hope was that Croatia would win her independence. Soon.

He'd walked a big loop around the centre of Zagreb. The fine morning mist penetrated the city's mood, leached right through him.

He had to do something about the car. It was a shame; he was getting to like driving a BMW. But Anzulović was right — the minute Strumbić was free, he'd have every cop in Zagreb looking for it. Della Torre would offload the BMW after he'd had a bite to eat.

There was a decent sausage stand at Černomerac, near the garage Anzulović had told him about. He drove there, parked just off the square, and bought a fat steamed kobasa, pinkish red and swollen to bursting out of the ends of its skin. It came with a thick slice of white bread and a dollop of hot, smooth mustard. He bought a third-of-a-litre bottle of Karlovačka beer and, briefly, thought about the Bosnians. He wondered if they'd been found yet and whether any of them had survived. Certainly not the swimmer.

"Dead today."

"What?" della Torre said, startled out of his reverie by the sausage man.

"I said it's dead today. I mean, plenty of people around, but not a lot of business. I guess nobody eats anymore."

"The country's on a diet."

"Yeah, well, there's some that eat very well. All those Bosnian smugglers are onto a gold mine. They go south, they go north, but wherever they go, there's a Deutschmark to be made. They keep the business pretty sewn up too. Try and muscle in and they plant you in the ground headfirst. I hear there's whole fields of sprouting legs in the hills down south."

"Paints a picture. You seem to know a lot about it."

"Nah, just what I hear. Černomerac is where they all come through if they're coming this way or going that way," he said, pointing towards Bosnia. "Reason I mention it is because you look like you might be interested in something like that but might not know too much about how to set yourself up, if you know what I mean. For a consideration, I could acquaint you with people who could help make sure you don't get hurt."

"That's very generous of you," della Torre said. "Soon as I leave the police, I'll come straight to you."

"Don't mention it," the sausage man said, suddenly wary. "I mean that — don't mention it, and the sausage is on the house."

"Gee, thanks," said della Torre. "But I distinctly remember having paid for it already."

"So you did, so you did." The sausage man turned away, busying himself in the kiosk.

Della Torre noticed that there were indeed many Bosnians about. All those slightly too short trousers, white socks, and dark shoes. Was there really a uniform? he wondered. He washed down the last bite of sausage with the beer and entered a stall that fringed the Dolac market. He picked up a cheap imitation leather shoulder bag, something to hold his passport, wallet, Beretta, and carton of Luckys minus a pack. He lit one and sauntered over to the BMW, which he'd parked within sight.

He circled around a bit before he found the entrance he was looking for. It was a narrow, unmarked carriageway that ran through a late-nineteenth-century block of flats. Once through he was in a large courtyard with rickety wooden garages all along one side. He supposed they must have once been either stabling or cover for carriages and wagons. An old and very large walnut tree grew in the middle of the courtyard, and beyond it was a car repair shop. The courtyard was surrounded by five- and six-storey apartment buildings with the same thick walls, dormer windows, and red-tiled roofs as his own. They formed the perimeter of a rather large city block. Della Torre suspected there was another carriageway leading through the apartment block on the other side, though he couldn't see it. Cars, mostly decrepit Zastavas and Yugos, littered the yard.

Della Torre drove slowly around the walnut tree and stopped near the repair shop's open entrance. Someone was standing in the mechanic's pit, underneath a Citroën, hosing it with compressed air. Della Torre wandered into the oil-stained workspace, where he spotted a man sitting at a desk in a corner office. He realized he'd forgotten the name of the man Anzulović had told him to talk to. He hadn't even written it down. He cursed himself.

The man looked up. "What can I do for you?" he asked between blasts of compressed air.

"I wanted to talk to somebody about my car."

The man got up and moved close enough to della Torre to see that the car in question was a BMW. He was short, solidly built but not fat, and about ten years older than della Torre, with a big widow's peak and watery blue eyes. A friendly-looking fellow.

"I'm afraid we're pretty booked up for repairs. Wouldn't be able to see to your car for a couple of weeks, and then it might take a while to get parts. You know how it is. You've got to pay the suppliers with marks first, and then a week later they tell you they haven't got it in stock and they have to order it from Germany. You might try the Mercedes garage on the Samobor road. They do all the German cars. Should be able to sort you out," he said, edging back to his desk.

"You must be the only people around with a full workload. Outside of the hospitals," della Torre said.

The man shrugged. "Lead a good, clean life and the Lord rewards you."

"I'm not really here to get my car serviced. Actually, I was told that you might be interested in buying it."

The man walked back towards della Torre, passed him, and did a little turn around the car.

"Nice Beemer, good condition, what is it, last year's model? I'd be tempted to buy it for myself if I had the money. But I don't. And we only mend cars here."

"Shame, really. A friend of mine said he'd used your sales service and found it impeccable."

"That's nice of your friend, but either he's pulling your leg or you've got the wrong garage."

"Sorry I wasted your time. I'll tell Mr. Anzulović that the garage no longer does the special service he promised me."

"Anzulović, you say?"

"Yes, Anzulović."

"Colleague, is he? Or a neighbour? Or somebody you met in a bar?"

Della Torre considered his answer and decided the truth was as good as anything.

"I work with him."

"And what line of work might that be?"

Della Torre was at a loss. He hadn't expected this question and didn't know how to answer it. Had Anzulović been on an official job here? Had he told them what he did or had he used some cover occupation?

The man rubbed his stained hand against his overalls and pointed it at della Torre. Della Torre wasn't sure what had happened.

"My name's Fresl. Come on in."

He shut the door behind him and signalled della Torre to sit. Della Torre offered Mr. Fresl a Lucky from his new pack, figuring the full ashtray on the man's desk wasn't just there as an *objet d'art*.

"Thanks, but I prefer my own Player's," he said. "I can see from your inability to answer my question that you are in fact in Mr. Anzulović's line of business," he added, laughing. Della Torre was still none the wiser.

"Not many people go around advertising that they're secret policemen."

Della Torre smiled uncertainly.

"If Anzulović sent you, either you're sound or my number's up. Not much I can do about the latter, but if it's the former, we can do business."

And then it dawned on della Torre. Anzulović had been selling the UDBA's official Mercedes to this outfit. And he'd been reporting them stolen to recoup more cash from the State insurer. It was one of the ways he'd managed to keep his staff paid. Another dangerous game.

"We can do business."

"Great. So, you want shot of the BMW. Can I assume there is something, how shall I say this... tricky about the sale?"

"You can assume it's tricky. The car's stolen."

"Ah. I like a man who doesn't beat around the bush. Because if it was a legit sale, I was going to warn you that there are many places you could get a better price for it. Many, many places."

"I'd like to trade it in for something that is legit, has all the right documentation. If you have something."

The man thought hard. "I've got something, but unfortunately, it's not the same calibre car."

"Does it run?"

"Runs perfectly."

"Is it falling apart?"

"Excellent nick."

"So what's wrong with it?"

"It's a Renault 4."

"A Renault 4?" Della Torre was incredulous. He was offering to trade a BMW for a farmer's runabout, a car even less fashionable than a Yugo, though he had to admit the Renaults were much better built. And with a top speed somewhere around seventy kilometres an hour and what were effectively motorcycle tires, it wasn't much of a getaway car.

"A Renault 4. But all the papers are pristine. They ought to be, it's my car," said Fresl.

"A late-model BMW coupe for an ancient Renault 4 is hardly what you'd call a deal."

"Oh, I'd throw some money in too."

"How much?"

Fresl thought for a little while and then said, "Two hundred thousand."

"I take it you're not talking Deutschmarks."

Fresl almost choked with laughter. "That, my dear sir, is probably the funniest thing I've heard this month."

"So what am I supposed to do with two hundred thousand sheets of toilet paper?"

"It'll give your ass something to laugh at. I'm afraid, as a patriot, I can only deal in our country's currency," he said. "On the other hand, I can direct you to some *bureaux de change* that offer favourable exchange rates."

"I'm sure you can," della Torre said sourly. Once he had been fleeced by the money-changers, he figured he wouldn't get much more than two thousand marks. He doubted the Renault would be worth as much again. Clearly Fresl was taking advantage of him. He shook his head and thought, *What's the world coming to when people no longer respect even secret policemen?*

"Do I take it the deal is not agreeable to you?" Fresl asked.

"No, it's not that. Look, I'm not going to haggle. It's not even my car, so hell, a Renault 4 and two hundred thousand dinars is more than I had this time yesterday."

"Excellent." Fresl held his hand out and della Torre shook it again. But he stayed in his seat.

"Just out of curiosity, what are you going to do with it?"

"Ah, trade secrets."

"Come on. Who am I going to tell?"

"Well, I suppose it doesn't matter. We'll put Greek plates on it —"

"Greek plates?"

"Sure. A guy drove up with a vanload of them and adequate blank paperwork to make the cars legit."

"Wouldn't the Greek licensing people be able to cross-reference against their records?" Della Torre reached over the desk to flick ash into the ashtray, but it just rolled off the heap onto the floor.

"Greek records? You are pulling my leg. The Greeks make us look like Germans. As far as I can tell, the Greek licensing archives are a dry well into which they drop any official paper the goats won't eat. As long as the documents are filled in properly and have the right stamps—and our van driver brought the right stamps—then the papers are legit."

"Won't it seem suspicious when Zagreb is full of expensive cars with Greek plates?"

"It would be if we resold the cars in Zagreb. But we don't. We have drivers who take the cars up to Austria or Germany, where we sell them. The Germans take the Greek documents, change them into German documents, and presto, they've got legit cars and we've got Deutschmarks... which, we, ahem, change into our national currency."

"Naturally."

"Naturally."

"So, before I forget how this works, let me run it back by you to make sure I understand. You take German cars we've imported. Put fake Greek plates on them. And sell them back to Germans." Della Torre admired Fresl the way he might have admired a well-executed painting. Worth millions.

"We'd do it with Zastavas and Yugos too, but for some reason the Germans prefer their own Mercs and Beemers. Volkswagens and Audis in a pinch. Opels aren't worth the effort."

Della Torre shook his head again. Socialism might have been a crap system, but at least you knew where you stood. If you were one of the chosen, you got to choose. If you weren't, somebody made the choice for you. Capitalism, on the other hand...well, it meant selling stolen German cars with Greek plates back to Germans.

Fresl unlocked a drawer in his desk and pulled out a stack of dinars. Della Torre didn't bother to count them. He handed Fresl the chain of Strumbić's keys. Fresl separated the one for the BMW from the rest.

"This one I can use. But until I figure out how to ship apartments from Zagreb to Munich, these keys you can have back."

Della Torre shrugged and put them in his pocket. He gave the BMW a fond stroke as he passed.

"Nothing of yours in the car?"

"Nothing."

"In that case, let me introduce you to your new love," Fresl said, waving della Torre towards three cars that at first sight looked like abandoned wrecks. On second sight it was two wrecks and a red Renault 4.

"You know how to drive these, with the gear lever on the dash?" Fresl asked as della Torre got in.

"My father has one."

"So your father knows how to drive one. What about you?" He gave della Torre a big smile. Almost as if he felt bad about fleecing the secret policeman. "Key's in the ignition. Every day I pray somebody will steal it. And what does God do? He replaces it with a Beemer."

"I see this has only half a tank of petrol. Any chance of topping it up as a way of thanking God?"

"I'd love to, but I'm an atheist. Good Communist upbringing."

Della Torre pulled the door shut and had turned the ignition key when a thought occurred to him. He slid the window forward.

"You don't happen to know anything about some Bosnians in a big Mercedes saloon with Greek plates?"

"Might do. What colour is it?"

"Blue. Cream interior. Smells straight out of the showroom. Driver's called Besim."

"Sure," Fresl said cagily. For once his smile had left his face. "Why, what do you want to know about it?"

"Your car?"

"Maybe I've got a share in it."

"Going to Munich?"

"Vienna."

"Not anymore it isn't. It decided to become a bit of landscaping near Samobor. Maybe God's an atheist too."

Della Torre put the car in gear and pulled away from the garage, sounding as if he was in a sewing machine on wheels.

15

IT HAD BEEN a long morning, and his brain was starting to dull. He was snapped back into alertness by the two marked police cars on either side of the one-way Avenue of the Yugoslavian National Army, about a hundred metres from his apartment.

Someone was pulling out from the cobbled pavement between two plane trees by his front entrance. It appeared the driver had tried to pull into a parking spot but was now being made to reverse by an officious-looking pedestrian. Della Torre would have bet every last dinar in his pocket he was a plainclothes cop. The woman trying to park was having none of it. Even in those days of gloom and uncertainty, good parking spots in central Zagreb came at a premium. So there was an impasse and the usual chorus of car horns and waved fists as a jam built up on the street.

The woman got half out of her car to remonstrate with the man on the pavement, who was holding his hands in front of him, palms towards her, miming a pushing motion. A truck driver tried to pull around her but misjudged the passing space he needed, effectively boxing the woman in. She'd have to pull forward to let the truck pass, but the cop on the pavement wasn't letting her. Della Torre couldn't help but feel this stupid farce was a metaphor for Yugoslavia, but he couldn't quite decide who each of the three actors was playing.

As he sat back, waiting for the situation to resolve itself, he started counting the blue Zastavas clustered in front of his building and on the pavement opposite. About six years back, the Zagreb police had bought a whole assembly line of blue Zastavas to use as unmarked cars. Now the first thing anyone thought on seeing a blue Zastava was "unmarked cop car."

Once traffic started moving, della Torre let it carry him along. He wasn't chancing going back to his flat.

He drove on at a leisurely speed, turned the corner, and passed a pair of marked cars, one on either side of the road. No one paid him any attention. He carried on, as calmly as he could.

Of course, it could have been just a coincidence. Maybe someone had forgotten to pay a speeding ticket. After all, could Strumbić really have got out of the cellar and set the Zagreb police on him in a grand total of what, fourteen, fifteen hours? Then again, Strumbić was full of surprises.

There was a time when della Torre would have been best off going straight to his office, where he'd have the protection of the secret police apparatus. In the old days, the UDBA would jealously guard its rights and those of its employees. Normal police couldn't touch them. They wouldn't have tried.

Della Torre remembered a middle-ranking UDBA officer who'd got a tiny bit drunk one afternoon at a countryside inn not far out of town. He'd been drowning his sorrows over some domestic disaster and became obstreperous, eventually chasing out the rest of the clientele and smashing a couple of chairs. When the proprietor finally had had enough, he called the local police.

It was bad luck for the cops that they were young and dumb farmers' boys. They dealt with him as they always dealt with difficult drunks, and then, when he'd beaten his head against their knuckles long enough, they arrested him for assaulting an officer.

It would have been an understatement to say they panicked when, on reaching into his wallet for the money to cover a fine and an additional gratuity for the call-out, they found the UDBA man's official ID. One fled to a wine hut in the woods. The other two drove him to the nearest hospital and then knelt by his bedside, weeping and praying, until the man's UDBA colleagues arrived.

Those colleagues took the rural cops off for questioning, where the farm boys learned the answer to a question they'd never realized existed. Namely, the difference between amateur and professional assault.

They served eight months in an UDBA prison, after which it was hard for them to find anything other than menial work, on account of the political black mark against their names. And much of the menial work they did find, they couldn't do, because not all their bones had healed straight. It took the UDBA a fortnight to track down the cop who'd scarpered into the woods, whereupon he suffered an unfortunate but unspecified fatal accident.

The irony was that the UDBA officer who'd started the whole fiasco was arrested even before he'd got out of his hospital bed. He'd long been under investigation for his part in an export fraud. He'd needed the money to keep his wife off his back. It was her nagging that had driven him to drink and to overstep even the UDBA's relaxed approach to corruption.

But times had changed. These days della Torre wasn't so sure how much obeisance the police would give to the UDBA. He suspected not much. The regular police had become the Croatian government's militia, while the UDBA were agents of the enemy federal state.

And the men in front of his building clearly weren't the UDBA. They were ordinary Zagreb cops.

Della Torre drove to Irena's. There too he saw a blue Zastava, parked on the corner of the narrow road that wound its way up the hill past her building. As he passed, he spotted a marked car further up the hill. Bottling operations in front of his place and his wife's. Nice.

Della Torre drove around for a while, gathering his thoughts. But it was like scooping sand with a rake. He stopped at a phone box and rang the hospital. It was a long shot, but sometimes Irena was at the desk writing up notes; if she wasn't, there might be somebody to take a message.

The phone rang for a long while. He hung up and tried again. It was the fourth go when somebody finally picked it up.

"Yes," said the exasperated female voice.

"Could I speak to Irena della Torre?"

"No."

"Can you get a message to her?"

"No."

"Oh, come on."

"I can't because I don't know where is she. She not back from lunch yet."

"What do you mean she isn't back from lunch yet? It's half-way through the afternoon."

"You're telling me. Maybe she gedding her hair done," the woman said sardonically.

Every morning, Irena did a fine caricature of an Albanian nurse in her department. "Doctor," the nurse would say with an utterly deadpan expression, looking up from one of the fashion magazines she always had on hand, "you are young woman. Your hair looks awwwfoool. Ged it cut."

Maybe this was her.

"Okay, well, thanks anyway," della Torre said, hanging up.

Irena was not in the habit of being late for work.

He called her apartment. This time, the phone only rang twice.

"Yes?" Irena sounded strained. There was a warning in her voice.

"Mrs. della Torre?"

"Doctor," she said, not letting on she recognized his voice.

"I'm afraid you are mistaken. I'm not a doctor," he said, playing the game.

"But I am."

"My apologies, Dr. della Torre, this is the pest exterminators. I understand you have problem with vermin," he said, putting on a rural accent.

"You can say that again. This isn't a good time to arrange an appointment, though."

"When would be good time to call back?" There was a long pause during which he could hear a muffled conversation in the background.

"I'm a bit engaged for now. How about in forty-five minutes, but be prompt because I need to be at work by four o'clock. Otherwise you'll have to call at lunch tomorrow."

"We'll try to call back by four o'clock then, We're the firm that work for the cathedral, by the way."

She hung up.

Della Torre cooled his heels for a while, picking up a pastry from a café to occupy himself. He left half of it; the synthetic flavour reminded him that cakes had tasted better under Communism.

Around twenty minutes before the agreed time, he ducked into a phone box not far from the cathedral, noted its number in his little notebook, and then went to another one on slightly higher ground, from which he could see the first phone box without much difficulty. They'd made this arrangement years before, in case of emergency. Working for the UDBA made della Torre always think in terms of contingencies.

When he spotted her, he popped a coin into the slot and rang the number.

"Hello?"

"It's me. What's going on?"

She gave him the rundown with the same precision as when she wrote patient notes. Pithy and relevant.

She'd come back from the hospital for lunch. It was late and a bit of a walk, but she liked to do it; it helped clear her head. And the food at the hospital canteen might be cheap, but it was also inedible.

She knew there was something odd when she saw the man leaning against the wall opposite her building. On that side, the road was narrow, and there was no pavement, so it wasn't the sort of place where anyone loitered.

But she shrugged it off and went in. The door to the flat was shut but unlocked, which made her think della Torre was in. Instead she was confronted by three strange men, two looking so much like cops it was as if they were from central casting; the third looked like some German fantasy of an *Übermensch*.

The *Übermensch* spoke, without bothering to introduce himself. "Where's della Torre?"

"You're speaking to her," she said.

"Your husband."

"My ex-husband."

"I didn't know you were divorced. It's not in the files."

"We're not."

"So he's your husband," said the *Übermensch*, who seemed to be running things.

"Don't tell me: you're a marriage counsellor."

He ignored the comment. "Where's della Torre?"

"I don't know."

"Has he been here?"

"When? I've been at the hospital."

"Last night."

"He was here."

"What was he doing here?"

"Sleeping, mostly."

"Why? I thought you said he was your ex-husband. Doesn't he live in the apartment on the Avenue of the Yugoslavian National Army?"

"Yes."

"So what was he doing here?"

"Is there a law against a husband spending a night with his wife?"

He regarded her as he might have done an unusually big moth in a museum exhibit. "Your neighbours reported noises coming from the balcony late last night." He pointed to the building next door.

"Oh, I see, so you're here investigating whether there's been a burglary. Well, if you let me have a look around, I can tell you if anything's missing."

"What time did he arrive?"

"I don't know. I was late back from the hospital. He was here, smoking. On the balcony. Maybe the neighbours heard him exhaling."

"What were you doing at della Torre's flat this morning?"

"Who told you I was at my ex-husband's flat this morning?"

"Never mind. Why were you there?"

"I went to pick up some of his things."

"Did he ask you to?"

"No. He was asleep."

"What did you collect?"

"Some clothes."

"Why?"

"Because the ones he was wearing smelled and he didn't have any spares here."

"What happened then?"

"He got up, and then I assume he went to work."

"Why do you assume? Aren't you sure?"

"I assume because I also assume that if he were at work, you wouldn't be asking me where he was."

"What did you do when he left? Did you go to the hospital?"

"No, I went to my office at the university."

"We'll be able to verify that with the reception there, will we?"

"No, because I used the back entrance. I usually use the back entrance when I come from this direction. Saves me having to walk all the way around."

"So there's a key for the back door that you've got?"

"No. The back door's broken. It's been broken since I was a student. You go down the basement around the plant works, and there it is. Would you like me to show you?"

"And there's nobody who can vouch for the fact that you went to your office?"

"No," she said.

"What were you doing there?"

"That's where I keep most of my medical books. Look, you're taking a very close interest in my morning. A closer interest than I took in it. You wouldn't mind telling me why or what you want with my ex-husband?"

The *Übermensch* signalled to one of the cops.

"Do you know what this is?"

"It looks like a leather coat. It's a very nice leather coat. Would you like fashion advice about what goes well with it?"

"Is it your husband's?"

"I doubt it's my ex-husband's."

"Why do you say that?"

"Well, for one thing, he can't afford it. And it's pretty clearly the wrong size, he'd look about as elegant in that as you would in a bustier."

"A what?"

"Something uncomfortable that ladies wear to look shapely for their men."

"Oh."

"That was a joke, by the way."

"Why is the coat in the apartment?" he pressed.

"I don't know. Did you ask it?"

"When do you expect to see della Torre next?"

"Probably Friday. He usually comes over for supper on Friday evening. It's sort of a tradition in my family. He likes it because it means he gets fed at least once a week."

"I thought you said he was your ex-husband."

"Even ex-husbands get hungry."

"So you don't know who this coat belongs to?"

"No. Listen, do you mind if I get something to eat? Then I need to go back to the hospital."

"You can fix yourself something to eat, but I think we'd like you here for a little longer."

She'd lost her appetite but forced down a boiled egg and a bit of bread. While she was eating, two of the men went to talk to the old widow downstairs, who hadn't seen or heard anything since at least the mid-1970s.

The men came back and started on Irena again.

Then the phone rang.

"Pick it up," said the *Übermensch.*

They listened intently to her part of the conversation. When she hung up, she asked how much longer they would be keeping her.

"Only about another half-hour. But I'll post one of our men here."

"He can stay in the stairwell. I'd rather nobody made themselves at home," she said.

It wasn't something she left room for debate on.

"You told them I was there last night?" said della Torre, shocked.

"Sure. But I also said it was nothing out of the ordinary. As far as they know, I don't know anything. And it's true; I don't really know that much. It's serious, isn't it."

"There's a decent chance they didn't believe the pest control routine. Your line will be tapped anyway. Can you do me a little favour though?"

"What?" Irena sounded worried. And that worried della Torre. She was the coolest person he knew.

"Pack an overnight bag for the hospital tonight. Put the things in your locker. Pack it again with some more stuff tomorrow, but don't overfill it. Don't let anyone notice. Do it for a couple of days, until you've got enough of what you might need to take to London. Then, on Thursday or Friday, work the night shift. Go into the hospital, be there for about an hour, and then go. Don't use the Slovene borders; there's too much military and police activity since they had that independence vote. Go north up to Austria. It's the long way around, but the Austrians will be friendlier than the Slovenes, and the guards on this side of the border will be less picky."

"I can't just leave my patients."

"Darling, one way or another you will have to leave your patients. And let me tell you, you'll be less useful to your colleagues sitting in a Zagreb police station than you will in a London hospital. At least that way you can find all of them jobs when they follow you out of the country. You've got some money. Have you got a visa for Britain?"

"Yes, that's been done for a couple of weeks now."

"Great. Don't tell anyone what you're doing. Just do it. Send them all a postcard once you get there. And let my father know where you are so I can get in touch with you."

"Okay." Irena often relied on the fact that, as a secret policeman, della Torre knew what he was talking about.

He did, but not as well as she might have thought. He wasn't one of the hard men like Messar. And from Irena's description, it sounded like Messar was on his case.

No one looked as much like a German hero of the Reich as Messar. Unlike Germans, though, Messar didn't have a sentimental streak. Or their sense of humour. That they'd set Messar on him was a worry. As far as della Torre knew, Messar was incorruptible. He could afford to be; he had family money from just after the Second World War. A proud, upstanding Communist family. With property abroad. Even worse was that he seemed to be working closely with the Zagreb cops. Times really were changing.

Strumbić had properly stitched up della Torre. *Next time,* della Torre thought, *I'm not just going to shoot him in the leg. And I'm going to use a gun that works.*

"I love you," she said, catching him off guard. He hadn't realized she was still on the line.

"I love you too," he said. "Take care. Take care in your new life. I hope it's better than the old one."

16

DELLA TORRE'S OPTIONS had narrowed. To one.

Clearly Strumbić had turned up. With Messar working on the case, there was no chance of laughing it off over a beer and sausage, or burying it somewhere in the UDBA archives. And with the Zagreb police involved, it meant Strumbić's side, whatever story he'd told them, would feature high up in the credits.

His best bet was to stay out of reach and then, from a safe distance, think about what to do next. A little trip to Italy. He'd explain himself to Anzulović once he got there.

A thought crept into his head. It might be time to return to the U.S. There was always a danger the UDBA would track him down. The firm was savage with apostates. They'd killed dissidents and defectors across Europe—Spain, Italy, Germany, France, England—and as far as Canada, the U.S., Australia, and Argentina. He'd investigated more than twenty of the hundred or so killings that he knew about. But there where whispers of more, many more. Foreign police seldom investigated closely. Western governments never wanted to make too much of an issue about it. Everyone had wanted to be on the good side of the only Communist country in Europe not within the Soviet orbit. Tito's secret police had been allowed to act with impunity, so much so that it left dictators the world over aggrieved at how much the UDBA was allowed to get away with. Libya's Gaddafi and Romania's Ceauşescu had protested on separate occasions to various European governments at the free rein given to Tito's agents when their own were treated harshly.

Della Torre's next thought was how far the Renault 4 could get him. Out of the country for sure, if he was clever about it. Assuming the car didn't shake his teeth out first.

It would be difficult to drive through any official border crossing. The political situation made guards on both sides of the fence jumpy. If anything, it was worse in Slovenia, Yugoslavia's westernmost province, which stood between Croatia and Italy. The Slovenes had developed a taste for independence and were becoming difficult with any non-Slovene Yugoslavs. And the Yugoslav army units stationed in Slovenia were belligerent in return. This ruled out the shortest route to the Italian border, along the Zagreb-Ljubljana motorway. He could go north to Vienna, from which he could fly direct to the U.S., but he didn't want to curse Irena's escape route if he were caught. But another way came to mind. And it was all the more attractive because it meant driving through Istria.

Istria meant going home, however briefly. Della Torre's family was from that little triangle of land on the northern reaches of the Croatian coast on the Adriatic Sea, south of Trieste.

That's why he had an Italian name. Istria had been Italian or Austro-Hungarian or Venetian long before the Yugoslavs took over the area after the Second World War. And although in the early 1950s there had been an exodus of much of the Italian population, many remained, especially those with long ties to the land, centuries old in the case of the della Torre family.

The della Torres had always stayed, despite Istria's frequent changes of ownership. Which happened often. Political maps showed that in her ninety years, della Torre's grandmother had lived in six different countries without once moving from the village in which she'd been born.

Istrians spoke Italian and Croatian; some spoke Slovene too. But above all the people spoke Istrian, a mash-up of the other languages with plenty of its own special flavours. They were a stubborn people, notoriously stingy because they worked hard and knew the value of their labour to the last dinar. And they were averse to politics, to politicians, and to other people's wars.

Della Torre was fond of the place, its red soil, its vineyards and forests, its hilltop towns and beautiful, ancient Venetian cities on the coast. It was where his father now lived. They'd bought the old farmhouse, a wreck not far from his grandparents' village, when they'd come back to Yugoslavia. Della Torre's mother had died in Ohio, and his father was so griefstruck that he had abandoned his academic post and returned with his twelve-year-old son to his homeland. The son who had become a thoroughly American boy.

They moved to Zagreb, where his father was welcomed back to the university. He'd always been well liked and had been warmly and honestly congratulated when he'd won a fellowship to an American university to research and teach the development of central European Slavic languages

Long weekends and holidays, the two della Torres, man and boy, would drive to the house in Istria, rebuilding it up from the large wine cellar on its ground floor and its antique ten-thousand-litre wooden wine barrels to the the oval windows just under the eaves. The house was a small fortress of stone blocks and heavy lintels, but on the inside it was open and spacious and had all the American luxuries. People came from every corner of Istria to wonder at a machine that washed dishes, a refrigerator as big as a larder, kitchen gadgets that did strange things, a hot shower as powerful as a rainstorm.

The house stood in splendid isolation on a small hill, surrounded by woodland, vineyards, and fields. There was a village nearby, where his father's family lived. Almost every name in the village was della Torre. They were farmers and winemakers, most of whom had many hectares of unregistered land to get around Communist restrictions on the size of holdings. Sometimes they visited the old village, but mostly he and his father kept to themselves.

So father and son worked on the house and on their dozen or so rows of vines or the small orchard of peach, fig, apricot, and plum trees, and when they were in Zagreb they had an old hand to tend to the land.

Sometimes they'd drive down to the coast and spend the day swimming, careful to avoid the spiny urchins that made a hazard of the stony sea floor. They'd picnic on one of the salty hams his uncle cured and gave to them every year as a Christmas gift, on cheese they had bought from neighbours, and on their own fruit, while sitting on cushions of stacked Mediterranean pine needles. They had a small wheat field that produced enough flour for them to bake their own bread.

At the peaks of the tourist season, they'd avoid the coast and stick to the empty countryside. When the tourists went home, they'd go back to Poreč or Rovinj and sit in cafés in the old parts of town, the broad, smoothed blocks of white Istrian stone underfoot, in among high, narrow, Venetian-styled Renaissance houses with their ogee windows. He'd drink Fanta and his father would speak English or Italian to him, the languages they'd always spoken at home in America. But as the years passed, della Torre increasingly took to responding in Croat.

After his father retired and moved to the farmhouse, he'd become, if anything, even busier. Della Torre's father discovered a facility for explaining the intricacies of central European history to non-specialist audiences. He wrote well-received articles for highbrow Western publications explaining the region's modern politics within a historical context. As Yugoslavia went through its paroxysms after Tito's death, he focused his writing on local matters but broadened it to a more general readership.

He became a major contributor to the popular international press, writing in Italian, English, and German, explaining what was happening in the country with an almost uncannily neutral perspective. The secret police left him alone not only because his son worked for them but because they, like just about everyone, valued his insights. People might not have liked some of what he said, but no one accused him of political or nationalist motivations. He was Istrian, after all.

His father's intellectual rejuvenation heartened della Torre. He hoped one day to earn similar contentment. But he had a feeling it wouldn't come anytime soon.

To get to Istria, della Torre first had to head southwest, towards the tense border country between Bosnia and Croatia where large communities of Serbs resided.

Della Torre drove back through Zagreb's suburbs. He avoided the highway to Karlovac, instead taking a narrow, slow parallel route. It was just as well. He counted two police roadblocks on the highway, and there were probably more that he couldn't see.

Further south, the road joined the main highway in a bottleneck, which was where the police tended to focus their effort. He took the westward fork well before the junction. The road rose from the flat Karlovac plain into deep pine forests that marked the genesis of the high spine of mountains dividing central Croatia from its coast.

Traffic was light in the mountains. There weren't many people travelling to or from the seaside midweek in the early spring. It gave him time to think.

He wondered what it would be like to go back to America. To live there.

It almost made him laugh. What could he possibly do in Ohio? Did Cleveland have a pressing need for secret police-men who spoke Croat? True, he'd trained in law. But he couldn't see himself opening a practice in some small mid-western town. *I'm sorry, sir, unless you're inquiring about contract details pertaining to assassinations on foreign territory or the limits of dissent in Communist autocracy, you might be better off speaking to someone else.*

He'd never returned, refusing as a child to go on either of the trips his father had taken to America to visit old colleagues and his wife's grave.

What could he remember of Ohio? What could he remem-ber of his mother? Or his first day at his American school, a new immigrant with no language, sitting on the floor by the piano with the other kindergarten children, listening to his white-haired teacher playing songs he'd never heard before and weeping quietly to himself because he needed to go to the toilet but didn't know how to ask. Wept and then wet himself. What could he remember?

Had it been any easier when he'd come back to live in Zagreb?

Superficially Croatia wasn't foreign. He'd spent most sum-mers with his relatives and spoke Croat almost as well as Italian, though neither with quite the fluency of his English. But when he'd moved there permanently, he'd been treated like a freak. Though plenty of Yugoslav kids had lived in Germany — their parents were *Gastarbeiters* working for the Mercedes factory in Stuttgart or at one of the other big engineering firms around Munich — no one had ever met an American. A gringo.

Did he ride horses to school? Did the Indians ever try to scalp him? Everyone was rich in America, so why didn't he give them some money? He thought he was too good for them, didn't he. Because he'd lived in America. He always managed to defuse the antagonism through self-deprecating humour or a goofy, vulnerable charm. But he'd always felt foreign.

Funny—what had bothered him most as a kid was that he didn't understand the sports. Especially football, or soccer, which wasn't the American football he knew. He'd known nothing of Dinamo or Red Star or Partizan or Hajduk or Lazio or Real or Barça or Juve or Arsenal.

Arsenal. He patted the shoulder bag by his side, trying to remember when he'd last fired the Beretta.

The light was fading; he was hungry. Just as well he glanced down to look at the fuel gauge. The warning light was flickering. He pulled into a petrol station in a clearing in the mountainous woods, giant pines looming all around, where an attendant, a teenage girl, filled his tank. He paid her out of the pile of dinar notes he'd got for the BMW, hoping they weren't forged. It'd be a shame to accidentally rob this little place.

There was a good rustic restaurant at the other end of the clearing, so he parked the car, grabbed his overnight bag, and strolled over through dewy spring grass by the side of the road.

The place was nearly full, the smell of slow-roasted lamb suffusing the air. He ate what everybody there was eating: lamb with *ajvar*, a pulped relish of roasted red peppers, eggplant, and garlic; proper fried potatoes sprinkled with rosemary; and a salad of finely chopped cabbage with oil and vinegar. It reminded him of all the times he had stopped at this place with his father. Talking about everything and anything. Or maybe not everything... Had they ever spoken about his mother?

He ordered a small pitcher of slightly sour, strong white wine, which he watered with sulphurous fizzy mineral water. Somehow the mixture produced something satisfyingly drinkable.

It was dark by the time he left, and he was tired. His knee throbbed, though if he didn't move his left arm the rib didn't hurt much. He wanted to press on, but a fog had started to drop on the mountain and he didn't want to drive into a ravine. So he folded down the Renault's seats and made himself as good a bed as he could, using the bag with the Beretta as a pillow.

He had drifted off into half-dreams when he was suddenly woken, startled by a pounding noise over his head. The car was rocking. Della Torre half opened his eyes, wondering how and why he'd driven the Renault into the sea. There was no sign of morning under a low lid of cloud picked out by the petrol station lights. He sat up and slid the window open.

"You can't sleep here," said a half-bear, half-man.

"I just did."

"Well, you can't."

"Why? Was I snoring?"

"It's not allowed."

"Because?"

"Because it's the rule."

"Whose rule?"

"The people-who-run-the-petrol-station's rule."

"Who's that then?"

"That would be me. And I don't want people breaking my rules when I come on my shift."

"What's the time?"

"Five o'clock."

"You mean it's tomorrow already?"

"If you don't get a move on pretty quickly, I'll send you back into yesterday. Understand?"

"Understood. And thanks for the hospitality."

"Gypsy bum."

Della Torre decided it was just as well he pushed off. The fog had mostly lifted, though a few wisps clung to the trees or swept across the road where there were clearings. He'd stop for a coffee once he'd got to Rijeka, a large port city on a wide gulf situated in the inner elbow between the top of the Dalmatian coast and Istria.

Once past Rijeka, he decided to follow the coastal road

rather than go through the Ucka tunnel. It would add about an hour to the drive, but there was often a police roadblock at the tunnel entrance.

The sun rose behind him, sharp and clear, casting a bruised pink light across the Adriatic Sea in front of him. Down at the bottom of the cliffs, night had clung on.

Eventually he cut inland and drove through the heart of Istria. As he travelled north he grew tempted to call in at his father's for breakfast and a chat, but he knew that would be fatally stupid. The UDBA would be waiting for him.

Instead, he stopped for a few minutes by the side of the road a few fields away from the house and smoked a cigarette. From a distance in the morning light, the house looked pristine, though he knew all its little imperfections. The cracked stone lintel over the main door. The temporary, now semi-permanent wooden cover over the wellhead on which was inscribed "della Torre 1877" — the house had been built by another branch of the family. The rusting iron frame holding up a massive spread of vines that kept the big cellar and a broad first-floor terrace shaded. The conical pile of builder's sand at one end of the front courtyard. The silt of papers and books and oddments that clogged the lives of single men.

Then again, there were some imperfections he wouldn't want to change. The slight asymmetry of one of the oval windows under the roofline. Or the blocks of stone in the house's façade that had been splintered by German machine-gun bullets. It was funny how every memory in this part of the world eventually ambled into a war.

Della Torre headed back north by northeast towards Italy, where his mother's family had come from. None of them were left, or no one close; all were either dead or scattered into the winds. But he knew the countryside well. He stayed off the main roads, following a small track into the Slovene part of Istria. Since the vote, the Slovene police had taken to stopping

cars at the border, almost as if it were an international boundary, and the Croats were beginning to reciprocate.

There was only a narrow corridor of Slovenian Istria separ-
ating Croatian Istria from Italy's Trieste. Once in Slovenia, he
stopped for breakfast and made a phone call.

"Anzulović?"

"Gringo, is that you? Where are you?"

"Umm, I think I'd rather not say, though you'll know soon
enough."

"Feel like explaining yourself? Seems you neglected to mention a teeny, tiny little thing to me yesterday."

"You mean about Strumbić?"

"Something like that."

"I didn't want to burden you with details."

"So generous of you. If you'd rather tell it to Messar instead..."

"Not really. Listen, I know you're an upstanding Communist,
but would you do me a little favour — would you pray for me?"

"Anything for you. Where?"

"How about at the cathedral. Nine o'clock. Wait for the bell
to chime and maybe you'll answer my call."

"I think the spirit may move me."

Della Torre hung up. Anzulović had understood. Everybody's telephone calls, including Anzulović's, were recorded.
The only line that escaped being monitored was the fax line to
their secretary's office, which for some unfathomable reason
caused the UDBA's recording devices to develop the mechanical
equivalent of epilepsy.

These prodigiously strange phenomena were fairly usual in
Yugoslavia. Some things never worked, however much effort
was made to mend them. Some things only worked in certain circumstances. And some things worked perfectly. And then didn't.

Della Torre thought he'd use the UDBA's phone tapping to his
advantage. They'd be watching for him at the borders. He was
less than ten kilometres from the Italian crossing at Trieste,

the most obvious route out of the country. It was also manned
by the federal border police and therefore under UDBA control.
He'd make it easy for them. He called his father.

"Dad."

"Marko? What are you doing? Some people were here looking for you this morning."

"Never mind them. I haven't got long to talk —"

"I said you were in Zagreb," his father said. "To try you there.
Have I told you about the researcher?"

"What?"

"An American. There's an American researcher who's taken
an interest in my work. Not the work I do now, but linguistic
research. We've developed a lively correspondence. She says
she might be doing a doctorate on my comparative language
analysis. She said she'd be coming this summer probably, if not
sooner."

"That's great, Dad, but I really can't talk."

"It's been a while. I mean, my work is solid but it's no longer
cutting edge. But she seems interested anyway. Maybe I'll go
to Zagreb to catch up with developments of the past few years.
I shouldn't have dropped out of academics so completely, but
the political writing has been so much more rewarding."

"Listen, Dad, I've got to go now. I just wanted to say I'll have
to stay out of touch for a while. I'm on a case."

"Let me know when you get back. Maybe I'll call Irena to say
I'll be spending some time at the apartment. She never minds.
It'd be nice to see her. I miss her coming to Istria."

"You do that, Dad. Bye." It was as long as he'd dared to stay
on the phone. They'd spoken in English. It had always been
their secret language in this country, but the UDBA would have
had an English-speaker on hand to listen in. They'd have also
immediately traced the call.

From where he was, the most obvious route was along the
main road and on to the Trieste highway, little more than ten

minutes to the border. But instead he went cross-country, along
the little roads where a rusty Renault 4 would be as unobtrusive as a peach tree in an Istrian orchard. Rather than head
towards Trieste, he made his way towards Piran, the northern-
most of Yugoslavia's pretty Venetian coastal towns.

As a tourist town, Piran had regular passenger ferry services
to Venice and Trieste, even out of season. National pride demanded that the boats run continuously, despite the heavy sub-
sidy that entailed. But because few people took the ferries in
the winter — generally only locals with relatives on the Italian
side — there was hardly any passport control. It was left to the
municipal police to monitor the few people who came and
went until the summer hordes arrived and the federal border
guards took up their officious places again.

It took him less than half an hour to reach Piran. He parked
the car on the main square. He checked his notebook for the
number of the telephone box in front of Zagreb's cathedral.

"Hello." It was clearly not Anzulović. It sounded like an old
woman.

"Madam, I'm calling for someone else."

"Well, I'm the only person here."

"Is there a man waiting there? About fifty-five, black-and-
white hair, shrubs growing out of his nose and ears?"

"What?"

"I'm calling for someone else. Is there a man there waiting
for the phone?"

"No. Just me."

"Lady, can you do me a favour? Can you see if there's someone waiting by the phones on the other side of the cathedral?"

"I can't see that far."

"Listen, if you go over there, you'll see a man who's waiting
by the phones. Tell him to come to these phones in ten minutes'
time and he'll give you fifty dinars. I promise. Just tell him I
promised you fifty dinars."

"A hundred."

"Alright."

"He'd better give me the money."

"I promise, lady."

Della Torre called again ten minutes later.

"Hello?"

"Anzulović?"

"That you, Gringo?"

"Did you pay the old lady?"

"Three hundred dinars that cost me."

"Should have been standing by the right phones. Anyway, I owe you."

"You owe me more than that. Why didn't you tell me about shooting Strumbić?"

"Didn't I?"

"I think it's something I'd have remembered. Shall I describe the shitshow that came down when Strumbić showed up in hospital yesterday morning? You've left me with a migraine bigger than my wife's ass."

"Sorry. I didn't want to complicate things."

"Complicate things? Gringo, you knew very well that shooting Strumbić wouldn't make things easier. It's hard enough for me to give you protection without having the regular cops after you as well as everybody else."

"It was an accident."

"I'm sure it was. And you used a crap gun. A slingshot would have been more effective. But the fact of the matter is that you shot and imprisoned a Zagreb detective. That immediately called for an UDBA investigation. The Zagreb cops — well, do you remember that Kubrick movie 2001?" Anzulović asked. Della Torre vaguely knew about the film, though he wasn't sure he'd ever seen it.

"Yes," he said.

"You remember at the start when all those apes see the big

black stone, the monolith, and start freaking out? Well, the Zagreb cops made them look like they were on sedatives. Can you imagine how happy they'd be to get an UDBA scalp? We're taking over the case slowly, but it's not a lot of fun."

"How's Strumbić?"

"Angrier than a bull that's having its balls cut off. He's in my office right now being self-righteous."

"What story has he told you?"

"Originally, that you were trying to sell him state secrets, and when he turned you down—shock, horror—you and your Bosnian gang tried to kill him. He's also got you down for stealing his car. And three cartons of Lucky Strikes. But with a bit of help his memory's starting to improve."

"I took his leather coat too."

"Well, he seems not to have noticed. I'll mention it to him, shall I?"

"Didn't fit."

"Well, that's a crying shame."

"What happens now?" della Torre asked.

"Officially I'm hunting you down like I'm the whole bloody Mossad and you're Eichmann. Messar's on the case, and everybody trusts him to do the job properly. Which he will. My worry is that the minute he's got a hold of you, whoever your friends are in Belgrade will ask for you to be handed over to the UDBA headquarters, after which you'll never be seen again. If you end up with the Zagreb cops, either they'll do the Bosnians' job for them or somebody else will pay for the privilege. I suggest you disappear until Belgrade no longer has any say whatsoever in Zagreb. I'll see if we can't get some dancing fairies into Strumbić's story. By the way, you haven't heard any of this from me."

"Thanks."

"I don't know why I'm doing this for you."

"Maybe I'm the son you never had."

"Every day I look at my daughters, I thank God I didn't have boys too. There's only so much disappointment a man can handle in one lifetime. I'm doing it for your wife; Lord knows you don't deserve her."

"I know. I'm a disappointment to her as well. Will you keep an eye on her?"

"Yes. She ought to go away for a little bit too. I'll make sure that if she does, nobody bothers her too much."

"Thanks. So now I disappear?"

"You disappear until Messar finds you or until we start playing cowboys and Indians with the Serbs. I wish I didn't have the feeling we'll end up as the Indians. Apart from Custer, they didn't do so well. Anyway, we'll be needing you here then."

"What about the UDBA?"

"We are the UDBA."

"No, I mean the people who kill people."

"The wetworks? What about them?"

"Won't they be after me if they find out I've run away? They don't have much of a record of forgiving defectors from their ranks. And they're not known for missing their targets."

"Messar has people on you, but I've made sure Belgrade isn't getting too interested. The Zagreb police don't talk to the federal agencies, and as far as I'm concerned you're officially on a sabbatical and there's just a little logistical problem keeping you from coming back in to explain yourself."

"Thanks, boss."

"I'll tell you what. Maybe you can put those brains of yours towards staying alive for a couple of months or so. And if everything goes tits up over here, don't worry, you'll get plenty of chances to pay me back by getting me out of the country too. But you'd better get moving. Messar has people looking for you in Istria. He's very persistent. And smart."

"My luck to have the only honest secret policeman south of Vienna on my case."

"You think they're honest in Vienna?"

"Did they find the Bosnians in the ravine, by the way?"

"Just a Merc welded to a tree."

"Any bodies?"

"No. Bit of blood but no corpses. On the other hand, some poor farmer from the village had his car stolen from him. The cops found him squatting in a stream with his trousers over his head. It'd be funny if he hadn't had to be hospitalized for hypothermia. Barely got a statement from him, his teeth were hammering so hard. It seems your Bosnian friends hijacked him. You'd better get going."

"You're a friend, Anzulović."

"Maybe one day the favours will stop flowing in one direction. You make my life more difficult than all the women in my household put together."

"Thanks."

"Stay alive long enough to pay me a commission on Strumbić's car. He's angling to get it back. He probably will, knowing him."

Della Torre noticed two men in leather jackets taking an interest in his Renault on the other side of the square. Had it been a Ferrari or on fire, it might not have been surprising. But they weren't handing out tickets or admiring the bodywork. He was taken aback. It couldn't be Messar already. But there was no other explanation. It was time to go.

"Gotta run."

"Good luck."

He hung up and walked as casually as he could towards the dockside.

17

DELLA TORRE DIDN'T look back at the men. There were people about, but out of tourist season he would be found before long. Piran wasn't a big place, and worse still, it was on a narrow promontory. It would be easy to get bottled up there.

He stuck to the shadows of the town's Renaissance stone buildings. Early spring flowers were erupting over the tops of walled gardens. There was a little graffiti about, but mostly Piran was clean and well maintained. He hardly noticed, instead keeping his senses alert to anyone following. At the long quayside, he ducked into a kiosk. A doughy, youngish woman sat on a stool behind the counter, reading a garish gossip magazine.

"When do the ferries run to Venice or Trieste?" he asked in Italian. She looked up, barely able to lift the weight of indifference from her expression.

"It's on the board," she said, pointing offhandedly at the schedule printed up on the side of the kiosk. "Regular ferry to Venice left at nine. Another one tomorrow. They don't go to Trieste any more. Take a bus."

"Shit," said della Torre.

"Winter schedule."

145

"Any boats going anywhere this afternoon?" he asked.

"There's a boat at three-thirty going to Zadar, Šibenik, and Split."

A coastal boat. He'd be picked up somewhere along the way.

"Anything else?"

"No." She glared at him. "Except for the weekly catamaran. That's at midday."

"Catamaran? Where does that go?"

"Where it always goes. Venice, of course."

Had della Torre lived in any other country, he'd have been astonished at her rank, almost evil unhelpfulness. But she'd behaved no differently from any other Yugoslav. That was the thing about Communism. In the eyes of its public servants, everyone was equally contemptible.

He paid for a ticket.

"Do I need to be early for passport control?"

She stared at him for a long moment.

"No," she finally said.

Della Torre gave her a forced smile and wandered off. He had around two hours to kill while staying as unobtrusive as possible. He found a café in a jazzed-up old wine cellar, and was sitting in the gloom at the back when the two men who'd taken an interest in his Renault walked past. One looked in. He was in his early thirties, either very fair or prematurely grey; it was hard to tell from his military buzz cut. He had a peasant's flat and heavy face. He didn't see della Torre, who'd pressed himself into the shadows behind a pillar.

If they were UDBA, della Torre knew they'd probably do a quick circuit of the town and then a slower one, going into shops and bars. There was sure to be another team, which would stick closer to the car. This other team would circle the edge of the old town across the neck of the promontory to ensure he didn't escape landward.

The guys he was seeing now would try to winkle him out.

They'd ask around about him. Knowing Messar, they would have a faxed photograph. It still astonished him that Messar was focusing any effort on this little town. Then again, he was thorough. He probably had people in Poreč and Rovinj too, though he'd be focusing his efforts on the Italian-Slovene border.

Even before they'd voted for independence, Slovenes had been prickly in their dealings with other Yugoslav nationalities. They'd always considered themselves Mitteleuropeans rather than Balkans, with a German work ethic and German aspirations. Now they were cutting themselves off wherever and however they could. Messar couldn't take for granted that the local police would co-operate with the UDBA. Much as the Zagreb police were proving less than helpful to UDBA headquarters in Belgrade, Slovenes had become even less compliant with any of the federal government's agencies. And for that matter, with the Croat police.

That was a major reason della Torre had decided to go this route. The Slovenes would be as helpful to Messar's investigation as sand in a gearbox.

Della Torre didn't so much kill time as strangle it slowly. With most of the town shut until the start of the tourist season, there just weren't enough places to hide. He almost bumped into the UDBA team, but he spotted them in the reflection of a shop window, only just getting out of their way in time.

The pursuit traced ever-tightening circles towards the crest of the town, where Piran's modest cathedral stood at the edge of a bastion rising forty metres from the sea, a white stone insect pinned to the earth by the needle of its tall bell tower. The UDBA men weren't letting up. They hadn't seen him yet, but they kept on his trail, tracking him as if by smell.

He ducked into the church's gloaming. It was empty. A row of three wooden confessionals was tucked in along one wall. He doubted any priests would be expecting to hear confessions on a mid-week morning, though Easter was coming. Palm leaves bent into crosses still decorated the church and whole palm fronds circled the altar. He stepped into one of the boxes and pulled the door behind him, a dim light coming on in the coffin-like box. Its dark wood had recently been polished with beeswax; he could smell it, feel its smoothness on the small bench.

For a time there was silence. And then he could hear foot-steps on the stone floor. One pair. A second. Men's hard, heavy steps. They circled the church. Della Torre quietly unzipped his shoulder bag and took out the Beretta, checking by feel that it was loaded with a magazine. And then there was the softer brushing sound of a third set of shoes, or, more likely, slippers.

Della Torre froze. The door to the other half of his confes-sional box opened. He chambered a bullet, but the metallic click was covered by the door banging shut again. He raised the gun to the wooden screen.

"Have you come to make a confession?" asked a voice from the other side of the wooden grille. It was a young man's voice, speaking in Slovene.

"Yes, Father, forgive me, for I have sinned," della Torre whis-pered in Italian, lowering the gun, rocking forward with relief so that he could taste the beeswax on the latticework against his lips.

"Ah, Italian. Good. We shall speak in Italian," said the young priest. His accent wasn't fluent but clearly he understood the language well enough. "May the Lord be in your heart to help you make a good confession. How long since you have last con-fessed your sins?"

Della Torre thought hard. Was it when he was twelve, or thirteen? It was sometime not long after his mother had died. This much he knew.

"Six months, Father."

"That's a long time between confessions, my son. And what are your sins?"

"Many, Father. I've taken the Lord's name in vain many times. And I've done too much coveting. I stole a hoe from my neighbour and then lied when he asked whether I had it. But something else is weighing on my soul."

He paused for a long time, as if he were bringing himself to admit something. He wasn't. He just couldn't think of anything that would keep him in the confessional until the footsteps went away. He didn't particularly feel like mentioning he'd caused the death of one man or shot another and stolen his car. "It's to do with my wife. I'm not really sure I know how to explain it."

"Have you been adulterous or had impure thoughts about other women?" Della Torre listened. Footsteps had drawn close to the confessional boxes and then paused.

"Oh no, Father, It's not that. No, I'm not even sure it's a sin against God what I did."

"What is it that's a sin against your wife but not a sin against God?"

"Well, you see, it's embarrassing." Whoever it was pacing the church wandered away.

"Confession should not be embarrassing. It should be an unburdening, an opening of yourself to God."

"This might be a new one on God. I don't really know how to say it."

"Say it as simply as you can."

"Well, Father, my wife caught me this morning trying on her clothes."

"You were trying on her dresses?"

"Not her dresses, Father, not exactly. Her underwear."

"Her underwear?"

"Yes, her bra and underwear and stockings and suspenders."

"You wore her undergarments?"

"Yes, Father. Surely that's not a sin."

"Were you putting them on for unnatural purposes?"

"Sort of, you might say."

"For sensual gratification?"

"Oh no, Father, they were very uncomfortable. Pinched every-where."

"Had you done this before?"

"Never, Father."

"So why did you put them on?"

"Well, you see, Father, I'd been telling my mates at work that my wife has got very fat since we married. So fat that I could fit into her clothes. They laughed it off; they didn't believe me. I mean, I'm not a tiny fellow. Not overweight or anything. Just not tiny. So, you see, it got me thinking. And since she'd gone off shopping this morning and I didn't need to go to work, I thought I'd give them a go. Her clothes, I mean. Except she'd forgotten something and she came back. And caught me."

"You tried on your wife's clothing to prove that she was fat?"

"Yes, Father."

"And not for sensual reasons?"

"No, Father."

"I see."

"The complication is, Father, that if she thinks I did it because I like to dress in women's clothes for sensual reasons, as you put it, she'll be worried sick. Furious, but worried sick. But if I tell her it's because I wanted to prove how fat she's got, she'd want a divorce. And that wouldn't be good for either of our souls." Della Torre spoke softly, hesitatingly, listening for sounds in the church the whole while he spun his story.

"No, indeed not."

"But what I really need now, Father, is somewhere to hide so that she can't find me. I'll go home once she's cooled down and try to come up with some reason for her."

"Maybe you should tell her that it was an experiment but that you disliked it, and anyway you went to confession straight away."

Della Torre heard the door to the church bang with an echo. The footsteps were gone. "Thank you, Father. I knew you'd understand. But would you mind if I just stayed in here for a little while? Just to stay out of range of her frying pan?"

"By all means, by all means. We normally don't take confession on weekday mornings, but I was in the sacristy and heard some footsteps so I thought I'd make sure no one had come to steal the candles. They come to steal candles sometimes. The old ladies are the worst. And when I saw the confessional door was shut... Anyway, I'll leave you to it."

The priest had already started out of his side of the confessional when della Torre stopped him.

"Aren't you going to give me penance?"

"Oh, I'm so sorry. I'd forgotten," the priest said, hastily sitting back down. "How about a dozen Hail Marys and as many Our Fathers. That should cover the past six months. And whatever sin you might have inadvertently committed in putting on your wife's things. And now say the act of contrition."

"Lord Jesus, son of Mary and God, have mercy on me as a sinner." Della Torre marvelled at how much of the long-distant ritual he could remember.

"Your sins are forgiven; now go in peace. I mean, stay. As long as you like. And then go in peace. And I wish you well with your wife."

"Thank you, Father."

The minutes counted down. He wasn't tempted to leave the sanctity of the confessional. No one else seemed to come in that morning. No tourists, no penitents, no old ladies looking to steal candles. Half past eleven turned into twenty-five to. Then twenty to. Then a quarter of an hour. Ten minutes. He'd waited as long as he could.

He ran out of the church and through the town in a hobbling sprint, every step a bolt of pain. Out of the corner of his eye he could see somebody else running.

The catamaran loomed over the historic waterfront like a diabolical machine designed to drag the population of these sleepy little towns into worlds in which they did not belong. Passport control was in a building just past the kiosk where he'd bought the ticket. The catamaran's engines were running and quayside officials were preparing to lift the warps once the gangway was pulled up.

"You'll be lucky to make it," said the passport control guard in Slovene.

"Sorry," della Torre replied, pulling out his Italian passport. "I don't understand."

"You're cutting it very fine," the officer replied in rough Italian, looking through the passport. "Where's your entry stamp?"

"My entry stamp? I don't know. I didn't notice them put one in."

"Did you come through here?"

"Oh no, I came with a friend from Trieste. We drove down. My friend's Slovene. I don't know why, but they didn't stamp me at the border."

"Criminal how negligent they can be. They get so much traffic up there that they just stop bothering sometimes. Wouldn't catch us doing that."

He looked back. He could see another man rushing towards the building, the young man with the flat peasant face.

"Next time, make sure the stamp's in there. You can end up in a lot of bother without one," the passport control officer said. Della Torre took his stamped passport and made a running leap at the gangway, terrified his left knee would give out on him, as the flat-faced man ran into the building.

"You, let me look at that ID before you go rushing through," he heard the border guard shout behind him. *Thank god for Slovene petty-mindedness*, della Torre thought.

He was on the boat before he dared turn around. The young man was remonstrating with the passport control officer.

Another man had only just arrived at the barrier. He stared up at della Torre, a shrug implicit in the way he stood. They might have missed him now, his eyes seemed to be saying, but they knew where he was going. And when he'd be getting there.

"**THIS IS ADDING** insult to injury. Pulling me away from my hospital bed when I've been grievously wounded and then leaving me to fester in your office without so much as a cup of coffee while you disappear for hours."

Anzulović had meant to get right back to Strumbić once he'd got off the phone with della Torre, but by the time he'd got back from the cathedral to the UDBA offices, he'd been stopped by Lieutenant Colonel Kakav, who wanted to know why they hadn't arrested the offending officer yet and whether Messar was really up to the job.

Anzulović had spent a long half-hour persuading the man to be patient. Kakav was little better than a politician. No. Worse, Anzulović reflected. At least politicians were occasionally funny.

But Anzulović knew what was bothering Kakav. Messar was incorruptible. He was efficient and successful, and when Kakav would want to control him he'd be out of reach. Messar never even let a barman stand him a drink.

By the end of the meeting with Kakav, Anzulović felt like washing his hands and changing his shirt.

"Julius, don't give me grief. Three hours is how long you cops keep people waiting just to ask where to take a piss in that station, so don't be complaining to me."

"It's a matter of professional courtesy."

"If you were a professional, I might be courteous," Anzulović said with more venom than he'd intended. "I'm sorry about that, Julius. It's been a hell of a couple of days. Have you written up that statement for me?"

Strumbić handed a couple of badly typed sheets of paper to Anzulović.

Even before reading it, Anzulović said, "It's not signed."

"It's not a fair copy," Strumbić said.

"Doesn't surprise me."

"I'm not here to be insulted, Anzulović. You know very well what I meant is that it needs to be typed by somebody who can actually type. I'll sign it then."

Anzulović knew Strumbić was stalling. He read the pages.

Strumbić had done what he'd been told to do. According to him, della Torre had been with the Bosnians but hadn't shot Strumbić. On reflection, della Torre had been standing in the wrong place to have shot him in the shin. It must have been one of the Bosnians. The tall one.

Strumbić gave descriptions of all three, but they were generic enough to be useless. He gave a better account of the car. Which was exactly the one stuck to the tree in the gorge near his weekend cottage.

Best of all, he indicated clearly that he thought della Torre was there by force. It seemed the Bosnians wanted something out of them both. What it was, Strumbić didn't elaborate.

After the shooting, the Bosnians disappeared with della Torre. The implication being that they'd kidnapped him.

"It's good as far as it goes. Not Shakespeare. More like Three Stooges. But the audience ought to buy it," Anzulović said. "There's just the little matter of your thumbprint."

"I'll sign a fair copy in duplicate. I sign this and give it to you, who knows how you'll change it to suit yourselves."

Anzulović shook his head. Why was it that nobody in this country ever trusted anyone else?

"So what's to keep those Bosnians from looking you up again?"

"I have a feeling they've been taken care of."

"What about the people who sent them?"

"My colleagues on the Zagreb force are taking a close interest in my welfare."

"I'll tell you what. How 'bout I photocopy this and you sign both copies."

Strumbić shook his head, but before Anzulović could start grinding away at the detective, there was a knock on the door.

"Come in," Anzulović said.

It was Messar. He looked down at Strumbić and then back at Anzulović.

"We tracked della Torre to Piran."

Anzulović nodded.

"But he got away."

"Oh?" Anzulović tried not to look pleased.

"He got on a ferry to Venice. The Slovene police and port services wouldn't help, and by the time my men got through to me, the ferry was in Italian waters."

"What happens now?"

"We'll have men waiting for him in Venice." Messar was one of the few Department VI people to refer to the UDBA as "we." "The ferry will be there in about an hour. We'll pick him up and arrange for transport back."

"They can do it quietly, can they?"

"They'll be quiet."

Anzulović nodded. It was out of his hands.

When Messar left the room, Strumbić looked at Anzulović. The old cop seemed to care about della Torre. The saddlebags under his eyes hung lower than ever, his pallor looking even more like badly cooked veal.

"So it looks like Gringo will be back with us soon," Strumbić said. He was pretty sure he was unhappy with this state of affairs. Anzulović was right. Della Torre could make life hard for him.

"Mind if I make a phone call?" Strumbić asked.

"Go ahead. They're monitored, in case you're thinking of calling your lawyer."

"Even yours?"

"Especially mine."

Strumbić nodded.

"The secretary's fax machine is beyond our surveillance people's capabilities."

"Not monitored?"

"No."

"I'll use that then, if you don't mind. You don't have Gringo's photo by any chance, do you?"

"Why? Missing him?" Anzulović asked.

"No. But I'm hoping Messar will be."

19

VENICE ROSE OUT of the distance, the tall finger of the Campanile marking its spot on the broad horizon. Della Torre had always been indifferent to the city. Massed tourists irritated him. But mostly he disliked the deep vein of cynicism that spread through anyone who'd lived in Venice long enough. The city was beautiful. Accessible. But somehow unreachable, like those Hollywood actresses on billboards.

Everything was expensive. The food was a disappointment. There was tat everywhere. Ultimately it offered as little choice as a socialist supermarket. But the setting was, he admitted, easier on the eye than anything Lenin or Engels had ever inspired.

A little more than an hour and a half after the catamaran left Piran, Venice's great landmarks passed along its starboard side. It docked at San Basilio. Della Torre wondered what sort of welcoming party Messar might have arranged for him on such short notice. He'd hoped the catamaran's speed and Piran's proximity to Italian waters would be enough to escape interception by the Yugoslav navy. But he also knew the UDBA had people in all the major Italian ports along the Adriatic. He took his time getting off the boat. No one in particular seemed to be looking for him in the dockside crowds, but that didn't mean anything. Passport control was a formality. Della Torre slipped into the Venetian alleys, and only when there was no sign of anyone tracking him did he think about lunch.

The plate of spaghetti puttanesca was par for the Venetian course. Only just edible. The Italian beer was revolting. A few other tables were occupied, but the restaurant was mostly empty. Della Torre watched a man come in. He wore a suit in the way a travelling salesman wore a suit. As if he slept in it, bathed in it, wore it to the beach.

"Mind if I join you?" he said in an accented Italian, pulling up a chair after glancing at a shiny, folded piece of paper that he then pocketed. He lit a cigarette, ignoring that della Torre was still eating. Della Torre pushed his plate away.

"I take it you've got a message for me from friends," della Torre answered in Croat.

"You got friends? Not the way I hear it." The man flagged down the waiter and ordered a beer.

"Messar's quick."

The man shrugged. He looked world-weary. On close inspection, he had "retired cop" written on his features. It must have been an early retirement — he couldn't have been past his early fifties. But his papery skin, watery eyes, nicotine-stained fingers, and large belly suggested to della Torre that his retirement wouldn't last much longer. Overdue for a stroke. He looked like somebody in a holding pattern, waiting for the tag to be put on his big toe. Maybe a freelance was the best Messar could do on such short notice.

"So you've come to tell me that you want me to go with you quietly to whatever transport you've got arranged for me or I'll be going back in a box, right?"

"Nope."

"Oh, apologies. I've got you mistaken for somebody else. You'll be hoping to sell me a set of encyclopedias, then."

"An old buddy of mine suggested if I got a bit lonely I'd find somebody who looked a lot like you stepping off the Piran ferry."

"Your old buddy's a perceptive fellow. And who might he be?"

"My old buddy also suggested, some other people might be looking for somebody who looked like you stepping off the Piran ferry."

"Were they?"

"They might have been. But they had a little problem with the local cops. Something about having been seen picking pockets. They're just having a conversation now. It's a shame that the conversation won't last very long, unless they're very naughty boys and by some happy accident are found packing guns. But I doubt it. They looked like they knew what they were doing. And they won't be too far away."

"Maybe I should pick up the bill."

"Maybe you should."

"Mind if I stand you that beer? The least I can do."

"Beer? Is that what it was? I thought it was piss," the man said.

Della Torre paid up and the two men slipped into the Venetian alleys.

"So who can I thank for this timely intervention?"

"A friend. Of mine. A friend who suggests you make yourself scarce somewhere that's not Zagreb. Or Venice. He said it'd be really unfortunate if you found yourself floating face down in a canal tonight."

"Is that what would happen if I didn't make myself scarce?"

"Could be."

"So what do you suggest I do?" asked della Torre wearily.

"Train station's that way. And so's the airport."

"My regards to your friend."

Della Torre didn't think too hard about who had sent this peculiar guardian angel. Anzulović, maybe. But he knew quality advice when he heard it. He walked to the station. He briefly contemplated a train but decided a flight would probably be the thing, so he hopped a bus to the airport, passing on one of the expensive water taxis.

Riding over the long bridge Napoleon had built, a sort of drip line feeding the city the endless stream of tourists that kept it from dying of old age, he felt the thrust of fate pushing him farther. Della Torre knew he had to go to America.

He decided he'd take the first flight to wherever he could catch a plane across the Atlantic. For a short sojourn. The departures board offered slim pickings, though there was an evening flight to London on British Airways. The thought of London made him cringe, but at least it was easy to get to other places from there. First, he had to buy some clothes and a small suitcase. He'd break down the Beretta and put it into the case to be checked in for the flight. He was pretty sure security wouldn't like his carrying a gun on board in hand luggage.

Getting a suitcase was no problem, but apart from ties and handkerchiefs, he had no joy finding someone to sell him a new wardrobe. He'd slept in his clothes, sweated in them, smoked about fifty cigarettes in them, and he guessed he'd be about as welcome as a ripe cheese to whoever would be sitting next to him on the flight. But it didn't matter. If London was short on charm, at least it wasn't short of shops.

As it happened, there were only a handful of people on the flight, which may have explained the delay. They were meant to take off at eight p.m. but left the ground not much short of midnight. It was well after two in the morning English time before he'd got through customs and immigration at Gatwick Airport. And then he had to wait until half past four for the first train into Victoria Station. He could have taken a taxi, but he'd decided not to bother to change much money. He'd convert his Deutschmarks into dollars at Heathrow, where he'd get a flight to Chicago.

So he stuffed the envelope full of German cash into his back pocket, took a seat on the first train into town, one of the old-style slam-door trains dating back to the war, and slid his small suitcase — which contained nothing more than pieces of a handgun, a box of bullets, a carton of Luckys, and some scrunched-up newspaper to fill in the space — into the overhead locker. He kept the shoulder bag with the remaining cigarettes and travel documents next to him and shut his eyes, preparing for the hour's journey it would take to get into London.

The carriage was almost empty except for a group of teenagers who filled a couple of rows at the opposite end. The door slammed next to him. He opened his eyes. A woman, or at least he was pretty sure it was a woman, sat down opposite him just as the guard blew his whistle and the train pulled out with a lurch.

She had close-cropped hair, three earrings in one ear, and none in the other, and was dressed in jeans and a leather jacket. In one hand she held an open tin of beer. Her build was almost entirely block-like, matching her rather cubic head. He couldn't even guess at her age. She could have been a couple of years older than him or a decade younger.

She leaned forward in her seat, rocking more than the train's motion warranted. She struggled to bring him into focus.

"Travellin', eh?"

Della Torre tried not to nod.

"Yeah, I like travellin'. Used to do lots. Up to Newcastle. Been to Cardiff too," she said.

Della Torre thought, *Maybe if I shut my eyes, she'll take the hint.*

"Where are you from?" she asked.

"Cardiff," he said at last.

"Thought so; you sound Welsh. Or West Country, anyway." She took a swig from her tin. "Want some?"

Della Torre wondered if there was anything in the world he wanted less.

"No, thanks," he said, resigned to his fate for the next hour.

"Can't say I blame you," she belched. "Tastes like piss."

Maybe all beer in the world except for Karlovačka tastes like piss, he thought.

She was quiet for a moment, her eyelids struggling against gravity. Della Torre found it hard to keep his own eyes open. At least she'd distracted him from the chest-tightening feeling the return to London gave him. His exhaustion was fed by the soothing rhythm of the train's clacking wheels. He didn't notice falling asleep until someone punched him in the head.

He started out of his seat, but a second blow knocked him back down. Three youths were standing over him, two holding knives. He could hear others elsewhere in the carriage.

"Yo money, be fass. Everything out yo pockets."

Della Torre thought longingly of the Beretta in the suitcase overhead. Out of reach and in bits. Would he ever have his gun when he needed it? A blade pushed against his neck hurried him. He took three sets of keys out of his pocket. His wallet came next. They took all the notes out of it, all the sterling he'd only just acquired, some lira, and the nearly worthless dinars. And they took the envelope full of Strumbić's cash. Other than what he'd spent on ferry and plane tickets, the rest of the money was still there. The best part of fifteen thousand Deutschmarks.

"Hey, what's this, bro?" one of the teenagers asked another.

"Don't you know nothing? That's German money."

"Yeah? You buy anything with it?"

"Yeah, you buy a BMW with that shit."

"BMW, that proper nang."

They turned back to della Torre, "What else you got?"

They ignored the suitcase but dumped the contents of his shoulder bag on the floor.

"Smokes in this one and some diary thing," one said, throwing the notebook aside and helping himself to as many packs of Luckys as he could hold in one hand.

"Time to peg it, this our stop," one of them said, his head hanging out of the window. A kid pulled the emergency stop cord and before the train had quite screeched to a halt, they were gone, across the tracks and into the night, carriage doors left flapping open. Gone with Strumbić's money. No, gone with della Torre's money.

He lit a cigarette and stared out into the cold darkness, too tired even to think of chasing the kids. Pointless, really. They were at some junction, without a station in sight. At least they'd left him some cigarettes. He put the keys and his empty wallet back in his pockets and replaced the items in the overnight bag.

The police, when they finally came, were sympathetic. Another single male passenger and a middle-aged couple on the carriage with him had also been robbed. Della Torre's companion had been left alone. In fact, she hadn't woken up until the police got there, and then complained bitterly about how they were persecuting her.

They wrote down her details and left her to take the next train into London.

Della Torre went to the police station to give a short witness statement. The policeman said he'd be contacted for a longer one later on. For some reason, maybe because it popped into his head, della Torre gave his childhood address in Ohio.

Even now he couldn't really remember what the kids looked like. Big teenagers. Two black, one white. For a while the investigating officers got excited when they saw him limping and the way he favoured his left arm. They were disappointed when he said his injuries had nothing to do with the robbery. The punch to his head had left no visible bruising, so there was no chance of a grievous bodily harm conviction.

"There's been a lot of 'steaming' on trains in this part of London," PC Nicholas said. "That's what they call it. Gangs of teenagers rampage through carriages late at night, robbing passengers and then pulling the emergency cord between stations. It's mostly a south London thing."

He had short ginger hair, protruding ears, and an innocent, open expression. He couldn't have been much more than a teenager himself.

"Usually it's late at night. This is the first time I've heard of them doing it this early in the morning. It's not very nice for a visitor from abroad. It's not very nice for anybody. Have you been to London before?"

"I've passed through once or twice," della Torre said, nursing a bland cup of black coffee.

"Have you given any thought to what you're going to do? I mean, the Italian consulate might be able to help out, at least to get you back to Italy. I'm not sure what they can do about getting you to the U.S. You haven't got travel insurance, have you?"

"No," della Torre said.

"They don't always pay out anyway. Not if you've been robbed of cash."

Della Torre had counted up his resources. They'd taken everything out of his wallet and the envelope full of Deutschmarks, but they hadn't touched the passport wallet in his overnight bag. He'd always kept some emergency cash in various currencies in it, though, feeling flush with Strumbić's cash, he'd given most of his reserves to Irena. All told, in Deutschmarks, dollars, and lira, he had around four hundred pounds sterling left. It might be enough to get him a one-way ticket to the U.S., but then what?

If he husbanded the money carefully, it would last him about three weeks in London and then might even leave him with enough to catch a coach back to Zagreb. He was pretty sure he'd be fed on Goli Otok, or whatever the equivalent was now that they'd shut the penal island for good. At least until whoever'd hired the Bosnians got to him. He lit a cigarette.

"Would you like me to drive you somewhere? Anywhere within reason. I mean, anywhere in central London or to Heathrow?" asked PC Nicholas.

Della Torre fiddled with the keys in his pocket. He took out all three sets. His apartment keys. And those for the Renault. The UDBA was sure to impound it. And then there was Strumbić's set, the ones that had been on the ring with the key for the BMW. And a thought dawned on him.

"Do you know where Hampstead is?"

"Sure, north London, big park. Very nice. Very posh."

"Can you drive me there?"

20

ANZULOVIĆ WAS SLUMPED against the back of his chair. His long face had the look of an antlerless moose. He'd always had the habit of getting in early. He laughed it off whenever a colleague mentioned it, saying his wife and daughters drove him out of the house. There might have been a little truth to that. But the reality was that, outside of the cinema, he'd never liked to be surprised. He liked to know what was going on, to be able to plan and organize, to stay on top of things, so that when the inevitable shovelful of rusted nuts and bolts was thrown into the machine, he knew how to sort things out.

Not that there had been much to do during recent months. They'd stopped receiving orders from Belgrade, and much of the UDBA's normal operations in Zagreb had shut down as the many Serbs on its staff left the increasingly hostile atmosphere. He felt sorry for those in mixed marriages, especially where it was a Croat married to a Serb, or either married to a Bosnian Muslim. Those families were going to suffer trying times. They were suffering already.

Della Torre came into Anzulović's mind just as there was a knock on the door.

"Come."

It was Messar. He shut the door behind him but remained standing.

"What's the news?"

Messar looked at him for a while.

"My men were stopped by the Italian police. It wasn't random. Somebody had put them up to it."

"Do you think Gringo planned ahead to make sure he didn't have a welcoming party?" Anzulović asked neutrally.

"Maybe. But I think he had help from this side."

"Oh?"

Messar just shrugged.

"So what now?" Anzulović asked.

"There's the Bosnians. From what I've been able to find out, they're back in Bosnia."

"Can't you get someone to track them down and pick them up?"

"No, they're from near the border, by the Krajina," Messar said, referring to the swathe of Serb-occupied lands in Croatia next to Serb-dominated parts of Bosnia. There was no chance a request from Zagreb would hold any water there.

"So what do I tell Kakav?"

"I don't think you need to tell him anything. We'll monitor both della Torre apartments and his father's house. We'll track him down when he gets in touch."

"And what do we do when we've tracked him down? Leave Zagreb to sort out an extradition? Good luck to them," Anzulović said. Croatia was still part of Yugoslavia, and as such any extraditions would have to be organized through Belgrade.

"Or we get the UDBA to do it the old-fashioned way," Messar said.

"Ah yes, make him an offer he can't refuse," Anzulović said. Messar stared at him. "That's from *The Godfather*, by the way." Messar still didn't react. Why did none of his staff ever watch any decent movies? They lapped up Laurel and Hardy, and local crap, which usually involved some superhero partisan and a dose of soft-core or alternatively was an ersatz western. But that was it.

"Until then we'll keep a lookout for the Bosnians. And a close eye on Strumbić. There's more to this story than he's telling us. My best guess is that he and della Torre were involved in some dirty deal and then fell out."

"Anything else going on?"

"With this case?"

"With the world," Anzulović said and then quickly added, "Never mind. Keep me posted."

Messar left without saying anything.

Anzulović looked around the office. It was, he supposed, grand. The proportions were, anyway. Tall windows looked out across a park. But like most of Zagreb's late-nineteenth-century buildings, it had been badly adapted to the modern world. The ceramic stove in the corner of the room had been converted from wood to gas, but the process of keeping it lit and running smoothly was beyond him. Rather than freeze, he kept the room too hot but left a window slightly ajar. Which meant there was always a cold draft.

Yugoslavs had mostly lived well during the past couple of decades. Before that, the poverty had been palpable. And so had been the oppression of living under a Communist ideology in a police state. But the 1970s and '80s had been better. Not like in the West. Still, people had cars and televisions, and most ate meat more or less whenever they wanted it. Those who did well, the professionals, could save enough to buy Volkswagens and German washing machines. They could even travel abroad, though it was expensive.

The past year and a half, though, had brought back memories of those difficult times. He could feel them coming back, the deep, brutal poverty of his childhood, when children from the villages in the hills didn't have shoes, when food was little more than cabbage or beans with the occasional scraping of pork fat to flavour it. Mean times.

And mean times made people angry. There was solidarity with those they considered their own, but strangers would suffer.

Anzulović looked up at the peeling and chipped white-washed walls, dingy with dust towards where they reached the ceiling in a gentle curve instead of a cornice. Maybe the answer was for the people to save themselves. It was too late for him. His daughters? No, they'd never go anywhere else, fearing the world beyond their narrow borders.

But it wouldn't be too late for Gringo. Or for Irena.

21

"**S** ORRY, THIS IS a non-smoking car," said PC Nicholas when della Torre popped open another pack of Luckys.

"Clever car. It'll live longer that way," he said, reaching for his matches.

"Sorry. You don't understand. People aren't allowed to smoke in this car," said PC Nicholas.

"You're not Bosnian by any chance, are you?"

"What?"

"Never mind. I'll chew my fingernails instead."

"Did a mugging here last week," PC Nicholas said, pointing to a nondescript street corner.

"Is that really something you should be admitting to? You being a policeman and all?"

"What? Oh. No, it was a case I took on. I didn't mug anyone. Someone else did," he said, slightly flustered. "There's been a wave of bag-snatchings along here. A couple of kids on bikes. My case."

"Any luck so far?"

"Not really," he admitted, but then quickly added, "It's just a matter of time."

"Wait long enough and you might get a deathbed confession."

A minute later PC Nicholas let out a honking laugh. "I get it. I didn't know Italians were so funny. Though you sound pretty American. I'll have to use that one."

"Have it on me," della Torre said. The police radio cut in and out in the background, parcels of static.

Despite the misery of his circumstances, he had warmed to this young cop. There was no affectation. No fake toughness. Just a keen earnestness and concern.

Had the train robbery happened in Zagreb, the police would have shrugged their shoulders and said he ought to have paid more attention before getting into a carriage full of teenagers. But only after leaving him to rot in the station waiting room for the best part of a day. On the other hand, he didn't know of a cop car in Zagreb that was without a full ashtray.

It was a slow drive through London's nondescript and rubbish-strewn southern suburbs; rush-hour congestion kept them crawling for long stretches.

"Wouldn't it be quicker with the lights flashing and the siren on?" della Torre asked.

PC Nicholas looked scandalized. "Not unless it's an emergency. And I'm afraid you don't count."

Della Torre wondered whether the young cop would feel the same in ten years' time, when he had to get his kids to school and everyone was running late—PC Nicholas had proudly told him his wife was pregnant. But della Torre kept his mouth shut. At least the cops here started off honest.

They crossed the Thames at Blackfriars Bridge. Della Torre admired the way the river seemed to bend around them. For a moment, London offered up the stately beauty the tourist brochures always promised. He caught a glimpse of Westminster to his left, and on the other side St. Paul's and Tower Bridge. It brought on a prickling of unwanted memory.

Then they were back in the endless monotony of the city's dirt-grey Georgian and Victorian architecture, punctuated by socialist-inspired bits of concrete functionalism.

But it was different when they got to Hampstead. They eased into an elegant world of white stucco villas and cottages that might have been transported out of country villages onto this expensive film set.

"Welcome to Hampstead. Do you know where you're going?"

"It's a building set into the park, up on the hill. Do you mind driving round?"

PC Nicholas didn't mind. He seemed to enjoy marvelling at the big houses the rich people lived in, guessing at how much they might cost.

They made a circuit of the vast park called Hampstead Heath, looking for a likely building. They briefly got lost on the Highgate side, up a steep, narrow lane bordered by heavy cast-iron railings and overhung by ivy-strangled trees, where they caught glimpses of weathered stone angels in the shadows. It was only when they passed the gates that della Torre remembered. Highgate Cemetery. Eternal home to Karl Marx. They muddled their way to the road at the wooded top of the Heath and then drove down its eastern side.

"There," della Torre said. "Stop here." He'd remembered Strumbić's description. It was five storeys high, red brick, and built around the turn of the century — the southernmost of a pair of buildings that dug into the Heath, surrounded on three sides by the parkland and on the fourth by a narrow road. Crowned with white dormers, which della Torre had kept his eyes on from the top of the hill.

They pulled up directly in front of the building. Della Torre got out and tried the keys on the front door. One of the Yales worked.

PC Nicholas seemed disappointed that they had arrived so soon; he'd have to drive back into the depths of south London now. Della Torre came back to grab his suitcase from the car and shook the officer's hand with heartfelt thanks.

He carried his near-empty suitcase and his shoulder bag up the stairs, ignoring the lift. He tried to remember—had Strumbić said the third floor or the fourth? Whichever it was, he knew it had a long view over central London, which put it on the south side of the building.

He worked his way methodically along the parquet-floored hallways, knocking on doors and, when there was no answer, trying the keys. Once a maid answered, but she didn't seem to speak English. Otherwise, no one seemed to be around. When he'd run out of doors on the third floor, he went up the stairs.

The security key fit the corner flat. Although he heard the deadbolt clank and the Yale turned in the door handle, he couldn't open the door. He tried to force it but the wood protested against his weight. And then he remembered the Chubb lock.

The apartment was spacious and light. A small entrance hall opened into a large sitting room, which bent around in an L shape. The bottom leg of the L was a dining room, and there was a galley kitchen in the angle. The windows, covered by fine muslin curtains, looked to the south and the east over a large expanse of woods, rolling meadows, and ponds glinting in the morning light; beyond, the hill ended and London's vastness took over. The apartment was furnished along simple lines, the way he'd seen in Swedish houses. Nothing looked cheap, but it was all understated, with spare lines. There were a few older mahogany pieces, but none of the fake, heavy rococo that was all too common in Italian households. He wandered along the hall, looking into one, two, and then a third bedroom, the last with its own bathroom.

The apartment was vast. Had Strumbić said two hundred square metres? Della Torre could easily believe it. There was nowhere like it in Zagreb that he knew of. Come to think of it, he'd only ever seen places like this in magazines, as backdrops to celebrity photo shoots. He'd long known Strumbić was a crook, doing dodgy little sidelines here and there, but he never imagined it could be on such a scale. The apartment was worthy of a Mafia kingpin.

He'd have felt comfortable camping out for a couple of weeks while he decided what to do, but it was obvious someone was living here. The flat was spotless but the refrigerator was full of food. Stockings were hung up to dry in one bathroom, and the other was full of well-ordered toiletries. There were women's clothes in the closet of the main bedroom. The decor was neutral or slightly feminine.

He went back to the front door and tried all the keys again. There was no mistake — this was Strumbić's apartment.

Della Torre sat on a cream sofa and was about to light a cigarette when he noticed there was no ashtray. He found a saucer in the kitchen and brought it back to the living room.

He was tired and he smelled. He wished he had a change of clothes, but then he remembered seeing a washing machine and dryer in the bathroom. Maybe Strumbić had a mistress whom he kept in the place. He'd never mentioned one. In fact he'd said it was empty, waiting for him.

The only woman in London Strumbić had mentioned was the agent who handled the apartment for him. Della Torre remembered the conversation. He'd asked how much the apartment had cost.

"You don't want to know," Strumbić had said. "On your salary, you'd probably have to work for the next 250 years to buy it — that's if I gave you a sixty percent discount and you didn't eat or pay taxes along the way. It's not cheap to run, either — the building charges, taxes, utilities . . ."

"Who's handling it for you?"

"All the bills get paid automatically out of an English account I've got set up. There's enough cash in it to cover costs till I'm a great-grandpa. The agent who sold it to me has it all furnished. Real nice. Not cheap. She's got taste. Which means

I've got taste. I give her a call a couple of days beforehand and it's all ready for me when I get there. Clean, tidy; beds made, dusted, sorted, and nice little touches like flowers, fruit, milk in the fridge, and that feminine smell that makes a place feel like home."

"She sounds a dream."

"Not bad-looking, either. Bit older than the ones I usually go for."

"You mean she's not sixteen."

"I'd put her at around thirty," Strumbić had said, ignoring the comment. "Blond—real blond, not the bottled stuff. Not married, though I don't know why. She's put together pretty well, though her tits aren't as big as I like. A bit on the tall side. She'd suit you better than me. Still, I'd nail her."

"Except what? It'd ruin your professional relationship?"

"My English isn't good enough to explain just why it would make so much sense for her. My seductive technique relies a lot on getting the right message across. Maybe I'll bring you along as translator."

No mention of any mistress.

Della Torre would just have to sit there until the mystery resolved itself.

But he smelled. And having finally found a quiet bit of comfort, he minded. He decided to chance it, throw his clothes into the machine and then try to explain his way out of any awkwardness later. He was too tired to think straight.

Della Torre stripped and shoved everything into the machine apart from his wool cardigan. He decided to burn it once he'd bought himself a jacket. He took a shower in the en suite bathroom, luxuriating in the lavender soap, using a lady's razor to shave. He dried himself on a big towel folded over the heated towel radiator, a hitherto unknown luxury.

He wandered into the bedroom, where he found a dressing gown made of heavy damasked grey linen. It fit perfectly.

Either the woman was a giantess or she liked flowing robes. A thought flitted across his mind. Maybe he should try on her underwear to see how big she really was. He laughed. The poor priest. The secrets of the confessional meant that he wouldn't be able to share the story with anyone else. Or would he? Maybe priests kept secrets in the way that secret policemen kept secrets. Which was to say usually, but not always.

Her scent was on the robe. Not a perfume, but her—a light, delicious fragrance. It reminded him of his tiredness. He went into one of the spare bedrooms and lay down. "To stretch his legs," as his father would confusingly say, mangling the English expression.

It was late afternoon when della Torre woke to the sound of birds. He resisted at first, wanting to prolong the feeling, to rest his bones until they'd savoured every last possible grain of sleep. But he knew he had to get up. Nearly four o'clock. He was hungry.

He went to check his clothes and cursed. They were sitting in a machine full of water. He'd neglected to switch on the spin cycle. They'd need drying too.

Nothing to be done. His stomach rumbled, so he went into the kitchen to see what he might be able to rustle up and fixed himself a couple of fried eggs with bread. He opened a beer and was surprised to find it was drinkable. No wonder: it was Czech. He was enjoying a cigarette when he heard a key click in the door. Once again, he thought of his gun too late. It was still in pieces inside his suitcase.

He was standing, facing the door, when the woman stepped in. She stopped, pulled back into the doorway, and stood there, holding the frame as if she was going to push off it when she bolted. She paused before speaking.

"Who are you, and what are you doing here? And why are you wearing my dressing gown?" There was a tremor in her voice.

He held his hands up in a show of peaceful intent.

"I'm a friend of Strumbić's. He gave me the keys to his place and told me I could stay here while I was in London."

"Who?"

"Strumbić, he owns this place. I used his keys to get in."

"I don't know anybody with that name."

Della Torre shrugged.

"I think you might have to leave."

"Let me explain."

"I think the only thing you have to explain is why you haven't gone yet."

"Can I keep your dressing gown, then? My clothes are in the washer. You see, I flew in from Italy last night and I was robbed of my money and my things."

She watched him, her eyes alert, fearful. And cold.

"I know what it looks like, but I promise you it's not how it seems," he said. "Listen. You stand there. I'll stand here, right up against the wall. I'll turn around if you like. And maybe we can talk. Put a chair in front of the door if you like. But I promise you, I'm pretty sure I have as much right to be here as you."

She considered him for a long time, tense, poised to slam the door shut and run. But she stayed.

"I'll listen," she said slowly, "as long as you do one thing first." She'd loosened her grip on the door frame but continued to watch him intently, unblinking.

"Tell me."

"Do you see that little wooden bookcase beside you?"

Della Torre looked at the simple three-shelf stand, then turned his attention back to her, puzzled.

"Think you can pick it up?" she asked.

"Sure," he said. Only the bottom shelf was full, a few broken-spined paperbacks skulked on the other two.

"Pull it out from the wall a little. Then get behind it and pick it up."

"Pick it up?"

"Pick it up and don't let any of the books fall off," she said. There was a determined air about her, a hard, metallic edge, despite her obvious unease.

He did as she demanded: stood behind the bookcase and picked it up. It was heavier than he'd thought. His back didn't thank him. Nor did his ribs or knee.

"Now put it on your feet," she said.

"On my feet?" He looked down at his bare toes and couldn't avoid wincing. "Is that really necessary? I mean —"

"If you want to talk, you keep that bookcase on your feet. Otherwise I go straight down to the porter and he calls the police."

Looking at her, he knew there'd be no give. He shrugged and then regretted it; the muscles in his shoulders complained at the weight. So he lowered the case onto the tops of his feet, taking some of the strain with his arms to prevent it from crushing his arches and to keep the books from piling onto the floor.

"I see a book fall and I'm out of here," she said.

He made a poor attempt at a smile. This was going to be a painful conversation.

"So talk now." She'd regained control of her voice but tugged on her clothes nervously.

"My clothes are in the machine, the rest were stolen from me this morning when I came in from the airport. I didn't know this was your dressing gown. I didn't know anyone was living here. Strumbić didn't tell me."

"Who is Strumbić?"

"Strumbić? Julius Strumbić? He's the owner. He owns this place."

"I know the owner and his name isn't Strumbić."

"Not Strumbić?"

"No."

She had wavy flaxen hair down to her shoulders and the bluest eyes he could ever remember seeing. She was slim and small-breasted. Her skin was pale, though her cheeks had coloured, and she had full, red lips. He'd have put her in her late twenties, thirty tops.

"You wouldn't happen to be the agent who handles this place for Strumbić, would you?"

"I'm an agent. But I don't know anyone named Strumbić."

"He's about forty years old, a couple of centimetres shorter than you, big belly. The hair's thinning a bit, but it's mostly curly and sort of sandy coloured. Piggy eyes, fat cheeks, and smokes constantly. He might have tried to pinch your bottom. That's his style, anyway. Carries a big roll of cash and likes to show it off." His lower back was aching and the edge of the wood was cutting into the tops of his feet.

"It sounds like the owner. But that's not his name. I suggest you get your clothes and leave before I call the porter and he calls the police."

"The porter?"

"Yes, the one downstairs. How did you get past him?"

"I didn't see anyone downstairs."

"Well, he'll hear about this," she said. "Anyway, it was nice to meet you but really it's time for you to go."

He was tempted to leave, if only to get out from under the bookcase, but he kept at her.

"Just out of curiosity, what right do you have to be here? You know the owner. Are you a tenant?"

"This isn't about my right to be here. This is about you having to go now."

"I'm just curious. You see, Police Constable Nicholas, who drove me here this morning, knows that I'm staying at a friend's place. He saw that I had the keys and he knew that I'd flown in this morning. So I think he'd vouch for me. I could also give Strumbić a call, and he could call your office and confirm that he offered to let me stay," he said, hoping the strain from holding the bookcase meant his eyes didn't give away the bluff. "Could you get the owner to agree that you've got the right to be here? Whoever that might be."

She contemplated him.

"Why don't you call down to the porter and tell him to come up in half an hour or twenty minutes if you don't call back down again," he said. "That way you'll know a rescuer is at hand. And then why don't you shut the door and sit down and we can talk, and I can take this thing off my feet before it cripples me."

Her eyes didn't leave him. She ran her hand over her forearm. She took a deep breath and then shut the door behind her.

"So what does he call himself, the owner of this very nice apartment?" he asked.

"Julius Smirnoff."

"Like the vodka?"

"Yes. He said that it had been a family business."

Della Torre laughed. "You could certainly say it runs in his veins. But so does just about any alcohol you could name, and some you couldn't. Can I take this thing off my feet before they start looking like flippers?"

She barely nodded.

"I didn't think it was his real name."

Della Torre edged his feet out from under the case and then settled it on the floor. He shook each foot a little and balled and unballed his fists to work the blood back into them.

"What did he say he did?" he asked, edging his way from behind the bookcase but not moving any closer to the woman.

"He said he was a businessman. He's from east Europe, but he wouldn't say where."

"I can tell you that he's a businessman. Whatever else he is, he's certainly a businessman. A Yugoslav businessman."

"Maybe that explains the contact address."

"Oh?"

"We handle his affairs, his bills and things, but we send

invoices and statements to an address in Mestre—that's just outside of Venice. That's not too far from Yugoslavia."

"I know, I came through it last night. Sorry, I didn't catch your name."

"Henrietta. Henrietta Martingale. Everyone calls me Harry."

"How do you do, Harry. I'm Marko della Torre. Nobody calls me Marko." He held his hand out but she showed no interest.

"What do they call you, then?"

"Plenty that's unprintable. But you can stick to della Torre."

"How do you do...della Torre. You're American, or you sound American, but not completely."

"You're right. I'm American. But the accent's changed a little. I grew up in Yugoslavia and spent most of a year here as a student. I did international law in London."

"Is that what you are? A lawyer?"

"Yes. Among other things."

"What might those other things be?"

"Oh, I find things out. Are you going to call the porter?"

"No. I think we'll be fine for now."

"So you live here. Does Strumbić know?"

"No. Are you going to tell him?"

"No. He and I...well, we've got what you might call an on-again, off-again friendship. We're off again."

"So how did you get the keys?"

"Long story."

"Entertain me."

"Mind if I smoke while I do?"

"Yes."

"Do you tell Strumbić not to smoke in his own place?" He hoped he hadn't damaged his feet. Holding the case up had made his rib hurt again. And his knee was still swollen.

"No. But I air it out when he leaves."

"Do you mind if I sit? I was in a car accident a couple of days ago and I'm still sore," he said.

Her face registered a brief flash of concern but then she brought it back under control. He could see her thinking it probably served him right.

"So how do you rig it? I mean, staying here without him knowing?" he asked.

"He calls about a week before he comes, and I move out until he leaves."

"All your stuff?"

"Most of it stays, except the clothes."

"How do you explain it away?"

"I offered to furnish the place and he liked what I did."

"He bought all this furniture?"

"Oh, no. I took it when I moved out of the place I was sharing with a banker boyfriend. He owned the flat and I owned everything in it."

"Don't tell me: Strumbić bought this place around the same time that you split with your boyfriend and it was just too tempting to move in, seeing as he was never going to be here."

"Okay, I won't."

"So what happens when he moves here permanently?"

"It doesn't sound like he will for a while. That's what he told me. It was for his retirement and he didn't look that old. But when he does, I'll move out and take my stuff with me."

"So what'll you tell him? Sorry, but your furniture is gone? Here's a camp bed?"

"He's renting the furniture for now, just to keep the place homey."

Della Torre stared at Harry, astonishment washing over him like a cold shower. "He's renting the furniture from you?"

"Yes."

"And you're not paying him to stay here?"

"No."

"How much is he paying you?"

"Not much. Just a couple of hundred a month. That's all."

"He's paying you a couple of hundred pounds a month so that you can live in his flat."

"He's not paying me to live here. He's paying for the furniture."

Communism was a pig of a system, but at least he understood it. Capitalism was something else. He pulled out a cigarette and lit it.

"Mind if I smoke?"

"Yes, I do," Harry said. She walked round and opened the window behind della Torre. "So where are you planning on staying?" She sat down at the far end of the table, away from him.

"You seem to have a comfortable spare bedroom."

"That's for friends."

"Of Strumbić's?"

"Of mine. You were going to tell me how you got the keys."

"I wasn't, but I will. I stole them. Sorry, that's not right. They were on the ring with the BMW key when I . . . um . . . borrowed his car."

"You stole his car?"

"No, he lent it to me."

"I thought you said you weren't on speaking terms."

"Only temporarily. We had a little disagreement, but I'm sure it's fine now."

"I see."

"But really, we're old friends. That's why he said I could stay here."

"He said he'd always be in touch before he came. He didn't say anything about lending the apartment to friends."

Della Torre shrugged. "Maybe he forgot . . . I have to say, you took it well, finding a stranger in your apartment wearing your dressing gown."

"My school taught us to be prepared for every situation."

"Some school. For commandos, was it?"

"A girls' school in west London. Much tougher than the army."

"Remind me to stay on your good side."

Della Torre wasn't a particularly sociable person. In fact, he preferred to be on his own. But his charm and easy smile made people want his company, made them want to talk to him. He prattled for a little while, admiring the apartment and the furnishings, asking innocuous questions she could answer easily until some of her wariness dissipated.

She gave him a long look during a break in the conversation. "You know, you remind me of somebody."

"Don't tell me, it was on a wanted poster."

"No. You look like...the name's on the tip of my tongue. George..."

"Washington?"

"Don't be stupid."

"The Third?"

"No, and not the Second, First, or Fourth either. No..." She wandered off to look for a magazine and came back, holding a page open. "Hamilton. George Hamilton."

"Never heard of him."

She showed him a picture of a man at least fifteen years older than he was.

"I'm not sure I'm very flattered."

"No, not how he looks now. How he looked in the late 1970s."

"Oh."

"You should be flattered," she said, colouring slightly. "Though your hair could do with a bit of growing out. And that moustache — I know they're popular in east Europe, but I think you'll find they're pretty unfashionable in the fashionable parts of London. In fact, they're unfashionable in the unfashionable parts of London too. They're sort of a minority interest. Although I'm told some men find them very attractive."

"Oh," he said, feeling the bristles under his nose. He'd had the moustache since he'd been conscripted into the Yugoslav army after university. Irena wasn't a particular fan, but most of the men he knew had one. "My clothes are in the machine. Do you mind if I finish washing them before I go? Otherwise, I'll have to take your dressing gown. I don't feel like getting arrested for indecent exposure."

Harry got up and checked on the machine.

"You've been running it on a delicate woollens setting. I had to start it up again," she said when she got back.

"Sorry. It's an unfamiliar machine. So how long will it take?"

"To wash and dry? About three hours. You sure you don't have any other clothes?"

"Just an old cardigan."

"Well," she said, giving him a long, hard look, "you might as well stay for supper."

22

ANZULOVIĆ DIDN'T DO stakeouts. He was too old. He'd done enough of them as a young cop to have lost any vestige of a romantic illusion about the routines of detective work. That's why he'd taken the UDBA job. It meant he'd never have to run up another set of stairs again unless it was to catch a movie. It was a pen-pushing job. Sometimes arm-twisting. Or politician-stroking. But those were the limits of the physical work he wanted to do.

So why, he asked himself, was he watching it drizzle in the forlorn Dolac market, waiting like some hungry, near-toothless wolf? Why wasn't somebody else doing it for him? Somebody who could write a nice crisp report that he could read over a freshly made coffee in a warm, dry office?

He didn't have to answer himself.

Messar had lost track of della Torre. And he'd been irritated when Anzulović had let Irena leave, though Anzulović mol-lified him slightly by pointing out that they might be able to track down della Torre through her. The UDBA had some lever-age over the friend she was staying with in London.

Messar was also managing to accumulate an interesting dos-sier on Strumbić. As well as bits and pieces about the Bosnians, though they were out of reach. But so far he hadn't found out about della Torre's little money-making sideline with Strumbić, nor about della Torre's hobby files. Anzulović had tidied those up himself.

Anzulović found it strange to be directing an operation that, he was, at the same time, trying to subvert. Or maybe not so strange. Those things happened in the UDBA.

Belgrade was still only peripherally involved. Messar had used UDBA agents to track della Torre and to monitor various people, but as far as Belgrade was concerned it was still a routine investigation. Internal witch hunts were frequent enough that they didn't tend to generate much interest from the top brass unless one of them was involved.

But if the Belgrade hierarchy became interested, if Pilgrim proved to be not just a bee in some old Communist's bonnet but a nest of vipers, then none of them would be safe. Not Gringo. Not Strumbić. Not Anzulović. Not even Messar.

Anzulović hoped the Dispatcher would give him some clues. He had to be the old man Strumbić had met at the Metusalem Restaurant. No one else fit the description. But having reviewed what there was of the old man's file, he questioned how much he'd know about Pilgrim. He'd been called the Dispatcher for a reason. Under Tito, he had merely taken orders and passed them on.

There was only one way to find out. And that meant waiting in the near-empty Dolac market on a damp early spring day, lighting one cigarette with the embers of the last.

Dolac was the old town's open-air food market, a walk along a broad promenade between flower stalls from Zagreb's main square and up a flight of stairs. A shorter flight at the opposite end of Dolac led to the city's twin-spired cathedral.

In normal times, the market was packed from first light to midday, when it shut. Professionals, wholesalers, and restaurateurs would get there early for the best of the day's produce, while later it was thick with housewives and grandmothers circulating

between the tightly packed tables laid out with fruit and vegetables, homemade jams, cakes and cordials, nuts and sweets,
honey and beeswax candles. The meat, dairy, and fish stalls were
in covered arcades that formed two sides of the square.

But uncertainty about the future, the war, steep inflation, and
general economic malaise had crippled trade. Few people had
the money to buy, and those who had something to sell tended
to keep it for themselves, insurance against even worse times.

Anzulović knew all that. Even so, he was shocked by the state
of the market. He hadn't been in months. His wife or daughters did most of the shopping, and he'd long since stopped listening to their complaints about how little they could find.

Early spring had never been a good time to buy fresh food,
but these were the Dolac's hardest days since Tito had broken
with the Soviets.

Only one stall in three was manned; those missing made
for forlorn gaps. A few old ladies wandered around the square,
wilted beetroot leaves or limp kale hanging out of their woven
plastic baskets. The produce on offer was either more of the
same or too dear. Beetroots. Potatoes indistinguishable from
clumps of mud. Tired leaves.

It was even worse in the covered part of the market.
Anzulović counted six open stalls, each with slim pickings. A
bucket of sardines, a few squid, and an unidentifiable white-
fish fillet were displayed at the fishmonger's. The two butchers
were no better, one limited to formless lumps of red meat that
could have come from a horse or an ox, and the other selling
waxy-looking pig oddments. Anzulović was too depressed to
even bother with the cheese stalls. Only those with money and
connections in Zagreb could still get good food. He was beginning to forget what normal times had been like.

What it must be like to shop in an American supermarket!
Though he'd always suspected the ones he saw in movies were
figments of Hollywood's imagination. Della Torre had told

him it was true, the supermarkets really were like that, but Anzulović put it down to unreliable childhood memories.

He wandered around the square, keeping his eyes on the steps up to the old town. It was getting towards noon, and he worried he'd missed the old man.

The Dispatcher had been Tito's hangman. He'd made sure the right people were there at the end with the nooses around their necks, that the rope was sufficiently strong and long, and that the hinge on the trapdoor was well greased. It was said his tendrils reached into all corners of Yugoslav life, through the army, the political establishment, the criminal underworld. Even the Church.

He'd been a man in the shadows. But in the late 1960s he'd completely disappeared from the scene, not long after Tito discovered someone had been tapping his telephone calls, bugging his office and car. The files said the Dispatcher had been sent to Goli Otok. But unlike most, he came back from the island of the living dead alive. Alive and even more powerful than he'd been before.

In the early 1970s, when Croatia's reawakening national identity threatened to become an independence movement, Tito found he needed the Dispatcher. Once he'd reappeared, high-minded Croat liberationists found themselves breaking stones on Goli Otok, or in exile, hounded by the UDBA's murder squads.

And then, after Tito's death in 1980, the Dispatcher had disappeared again into a quiet retirement in Zagreb, where the UDBA kept half a sleepy eye on him.

Retired? Anzulović shook his head. Do people who have swum in blood all their lives ever retire? Or do they lurk in the shadows, waiting for the next opportunity to drink from the infernal pools? The times were becoming ripe for Yugoslavia's vampires to rise once again. A sketchy observation report noted that the Dispatcher had been more active lately. His telephone, long silent, had begun to ring again. And there were visitors. The old man's days once again involved more than just a morning routine of going to the Dolac market to collect his cigarettes and newspaper and cutlet for lunch.

Anzulović was skulking in the covered market when an old man made his way down the shallow flight of stairs from the old town. He was limping, walking with a stick, his wispy hair looking like a wreath of white laurel. The square, dark-plastic-framed glasses that magnified his eyes were unchanged, and he looked at least a decade younger than his eighty-plus years. Though his file photograph was a dozen years out of date, there was no doubt this was him.

As the Dispatcher was buying his cigarettes and newspaper, Anzulović mulled over how to approach him. He had hoped to do it in the thick of the crowds. Pull him aside for a quick chat. But he didn't want to expose himself now, where even a casual observer wouldn't fail to notice him bending over the ancient gnome.

Anzulović's difficulty resolved itself as the Dispatcher made his way towards the covered part of the market. Anzulović backed into a metal shutter, where he was sheltered by some concrete arcading.

"Excuse me, you wouldn't have a light?" he asked as the old man passed, the ember on Anzulović's cigarette clearly glowing in the gloom of the arcade.

"Seems to me that you're wanting either a lesson on how to smoke or a conversation about something else."

"Very perceptive of you, sir." Anzulović used formal language with the old man.

"When you get to my age, you're surprised if you've seen something only twice. There used to be a time when it wouldn't be safe for a stranger to stop me in public. Not a chance. Not safe at all. But these days, well, how much supervision does a pensioner need, anyway?"

"So you know what I'm going to ask about?"

"I've got a general idea you're not looking to pass the time of day about the weather or how Dinamo did over the weekend. And I suspect you know who I am. So what can I do for you, bearing in mind I've mostly forgotten anything remotely interesting to anyone?"

"I'm pretty sure you won't have forgotten this."

The little man's owlish eyes stared up at him.

"Sometime in the last month," continued Anzulović, "three amateur Bosnian criminals tried to kill a man called della Torre. I'm trying to find out why."

"I wish I could say the name rings bells. But it doesn't. And as I may have mentioned, I've been retired more or less since Tito died. Write your number down for me, and I'll give you a call if anything comes to mind. I'm often fresher in the afternoon, after I've had a little siesta." He made to leave, but Anzulović put a hand on the old man's shoulder. A firm hand.

"The Bosnians are now ex-Bosnian ex-hitmen, as I'm sure you know. But before they ex-pired, they ex-plained a thing or two about what had happened. They mentioned being hired by a certain elderly gentleman."

"How indiscreet of them. But even so, I'm not sure how I can help. I don't know any old gentlemen. They're all dead. And some might say that when they were alive, they weren't gentlemen." The Dispatcher looked at him, bemused.

"What I don't understand is why an old professional like you should employ such abject amateurs."

Was that a flicker of embarrassment Anzulović saw crossing the old man's face? Or had it been merely irritation?

"Are you taking issue because you think I did a job badly? I thought the man was your friend."

"No, I'm glad you made a mistake." Anzulović smiled. "I suppose anyone coming out of retirement might be a bit rusty. But really, what I want to know is who you were acting on behalf of. And why."

The old man turned away without responding.

Anzulović sighed. "I suppose this conversation could be much less cordial," he said.

"Are you making a threat? If you are, you must make yourself clear. I need things spelled out. Vagueness won't do. I'm afraid the subtlety is all gone." The Dispatcher shrugged, showing no fear, his expression returning to an ironic half-smile.

"Perhaps."

"Then I must warn you. Someone who spent four years on Goli Otok fears very little from life."

"You had a daughter."

"I had a daughter."

"When Tito packed you off to Goli Otok, you thought that at least your daughter was safe because she was in Munich. But she wasn't, was she."

"Yes?"

"And she had two children. And because Munich was too close after all, they moved to Canada, didn't they."

"Did they?"

"You still speak to them once a week."

"Ah, I see what you're getting at. You must forgive me. The years constantly creep up on me. Canada, yes. But I'll give you a little advice for free. You're a policeman...or something." Anzulović showed no sign of agreeing or disagreeing. "If you speak to your people, you will understand very quickly that I am not a person to abuse lightly. I have many friends who still have considerable influence."

"Even in Zagreb? Even now?"

The old man shrugged. "Even in Zagreb. Even now."

Did the old man still have ties to the UDBA? The Croat government? No one like that lived to his great age without the indulgence of a powerful protector.

"What happens when Croatia becomes independent? What happens when your friends in Belgrade can no longer help you?"

"My dear boy, that you approached me as you did tells me you're working alone," the Dispatcher said with amusement. "You should think a little more about the risks you're taking rather than being concerned about me."

The Dispatcher's ironic smile was beginning to grate. Anzulović had come prepared for a simple game of draughts, only to find himself on the wrong side of a fool's mate. He'd never been particularly good at threats. Had he been Messar, he might have taken a swipe at the Dispatcher. And if his papery skin and desiccated bones crumbled into dust, well, that'd just save the cost of a cremation.

"Son, I forgive you because you are clearly impassioned over your... friend's misfortune. But you are sadly mistaken in the role you attribute to me. It's like blaming the man in the control tower for the engine that fell off the plane. Now, if you permit me, I would like to buy something for my lunch before the butchers close."

"Who are you working for? Who is it in Belgrade that's worried about Pilgrim? What does it have to do with the Montenegrin and centrifuges?"

"Perhaps you should ask the Montenegrin yourself."

"He's retired. On the wrong side of the border. And he's never liked to talk very much. You, on the other hand, are here."

"Maybe you should send him a postcard."

"What's Pilgrim? Perhaps you can explain that to me?"

"Pilgrim? Isn't that someone who goes on religious voyages? We had in our grasp enlightenment, the purity of socialism, and the brotherhood of workers. And now we slip back into superstition and the false comfort of fascism. We are all pilgrims heading into our ugly past, don't you think?"

Without a further word, the old man carried on to buy a little pork cutlet. But only a very little one.

23

"**P**LEASURE," **SHE SAID** and her eyes told him she meant it. They were a blue-green as clear as the Adriatic, so astonishingly clear that he stared into them unembarrassed, like a child. He realized what he was doing and looked away and then looked back.

She was without question beautiful. She'd dressed simply, in a blue knitted jersey, cream trousers that tapered to her ankles, and a pair of old blue and white deck shoes. There was little evidence of make-up, though he'd been fooled before. Her dark eyebrows contrasted with her hair, a deep flax when the light caught it.

He seldom cared about how he dressed, but he felt out of place in this restaurant wearing cheap Yugoslav trousers and an indifferent shirt he'd bought at Marks & Spencer. It didn't matter, though, because nobody was looking at him. All eyes drifted towards Harry, pulled away, and then drew back. Glancing around the room, it was impossible to miss the attention directed at her. Reflexively he ran his hand over his face. He was no longer shocked to feel a smooth top lip. He was growing used to not having a moustache.

They'd grown used to each other over the past few weeks. She'd come to accept her accidental flatmate and he enjoyed her company. She was funny and entertaining. He'd even learned a thing or two from her about music and books and art. So when she suggested going out to dinner—her agency had an account at the West End restaurant—there was no chance at all he'd turn it down.

"Tell me," he said as they had their coffees and petit fours, "how is it that such an astonishingly beautiful woman seems to be single?"

There was a trace of irony in her smile. "I don't know. Maybe you can tell me."

"I can only think it's because you choose to be."

"Maybe that's because there's so little to choose from."

"In the whole of London?" he asked, shaking his head at the absurdity of what she'd said.

"The banker was a failed experiment. I decided that I didn't want to settle down and become an upper-middle-class housewife."

"And you couldn't find anybody else exciting enough?"

"The problem with exciting men is either they're profoundly stupid or they're sociopaths or narcissists or just really dull except when they're throwing themselves out of airplanes or shooting lions or driving very expensive cars very fast," she said. "Besides, I'm too broke to move in those circles these days. There comes a point where if you're not paying your way, you start to feel like a whore."

"Doesn't your job pay?"

"You may have missed the news, but we're in the deepest recession since the war. House prices in London have crashed, and nobody's selling or buying. The only things keeping me afloat are the fact that I don't pay rent and what I get from your Mr. Strumbić-Vodka for the furniture. Just about anything I earn at work gets ploughed back into the agency. I made the mistake of becoming their most junior partner at the very worst possible time."

"Can't you sell out of your partnership?"

"Who'd buy?"

"So you're broke?"

"I'm worse than broke. I'm sitting in a riptide of debt and the current is taking me far away from shore."

"But you stay away from rich men?"

"Mostly."

"What about poor men?"

"They're the same. But have less money. Some even steal the change off one's bookshelf," she said, laughing.

"Sorry. I thought you wouldn't notice."

"Never mind."

He scraped up some of the sugar that had stuck to the bottom of his cup and sucked it off the tiny, spade-shaped silver spoon.

"So, what kind of excitement are you talking about?" he asked.

"After university I taught English in Papua New Guinea. What they say about cannibals isn't true."

"What do they say about cannibals?"

"That they have good taste."

"How long was that for?"

"A year. I came back to work at a publishers. It was fun if you like cheap and tepid white wine, being paid badly, and spending time in confined places with neurotic people."

"So what'd you do after that?"

"A friend's father owns a diamond mine in South Africa."

"You mined diamonds?"

"No. They also had a game reserve. She set up a company that took rich men on big-game hunts."

"Sounds fun. Is it dangerous?"

"It is when you do it from horses. Which is what we did."

"Oh," he said. "Well, at least there were rich men there."

"Yes. Rich men with big guns."

"Were they interesting?"

"Some. But by and large, they weren't nice people. Nothing

to do with shooting animals. You just had a feeling that if they could, they'd have been happier hunting people. On the other hand, that might not be a bad idea — if they went after those willowy, self-obsessed boys in the publishing industry who are so full of existential despair."

"So you're looking for somebody rich, clever, and flawless?"

She laughed. "You make it sound like a tall order. No, he doesn't have to be flawless, but there has to be something there. I probably want a cowboy: a man on a horse, book in one hand, rifle in another, and wilderness in front. Only not the sort who goes to South Africa to shoot buffalo. Or the ones who work in banks."

Della Torre shrugged. He'd never really given much thought to horses. Or bankers.

"But at least I didn't want for trying. Though not lately, of course," she said.

"Oh?"

"Going from an all-girls school to university is like being a child with strict parents who's taken to a candy shop by a favourite uncle for the first time. It's very hard not to sample a little of everything."

"And the sampling stopped with the banker?"

"Yes. Though he didn't last that long either. I decided to have a little break after him. He was about as sexy as Luxembourg, but not as interesting. Maybe I'll do some travelling when the money starts flowing again. I miss travelling since I've been poor. I only get to stay at friends' country houses or their French or Italian villas or chalets. Not the proper sort of travelling, where you go somewhere you can't spell and eat things that make you sick for a week. Maybe the man of my dreams is waiting for me in Alma-Ata. What about you?"

Della Torre thought about Irena. If she wasn't in London already, she'd be coming soon. The UDBA would keep their eyes on her. Messar would expect him to find her. And then they'd find him.

"I was married."

"And?"

"It ended."

"Children?"

"No."

"Messy?"

How could he explain it when he didn't understand himself what he felt?

"No."

"Does that mean you don't want to talk about it?"

"It just means there's nothing really to say. We were married. But now we're not. We don't put pins into each other's wax effigies, and we don't try to wish each other out of existence either."

She nodded.

"What are your plans?" she asked. "How long are you staying? Not that I mind. Other than the cigarettes and the fact that you're barely housebroken, you're not too bad to have around."

"Thanks," he said. "I don't know. If I eat plain boiled rice and eggs I'll have enough to live off for a few weeks. Shame that Lent's over. I could have made it into a religious observance."

"And then?"

"Well, I can't really look for a job here. My intention had been to go to the States, but that seems unlikely unless I can mug those little bastards who have my money. I'll probably have to go back to Yugoslavia. Maybe I'll call up Strumbić and ask him for a loan," he said, laughing at the thought.

"He certainly doesn't seem to be short a penny or two," she said. "I don't need to tell you how much running his apartment costs. The service charges, council tax, utilities — everything adds up."

"Not to mention what he pays for your furniture."

"I didn't mention that on purpose."

"He must get cramp writing all those cheques every month."

"Oh, he pays by direct debit."

"Direct debit?"

"Yes, it just comes out of his account. I helped him sort all that out."

"He does a direct debit to you for your furniture?"

"Sure. All the bills."

"How exactly does he set that up?"

"There's a form from the bank. He fills it in, signs it, and sends it to the bank, and then the bank takes over from there."

"What if the bills go up?"

"Then the bank pays whatever he gets billed."

"So some months it's higher than other months?"

"Well, there was a bill from the management association last year to sort out some unanticipated building works. They needed to replace part of the roof and it wasn't covered by insurance or the general maintenance fund. I remember they sent us a statement as his agents."

"So you sent Strumbić the bill?"

"We sent him a copy of the invoice, but the money just came out of his account. As managing agents, we drew it out of his account and then shifted the money to the company that did the work. He never said anything. I wonder if he ever looks at his bank statement. Most rich clients don't seem to."

"So you could charge him more for your furniture?"

"I suppose I could."

"He once told me he had enough money in that account to keep his great-grandchildren happy."

"I didn't know he was that old," she said, laughing.

"He hasn't got any kids. At least none that he knows about, but you never can tell. His wife is as parched as the Gobi, he says."

"He's not fond of her?"

"He respects her the way an infantryman respects the general

who wins battles, but I don't think it's one of those romantic marriages, if you know what I mean. Come to think of it, Strumbić
and romance are like flippers and wheels. Very hard to hold in
your mind at the same time."

"Well, that's all very nice for Mr. Strumbić-Vodka, but we're
stuck eating plain rice or going to restaurants that serve main
courses that cost as much as a pair of handmade shoes," she said.

"No. I think Mr. Strumbić is stuck in Zagreb for the next little while, if I know a certain Mr. Messar. Mr. Strumbić, you
see, will be having a little trouble with the Yugoslav law. If he
doesn't notice what comes out of his account, what's to stop
you increasing what you charge him for the rent on your furniture? Or to invoice him for further work on his property?
Create an account, set up a company, and then charge him for
redecorating. Or whatever."

"Because that, my dear Mr. della Torre, is dishonest. It's fraud.
And people go to jail for fraud."

"Ah, but Mr. Strumbić's money isn't his. Or should I say, he
would never admit to having the money he has here because
it is derived from his corrupt and criminal activity back in
Croatia. So he isn't very likely to go to the London police to
complain that somebody's stealing money that he himself stole.
Especially when he's here under a fake name. You see, it's only
fraud if somebody says it is. Otherwise, it's just a normal commercial transaction. And since he can't leave Croatia, the only
thing he can do is transfer his money out of his British account
if he's unhappy."

"You are a very devious man, Mr. della Torre. A very devious man."

"I am a very broke man speaking to a very broke woman
who has the keys to a very rich man's bank vault. A very rich
man who really doesn't deserve his riches."

"And what happens when Mr. Strumbić-Vodka notices that
he's been had?"

She was playing with the silver coffee spoon. He put his starched white napkin on the table. They were the last diners in the restaurant. The waiters stood aloof, unhurried. Natural light filtered through the room from the frosted skylights overhead, turning the leaves of the potted lemon and orange trees into a green that almost hummed. An artificial world set against the early spring chill. For a moment it crossed della Torre's mind to go to Mass; and then, following directly behind that thought, was a memory of the Croatian service at the Brompton Oratory. Della Torre shuddered and put religion out of his mind. After all, it wasn't long since he'd last been to confession.

"What happens is that he tips his hat to somebody who's better at doing something he does quite a lot. He's a little poorer and we're a little richer. And we make sure we're nowhere near him when he finds out. You did say you liked travelling, didn't you?"

24

"WHEN ARE YOU going to fix that bathroom light switch? I'm getting tired of having to use a flashlight to go. It's like my grandparents' outhouse."

"My leg's still sore, woman. What do you want, for me to have a relapse?" Strumbić shouted back at her from the living room. The smell of butter and cooked apple drifted in from the kitchen.

"Didn't stop you going out last night."

"That was work."

"So why'd you come back drunk?" Mrs. Strumbić shouted back.

He turned the television up. The news was about how Serb rebels had taken over the Plitvice Lakes and shot up a bunch of Croat police. It showed an Italian tour group babbling and throwing their arms around just because the windows of their bus had been shattered. It wasn't as if any of them had taken a bullet. They might have had something to complain about then. It was more than a month and his shin was still sore.

The phone rang.

"Can you get that? I've got my foot up and I'm watching the news."

"You answer it. What am I, your servant? Isn't it enough that I'm getting your dinner ready without having to be your secretary as well?"

"How do you know it's for me?" he shouted back, but got no response.

The phone kept ringing. Finally he gave up and clicked the mute button on the remote.

"Hello? Hello? Who's that? Can't hear a bloody thing." Strumbić held the phone away from his ear. "What?" The noise seemed to be coming from a full bar. A jukebox was playing in the background. Maybe it was a prank. He tried listening again but gave up and put the receiver down.

The telephone rang again.

"What?" Strumbić shouted into the handset.

"Mr. Strumbić, don't hang up." Music was still playing in the background, but it wasn't so overwhelming now. The man sounded like he had a country accent. Bosnian maybe.

"Who is this?"

"You set us up. We don't like that. And you owe us money."

"Who the hell is this?" Strumbić asked.

"You were dishonest with us, Mr. Strumbić. We don't like that."

"Who are you, before I tell you to fuck off?"

"We want the money you took from us." Strumbić heard the sound of a toilet flushing.

"What are you doing, calling me while you're taking a crap?"

"It's a little quieter in here, Mr. Strumbić."

"What the hell do you want?"

"Pay us or we'll shoot your wife, Mr. Strumbić."

"Go ahead. You'll be doing me a favour," he said, looking towards the kitchen. Maybe he was being harsh. She had shut up for a change. And it smelled like she was making him a strudel.

Fair or not, it stymied the caller for a moment.

"You'll be next," he finally said.

"Way I hear it, if you're the planks I think you are, you've got a peashooter. You'd do more damage driving me into a tree. That fucking car was worth twice what you want from me."

He shouldn't have lost control. The UDBA were listening. He knew they were monitoring his phone, his mail, and all his contacts. He couldn't pick his nose without somebody checking his finger. That Nazi bastard Messar had somehow managed to get the Zagreb cops to fetch his slippers when he whistled.

Strumbić should have pretended not to know what they were talking about. But he couldn't help it. These idiot Bosnians had been calling him every day for the past week. How'd they get his number anyway? Didn't matter.

Good thing Mrs. Strumbić didn't pay too much heed to people demanding money. As far as she was concerned, bills were paid only by people without the imagination to avoid them. She'd have shouted them down.

He should have kept his mouth shut. He didn't want the UDBA on his case any more than they already were. As it was they were treating him like he was some sort of suspect. Talk about victimizing the victim.

He couldn't help it, though. Being at home, being watched from all corners, being nagged constantly about fixing this or not drinking too much or not smoking on the john or how at his age her father had already become a police superintendent rubbed his fuse down to a frayed stub.

Worst of all, he barely got a chance to sneak out. He had to find some way of seeing Renata. His leg was well enough that he needed a bit of the other kind of relief. He'd sent round one of his squaddies to find out what she was up to, but when he came back he just said, "Washing her hair." Strumbić had to send the man back twice to get his mail from the flat he was letting her stay at.

"You also owe us for Besim's cousin's funeral. You pay us all that, we might leave you alone. We might even forget you set us up, Mr. Strumbić. Do you want to talk about how you can get the money to us? We'll meet you somewhere. We take cash, Mr. Strumbić."

"Whoever the hell you are, I'm going to arrest you the minute I find you. One, for threatening an officer. Two, for threatening an officer's wife. Three, for trying to blackmail said officer. Four, for attempted murder. And five, for depriving three Bosnian villages of their idiots."

Strumbić slammed the phone down. Jesus, he was starting to get hoarse from shouting so much.

He sat back down and turned the television back up.

"No wonder you have to yell if you leave the volume on so high," his wife said, coming into the room.

Strumbić didn't look at her. "Any of that slivovitz left?"

"After dinner."

"Yeah? And what's for dinner?"

"Stuffed cabbage leaves and mashed potatoes. If you're lucky you might get some strudel."

Strumbić looked up at his wife. What he couldn't get over was how such a skinny, desiccated, sour woman could cook such delicious food. Just looking at her made him flinch. She had her father's face—the old chief of the Zagreb police, a brutal man who'd been one of life's great haters. Legend had it that when one of the horses he'd been inspecting during a parade tried to bite him, he'd knocked it out with a single punch. It was true. Strumbić had been there. But what people didn't realize was that the old man had been holding a granite cobble.

His daughter had been his one weakness. "But if you continue to be a pain in my ass, I will give the whole of the strudel to Mrs. Gospodin downstairs," Mrs. Strumbić said.

"That hag. What are you feeding her for?"

"Because she hasn't got any family, and if we're nice to her, we might be able to get her apartment cheap when she has to go into a home."

Hard to argue with that, he thought.

"When are you going back to work? You're getting underfoot."

"Maybe I'll take myself off to the coast for a little while to recuperate."

"This time of year?"

"Šipan's pretty mild in the winter."

She shuddered. "You know I hate boats."

Why do you think I bought a house on an island, you silly cow? He didn't dare say it.

Now that the old man was dead, there was nothing to keep him from divorcing Mrs. Strumbić. But he'd never found anyone who could cook like she did. Certainly not Renata. He'd once watched the silly bint try to cook potatoes by slicing them directly onto a dry frying pan. Without a drop of oil or water. Never in his life had he imagined someone could burn raw potatoes.

He rubbed his shin. The doctors said it was nothing more than a bruised bone. How the hell does a bone get bruised?

Worst of all, Branko had forwarded a strange letter from his London agents. Something about needing to do emergency works in his apartment, though he couldn't understand it. It looked like a lot of money to him for emergency works. And there was the bank statement, which he didn't understand. Where the hell was his money going? As if he didn't have enough else to worry about.

Strumbić didn't like it when he couldn't stay on top of his affairs. Or on top of Renata. He'd have to slip his leash for a little while. Buy a bottle. Go up to the other apartment, check his mail, and do a little partying.

As long as Messar didn't get hold of the Bosnians or della Torre, he'd be able to find a way of making life bearable. He should have been given a medal for taking the bullet, instead of an endless pile of grief. As soon as he could, he'd go on a little convalescence leave abroad. Get away from the crazies shooting at each other. Problem with being a cop was that cops were being sent to get shot at by the Serbs. And Strumbić had had enough of being shot at.

FOR LONG STRETCHES they crawled along the motorway.

Della Torre read the paper. He played with the window, folding it up and down. He shifted in his seat, the springs biting into his backside. It was a ridiculous car, Harry's 2CV with a red and white–striped canvas roof, even more ridiculous than the Renault 4.

They drove north and east.

"This would be a great car for doing detective work. Quick getaways and very discreet. Should blend into any circus you might be staking out," he said.

"You're very welcome to walk. Or I could tie you to the bumper and drag you along."

"I'm not sure it's got the horsepower to do any towing."

"Shall we try?"

"No. I don't want to break your car."

"Considerate of you."

"Sorry. I shouldn't be rude. Not within its hearing. It might get offended and stop working."

"Is that meant to be funny?"

"This is the sort of car that women give pet names to. What's it called?"

"Are you still talking?"

"Only to myself."

"Good. I didn't think you had anything to say worth listening to."

Once on the motorway, they slipped into their own thoughts. The car was too noisy for conversation, its engine needling away as the wind buffeted its canvas roof.

For a while, the driver of an articulated lorry played silly buggers with Harry. He wouldn't let her pass but then slowed right down when she was behind him. She swore a running stream of obscenities, mostly under her breath.

"Wish I had a gun," she said.

"Oh?" he asked, glad she'd never found his Beretta.

"I'd shoot out this bastard's tires, and then when he stopped, I'd shoot him." She swore again.

"How do you know it's not a woman?"

"I don't. But whoever it is will be when I'm done with him."

She calmed down when they got onto smaller roads.

The afternoon shadows were spreading across the ground. The clouds had broken and the sun was out for stretches at a time. It was a mild day. *The time of year when Zagreb is probably starting to get hot*, he thought. It was a good time to go to the islands, get some sun, eat fish off the boat cooked in one of those impromptu restaurants that spread from people's houses to picnic benches on vine-shaded terraces: homemade wine, salad picked out of the garden, and the day's catch grilled just so.

He wondered how his father was doing, hoped he wouldn't be worrying too much about him. He never discussed his job, and for his part the old man pretended he didn't know that his son worked for the UDBA. It was a forbidden subject. Like his mother's death.

It was late May, the first warm weekend of the spring, and Harry had decided to celebrate their healthy and growing bank balance by heading to the seaside, a short break alone with della Torre before she went off on holiday to France with friends.

Della Torre had looked forward to having Harry to himself and at the same time regretted she'd be abandoning him. As if she owed him her companionship.

Their relationship had developed in a funny direction. He felt a charge when she was around, and missed her when she wasn't. The business with Strumbić had brought them close. They were conspirators. Yet somehow it had also made them keep their physical distance. It might have had something to do with a natural reserve they both had.

He was like most Istrians, who—strangely, for people who lived in a tiny corner between the Balkans and Italy--were noted for their emotional detachment. It used to bother Irena.

Harry, for her part, was an upper-middle-class Englishwoman. And upper-middle-class Englishwomen were unflappable, made no fuss; they'd been the true backbone of the empire.

For both of them, it seemed somehow wrong to mix business and pleasure, to become romantically involved with someone with whom they were engaged in a criminal conspiracy, though neither had ever said as much.

But they'd become close. He'd listened in fascination as she told him about the customs and traditions of her family and friends. And she had enjoyed his, albeit abridged, history.

When the money started magically to roll in, she'd taken him shopping. It had been less painful than he'd expected. They tramped around Jermyn Street and the Burlington Arcade, New Bond Street, and up to Selfridges. Fine cotton and linen shirts, silver and amber cufflinks, handmade chukka boots, chinos, blazer, an Italian-cut suit from Savile Row because, Harry had said, the English cut was for English men with big bottoms and narrow shoulders. The one choice he'd made on his own: a grey and heather-green Harris tweed jacket. Harry didn't protest too much.

She'd insisted he wear what he'd bought out of the shops, so he'd completely shed his tatty, cheap Yugoslav skin, which the sales clerks disposed of.

It had taken him a while to get her into the spirit of the enterprise, to convince her that it wasn't immoral to steal from Strumbić, because the money wasn't rightfully his in the first place. It would mostly be risk-free; they'd get well away before he came looking for them. He'd never use the law to pursue them, and he was unlikely to use other methods. Strumbić wouldn't want to jeopardize his safety net. He wouldn't be happy about being robbed, but ultimately he'd recognize he didn't have much of a choice other than to eat the loss. Strumbić, for all his faults, was clever enough to see his best advantage. The trick was to stop before he'd been bled too much.

She'd treated it as an intriguing joke for the first week. And then, during the second week, she thought carefully about it. The money would be easy. Almost as easy as writing a cheque. There was the frisson of danger about it too.

So at the start of the third week, she sent a debit request on agency stationery to Strumbić's bank and then transferred money from the agency into an account she'd set up for her and della Torre.

And at the start of the new month, the following week, she did the same again.

Now that they were flush, her mind had turned to holidays: the long-standing invitation to an extended house party in France. But first a short, quick jaunt to the coast. With della Torre.

Somewhere beyond Ipswich, they turned onto a straight road that went through gentle countryside bordered by copses of trees or by fields, mostly wheat or sugar beet, and then wilder gorse. In the distance he saw something shimmer, which Harry said was the river.

They passed through a small, neat suburb and then reached a square-towered medieval church made from knapped flint that looked like old tweed. The road dropped from there to show a vista of the North Sea over red-tiled rooftops.

She had the keys to a tall, narrow cottage on the front. A family place, she'd said, though he wasn't clear on the exact provenance. He put his bag in a guest bedroom overlooking a courtyard at the back. She took the main bedroom, with the big bay window offering an impressive view of the beach.

"We can go for a walk and then get some fish and chips for supper."

They strolled north on a tarmacked promenade among the other late-afternoon strollers, avoiding being knocked down by small children pedalling madly on their wobbly bicycles. The path ran along a low concrete seawall painted in a rainbow of muted primary colours, which separated the houses and cottages from a broad shingle beach that undulated down to the sea.

On the beach itself were little clusters of clapboard fishermen's huts blackened with creosote, and fishing boats winched up well above the high-tide line. The green-grey North Sea paralleled the flat landscape. The clouds had broken, and a light breeze blew in from the sea. They passed an isolated building on the front, surrounded by neat lawns and a boating pond to one side; behind it and up the hill was the church.

"Looks like toy-town Tudor," della Torre said, amused at how the architect had managed to impose every period cliché onto the building, from the jutting half-timbered first floor to the steep roof and tall, narrow chimney.

"It's real. Elizabethan. It's called the Moot Hall—it's where the town council meets. It used to be in the middle of the town; there were about three streets in front of it. This was an important port in the Middle Ages, but the sea ate it up. Without the seawall, the rest might disappear too."

"Atlantis."

"If you're looking for Atlantis, there's a town further up the coast called Dunwich. It was an even more important port, a proper city for those times. It had eight churches and half a dozen friaries. It's completely gone now. In my grandparents' time the sea had reached the last churchyard. As the sea eroded the sandy cliffs there, it exposed the graves. My grandmother said ancient bones used to fall onto the beach and then disappear at the next tide. There are a couple of houses left; one's a pub, but that's it. It's now all heathland and forest. They say on still nights you can hear the Dunwich church bells ringing out at sea. It's a spooky place."

They couldn't have walked more than a kilometre from the cottage before they reached the town's northern limits and the start of a flat, open marsh, green with its tall grasses and reeds. But that wasn't what caught della Torre's eye.

In the distance, hanging above woodland, was the massive grey-black block of a concrete building. Beach houses a couple of kilometres from where Harry and della Torre stood were dwarfed by the structure. Next to this massive bunker of a building and situated even higher up the cliff was an improbably bright white dome, almost translucent in its whiteness, that seemed to reflect the evening's light.

"What's that?" he asked.

"That's the nuclear power station, Sizewell. The dome is new—that's Sizewell B—but the block has been around my whole life. You stop noticing it; it's part of the landscape. Sort of familiar. I guess we'll get used to the dome eventually too."

"It's either huge or close."

"It's huge. It's about seven, eight kilometres up the coast."

They stared at it for a little while and then turned around. Della Torre was familiar with man-made blights in otherwise striking natural settings. Much of the Istrian coastline was punctuated by massive Communist hotels that looked like beached storm-worn ocean liners. But this spare and impossibly huge cube and half-sphere were geometric impositions on nature that even the Yugoslavs couldn't rival.

"The weather's supposed to be nice tomorrow. We could do some sailing if you like," she said.

He looked out over the sea. There were some big container ships on the horizon, and closer to the beach there was a small fishing boat trudging its way north along the coast, but not a sail to be seen.

"Doesn't look like there's much sailing to be done," he said.

She followed the path of his gaze and smiled.

"No, not on the sea. Just beyond the other end of town there's the river. We sail on that. Little boats; dinghies, mostly. Have you ever dinghy sailed?"

"No. I've been on ferries and motorboats and rowboats, but I don't ever remember setting foot in any kind of sailboat."

"You spent your life near the Adriatic and you've never sailed?"

"Sailing was for the bourgeoisie. We were good Communists. We rowed. Or just sat on the beach and drank."

"We can borrow a boat and a life jacket down at the yacht club, and I'll take you on the river."

They walked back through the middle of town, down its wide high street—more like a public square, though it was taken over by cars and parking spots—and stood in line outside a shop selling fish and chips. The best in England, Harry said. Della Torre didn't disagree. But it could just as well have been the worst; it was always a travesty what the English did to fish, he thought.

They ate on the beach, the way they were meant to, judging by how many of the chippy's other customers were doing the same, out of paper wrappers, the breeze carrying away the fried-fat smell. Harry gave him a brief geography lesson.

"That way is Holland. You can get a ferry to the Hook from a port a little way south. Over there is Denmark and up there is Norway."

"And Sweden? Somewhere between the two?"

"I guess so. The people who lived here a thousand years ago spent a lot of time worrying about what was coming from that direction. The Vikings, the Norsemen, raided and then ruled this part of England."

Sweden. He cast his mind back to the Pilgrim file. Since coming to London he'd spent time reading about AIDS and blood, trying to determine what role the Montenegrin might have had with the centrifuges. His mind was filled with all sorts of strange conspiracy theories about poisoning blood or taking the viral poison out of blood, and what role the UDBA might have in it all. But they were all so far-fetched as to be irrelevant. His research had been half-hearted and got him nowhere.

They went to the pub, where a couple of locals stopped to talk to Harry and size up della Torre. She introduced him as Marko. She seemed well liked, and they were stood pints of the local beer, served at the temperature of a cool late-spring evening. Della Torre found it bitter and not cold enough, missing his Karlovačka beer, and Harry chided him for not draining the whole glass.

They played a couple of hands of gin rummy back at the cottage, Harry having to remind della Torre of the rules, and then they read, with Harry playing Benjamin Britten's *Sea Interludes* and Bach cantatas on her newly acquired portable CD player.

"It's going to be expensive to replace my records with CDs," she said.

"I'm sure Mr. Strumbić will be happy to take the pain."

"I wonder."

"Well, maybe not happy. But not unhappy. If he doesn't know about it."

When it became sufficiently dark, they climbed the narrow, steep staircase to their bedrooms, Harry leading. He looked up towards the seat of her jeans. He had a nearly irresistible urge to slide his hand up along the insides of her legs. But seeing as she'd never more than laid her hand on his forearm, he thought better of it.

She stopped on the landing and gave him a wicked smile.

"If we're to catch the tide, we'll need to be up early," she said. "Sleep tight."

They stared at each other. She rose on tiptoes and touched her lips to his. He bent towards her, leaning into the kiss. She pushed him back.

"Let's get some sleep. We're up here to do some sailing. Remember?"

He nodded, running his hand over his top lip, missing the feel of the bristles.

"Can't think of anything I'd rather be doing this weekend," he said.

"Night night," she said, shutting her door with a soft finality.

26

WHEN HE WOKE, Harry was already up, reading a Sunday newspaper and drinking a cup of tea, dressed in one of his T-shirts.

"Hope you don't mind. I forgot my nightdress."

She must have gone into his room at night, when he was
asleep. Had she really just gone to find a T-shirt?

"I don't mind. You bought it for me, after all."

"Sleep well?" she asked.

"Is that a trick question?"

"Maybe." There was mischief in her eyes.

The ocean glistened like fish scales in the morning light. He
scanned through whatever bits of newspaper Harry wasn't
reading, looking for news on Yugoslavia.

Croatia's independence referendum had gone through. The
percentages looked like old-style Communist ones, 93 percent
in favour on an 84 percent turnout. Except he believed those
numbers. Many of Croatia's Serbs had refused to vote. And the
Croats were itching to sever ties with Yugoslavia. The Slovene
referendum had registered similar numbers a few months
before.

There was speculation that Croatia and Slovenia would
formally declare independence the following month. If they

did, della Torre didn't see the Yugoslav national army sitting
back, twiddling its thumbs. Its whole purpose was to defend
the integrity of the Yugoslav state. Take away its two wealthi-
est republics, and suddenly the Yugoslav state was not only a
lot smaller but a lot poorer. And the Yugoslav army's generals
knew who was picking up the tab for its tanks and jets.

The conflict was already turning bloody. There were a
couple of paragraphs about the killings in Borovo Selo earlier
in the month. A busload of Croat policemen had driven into an
ambush in a Serb-dominated Croat village on the Danube, on
the eastern borderland with Serbia.

Croatia's Serbs were becoming increasingly militant everywhere. The country was shaped like a boomerang, with the
western arm making up much of the Adriatic coastline. There
the Serbs had effectively cut the republic in two by carving out
an independent mini republic that stretched from the Bosnian
border to within a few kilometres of the Dalmatian coast. The
Yugoslav army had made it clear it wouldn't brook efforts by
Croatia's military forces to recapture the land and reopen the
republic's southern highway. Della Torre couldn't see how civil
war could be avoided.

What would he do? He'd disappeared effectively enough; no
one had tracked him down. But only at the cost of severing all
ties with his former life.

It wasn't just that. He still wasn't sure he could run to
America. The thought of going back somehow frightened him.
Was it the memory of his mother? Was it because in America
there were fewer excuses for failure? The country was a vast,
open wilderness waiting to swallow pilgrims... Pilgrims.

But his fate was tied in to Croatia. If Belgrade won, even
America wouldn't hide him. Better to die on a Croat battlefield
than be assassinated on a suburban street in Ohio.

He'd taken his coffee out to the seawall, where he could
smoke. He watched with astonishment as people walked down

the beach, dancing awkwardly across the shingle, and stripped off their dressing gowns and plunged into the North Sea.

"Already had my swim this morning. You were still asleep. I thought it best not to wake you," she said.

He looked at her horrified, though he shouldn't have been surprised. She'd been swimming in the Ladies' Pond on Hampstead Heath the past three Saturday mornings.

"Maybe you'd like to take a dip later, after we've come back from sailing."

"When I was in the army, they made me do things like that. The only reason I did was because they held a gun to my head."

"Would they have shot you?"

"You know, I think the commandos were crazy enough to. But I never wanted to find out."

"So you did it?"

"And I swore I'd never indulge in any form of masochism. Ever."

"None?" There was that wry, seductive smile again.

They followed a potholed gravel road that ran along the seawall at the opposite end the town to where it ended in a collection of sheds. The river flowed to within fifty metres of the sea and then turned away and flowed south, separated by a widening spit of land. Grassed river walls, protecting land-side meadows, had been built up on either side of the river. Looking inland, della Torre could see white triangles sliding above the green meadows. For a while he couldn't tell what he was looking at and then realized they were sails poking above the river wall.

The yacht club was a white, square building with a balcony overlooking the river and a three-armed flagpole overhead. Beyond it was the dinghy park's forest of masts. The dinghies ended just short of a fortress-like dark brick, curved building.

"Don't tell me, a mini nuclear power station," he said, pointing towards the structure.

"A Martello tower. A signalling fort from the Napoleonic era. This is the most northerly one, but they stretch down around the coast. The principle was you could see a lit beacon from one to the next. They were used as invasion signals. Those concrete blocks you see on top of the seawall here were Second World War tank traps, defences against invasion. As the French say, *plus ça change*," she said.

They walked behind the yacht club to a converted shipping container. Harry nipped in and got them each a life vest.

"I'll try not to capsize. But you might as well put this on anyway."

They stopped at a wooden boat near where the dinghy park ended and the landscape of low marsh grass began. Harry untied the heavy canvas cover, pulling it off the boat.

"So how does this work?" della Torre asked. "You just help yourself to a boat here?"

"I hope not. This is mine."

"Yours?"

"Yup, inherited it. It was built for my grandmother in the 1920s, when she was a girl. You only get these particular clinker-built boats on this river." She did some preliminary checks of the interior, and then they wheeled it on its trolley to a concrete ramp that led down to the river. Della Torre felt the smooth varnish against his palms. The wood was beautifully shiny, polished like fine antique furniture. The boat was almost five metres long—about the length of a big rowing skiff, but with a mast. At the concrete slipway, they stopped and Harry dealt with the rigging.

"Here, take this end of the sail and feed it through this little channel in the boom and tie it off."

He did as he was told while Harry dealt with a sail in front of the mast. Or as he thought he had been told.

"What sort of knot is that?" she asked.

"It's a knot. That's the sort of knot."

"It's a granny knot. Strictly forbidden on boats. Tighten it too much and we'll have to cut the rope to get it undone," she said, undoing his efforts. "Can you pull the main halyard up a bit while I feed the sail into the mast?"

He stared at the boat for a while and then asked, "Can I what the what?"

She laughed. "Sorry, you did say you'd never sailed. Here, pull on this thin little rope, steadily but not too hard, while I get this big sail sorted."

He did as he was told. When they'd got most of the little boat assembled, the sails flapping slightly in the breeze, Harry told him to take his shoes off and roll up his trousers. She hadn't equipped him with sailing clothes in London. They launched the dinghy onto the grey-green river.

Della Torre got into the boat uncertainly. It rocked under his weight, and for a moment he thought it might tip him overboard, but Harry made him sit still and then pushed them off, nimbly hopping into the boat before the water became too deep. With quick, assured movements she got the rudder biting into the water and tightened the mainsail so that the little boat jumped into the middle of the stream. Larger yachts were tethered to buoys like a string of giant thoroughbreds. Even secured fast, they emanated a feeling of speed, all pointing downstream, straining at their mooring lines.

"Drop the centreboard—that's the bit in the middle like a lever. Pull that back towards me," she said. "And when you've done that, can you pull in the jib sheet, please. There aren't many people around this morning for some reason, but it doesn't do to be sloppy."

Della Torre gave her a look. "I'll be happier if you start speaking English. Or you can practise your Italian on me. But I don't talk boat."

"Sorry. That thickish rope opposite you. Pull it in until the sail makes a nice curved shape and doesn't flap, and then come to this side and sit still until I tell you otherwise."

There was a decent breeze coming from the south and east, and the little boat heeled as Harry took it in hand. Della Torre grew nervous about being forced to swim.

"You sure we're supposed to be over like this?" he asked.

"Lean back a bit. Sit up on the gunnels and get a grip of that webbing with your toes so that you don't fall out. Your weight will balance us and you'll see how nicely she rips along for a little old lady," Harry said, beaming. "The tide's coming in. It's strongly tidal here, by the way, so we'll go against the tide for a little while, down to the south. The river doesn't meet the sea for another sixteen kilometres or so; that land on the seaside bank is a giant shingle spit, a long peninsula. We'll go down as far as the castle downriver, and then we'll run back in no time at all."

The river widened considerably, so that they could do long tacks. At first, della Torre was unsettled about having to swap sides of the boat, getting tangled in that cramped space, losing track of the rope he was meant to be responsible for. But before long, the exhilaration got to him as well. There was a real impression of speed as the boat beat into the stiffening breeze, the river's little waves breaking over the bows, leaving della Torre wet with chilly water and grateful for the sun.

The scenery was harsh and flat; even on a sunny day it had an unforgiving quality. There were low marshes on either side of the river, and the expanse of shingle in the distance. He looked up at the huge, open sky and remembered something from Dickens. He'd never read Dickens much, never liked it, but there had been something about the marshes that darted into della Torre's mind with the speed of one of the rock swifts above. Magwitch.

"What do you think?"

Della Torre thought for a while in silence. "Bleak...Bleak and at the end of the world. It's almost beautiful too."

"Britten loved it. A lot of his music only makes sense if you think of this place."

But here too, sharp intrusions pierced the scene.

"What are those?" he asked, pointing to rows of frail metal towers anchored to the ground by constellations of wire.

"Top secret. They're military radio masts. And if you look over there... Wait, let me tack and then you'll see them when the sail's out of your line of sight. Ready about, lee ho," she said, turning the bow through the wind. "There."

They were impossible to miss. Rising above the shingle was a group of massive concrete buildings with hat-like roofs held aloft by the most spindly columns. They looked like temples built by an alien culture.

"They're the pagodas."

"The pagodas? What are they?"

"They were used for atomic weapons research. Something to do with testing the bomb triggers. The pagodas were designed so that if something accidentally went wrong and the bomb blew up, the columns would collapse and those massive roofs would drop down, sealing the buildings."

"Atomic bomb testing," he repeated.

"Something like that. It's all off-limits, though they're supposed to be decommissioning the site. But if you go twitching —"

"Twitching?"

"Birdwatching. Some of the birdwatchers around here know a lot about the military stuff too. It's all top secret, but they'll tell you stuff about it if you ask nicely. Especially if you're a girl. A couple of those great big buildings... I can't remember what they're called." She thought for a moment and then gave up. "Something beginning with s. Anyway, the military people are meant to have refined uranium there. The machines aren't there anymore. The government's been winding the whole thing down, but there were lots of the machines, hundreds and hundreds of them. Nobody's supposed to know anything about any of it."

Della Torre mulled over the bleak landscape.

"Hard to hide a big site like this."

"Sure is. Even at the end of the world, like here."

The wavelets picked up and the boat became skittish.

"I think we might start getting back," Harry said. "The wind's shifted a bit so that it's behind us, which will make for quick going, but if it starts dancing around there's always the risk we'll jibe."

They were back near the Martello tower when the wind fluked, and Della Torre learned what it was for a boat to jibe. The boom, which had been sticking straight out over the water from the opposite side of the dinghy, swung around before he could register what was happening. The force with which it hit his head knocked him into the river. He bobbed up, choking on the salty water, the weight of his clothes countered by the buoyancy jacket. Harry had already turned the boat and was pulling up alongside him.

"Are you okay?"

He bared his teeth at her. "Lucky for you I felt like a swim. What did you say that was called? A jab?"

She laughed as she eased the dinghy next to him, the bow pointing straight into the wind so that the sails went dead. She helped pull him into the boat, though as she did, it rocked wildly. He slumped, sodden, into the vessel, rubbing his head and staring bemusedly at the wooden beam that had just felled him.

"It's a rite of passage, getting clobbered by the boom, though not everyone's lucky enough to be drowned," she said.

"I'm glad you think it's funny. Would have felt a waste otherwise."

He drew a few amused looks when they landed the dinghy.

"Hello, Harry. Been fishing, have you?" asked one wag.

"He's better than an old boot. But only just," she replied.

When they put the boat away, della Torre carried his shoes, hobbling uncomfortably on the gravel rather than get the leather wet. He was shivering and his feet were sore by the time they got back to the cottage.

She stuffed his wet clothes into a washing machine and led him, towel-clad, into the bathroom that adjoined the main bedroom. The main bathroom didn't have a shower and the bath was too small for him to have a proper soak, she said.

He'd left the door open in his rush to get warm and then felt self-conscious in the glass cubicle when he saw that Harry had returned to the bedroom. He turned away from her to face the white-tiled corner before he noticed she was smiling at him. The water was hot and flowed strongly; slowly, heat seeped back into his bones.

He dried off and wrapped himself in a towel before going to look for his clothes, but the sight of Harry stopped him dead.

She was lying on the bed, naked.

"Interested in some lunch?" she asked.

"Lunch? I wasn't really thinking about food just now."

"Shame," she said. "I'm feeling a bit peckish."

"You are?" he asked.

"Yes," she said. "Ravenous."

He dropped the towel and joined her.

They lay on their sides looking at each other. He'd never seen such flawless skin, snow-pale but for a scattering of faint freckles high on her chest to match the ones that were only just visible across the bridge of her nose. Her breasts were small, the nipples a flushed pink. The hollow between her collar-bones had reddened slightly, as had her neck and her cheeks. Her eyebrows were a shade darker than her hair, as was the small diamond of down between her thighs. But mostly what captivated him were her eyes; they caught his and refused to let go, the pupils widening and then growing larger still as he drew closer to her until he felt the perfect softness of her lips.

"I thought you weren't interested," he said.

"And what would make you think that?"

"I don't know. You just never seemed terribly approachable."

"Did you try?"

"No. After that first day, when you caught me in the apartment, I was afraid you'd —"

"I'd?"

"I don't know. I didn't want you to feel that I was forcing myself on you."

"I was starting to worry you had other preferences."

"You mean the moustache?"

"Maybe. But that's gone now. And I see the cold hasn't affected you too badly."

They missed lunch altogether. But as Harry dozed, della Torre stared out to sea, out towards where the Vikings had come from. Denmark. Norway. Sweden.

He looked down at Harry's shoulders and back, and then kissed the top of her spine. She purred.

His thoughts traced their mazy way to Irena, where a fine thread of guilt began to unravel.

27

ANZULOVIĆ SAT IN his office, sweating. It wasn't even mid-June, and already the temperature in Zagreb was becoming uncomfortable. It didn't help that he'd sold all the building's portable air-conditioning units.

He was feeling low. There were enough trivial things to do to fill his days, but he wasn't really doing anything of consequence, except making sure his staff didn't starve. Like everyone else, his attention was almost fully absorbed by Croatia's looming declaration of independence, which, according to rumour, would be coming as soon as the following week. What would happen then, nobody knew.

At the UDBA, it felt like Napoleon's retreat out of Moscow. Only a lot hotter.

What he'd been able to piece together was that once independence was made formal, the UDBA would be banned from Croat territory. Croats working for the main part of the organization would be absorbed into Croatia's new intelligence service, the skeleton of which had already been built by President Tudjman's flunkies.

But that didn't include Department VI. They'd be handed over to military intelligence. Except Croatia didn't have a military. It only had a police force, which was being hammered into something that might do as an army, in the way an oil drum could be made into a stove. Neither efficient nor very refined, but fit for a very limited purpose. What wasn't fit for the purpose was the Zagreb police's hitherto ludicrously unprofessional political intelligence unit. The one run by Lieutenant Colonel Kakav. Who, by default, would probably become Department VI's proprietor.

Kakav had been emboldened by the UDBA's decline in Croatia and by Department VI's failure to solve the Strumbić shooting. He'd come strutting around their offices twice a week, demanding an explanation from Anzulović.

Anzulović had Strumbić's unsigned affidavit that della Torre was not responsible for the shooting. Strumbić gave endless excuses, all of which either started or ended with the fact that he was on sick leave and couldn't be expected to legally commit himself to anything until he was fully healed. There was a time when Anzulović would have found it very easy to force Strumbić to sign. But not now.

He was lucky that Kakav was a coward. Kakav feared that Croatia would quickly lose any military action. People talked about Croatia crossing the Rubicon, but it'd be more a case of Yugoslav tanks crossing the Danube and heading straight for Zagreb. Anzulović didn't hold out much hope for Croat bulldozers and tractors against the armoured division's M-84s.

Kakav's fear of what would happen meant he dared not push Anzulović too far. For his part, Anzulović needed Kakav's goodwill to ensure that his Department VI people, him included, weren't dumped on the street when things kicked off. Otherwise he could see himself wearing a badly fitting junior officer's uniform, in a shallow grave somewhere near the Bosnian border, or east, towards the Danube.

But for the moment, Anzulović had to find something else to sell to keep paying salaries, as pitiful as they might be. They

couldn't last much more than another two months on the reserves he'd built up. He had one Mercedes-Benz saloon left,
only just back from a servicing. Fresl said the Austrians and
Germans would only take cars in top condition. There were
a few Zastavas. A donkey and cart were probably worth more
than one of those. At least you could slaughter donkeys for
sausages and break the carts up for firewood.

His windows were open, willing a breeze. What it would be
like in August, he dreaded to think.

There was a knock on the door.

"Come in," Anzulović said wearily. It was morning, but whatever the time, the only news he got these days was bad.

Messar walked in and shut the door behind him.

"Strumbić is on the move."

"Oh?" For once, here was something case-related. Something
that didn't have to do with politics or scraping around for
money.

"He bought a bus ticket for Dubrovnik, leaving tomorrow."

"Bus ticket? How many cars does he have?"

"Bus ticket. The slow bus. Express to Rijeka and then stopping everywhere down the coast."

"Jesus, how long will that take him?"

"Best part of twenty-four hours. The only road going south
that's still open is the slow one along the coast. And the bus
stops everywhere."

"I'm assuming he's going to his place in Šipan. Can't say I
blame him. Nice quiet island, well away from the fireworks
when they start. Don't see why he's taking a bus, though."

"I think he wants us to know he's going south."

"Oh?"

"Told his girlfriend he'd be away for a while. Gave her enough
money to keep the bills paid and herself going for six months."

"Seems a very long time to think he won't be coming back to
Zagreb. It's not like he's going to Timbuktu. If he'd taken his

car, the trip's what, ten hours tops?"

"Closer to twelve now that the Serbs have cut off the highway."

"I take it you've got his girlfriend's place bugged."

"Yes. But the bugs aren't working."

"Up to typical Yugoslav electrical standards. So how'd you find out?"

"The girlfriend told one of Strumbić's vice-squad cops. We've got him on what's left of our payroll."

"And why would she do that?" Anzulović asked.

"Because she screws him when Strumbić isn't around."

"Sometimes I feel sorry for the bastard. With that wife of his . . ."

"They've been having some — what do the diplomats say — free and frank discussions."

"You hear this on the bugs or is Mrs. Strumbić on the payroll too?"

"You don't need bugs. You can hear it standing on the street."

"So he's finally had enough."

"I don't think that's all. The Bosnians have been in touch."

"I thought they've been harassing him for a while."

"Yes. But now they're in Zagreb."

"Are they?" Anzulović perked up. Getting hold of the Bosnians would give him some leverage on the Dispatcher. After his singularly unsuccessful contact with the old man, he'd made no further headway. Archive files on the Dispatcher had been pulled or put on a security code above Anzulović's level and kept in Belgrade. Nobody in the organization was telling him anything. And he wasn't sure how to find out if the old man was playing ball with the Croats. No attempt had been made on Strumbić, but only a fool would have tried, with Messar's surveillance and Strumbić's police guard. Besides, della Torre had disappeared. If that's what the Dispatcher had aimed for at the start, he'd certainly got what he'd wanted.

"Have you managed to pick them up — the Bosnians, I mean?"

"No. We haven't got the people to find them, and we haven't mentioned it to the Zagreb cops."

"Why's that?"

"Because I didn't know whether you'd want us to," Messar said.

"Because?"

"Because the Bosnians are evidence the Zagreb cops might not want to keep around. Besides, I thought it might be interesting to see where Strumbić goes. I think he could lead us to della Torre," Messar said.

Messar was convinced that della Torre and Strumbić were involved in a criminal conspiracy somehow tied in with the Bosnians. Because he wasn't allowed to unlock Strumbić and he was sure the Bosnians were little more than thugs for hire, Messar saw della Torre as the key.

There had been no word from della Torre. No sign since he'd given Messar's men the slip in Venice. No calls to his father. Irena had rung della Torre senior to ask after her husband, and neither seemed to know anything. They both sounded genuinely worried. Anzulović was also becoming concerned. Not only because della Torre was his favourite.

"So you think Gringo's in Dubrovnik?" Anzulović smiled, knowing a stupid question like that would irritate Messar.

"No, I think Strumbić is getting off the bus in Rijeka, or somewhere like that, and then taking either a ferry to Venice or a bus to Trieste. My bet would be a bus. He figures, rightly, that we haven't got enough people to put a full team on him, which is why he's taking a bus. Easier to disappear, get off at an unexpected stop. I doubt he'll take a ferry from Rijeka, because of the security. But he'll figure that since the Slovenes have taken over the border controls in Trieste, he'll be able to slip through more easily. Besides, he's got a friend, an ex-cop, in Mestre. He'd be worth a visit. He sends a package to Strumbić's girlfriend about every month."

Messar was right. The Slovenes and the regular border security were staging a low-level pushing competition at Slovenia's borders, Slovenia exerting authority over its borders while the federal government tried to impose its own will without allowing things to spill into direct conflict. It was a messy situation that allowed plenty of people afraid of the looming situation to leave the country. So long as Italy would let them cross the border. And Mestre was a short drive from Trieste.

"Funny thing is, he's made some calls to London."

"Who?"

"Strumbić."

"What about?"

"I don't know. They're short calls, made from post offices. All to the same number. A property agency of some sort. What makes it even more interesting is that London's where della Torre's wife is."

Anzulović nodded. Even robbed of resources and in an environment of government hostility, Messar managed to do his job.

"He's chosen a good time to do a runner. What do you suggest?" Anzulović asked.

"I suggest we track him and find della Torre."

"Thought you might say that. With or without the Zagreb police?"

"Without. I think they're too friendly with Mr. Strumbić."

"So who do you propose to send?"

"Me. I'll take somebody on the team with me. I'll take the Merc. There could be a bit of driving involved. I'll also make sure we've got the documentation to give us easy circulation once we get to Italy," Messar said.

That meant he was going to use Italian papers and Italian plates. It was a standard UDBA solution to the little matter of getting around in western Europe.

Anzulović looked out the window. Still no breeze.

For the next five or six days they would be in a sort of limbo. Nothing was happening. And then everything would happen. For five or six days there was a hole in the universe.

"We have enough money to cover two men for about a week. Even if Strumbić leads us nowhere, it won't be expensive. Besides, I'm happy to pay for part of the expenses myself," Messar said, thinking that Anzulović's concern about finances had made him pause. Like everybody else in Department VI, Messar had been unsettled, enervated, by the inaction of the past few months. This was something real, a proper case.

"It's not the money," Anzulović said. Then he looked up at Messar, a half-smile on his lips. "You've got five days. The rocket goes up next Tuesday or Wednesday. That's when our lot and the Slovenes will declare war and the tanks start rolling in. You've got to be back by then, because I suspect that when things start to happen, they could happen pretty quickly."

Messar turned to leave. But before he got to the door, Anzulović stopped him.

"Oh, and another thing. I'm going with you."

28

STRUMBIĆ WAS IRRITATED enough even without having to spend an age wandering around the old hospital. It had turned into a hot summer, and he was getting tired of sweating. It took him two full circuits before he found the right room. He walked in without knocking.

The patient, a heavy mass of white flesh looking like something a whale had regurgitated, opened his eyes and smiled.

"Julius. Hey, how nice of you to visit."

"Branko. What happened to you? I've been calling for over a month now. You haven't sent me my mail. Nothing."

"Sorry, Julius." He shrugged apologetically, nudging the drip that ran out of his arm. Another tube ran into his nose. "I've been in here. Really. I couldn't do much about it." His voice croaked with disuse.

"You couldn't get anyone to organize my mail for you?"

"I had other things on my mind."

Strumbić sat down, slightly mollified. The man really did not look well.

"What happened to you?"

"Some thrombosis, some clot or other. I had bad circulation anyway, and things seemed to gum up. They had to take my

235

leg off. Stupid thing. Still itches."

"Scratch it, then."

"I can't. It's not there."

"What do you mean it's not there?"

"They cut it off."

"What?"

"My leg," the man said, pointing to where the sheet dropped flat against the bed, just above his right knee. "They took my leg off."

"Well, that should fix your itch."

"No, that's the point. It itches where my leg ought to be. I can't scratch it because there's no leg. But it itches like crazy. Drives me nuts."

"Listen, Branko, I'd love to chat, but I'm in a bit of a hurry. Where are your keys? I need to get into your place to pick up my letters. Something funny's going on."

"What's that? Nothing to do with me, I hope. I've been honest as the day is long. To you, anyway."

"In those last two batches you sent, the estate agents wrote they'd taken money out of my account. Ten thousand out of my account. Twice. I'm starting to get worried."

"Ten thousand lira?"

"No, pounds, you idiot."

"Wow. That's a lot of money."

"You're telling me."

"They can take money out of your account just like that?"

"Sure, they can do it. I just didn't expect them to. It's for emergencies. You know, if the windows all blow in or something, they've got the funds to fix stuff."

"Maybe some accident happened. Did they say why?"

"There's some big works needing to be done on the building, something about making sure it doesn't slide down the hill. It's been up there for a hundred years and there wasn't any sign of it going anywhere when I bought the place. I'm getting a funny feeling somebody's stitching me up."

"Why don't you call them up and ask them what's going on?"

"I did. That peach who's looking after it has been on holiday. They say. I hope she hasn't run with my money. As far as I can understand, the rest of the idiots in that office keep telling me that these things happen, that the woman'll call when she gets back. But I'm smelling a rat. If they've taken any more money, I'll pop a blood vessel. I'm going over to have a look."

"So you didn't come over just to visit me?"

"Course I came to visit you. How else would I get your keys? Jeez, Mestre is a tip."

"You know, Julius, you never paid me for that last little job."

"What's that, then?"

"You know, when your friend came off the boat and I made sure he didn't have any unwanted attention."

"Yeah, thanks. You sure I didn't pay you? I'm pretty sure I paid you."

"No, you didn't pay me."

Strumbić pulled out his wallet and put a couple of ten-thousand-lira notes by Branko's bedside.

"Listen, thanks. That'll be useful. I can't get around and I haven't got any cash to pay anyone to get me stuff from the shops. Cigarettes and a little drink and some magazines and stuff. It's gets pretty boring in here."

"Think nothing of it. I'll never know why you settled on such a craphole like Mestre. Must be the ugliest place in Italy. Took some sterling detective work to find a place like this in a country with so many beautiful towns."

"Hey, it was useful, wasn't it? I mean, close enough to Venice for me to get to your friend before anybody else did."

"What did you do with della Torre?"

"I told him to get lost. I pointed him to the train station, and that's where he headed."

"Haven't heard from him in months. You did a good job." He

pulled out another note and put it by the bedside.

"So you going to London?"

"Yeah. Needed to get out of Zagreb for a while anyway. Some UDBA guy is giving me serious grief, fucking Nazi. Looks like one too. And I'm being harassed by a couple of Bosnians who labour under the mistaken belief that I owe them. I'd kill them if I could just find them."

"How you getting there?"

"I don't know. I was going to drive. Booked a Merc from the car hire in Trieste. They kept telling me they had this great red sports car, just up my alley. Two-seater, soft top, pull all the birds I could possibly want. So I said put the red sports car aside for me. I get there and the bloody thing's pink. Not red. Pink. I had to drive to Mestre in a pink Merc because I'd already paid for it. Bloody pink Merc."

The man on the bed laughed until he choked.

"Were you talking in Italian?"

"Sure, those idiots don't speak anything else."

"You must have been saying *rosa* instead of *rosso*. Happens all the time."

"Thanks for nothing, Mr. Berlitz."

"You going to bring back the keys?"

"I'll leave them with the old hag concierge in your building. I nearly punched her when she wouldn't let me in your apartment."

"Too right. I don't want every Tom, Dick, and Harry walking into my place. Before you go, have you got any cigs?"

"Here," said Strumbić, leaving a packet by Branko's bed. "Just don't blame me if you get cancer. Make sure you do something about that leg."

"See you, Julius." But Strumbić had already left the room.

·   ·   ·

The morning faded into the early afternoon, the patient slipping into the state of semi-comatose boredom that had made up his days since he'd woken up from the emergency operation more than a month earlier. They'd wheeled him in a couple of weeks before that, but he didn't remember any of it.

His leg had been killing him, so he'd taken a taxi to the emergency room, and then when the doctor was checking him out, he'd fainted. Out cold for nearly three weeks. He was lucky to be alive. Or at least that's what the nurses kept telling him. He didn't feel so lucky when the matron came in to give him his painkillers after lunch and found the cigarettes by his bedside. She pocketed them. He was sure she was taking them for herself, but he wasn't in much of a position to run after her.

Strumbić was long gone and Branko was dozing when the glass door to his room slammed shut, waking him. There were never any loud noises in this ward.

"Hey, Branko." The nasal and aural foliage were unforgettable, but he couldn't quite pull the name out of his memory. "Branko, remember me? It's Anzulović. From the detective squad."

"Anzulović? So it is." Branko smiled. "What a treat. Nobody visits for weeks and then *bam*, two in a day."

"Branko, this is Captain Messar." Anzulović waved at a tall, blond man who looked as if he'd stepped out of some Second World War poster.

"Mr Krushka," Messar said.

"Branko, everyone calls me Branko. So, looks like my number's up. You guys finally found me. Unfortunately for you, it doesn't look like I'm going anywhere for a while, eh?"

"Mr. Krushka, we're here on other business," said the Nazi.

"Yeah? So I'm off the hook, am I?"

"No, the law will catch up with you eventually. But there are more pressing matters now."

"Listen, Branko, we're not here to give you a hard time," said Anzulović, soothing the sick man. "What's past is past. Times have changed. I mean, politics are all up in the air. I'm not even sure the indictment holds anymore. The courts would have to dig it up and make sure there's no political motivation behind it and that it was purely a criminal matter. And you know how long these things take."

"Yeah, it was entirely political. I had to run out of the country because of political persecution," said Branko.

"And there I was thinking it was because you were about to be done for corruption," said Messar.

"It was a frame-up. They could have had half the force up on charges worse than mine. And the only reason it was only half was because the other half were just too stupid to figure out how to make themselves a bit of extra dosh," said Branko.

"So which were you?" Messar asked Anzulović.

"Oh, I was definitely in the stupid half. That's the only reason the UDBA took me on. I got a sufficiently low mark on their intelligence tests," Anzulović replied, unperturbed by the insinuation.

"I can vouch for that," said Branko. "Never met a dumber cop. Haven't got a clue how he made detective inspector."

"Alright, you don't have to lay it on with a trowel," said Anzulović. "And if you're so smart, how come you ended up running to a shithole like Mestre?"

"I like to be near refineries; you never know when you might need to fill up."

"Enough of the pleasantries," said Messar. "We're here about Julius Strumbić."

"Who?"

"Strumbić."

"Name rings bells, but I can't put my finger on it."

"Shame when old age catches up with you and you can't remember your old partner on the force."

"Oh, you mean *that* Julius Strumbić."

"Are there many that you know?"

"Loads and loads. Used to meet a new one every other week. Got very confusing."

"It seems Julius Strumbić has been phoning a number in Mestre for the past few weeks. Yours, I believe. In fact, we got word he might be heading this way. Any idea what it's about?"

"Love to chat, but the throat dries up lying in a hospital bed. Water is such a poor lubricant, don't you think?"

"So what might be sufficiently soothing?" asked Messar.

"Oh, a nice bottle of whisky or brandy. One of the big ones," Branko said.

"Get him some cheap vodka, half-bottle," Anzulović said. Messar took one of the ten-thousand-lira notes from Branko's bedside table.

Branko stayed quiet until Messar got back, and then he drank down two fingers of high-octane spirits in a swallow.

"My thanks to you gentlemen. Gets the engine running. Haven't had a drop since they took the old leg off. It's like coming home after a six-month tour in the army."

"We were having a conversation about Strumbić," said Messar.

"Were we? Remind me, name rings a bell."

Messar got up out of the worn visitors' chair, the foam padding coming out of its torn covers, walked around the bed, and punched Branko in the stump, first shoving a corner of a pillow into his mouth to stifle his scream.

"Hey, Messar, all he needed was a couple more glasses of this stuff and he'd have been happy to talk. You don't need to torture the poor guy," Anzulović said, jumping off the windowsill where he'd been perched.

"Now, you are not going to shout and make a fuss, or you die of a suspected heart attack in the next ten minutes," Messar said. "And you are going to talk about Strumbić. Nod if you understand. Shake your head if you want me to keep the pillow in your gob."

Branko nodded vigorously. He'd actually developed a tinge

of colour. Didn't make him look any better. Messar left him to catch his breath.

"So why was Strumbić calling? What does he want?" Anzulović asked.

"I wasn't there to take his calls. I swear. I've been in hospital. Whoever's been monitoring his calls for you people should have been able to tell you that."

"He rang from phone boxes. All we got was the number, not the content of the conversation. Why would he be calling? What deal have you got going with him, other than the fact that you two did very dirty stuff together once upon a time?"

"Nothing. I swear. I'm just a post box for him. He gets mail sent to him here. I forward it, that's all."

"Where do you send it?"

"To some girlfriend of his. It gets packed with underwear for her. Frilly black stuff. Customs never bothers with that sort of thing. I don't think they know how expensive it is."

"Where's the mail from?"

"England."

"Where in England?"

"London."

"We can go back to my way of playing the game. Where in London?"

"How do I know? I just collect the stuff and send it on. If there's a real emergency, somebody might phone. But they know I don't speak English and nobody's ever had reason to call."

"Any more of these letters at your apartment?"

"I haven't been there to collect them in a while. I've been indisposed."

"I think we might check. Where are your keys?"

"Haven't got them. They must have fallen out of my pocket when they cut my leg off. Try the concierge at my building. She's a lovely, accommodating old lady."

"We've met her."

"Terrific. Listen, when you see her next, can you give her something for me?" Branko asked.

"What?"

"A pat on the back for telling you guys I'm here. With a tire iron. Visitors like you I can live without."

Messar got out of his chair.

"Do us a favour in return. Give our regards to Strumbić. And remind him that he hasn't asked to take any holiday time off. So it's unpaid leave," Messar said. "It's been nice chatting. Next time I see you it'll be either in the morgue or in the dock of a Zagreb courtroom."

"And you have a nice day too," said Branko through gritted teeth, the pain in his stump shooting up his side.

He'd medicated himself with the grappa bottle he'd hidden so that when Matron came to give him his painkillers, she didn't confiscate it. Eventually, the agony in his stump muted into a low throb.

.   .   .   .

It was after visiting hours when Branko felt somebody shaking him awake. At first he thought Anzulović and the Nazi had come back, but as his eyes drew back into focus he saw, instead, a pair of ghouls. The one shaking him was bent to the side like a banana, while the other was missing the whole top row of his teeth. Branko could tell because the man seemed able to breathe only through his mouth; his nose was mashed flat.

"We were told you were here," said the human banana with a heavy Bosnian accent.

"Who the hell are you? You shouldn't be here, it's after hours."

"That's okay. The nurse is fine about it. She might not be when she wakes up, though." His shoulders rose and fell as though he was laughing, though no sound came.

"I cannot tell a lie. You're right, I'm here. That still doesn't tell me who you are or what you want," Branko said.

"We think you might know where Mr. Strumbić is."

"I should have guessed it might have to do with Julius. What do you want?"

"He owes us some money."

"Look, he's usually good for it. Send him an invoice."

"Can you tell us where he is?"

"Everyone wants Strumbić. I've got no idea where he is. Hey, put that down," he said to the mouth-breather, who'd opened the bottle of grappa and was taking a long drink. The mouth-breather ignored him and offered the bottle to the banana, but the banana shook his head.

"He picked up a pink Mercedes in Trieste this morning. We lost him for a while, but then we saw his car pulling away from your building. Must be the pinkest Mercedes I've ever seen. Actually, I've never seen a pink Mercedes before. But we lost him again. It might be pink, but it's fast. So we went back to your place. The old woman said everyone'd been looking for you today. She didn't sound happy about it. We figured if Strumbić was looking for you, he'd found you and you might be able to tell us where he was going."

"You speak Italian?"

"Not a word."

"I'd have paid to hear the conversation you had with the old lady."

"Yeah, it was a real problem to make ourselves understood. We thought it was our accent at first. Didn't we, Besim?" The banana grinned, but the mouth-breather didn't say anything.

"So how'd she tell you Strumbić had been looking for me and where I was if you couldn't talk to her?"

"Took us a while but we got there, didn't we, Besim? She showed us."

"She's here?"

"Oh no, she's in the boot of the car. We'll drop her off later. I think she'll be okay, but she is pretty old. Where's Strumbić?"

"What'd you do to the old lady?"

"Doesn't matter. Where's Strumbić?"

"Hey, what are you doing there?" Branko said to the mouth-breather, who had unscrewed the top of the invalid's drip—one of the old-fashioned glass bottle kinds—and was pouring the rest of the grappa into it.

"Where's Strumbić?"

"Don't do that. Don't, that's not nice. I'm not a well man."

"You going to tell us or are we going to have to operate on you? Looks like they forgot to take one of your legs off. We can fix that for you."

"Christ almighty. He's gone to London. Somewhere in London. He's got a place on somewhere called E-A-S-T H E A-T-H R-O-A-D, that's all I can remember. I think it's a road or something. The place is an apartment building. It doesn't have a number, just a name. That's all I know, I swear, guys."

Branko's speech was already slurring and the room was spinning around his head like a helicopter blade. He felt numb. He certainly couldn't feel the pain in his stump anymore. In fact, he couldn't feel much of anything anymore.

As they went out, the banana helped himself to the ten-thousand-lira notes by Branko's bed. Branko didn't look like he'd be needing them.

"**S**O HOW WAS your holiday?" della Torre asked.

"Fantastic. Just terrific," Harry said. "Really relaxing. The food was delicious; they've got such a good cook. But even when we had to fend for ourselves, you'd always have nice cheeses, or pâtés for a picnic lunch, or cold chicken. A couple of times we picked mussels. You just pick huge mounds of them off the rocks and piers and then you collect as many dry pine needles as you can. You know, those Mediterranean pines with the really long needles? Once you get inland the ground's covered in them. You put the mussels on top of a big sheet of corrugated steel and then pile on the pine needles and set a match to them. The whole thing goes up like a petrol station. It's got to be on the beach, otherwise you'll burn the whole forest down. The mussels cook instantly and you eat them there and then, and they've got a pine-resiny flavour. Not something you'd order in a restaurant, but on the beach it was delicious with some of the local iced rosé. We'd have the pick of their cellar too, really yummy wines: Bordeaux reds and whites and some mind-blowing Sauternes."

"For somebody who spent two weeks eating and drinking, you don't look like you've put on any weight." Was it only two weeks? It had felt longer to della Torre. She'd gone when much of the Heath was in that fuzzy springtime, its hedges covered with pale green and white blossoms. But now most of the candles were gone from the horse chestnuts and the grass was waist-high.

"Don't you believe it," said Harry. "This frock just hides it well."

Della Torre's eyebrows shot up. He couldn't imagine the short, tight black cocktail dress she wore hiding so much as a Band-Aid. The thin cashmere cardigan she'd pulled over her shoulders merely drew attention to the lithe figure underneath the dress.

"So did you do anything other than eat and drink?"

"We swam all the time. And bicycled. That's mostly how you get around the island, on a bicycle. They've got these great long cycle paths and there aren't many roads. So we spent a lot of time exploring. We went swimming every day. They've got a pool at the villa, but the beach was only a couple of hundred metres down a path. It seemed like a hundred kilometres of sand. On the other side of the island there are these nice coves. It's rockier there, and that's where they keep their dinghies. So we'd cycle across and do some sailing. The cook packed perfect picnics."

"Back to food."

"You'd have loved it there, I'm sure. Had I known you longer, I'd have asked to take you along, but it was a group of such old and close friends that it's hard to bring somebody new in. What did you do with yourself? Were you lonely?" She paused. "Did you miss me?"

He looked at her. They'd met up for dinner at a fashionable restaurant in Chelsea, her recommendation.

After returning to London from their—what was it? a romantic entanglement?—they had hardly seen each other. Harry was busy with work and social engagements and then suddenly she was gone, off to France.

This was the first he'd properly seen of her since that weekend by the coast. He wasn't really sure where they stood with each other. For the moment, it didn't matter. He had her to himself.

The sun had turned her skin golden, making her eyes even bluer and her hair a richer, paler straw. The truth was he'd missed her very much, and he felt a pang of self-pity that he'd had so little of her to himself.

During that time he'd been in some sort of limbo. He'd gone to various clinics and medical libraries to do research on blood and AIDS but got no further with his far-fetched thesis. He monitored developments in Yugoslavia as best he could, growing anxious at being away from it. He knew he wouldn't be able to influence matters. But even so, it was worse to be watching from London. The collision was coming and, in his bones, he felt it was going to be a bloody one. He felt guilty at having run away.

"I read and took long walks on the Heath. It's a lovely place, easy to get used to," he said.

He'd indulged himself. He'd had more time to be alone with his thoughts over the past month than at any time since childhood. He didn't explore so much as let the Heath swallow him; he disappeared along the forest paths, through the meadows, past the ponds fringed with willows, where hardy swimmers almost inevitably twice his age braved the early morning chill. His ruminations kept company with the dog-walkers, birdwatchers, joggers. He'd walk to Kenwood, the grand country house at the top of the Heath, and take in the bucolic vistas. Keats's house was nearby, and he reacquainted himself with the Romantic's poetry.

He'd filled his mind with music — Wagner and Bruckner, Bach and Brahms, and always Beethoven. And with trashy novels. They worked best. He'd never had much patience with television. There was never anything worth watching in Yugoslavia.

Soon, ex-Yugoslavia. Would he ever go back?

"Isn't it just." Harry looked him over with soft eyes.

"What?" he asked, drawn out of his thoughts.

"The Heath."

"Yes, yes, it is."

A waiter discreetly interrupted them, and they ordered.

"I'm sorry about the past week. I had to shove all my appointments into when I got back. Stacked-up obligations are how you have to pay for having nice times."

"Is this an obligation?"

She stared at him hard. "No. This is pleasure."

"So, how many of you were there?"

"Oh, there were always at least a dozen, and for about four days there were nearly thirty if you count the babies. I mean, it's a big house, but that was a squash."

"Were they all old friends?"

"Nearly all. One or two newish boyfriends or girlfriends, but they were mostly out of place and got ignored. And the kids, of course, but they don't count."

"Where exactly is it?"

"It's off the west coast of France. It's where the smart French go on holiday. All the nouveau money goes to Saint-Tropez, but the old money goes west. It's much less spoilt and much more chic."

"I'll have to try it sometime."

"You'd fit right in."

They drained their glasses of kir and their first courses arrived. Della Torre figured he'd have been able to eat for the best part of a week in Zagreb on the money his scallops cost. It didn't matter. Strumbić was paying.

"When I got to the office, there were about a hundred messages from your Mr. Strumbić-Vodka. Apparently he was very irritated but not entirely comprehensible."

"I know, you'd said."

"Sorry. I forgot I saw a bit of you this week. It's been such a blur."

"His English isn't very good."

"It isn't, is it. His Italian's passable, though," Harry said.

"Just as well you speak it."

"I tried calling the number in Mestre to get a message through to him, but there was no answer."

"I guess he's onto us."

"I suppose so. We'll have forty thousand pounds next week, though. He won't know about that until he gets his bank statement and my letter. I won't send it until it's time for the last instalment. So how long do we keep going?"

"Not much longer."

"Next week? I'll get the furniture moved into my father's barn, but I don't want that to happen until we're about to leave."

He smiled, but it worried him that Strumbić was getting anxious. Della Torre had thought they'd have at least six months clear of him — that the investigation by Messar would more or less pin Strumbić down. Strumbić knew the UDBA would be keeping close tabs on him until they finally gave up searching for della Torre. But maybe with war starting he would have a chance of disappearing into the chaos.

Della Torre had wanted to find Irena. To see her, to tell her he was fine. But he'd stopped himself. The UDBA would track him down through her. And as long as he stayed away, she'd also be safe.

"So were there any interesting men?"

"Oh yes. Very interesting. Very, very interesting," she said with a mischievous smile. "One was an astronomer, so he told us all about the stars. We'd lie on picnic blankets over the pine needles at night and he'd point out the constellations in this sexy whisper... But it was lucky that stargazing is an outdoor pursuit. You didn't want to get too close because of his breath. He could strip paint with it. Another one was an Olympic fencer. Tall and supple.

But he's a good friend's husband and likes to keep his sword well sheathed, I'm told. And there were a couple of guys from the New York music industry. Very good-looking. Witty. Able to talk about anything intelligently. One has a Ph.D. in classical history and the other trained as an engineer." She paused for effect. "But gay, unfortunately. There was a writer and a whole bale of lawyers. I think that's what you call a group of lawyers. A bale. They certainly were baleful. You might have found them interesting."

"I'm sure I would."

"But, sadly, nothing to entertain a girl's fancy. Any luck with the women in Hampstead?"

"Are there any? I hadn't noticed."

"For shame. You won't find a better collection of trophy wives east of New York. All of them pining for a bit of adventure. But no, you've got your nose in a book and your head in the clouds. Did you read anything edifying?"

"Jilly Cooper. Dick Francis. Anthony Powell. That's off the top of my head. But there was a lot of unmemorable stuff too."

She laughed. "So you went right through the high end of my collection."

"I made up for it with the music. I learned to like Shostakovich and Britten. The Bach and the Brahms and the Beethoven I mostly knew, but the twentieth-century stuff I'd always been sniffy about. I suppose that's because I'd never really listened to it before."

"Bravo."

"Thanks to your collection."

"Did you try the sheet music?" She ran her fingers along an imaginary keyboard. "Do you play?"

"I don't know. I never tried."

She laughed as if she'd never heard the joke before.

After dinner, they flagged down a cab.

Della Torre was amused to watch another as yet undiscovered part of London go past. The city seemed endless and limitless. And then he was back in the brutally familiar.

The building was unmistakable, the Brompton Oratory's floodlit Baroque lines, its white stone a shroud of della Torre's memory, catching him unaware. The rush of images from his student days there came to him, uncalled and unwanted. Croatian Mass in the crypt chapel on Sunday mornings.

Svjet.

Della Torre shuddered. The memory gripped him. For a moment the pain became physical, girdling him with a pulse and then another one.

"Are you all right?" Harry asked.

"Sure. I probably ate too much," he replied, his eyes on London's passing lights. It took a force of will to forget.

The taxi stopped at the bottom corner of the Heath so that they could walk back, the late evening still shedding a soft glow. Della Torre threw the whole of his attention onto Harry. She watched in amusement the men, in singles and couples, who furtively made their way into the parkland's deep woods.

"Think of all the good times that are going on not much past the foot of our building," she said.

"Is that so?"

"The Heath is notorious. Don't tell me you hadn't noticed."

"I did rather wonder once or twice, coming back late at night. People seemed unusually . . . friendly."

"More than friendly, darling. Downright dirty. I'm sure they'd have loved to show you just how much," Harry said. "On really still, warm nights, if you put your head out the window, you can sometimes hear them. It's like a nature documentary."

Harry opened another bottle of wine when they got back to the apartment. Della Torre stretched himself along one sofa. Harry took the one opposite, facing him, her legs tucked underneath her. The light was muted, but clear enough for della Torre to see the high colour in her cheeks. Her lips glowed red, though she'd used only a bit of gloss.

He lit a cigarette, and for once she didn't complain. The windows were open and a faint breeze wafted the gossamer curtains.

"Cheers," she said, raising her glass. "Thanks for dinner."

"It was the least Strumbić could do."

"He's a very kind man," she said.

"No, he isn't. But he can be very entertaining."

"Like tonight?"

"Yes, like tonight," della Torre said. "By the way, I never properly thanked you for the weekend on the coast. I enjoyed it."

"You mean you liked being hit on the head and made to go for a swim in a cold, cold river." Her eyes glittered.

"Yes," he said, "that's what made the weekend."

They were watching each other across the room.

"So, plenty of men on your magical island, but none that suited. What's the line — water, water everywhere..." della Torre said.

"But not a one to lick."

"I'm not quite sure that's how it goes."

"It seems right to me."

"Should I be doing something right now?"

She shrugged. "Funny. I'd been pretty happy not to think about sex until you moved in," she said.

"Had it been long?"

"You mean since the banker? About a year and a half."

"And you'd given up thinking about sex since then?"

"Well, it had started coming back a little. Maybe in the past six months. It starts really randomly. Somebody gives you a look, and rather than just ignoring it or being irritated by it you feel a little ping in your diaphragm. Or a book. Sex scenes you might have skimmed over a few months before, you find yourself reading. Little things. And then one night you wake up to find your nightgown has worked its way up over your hips and you're on top of the duvet and suddenly you're aware that you're naked from the waist down. Or you sit down in the shower to shave your legs and you feel the coldness of the tiles and the heat of the water."

"I can picture it now."

"Can you?" The way she was sitting on the sofa had made the already short dress pull up past her thighs so that he saw a little crescent of tanned flesh at the top of her stocking. His breath caught. She could see where he was looking but didn't move to adjust her clothes. She just reclined there, watching him.

"It's funny," she said. "Any other time of my life, with any other man, I'd have expected him by now to be tugging my clothes off as if he were trying to skin a fish. And I'd be helping."

"You make it sound so dignified. Is that what you'd like?"

"No. Oh, no. I like this. Looking at you and talking. I think I like this more. Sex without sex," she said.

He gave a heartfelt laugh. "You are unquestionably and achingly beautiful. Would you like me to talk about that?"

"No. That sounds so dull."

"It sounds like you were building up during the past six months."

"I've been reminding myself. A little after you arrived. More on holiday, remembering you. My memory didn't do you justice. And then, since I've been back, I keep hoping that when I get home, you'll still be awake."

"I was, the other night."

"You were? I can't even begin to tell you how I cursed the crashing headache I had."

"I know something that helps headaches."

"So do I. But I don't know you well enough to hand you a prescription and ask you to fill it right away."

"So if you don't want me to tell you how beautiful you are, what would you like to talk about?" he asked, watching that little crescent grow as she shifted her leg.

"Tell me a story. Tell me the sexiest thing that's ever happened to you that doesn't involve sex."

"You mean food or some other sort of pleasure?" he asked, confused.

"No. I mean something that didn't involve your having sex with someone else, but that, when you think about it, makes you go weak at the knees."

Della Torre watched her, bemused. He filled up both of their wineglasses, lit another cigarette, and then lay back down on the sofa. The crescent had become a near half-moon, and he could see the lines of her black suspenders.

"When I was fourteen, I think—yes, it was fourteen—I went on a school trip to the seaside. We went for two weeks every summer. It was a big school, so it would only be two year-groups at a time. But for some reason it was three that year. We went to these huge facilities built for socialist workers, giant concrete blocks of dormitories in amongst the pines, just back from the beach. Usually you stayed in single-sex dormitories with about twenty boys to a cinder-block room. But this time, because there were so many of us, the pupils in the top year got rooms for just four people and some just for two. For some reason I was put in a room with a guy two years above me. He was a real heartthrob. All the girls loved him. He was very good-looking and the teachers really liked him, which was probably why he got a room for just two. I don't know why they put me in with him.

"It's funny. Because I'd lived in America, the teachers either hated me and would be as unpleasant as possible—maybe because I represented a threat to their socialist ideals—or they bent over backwards to be nice to me. I think those ones thought we'd be invaded by the U.S. in the next war and wanted a bit of insurance against the fact that they were all members of the Communist Party.

"Anyway, for whatever reason, I got to share the room with this boy. It was a tiny room. We had bunk beds, but you could only just squeeze between the wall and the bed. He took the top, as you'd expect. He was very nice, very kind, except that every night he told me not to draw the blinds and made sure the window was unlatched and a bit open. It irritated me because there were these yellow arc lights outside and they were on the whole night, and leaving the window open meant the mosquitoes got in. But who was I to say anything?" He stubbed out the cigarette.

"I learned why he had this arrangement the third night into the holiday. I'd been asleep, but I heard the window open and somebody come in. It woke me up, and I froze. I thought it was burglars come in to slit our throats, and for some reason I thought if I played dead they'd leave me alone. It wasn't burglars. It was one of the girls in the boy's year, one of those high school girls who looks like a ripe peach, who all the boys fantasize about but are too terrified ever to talk to. I saw her as she climbed up the ladder. 'Be quiet,' he said. I remember her saying, 'Don't worry, Gringo's asleep.'"

"Gringo?"

Della Torre could have slapped himself. "It's my nickname. Everyone calls me that. All Yugoslavs and ex-Yugoslavs are cowboys-and-Indians fanatics. They started calling me that because I'd lived in America. I don't like the name, but it stuck."

"I like it. It's better than calling you della Torre."

"Okay, I was defeated on this one years ago. At least my father and my ex-wife don't call me Gringo."

"You were telling me a story, Gringo."

"She said, 'Don't worry. He's asleep. I saw him.'" He paused, pulling together the memory.

"And what happened next?"

"What you might expect. Except that the whole while, she was narrating in one of those stage whispers that you can hear across an auditorium. She was saying exactly what she was doing to him, exactly what he was doing to her, exactly where and how he was touching her or she him or she herself. It was like one of those voice-overs that movies do for blind people."

"What did you do?"

"Nothing. I was frozen stiff."

"Stiff?"

"Well, yes. But I didn't dare move a muscle. I don't think I breathed for twenty minutes."

"Is that how long it went on?"

"I think so. Maybe not. But it certainly felt that long."

"And then?"

"When they'd finished, she climbed back down the ladder. It was right by my head. She got most of the way down and she stopped. She asked the boy for a last kiss and he obliged. They kissed for what seemed like eternity. And as they did she pulled up this long T-shirt she was wearing. I could smell her; it was the headiest, most musky scent I'd ever smelled in my life. And I could see her in the light of those yellow lamps. And as they kissed she kept rocking her hips forward and backward, forward and backward."

Harry swallowed hard and looked at della Torre, lips slightly apart, eyes wide. "Do you think they knew you weren't asleep?"

"The next day I was on the beach, just sitting and getting some sun, when she came over and sat next to me. For some reason I was alone just then. She looked straight at me from a couple of feet away, not saying anything but not even pretending to look at anything else. Finally I had to say hi, but I think I must have blushed like a boiled scampi. She said, 'So, Gringo, did you like our conversation last night?' I thought it must be some trap and I stammered, 'But we didn't talk. I mean, I don't remember talking to you last night.' And she said, with a straight face, 'You didn't talk, but I did. Did you like our conversation? The one where you were quiet as a mouse while I was telling you things. Do you remember that one?' I swear I felt like crying. I didn't know how to answer, so I didn't. Eventually she just got up and went away."

"Was that the end of your relationship?"

"More or less. But it was one of the most memorable ones I've ever had. So what's your story?"

She took a swallow of wine and put the glass down. The movement pulled her dress up, fully exposing her small black lace underwear and the bottom of her belly. Hard as he might try, he couldn't pull his eyes away. So he just gave up trying.

"I hope you don't think I always dress like this. Normally it's just ordinary white smalls and tights."

"I know. You hang them from the rail in my bathroom. You were about to tell me a story."

"Yes, I was," she said languidly. "After university and after I came back from teaching in New Guinea and moved to London, I used to do some art courses in the evenings. Drawing still lifes and nudes. At the end of the course we had a project. One still life and one nude. The bowl of fruit was easy enough, but I didn't want to draw another one of those saggy middle-aged models or skinny art students.

"It was funny. Some of the boys we drew were all penis, a skinny little body and a huge penis. There was nothing sexy about that. A friend of mine at the time was heavily pregnant and I got the idea that I'd do a demure drawing of a pregnant female form. We used to have coffee on weekend mornings and she'd spend her whole while complaining about being pregnant, about how she couldn't sleep at night and how her boobs hurt and her back hurt and how she didn't even know whether she'd like the kid when it was born, never mind all the worries about labour.

"But she looked so beautiful. She glowed with it. Some women look terrible when they're pregnant, their hair goes all lank and their skin goes bad, but she was just . . . well, I don't know another word to describe it. Anyway, I suggested to her that she might like to be a model for me. It was sort of a joke, because I didn't really think she'd agree. But she said yes, as if I'd asked her to bake me some cookies or something. No problem.

"No doubt I was nervous when she came over to my place. I had a futon on the floor and some cushions for her to recline on, and the apartment was nice and warm. We had a couple of glasses of wine and a little gossip, and then she said we'd better get down to it.

"I'd expected her to do as the other models did and get undressed in another room and come in a dressing gown. I guess she didn't know the form, because she just got undressed right there. She took her socks off, her shirt, her bra, and her trousers — those things with a tent in front of them that pregnant women wear. Her belly was really tight and her breasts were big, really big; her nipples were like out of some men's cartoon.

"She sat on the futon and reclined. I said, 'It's a nude, but if you want to keep your pants on that's okay. She said she was doing it out of consideration for my futon rather than any sense of shyness. I told her not to worry, so she stripped down. I'd expected to draw her in profile, but she said, 'Why? It's not a nude that way.' So she lay back on the cushions, with her legs a bit like this." Harry pulled one knee back and opened her thighs.

Della Torre felt his heart beating in his throat.

"It was hard drawing her, because she wasn't particularly still. She'd rub her belly because it itched or under her breasts or run her hand on her hip, or have another sip of wine." Harry took another sip of wine.

"She was talking the whole while about what it was like to be pregnant. She ran through all the stuff she'd ever complained about. But then she said one of the funniest things was that the bigger she got, the more she thought about sex. Her boyfriend is a sweet soul, but he wanted it less and less because he thought he'd hurt the baby. She was lying there saying she always felt ravenous for it. And as I drew her, she swelled. I mean, between her legs. She swelled so that she started to open up. I'd never seen that in another woman.

"It was deeply sexy to see someone in such a sensuous mood. I've never been attracted to women, and I wasn't to her either, but there was something so achingly delicious about her right then. She wasn't at all embarrassed. She just let me look at her and draw her. In the end I couldn't submit the drawing. I did one of her from memory in profile that wasn't nearly as good. I've still got the original, though."

"Could I see it?" asked della Torre.

The drawing was as she'd described the making of it. A strikingly featured woman with an insouciant gaze, her breasts and belly heavy, and then her voluptuousness. Harry knelt by him as he looked at it.

"You're a very good artist. A very good artist. I'm — I don't really know what to say."

She kissed him, long and leisurely.

"Did you like it when we went to the coast? Did you like what we did? Or have you forgotten?" she asked.

He stood up with the intention of walking her to the bedroom, holding her hand, anticipating a long night. But the depth of his hunger was taken over by something else, first slowly and then more rapidly.

It started under his right ribcage and then spread into his back, gripping his side like a deep, unyielding cramp that came on hard and left an imprint on him. And then it came back with redoubled force.

It was all he could do to stop crying out.

"Marko? Are you all right? What's happening? Marko? Gringo?"

But he was on his knees, breathing shallowly, the vise in his side squeezing ever harder.

30

HE'D WAITED IN the taxi queue at the airport for half an hour, and it wasn't getting any shorter. Were there really no taxis in London? Somebody from the airport's management said something about traffic problems on the motorway that Strumbić didn't quite understand, and about frequent trains into town, which he did. So he turned around, went back through the terminal entrance, and followed the signs to the adjoining rail station.

He was thoroughly pissed off. Nothing had gone right about the trip since he'd picked up the pink Mercedes. But at least he'd got out of the country without any problems. Strumbić had been quiet for months, had kept his head down. He'd even stopped shouting at the Bosnians. Their last call had worried him, though; they said they were in Zagreb, and he believed them.

Just as well the UDBA had relaxed their grip on him, what with all the other stuff they had to think about. It made it easy for him to slip out of the country. He'd always meant to be gone before the war came, and the war was coming damn fast.

He'd had to find Branko in hospital and then had to bribe the old crone to get his own mail. She refused to believe he was the

Mr. Smirnoff to whom the letters were addressed, and he didn't have photo identification to prove it. They were a poor likeness, but the pictures on the banknotes finally convinced her. When she'd seen enough of them.

It'd have been more satisfying to have called on Mr. Beretta. He felt the solidity of the shoulder holster under his jacket. He hadn't liked being without the gun; having to take it apart for the flight and hide it in his modest check-in bag made him uncomfortable. There were anxious minutes as he watched the luggage carousel go round, other travellers picking up their bags, before he saw his own solidly locked case. But he didn't relax until he'd reassembled the gun in the privacy of a toilet cubicle, not caring that others might have heard the hard, metallic clicks. Let them think what they liked.

Ever since della Torre had shot him and the Bosnians had started harassing him about the money, he'd kept a bullet in the chamber. If only he'd managed to find those bloody hicks, he'd have rid himself of most of his troubles. And maybe got a medal to boot. Delivering a couple of corpses identified as the Karlovac killers, with a probable Slavonski Brod witness confirmation and who knew what else, would have made him untouchable. The UDBA would certainly have eased off. As for della Torre, well, who cared.

Unfortunately, they weren't quite as stupid as Bosnian hillbillies ought to be. Either they had better connections than he had thought possible or they were both sly and lucky. It didn't help him that his moves were circumscribed by Messar. If Messar got wind that Strumbić was hunting the Bosnians, those UDBA bloodsuckers wouldn't leave him to fart in private. If they got hold of della Torre or the Bosnians before he did, or at least before he'd done a runner, he'd be breaking rocks on Goli Otok for the rest of his miserable life. Or whatever new corner of hell they were using to replace it. And then they'd probably hang him.

Life was a pain in the ass sometimes, he thought, boarding a rickety carriage that had a door by every pair of seats. He was disgusted. What kind of country was this? Even Yugoslavia had more modern trains. The ones that weren't were at least clean. He popped his suitcase in the overhead rack, taking care where he sat. It smelled of spilled beer, and black discs of dried chewing gum mottled the ancient blue and orange patterned seats.

Still, at least those crowds waiting for taxis hadn't shifted to the train en masse. As far as he could tell, the carriage was mostly empty, meaning he wouldn't have to deal with any of those endless brown, yellow, or black people London seemed so full of. True, pretty girls of all colours fascinated him; the more exotic, the more they intrigued him, made him wonder if they fit together the same way as the girls back home. But the rest of them—the kids, the middle-aged and old folks, and especially the men—all looked like they belonged in zoos.

The train lurched forward. A wash of evening light showed him a bland, rubbish-strewn route towards central London. *These people really live like pigs. Thank god I found somewhere nice in the city, even if I had to pay through the nose for it*, he thought. That reminded him. Another thing to be pissed off about. The mail at Branko's confirmed his worst fears. The agents had taken another ten thousand pounds out of his account. He was going to have to discuss things with them. Forcefully. He'd see how they liked staring into Mr. Beretta's unblinking eye.

He was looking out the window when he saw, in his peripheral vision, four adolescent boys suddenly appear over him. They couldn't have been more than eighteen or nineteen, but they were bullet-headed and big. Two black boys, one brown, and a skinny white one with red hair. Two were holding knives. One punched him, a short, flat blow to the temple.

"Money. Give us your money or you get hurt. Understand?"

"Money," said another one, parroting the first.

"Quick, or we cut you, man."

"Giss yo money."

They were pulsating with aggression, crowding over him, the kitchen knives pointing at him. The one who'd punched him hit him again, knocking his head against the window.

Strumbić reached into his jacket. He clicked off the safety with his thumb and pulled the Beretta out if its holster. Most cops have a philosophy of showing the criminals they're armed, to let them know what they're dealing with, and then giving a verbal warning, and only then firing off a warning shot.

Strumbić belonged to the other school of thought. Every time he pulled the trigger, he made sure it counted.

He caught the nearest black boy twice in the middle, knocking him back across the aisle into the other set of bench seats. The brown boy got it in the ribs and the red-headed boy in the neck or jaw — Strumbić couldn't quite tell, because he more or less flipped over backwards.

They were all screaming like skewered pigs, especially the black boy who'd got away. There seemed to be more of them farther along the carriage. It was just a nine-millimetre gun, but it did a good job of spreading blood. He vaguely wondered whether the railway people would clean it off or just let it soak in with all the rest of the disgusting effluvia coating the train.

Somebody pulled the emergency cord and the train slammed to a stop in a section of line that had a dozen sets of parallel tracks. The carriage emptied of kids, all more or less like the ones he'd plugged, the doors left hanging open. How he could have not noticed them bewildered him, though he reasoned it probably had to do with the carriage's layout of mini-compartments and high-backed seats. They streamed across the lines, heedless of the possibility of being pulverized by any passing train, and ran up the embankment and then through a chain-link fence.

Strumbić grabbed his suitcase and followed them out, leaving the whimpering messes behind him. The drop from the carriage onto the tracks was longer than he'd expected. He was about to head in the direction the kids had taken when another train rumbled along on a parallel track, coming from where his train had been heading to. It stopped, cutting him off from the embankment. But that was no bad thing.

The train was exactly like the one he'd got off: a series of doors in a carriage that had probably seen wartime service. He shrugged, got his shoe onto a little foothold under one of the doors, opened it, pushed his suitcase in, and then clambered after it, slamming the door behind him.

The carriage, as far as he could tell, was full of Japanese. Row upon row of yellow faces and identical blue suitcases, each with a round red label stuck to it. They looked at him, startled, and looked away when he returned their gaze. He walked down the aisle until he found a free seat in a block of four, the three Japanese smiling and bobbing their heads as he sat down. They were so polite, he smiled and bobbed his head in return. The train moved off, the intercom crackling with a barely decipherable apology from the driver about signalling problems.

He got off at the next stop. Gatwick Airport. The taxi queue was marginally shorter than it had been when he'd left, but at least the cabs were once again flowing. He finally got in one but was then stuck for what to tell the driver.

"London."

"Big town, London. Anywhere specific?"

Strumbić mulled for a second as the car pulled away. He didn't have keys to the flat. His intention had been to get into town early enough to call in at the estate agency and get their set of spares, along the way maybe having a preliminary discussion about why they were looting his account. He didn't buy their story about the building sliding down Hampstead Hill. But they'd be shut this time of evening.

Still, it'd be no hardship to put up for a night in the hotel he'd stayed at before, on the recommendation of an Albanian he knew who did good business in London. There were always entertaining girls to be found at the bar and, failing that, it wasn't far to Soho.

"Piccadilly," he said.

"Bright lights. Big city. Piccadilly is a fine place to go for a good time."

Strumbić decided that taxi-driver patter in a language he barely understood was bad enough ordinarily, but with the loss of at least thirty thousand pounds hanging over his head, not to mention the railway slaughter, he felt entitled to slide the driver's little window shut, pull out a cigarette, and ignore the no-smoking sticker on the glass facing him.

31

"**C**AN YOU PUSH your belly up to touch my hand? That's good. When I touch you here, does it hurt? Good. I'm putting this needle in your arm. You'll feel a little prick. We'll leave the needle in because we can give you some painkillers through it. Some morphine. It'll work quickly. And then we'll put you on a drip; that way you won't get dehydrated. We'd rather you didn't drink now, in case we need to operate. I don't think we will. It doesn't seem to be appendicitis. We'll take some X-rays just to be sure."

Della Torre's contribution to the conversation with the unfeasibly young emergency room doctor was an occasional moan. Harry had flagged a passing taxi down to the hospital, though it was only a few hundred metres away from the flat.

The hospital was a bunker of a building at the bottom of the hill. The emergency room was full of drunks and Friday night revellers with bashed faces. Normally he'd have waited most of the night to be seen. But fainting out of his seat onto the floor seemed to speed things up.

The doctor turned to Harry. "Has he been drinking heavily or taking any drugs this evening?"

"No. We had a few glasses of wine, but that was it. We'd been out for dinner and then came home, and everything seemed fine until suddenly he just collapsed. He could barely talk with the pain," she said.

"It doesn't seem to be appendicitis. It doesn't usually come on that quickly, and the pains he has and the feel of his abdomen suggest it's not likely. I won't be able to tell until he's given us a urine sample and we've done an X-ray, but I think from the general location and type of pain, it's a kidney stone."

"A kidney stone?"

"Yes. The pain can come on dramatically. It's said to be on par with going into labour, but it's not usually dangerous. Normally it passes by itself in a day or two, but if it's a big one it might need an operation. Are you his next of kin?"

"We live together."

"Oh," he said, no clearer on the relationship. "I'm sure there really isn't any need to worry about him. Do you mind taking his wallet and any other valuables he has? Things have a habit of disappearing from this part of the hospital. You're welcome to come back in a bit, but I'd like to do more of an examination once I've given him some painkillers."

The conversation going on around him was as meaningful to della Torre as elevator music. Harry was still in her black dress. Through his pain he could still see how beautiful she was. It was comforting to be in her presence as he died so ex-cruciatingly. Maybe martyred saints had similar visions.

The morphine didn't work, so they gave him another dose. And then another one. Only then was he in a reasonable enough state to go through with the rest of the physical exam and to urinate in the pot they gave him.

He lay there in the examination room, curled up on his side, controlling his breathing as best he could, an occasional spasm working its way through him, though now it was just bearable. He was alone for at most a few minutes at a time, a nurse rou-tinely popping her head in to tell him the doctor would be back shortly. He didn't mind, as long as the pain stayed away.

"There's trace protein in your urine. You can't see it, but there's blood. That suggests a kidney stone is probably what you've got, but we're going to take some pictures of you just to make sure. Is it still hurting?"

"Better, Doctor."

"Is there anybody in your family who's had kidney stones?"

"My father... and my grandfather. I think my father's grand-father had them too," della Torre said, remembering how a few years before his father had called him from a hospital in Poreč to say don't worry, it's only kidney stones.

Only kidney stones? He wasn't ever going to tell anyone that he'd "only" had kidney stones. He was going to say it was like being shot in the gut with a cactus, like he'd been eating fishhooks and molten lead, like some creature had crawled inside him and was eating its way out. It wasn't "only" kidney stones.

They wheeled him on a gurney through the hospital's laby-rinthine corridors to a bit of hallway where he was left wait-ing behind another patient, an old woman on another bed on wheels. She was taken in and he was pushed to the front of a short queue of three.

Della Torre still felt the pulsing pain and then the low throb through the morphine and the bottle or so of wine he'd drunk during the evening. But it wasn't crippling anymore. They pushed him into a room where a nurse sat him up in front of a big machine. She left him and went into a glass cubicle, coming back to readjust his position: front, back, side. As he sat there having his last X-ray taken, he looked into the booth.

He stared hard for a long moment. The pain, the morphine, and the alcohol were playing tricks with his mind. It was dis-concerting not to be in possession of his faculties. The woman in the booth was such a spitting image of Irena that he almost called out her name. She looked up and caught his eye. The likeness was maddening. The only difference was the woman in the glass cubicle looked as if she'd had an electric shock.

"Marko?" she seemed to be shouting. "Marko?"

.   .   .   .

"So what now? You're in charge of the investigation. You call the shots," Anzulović said to the younger man. Messar, he thought, would rise high with his self-assurance, his unwillingness to be defeated. With his...momentum.

Messar gave him a glum look. They'd gone back to Branko's flat, but the concierge said Mr. Smirnoff had already picked up his mail. Mr. Smirnoff? He'd been driving a pink sports car, she said. Pink like a strumpet's underwear.

They couldn't imagine who the hell it was until she described him. As improbable as it was, it sounded like Strumbić. The hard-drinking, womanizing cop, always good for a dirty joke or a double entendre, in a flaming pink car? Then again, there was a lot that was strange about the whole case.

They dropped Strumbić for the moment and thought about where della Torre might have gone from Venice. They went to have a look at the ferry terminal where the two UDBA men had been held up by the Venice *caribinieri* when they lost della Torre. Messar had insisted on asking some questions, but neither of them spoke particularly good Italian and no one remembered one passing tourist among thousands after more than two months. After unsuccessfully showing della Torre's picture around a few bars and restaurants, they gave up and went back to the apartment building to see whether they could get anything more out of the old lady. Nobody answered either her buzzer or Branko's.

They drove past the hospital but decided not to stop in. It was late, after visiting hours, and besides, the nurses would have probably knocked Branko out.

"That's funny," said Anzulović.

"What's that?"

"There's a green Zastava parked at the corner just around from the hospital."

"So?" asked Messar.

"You don't see a lot of Zastavas outside of Yugoslavia," Anzulović pointed out.

"We're pretty close to the Slovene border. There's plenty of us Yugoslavs this side of it. Half of Trieste is Yugoslav. And everybody's going to be trying to get out of the country now."

"Yeah," said Anzulović. "Except there's something strange about that car."

Messar ignored Anzulović for a while, lost in his own thoughts. "If you were Strumbić, what would you do?" he finally asked.

"Find a brothel in Las Vegas. I always figured Strumbić was a Vegas kind of guy. Or Marseilles—there's something *French Connection* about him," Anzulović said.

"French? This is Italy."

"Yes, it's Italy. *The French Connection* is a movie."

"Oh." Messar nodded. Anzulović and his movies.

"Shame we couldn't get hold of the Bosnians," Anzulović said with a mild rap on Messar's knuckles.

"We will. Eventually. When we do, it'll be no thanks to the local UDBA in Bosnia," Messar spat. What was the world coming to? Nobody was co-operating with anyone else in Yugoslavia. It was all Serbs for Serbs, Croats for Croats, Slovenes for themselves. For someone who'd spent his life knowing that nationalism was the root of fascism, the way the country had turned was disgusting.

"Strumbić, the Bosnians, and della Torre—they've probably cooked up some sort of racket. Smuggling cars," Messar prodded back at Anzulović, "or drugs. Maybe they fell out. But you know they're tied into this together."

"I'd be surprised," Anzulović stressed.

Messar didn't know anything about the files or the Dispatcher but he sensed he wasn't being told everything. That Anzulović was keeping something from him. He considered Anzulović. Had the old man come along just to keep an eye on him? "Desperate men do desperate things," Messar said.

"Like rent a pink Merc."

"What was he thinking?"

"Maybe he thought nobody would think somebody running from the cops would do it in a pink Merc."

"Maybe we should look for a pink Merc."

"He'll be long gone by now."

They drove through the public car park at the Mestre railway station and the one at the end of the bridge in Venice. They drove past every hotel they could find in the phone book and every public space, spreading ever more widely from the centre of the industrial town. Eventually, it took them to the airport parking lot. Messar slowly cruised up and down the aisles, racking up short-stay charges.

"There." Anzulović bounced in his seat so that his head hit the car's padded roof.

"What?"

"There. A pink car."

"You sure? This evening light makes white cars look pretty garish."

"Not that colour pink."

They drove closer. A pink Mercedes convertible was parked in the section reserved for hire cars. There couldn't have been another like it in the whole of Italy.

32

"**M**ARKO, WHAT ARE you doing here?"

"Well, you see, I arranged this kidney stone as a clever ruse to find you because I couldn't be bothered trying the phone book."

They were in a private room. Irena had saved her questions for when they were alone.

"I always wondered what it would take to knock the flippancy out of you. Not a kidney stone, anyway. Though it seems to have knocked your moustache off. You look better without it."

"Thanks. I wasn't feeling very flip before the morphine."

"Yes, I'm told it's painful."

"Like labour."

"I wouldn't know."

"Sorry."

"Listen, Marko, we've got to talk. I'm glad you found me. Have you been in touch with your father?"

"No."

"I've spoken to him a few times. He's worried about you. He knows you're often out of contact when you're on a job, but the UDBA sent some people to talk to him a couple of times. He couldn't understand why they didn't know where you were."

"They've probably kept an eye on you too."

She shuddered. "I'll give you my details. I don't live far from here; it's just the next underground stop after Hampstead, a place called Golders Green. So you don't disappear again," she said.

"Oh, yes. I vaguely remember you talking about it now. I'd completely forgotten the name of the hospital. I kept thinking Partizan Pediatric Centre in Pazin or something. The irony is, I'm staying less than half a kilometre away."

"Where?"

"Strumbić's place, if you can believe it."

"Strumbić has a place in London?"

"In Hampstead, virtually in the middle of the Heath, about two hundred square meters of luxury like you wouldn't believe."

"Sounds like you fell on your feet."

"Sounds like it. Until he comes looking for us. Then there's a risk we end up on our backs, in a hole, two metres down."

"Us? What has this got to do with me?"

"Not you. Me and a . . . a friend."

"You have a friend?" Irena's eyebrows rose. "I guess that explains the moustache."

"It's not what you think. It really isn't," della Torre said, lying badly.

"Look, Marko, that's okay. I don't have a problem with it. You see, I think I've found somebody else."

"You've found somebody else?" Della Torre suddenly felt hurt, wounded in a way that got right under the painkillers. "How could you find somebody else? I haven't found somebody else." Harry wasn't somebody else. Was she?

"I didn't know I had to wait for you to go through the door first."

"You didn't. It's just, you know, kind of quick."

"It's three years, Marko."

"But we've had good times since then. Even better than when we were properly married."

"Yes, Marko. But that's because they were always a last waltz. Nostalgia. I don't know if this will lead anywhere. But it's got more of a chance of going where I want to be than I've had with you for a long time."

"Sure. Sure..."

"Listen, Marko, you need some sleep. The pain exhausted you and the morphine is knocking you out. It's not really the time to talk. But can you remember something?"

"What?"

"I haven't told this guy about you. I mean, I told him I'd been married but now I'm divorced."

"They say that fifty percent of all marriages end in divorce." Della Torre's mind ambled around the subject.

"Yes, and the other fifty percent end in death. Anyway, he's a doctor, he does emergency trauma here. There's no real reason he should visit you, but if he does, can you be my ex-husband's cousin who happened to be coming through town and just got unlucky?"

"Sure. Ex-cousin's husband."

"Ex-husband's cousin."

"Like I said."

"I'll be back in the morning. I'll go over the X-rays with you and we'll talk some more."

"Night night, love."

"Sleep well, Marko."

·   ·   ·

"Where do you think he flew to?" Anzulović asked, having confirmed that somebody who looked a lot like Strumbić had dropped the car off, paying the additional fee for not returning it to its original hire location.

"London."

"Yes. It's likely."

"Have you got the address of the place he was calling in the files?" Messar asked.

"It's somewhere in the centre, near Piccadilly—you know, where all the lights are and there's that statue of the angel trying to skewer people." Anzulović had been to London a few times, including once on a holiday with his wife. His English was rudimentary, but good enough to order in restaurants and to find his way around town. Messar didn't speak any at all.

"London's where della Torre's wife called his father from too, wasn't it? Looks like the criminal conspiracy might be meeting up for round two," Messar said

"So what now? Do we follow? I don't trust any of the UDBA people in London. I doubt the Yugoslav embassy would have anything to do with us anyway. So it's either us or nobody," Anzulović said.

"We go. We drive. Tonight. We can get through to France by the morning and then to London by tomorrow night. One sleeps, the other one drives."

Anzulović nodded, expecting nothing less of the younger man. "We have three days. That's it. That's as much as we can justify. Then we go back. Somebody's going to be needing us after that. Maybe Zagreb," Anzulović said, watching Messar. "Or maybe Belgrade."

Messar's lip curled with distaste. The politicians in Belgrade were no better than the ones in Zagreb these days. When religion dies, everybody's an apostate.

"How's your English?" Anzulović asked.

"It's not. Yours?"

"I can order food."

Messar shrugged.

"We'll learn on the way," Anzulović said encouragingly.

"We'll hunt them down and bring them back even if we have to use sign language to do it," Messar said. "And even if they're in bits and in the boot."

THE PAIN WOKE della Torre. Irena was already there, sitting, reading some notes.

"Ow, Jesus, does this never stop?" he said, clutching his side.

"I've got good news and good news for you."

"Don't tell me. The suffering will end soon because I'm going to die. And the other good news is that you won't need to divorce me then."

"Pessimist. Take this tablet and stick it up your rear end. I'll leave you in privacy while I get a coffee."

He did as he was told. She was gone longer than he'd expected, but even before she'd come back, the pain had completely disappeared. It was as if he'd never suffered at all. The agony of the previous night seemed an abstract memory.

"Wow. What was that?" he asked, smiling when she walked back into the room.

"That was your first bit of good news."

"Powerful medicine. Works miles better than the morphine. What was it?"

"Ibuprofen. A pill you take when you've got a sore head. It merely confirms where yours is."

"Ha," he said, though his smile was genuine.

"It's a very effective anti-inflammatory."

"So what's the other good news? I'm assuming it doesn't also involve my head being up my ass."

"No. Your X-ray shows that your stone has almost dropped out. A couple of hours and it should be gone completely. You'll pee it out and it'll be as if it had never been there. Even better news is that it's the only one. You might get another one in the future. If you don't take care of yourself, you will. But it might not happen for a long time. And I had a look at your lungs as well while I was at it. Clear as a baby's, though I haven't a clue why."

"I keep telling you, my great-grandfather on my mother's side smoked from before he could talk, wasn't sober a day in his life, and lived to be ninety-six."

"Somebody has to win the lottery. But it's a bad basis on which to plan your future."

"Speaking of tests, I meant to ask you something in Zagreb, but there wasn't time."

"It's too late, Marko."

"Too late for what?"

"For whatever you wanted to ask."

"About centrifuges?"

"Oh, sorry, I thought it was something else." Irena blushed slightly. "So ask me about centrifuges."

Della Torre was momentarily puzzled but then ploughed on. "What do you know about them?"

"Centrifuges? They're a spin cycle on a washing machine."

"No, real ones. The sort you use in hospitals."

"What about them? They separate solids out of liquid solution. Blood, mostly—they spin the blood cells and platelets out of the plasma. You can test each component separately. Or at blood centres they use it to separate the products so that plasma, red cells, and platelets can be transfused to people who need them."

"Do they use it to get rid of AIDS from blood?"

"Are you worried about becoming infected? You don't need a transfusion, you know."

"No, it's not about me. I want to know why somebody would want a whole bunch of centrifuges, whether it might have something to do with AIDS."

"As far as I know, AIDS is viral, and I'm not sure they'd be willing to use suspect samples for transfusion. I don't know anything about purifying contaminated blood with centrifuges. How many is a whole bunch, by the way?"

"Thousands."

"For blood? That really is a lot. I doubt there's a thousand centrifuges in all the hospitals in Yugoslavia."

"I don't know that they're for blood. I'm just guessing. But I don't know what else they'd be for."

"What kind of centrifuges are you talking about? I mean, what do they look like?"

"Tall, fairly narrow cylinders, as far as I can remember. About two metres long, and they look like water-mains pipe, I think."

"And lots of them?"

"Yes, apparently there were a few thousand sent from Sweden to Belgrade in the mid-1980s. I thought they might have something to do with AIDS."

"They don't sound like hospital centrifuges. They sound more like the ones they use to purify nuclear fuel. What level of purity you're looking for and how much of the fuel you want determine how many centrifuges you need."

"Nuclear fuel?" he asked, puzzled.

"We've got some at the university in Zagreb. About a dozen or so. That mostly covers what we need at the hospital for radiotherapy and the physics department's uses."

"I'd forgotten you did nuclear medicine."

"Oh, it only took up three years of my life."

"I was in London for one of them."

"Yes. Anyway, that's the prime reason they gave me this X-ray job without demanding any training. I guess having most of the coursework towards a Ph.D. in a subject lets you off lab technician qualification," she said.

"So tell me more."

"What more?"

"I mean, would anyone need more than a dozen?"

"Sure. You need a few hundred to purify the fuel for a power station. And a couple of thousand to make a bomb."

"A bomb? We never made a bomb in Yugoslavia, as far as I can remember."

"We had a program. I remember in the late seventies having to compete with the national weapons lab for equipment and radioactive material. And people. I don't think it was a big secret. Tito talked about it in the papers. But it mostly ended when he died, if I remember well. It was too expensive to keep going."

"Maybe Belgrade restarted the program in the mid-eighties."

"Maybe. But I'm pretty sure they didn't. We'd have noticed at the university. They'd have taken our physicists and equipment, like they did in the seventies. But there wasn't any interference with my radiological work. So unless it was top secret and somehow conjured a couple of hundred experts out of thin air, I doubt there was any program."

"Oh. Now that you mention it, I think they were mostly exported again."

"There you go. Yugoslavia bought the centrifuges from Sweden and then sold them on to some suspect Third World dictatorship afterwards," she said. "Capitalism with a Communist face."

"Would we have been allowed to?" he said, mostly to himself.

"Not really. These things are tightly controlled. The West let us have a program because they knew we were more scared of the Soviets than we were of America. I don't think they'd have been happy for us to sell the equipment on to some tinpot dictatorship," she said.

"Some *other* tinpot dictatorship."

"That's what I meant."

"So we'd have been doing it quietly."

"I never heard anything about us buying thousands of centrifuges. And I know a lot of physicists."

There was knock at the door. Irena opened it.

Harry stepped into the room, her expression for all the world looking like Billy the Kid's when he ran into Pat Garrett that last time.

"I can come back when you're free," she said. She was wearing a severe skirt, cut just above her knees, and a cotton jersey. Her hair was pulled back. There was a certain bloodlessness to her expression. She smiled, but her eyes had a wariness in them.

"No, that's fine. Come on in, Harry. This is my radiologist. She happens to be my ex-cousin's husband's wife."

"His cousin's ex-wife."

"That's what I meant."

"Must have been a surprise. Finding each other in the same hospital," said Harry in a tone suggesting nothing was about to surprise her.

"A big one. For both of us," della Torre said.

"I'll be back in a bit. When the urologist comes," Irena said in English, leaving the room.

"Hi. Do I get a kiss?" he asked.

Harry stared at him without answering. She reached into her bag and pulled out his wallet.

"When I got home, I went through your wallet. In case I had to find your next of kin."

Della Torre winced, suspecting what was coming next.

"I noticed an ID with your picture on it. It said UDBA. I had no idea what that meant, but it looked pretty important. I mean, it clearly wasn't a bus pass. So I looked it up. It's handy having lots of modern history books. And do you know what?"

"Look, I can —"

"Please let me finish. Do you know what they say about UDBA? It's the Yugoslav secret police, notorious for domestic repression, running concentration camps, and killing dissidents in foreign countries. Is that what you are?"

"Harry —"

She held her hand up to silence him. "Of course you are. Once I got over the shock, I looked at your things. Italian and American passports? They look real. Are they? A gun and bullets. Do you know you can go to jail in this country for having an unlicensed handgun? Who'd you come to kill?"

For some reason, he'd put the Beretta back together while she'd been away. Out of boredom. Or maybe unease at being alone in the apartment. It crossed his mind that she might not have recognized it for what it was had he left it in bits. Though it would have been hard to justify the bullets. They looked nothing like earplugs.

There was a long silence. Her look was cold, and underneath that it showed fear.

"I have some explaining to do. But I didn't lie to you."

"You'd need to be a lawyer to argue that," she said in disgust.

"Okay, maybe there were a couple of little white lies. But most of what I told you is true. I am a lawyer, though I work for the UDBA. But I'm not one of the bad guys. I investigate the secret police for corruption. Actually my job is—was—to investigate UDBA killings, the ones you mentioned. About five years ago, an internal department was set up to prevent the UDBA from becoming a law unto itself. I'd been in the prosecutor's office and I joined from there. A lot of those killings, I'm sorry to say, were legal. I mean, within Yugoslav law. My job was to find the ones that weren't."

"So if they had somebody to kill, they'd go to you to make sure all the paperwork was done properly," she said bitterly.

"No. No. I investigated past assassinations. I had nothing to do with current UDBA operations. Really, I didn't."

She looked sceptical.

"It's a hard job, Harry. Everybody in the UDBA hated us because they were afraid we'd find out what they were up to. But as far as the wider world is concerned, we're as bad as the rest."

"My heart bleeds. Nobody made you do it." She stood with her back against the wall.

"You're right. But to tell you the truth, it was one of the few jobs where I really felt as if I could properly serve justice. And I did. We caught killers and had them put away —"

"In concentration camps?"

"Living under a dictatorship means compromise. For everyone. You can't lead a pure life. It's just the way it is. I'm sorry."

"So why did you come here? Was it a holiday?"

"I was running. Somebody wanted to kill me for something I knew. Even now I don't know what."

She didn't look convinced. He shrugged.

"Somebody wanted me killed and Strumbić helped to set me up. So I shot him. Accidentally. But now I've got killers and the police — Strumbić is a cop — after me. I had to go."

"We've been stealing from a killer?"

"No, I don't know of anybody Strumbić has ever killed. But he's a crook. That's where he got all the money to pay for the place in London. We just stole it back from him."

Her eyes had turned a grey shade of blue. They were wet. She looked as pale as he'd been the previous night on the hospital gurney. He worried she'd faint.

"You're right, I didn't believe you. I just thought you were running some scam. That you were some con man."

"Look, Harry, I'm sorry. I don't think you're in any danger. Strumbić will be tied up in Zagreb for a long time yet, and when he does come, we'll be long gone. As far as the money goes, he'll just eat the loss for a quiet life."

"I hope you're right."

So do I, thought della Torre.

"What about your second cousin's ex-husband's mother-in-law's niece who works at the hospital just accidentally?" Harry watched him expectantly. Della Torre scratched his head and sank further into the bed.

"If I were to tell you she's my cousin's ex-wife's best friend, would you believe me?"

"No."

"What about a long-lost great-aunt?"

"No."

"What sort of answer might be satisfactory?"

"Maybe telling me she's your ex-wife, and whether she's really still your wife."

"Why would you think she's not my ex-wife?"

"Her ring finger has fresh marks. It looks like she's only recently stopped wearing it. Have you got divorced since you've been here?"

"You're sharp. Ever think of becoming a secret policeman?" His smile got no response. "It's very amicable."

"I'm sure it is amicably ambiguous. If it weren't, you'd probably be glowing by now."

"Glowing?"

"She was the one who operated the X-ray machine on you, wasn't she?"

"Ah, yes. Glowing. We've been meaning to get divorced, but, well, neither of us really had a good reason. But now she seems to have found herself a very smart and very nice doctor. I might get to meet him."

"How convenient. To go from a husband who puts bullets in to a boyfriend who takes them out."

"He probably specializes in hemorrhoids. It won't last. He'll bore her. Like they say, you can take the girl out of the ex-Communist totalitarian war zone but you can't take the war-zone totalitarian out of the girl Communist."

"You make it sound so romantic. Did she work with you in your secret police place? Like Dr. Mengele or something?" He could almost taste her bitterness.

"No. She worked in ordinary hospitals. And I'm not sure how thrilled she'd be to be compared to a Nazi torturer, seeing as she's one of the few remaining Croat Jews."

"Oh. Sorry. I didn't mean that."

"I'm sure there were plenty of Jewish secret policemen and worse working in east Europe. But none I can think of for the UDBA. Anyway, she's an X-ray techie here because that's what they allow her to do, but in real life she's a very good specialist. She does lungs. Special sorts of radiotherapy to fight cancer."

"Forget I mentioned it."

"Forgotten."

They watched each other: she wary, he with a mixture of pity and sorrow. For himself. A thought struck him.

"Harry, can I ask you something?"

"What?" She seemed unsure whether she wanted to hear what he wanted to ask.

"When we were away for the weekend."

"Yes?"

"And we were sailing."

"Yes?"

"You pointed out some buildings but you couldn't remember what they were called. They started with an s, you thought."

She seemed more bewildered by this question than anything he'd said so far.

"What about it?"

"Were they centrifuge buildings?"

She thought for a moment.

"Yes, I think they were." She sounded distracted, annoyed. Della Torre's question had been as perversely mistimed as asking the bereaved at a funeral for a pizza take-away's phone number.

They didn't have time for any more conversation, as the urologist interrupted. He was older, shorter, and fatter than della Torre, and balding besides. He shot lecherous looks at Harry, who was oblivious to him.

"Well, well, well, and how do you do." He was talking to della Torre but stayed focused on Harry.

"I need to go away for a couple of days," Harry said to della Torre. "I'll call you on Monday, but I need some time to think about all this." Her voice trembled. "We can sort some things out when you get out of here, with the flat and money."

"You're not staying at the apartment?" he asked.

"No," she said. "No. I'll stay with...friends. We'll talk on Monday." She glanced at her watch. "I've got to go to work now. I have some appointments..." Her explanation trailed away, unneeded.

She left the room.

The urologist's smile was short on sympathy. "Well, looks like this weekend just isn't working out for you," he said.

Della Torre was tired. He ignored the doctor.

"How long am I going to be in here?"

"I'm sure we'll want to keep you in here for a bit of observation. One more night, and I don't see why you shouldn't be out tomorrow morning."

Yesterday everything had seemed to be falling into place. Now it was falling apart. He'd started building a new life for himself in his mind. With Harry. He and Irena were too far gone. He'd known that. But Harry could have been...

They had nearly as much of Strumbić's money as they could reasonably want without risking bloody vengeance—enough to set up a new life. Della Torre felt sorry for himself.

"So, shall we get down to business?" asked the doctor.

"I've cleared my diary," della Torre said distractedly.

The urologist ran through della Torre's local difficulty and prescribed some medication, including more of the magic painkillers, with a warning that he shouldn't overuse them.

Irena returned. The urologist gave her a peck on each cheek, deeply un-English. "I take it we're still on for tomorrow night?"

"We're still on," she said.

Della Torre felt as if he were being stabbed from every angle at once. When he was alone with Irena, he turned to her, hurt and amazed.

"That's him? That's the guy you threw me over for. A gnome?"

She laughed. "And what if it were?"

"Because it would make me sad for the rest of my days that you'd fallen so low and I'd done so little to help."

"In that case, you can rest easy. I'm interested in someone else. In fact, he'll be stopping by to pick me up in a few minutes. My shift finished hours ago, and he's also done for the night."

"So you're going back to his place? On a Saturday morning? On your Sabbath?"

"And?"

"But that's adultery. We're still married."

"Does your friend know that?"

"She's merely my criminal accomplice. We aren't doing anything as contemptible as breaking marriage vows on a Saturday morning. Besides, I don't think she likes me anymore. She found out I was UDBA."

"I'm sorry to hear that. She's very attractive." Irena paused. "Listen, Marko, I don't want to make your life any worse, but we're going to have to go through with a divorce. We really are. I've been calling your father to find out where you were. I mean, I didn't want to break it to you now, so suddenly, but it's not sudden. It's something we need to get done."

"Your man?"

"I'm sorry, Marko. I gave you my best. I really did," Irena said. "It's just that I've got to start thinking of my future. I can have a new life here. A nice one."

"When do you want to do it?"

"When did the urologist say you'd leave the hospital?"

"He said they wanted to keep an eye on me tonight, just in case, but I'd be home tomorrow morning."

"He's being over-cautious. You'd have been home already if this was back in Zagreb. Anyway, I have a lawyer friend who's coming to dinner tomorrow. So is the urologist and a couple of other people. It's informal. Why don't you come? He'll give you a checkup there. Free."

"Gee, thanks."

"And after dinner I'll get the lawyer to stay back and we'll talk about what we need to file. He's very nice. He won't charge us for the consultation. Just a bit of background."

"What about your man? Won't he feel awkward having dinner with his lover's husband?"

"You won't tell him. Besides, he won't be coming. He's working tomorrow."

"Tomorrow," della Torre said dully. "Sunday."

"The very same."

"I can't really refuse you, can I?"

There was an apologetic cast to her mouth, which was drawn straight. Her eyes glistened slightly. But he could tell she was determined.

"I wouldn't refuse you, Irena. It's been a long time coming."

"Thanks, Marko." She kissed his forehead.

There was a knock on the door. A tall, slim man stepped in. He had a sharp widow's peak and small, round glasses perched on a finely chiselled Roman nose. His hair was flecked with grey, but he couldn't have been any older than della Torre.

"Marko, this is David Cohen."

"How do you do, Doctor."

"Irena's cousin. What an extraordinary coincidence you should pitch up here," he said in a rather sonorous voice.

"Her ex-husband's cousin's daughter's best friend, to be

precise. But we call it cousins," della Torre said, finding comfort in sarcasm.

David Cohen looked quizzical for a moment and then smiled. "I'm afraid I'm a little slow this morning. It's been a long shift."

"Don't tell me, you're an emergency urologist or dermatologist or proctologist or —"

"None of the above. I do trauma. And trauma tends to be very popular on a Friday or Saturday night."

"Is that so? Trauma in Hampstead? Let me guess, catastrophic hernias from people making the mistake of picking up their sacks of money. Or reaching up for a book on a top shelf and being bludgeoned by a misplaced gold bar. Or trophy wives discovering a friend is wearing the exact same dress to a party."

"You have to excuse Marko," said Irena. "He's an unreformed Communist, already nostalgic for the days when you could pass a whole leisurely morning queuing up for a loaf of bread."

"No, that's all right. That's pretty funny, actually. I'll remember to use it sometime. We get people from Hampstead — muggings gone wrong, domestic disasters, or car accidents, mostly. But we cater to a lot of poor neighbourhoods around here as well. And people have a nasty habit of getting into fights when they're drunk, whether they're rich or poor. But I spent most of last night in south London, working on some boys who got themselves shot in a train."

"Shot in a train. Don't tell me, they were minding their own business and somebody decided to use them for target practice."

"No. It seems they're part of a gang that robs passengers on trains."

Della Torre looked at him in astonishment. "I think they might be some long-lost friends of mine. I was robbed on a train in south London."

"You were robbed on a train?"

"Yes. Two months ago."

"I'm sorry to hear it. Not that it's infrequent, but it still requires a big dose of bad luck to have that happen to you. Not quite as bad, mind, as they had it, robbing somebody with a nine-millimetre gun."

"Nine-millimetre? Standard issue?"

"Probably."

"Were you just passing through? Is that why you got the job?"

"Oh, no. I specialize in gunshot wounds."

"David spent a year in your part of the States, Marko, doing on-the-job training," said Irena.

"I was in Chicago, patching up holes. It's amazing how many extra holes people in the U.S. develop. Are you from Chicago?"

"No, Cleveland."

"Not far, but I never ventured. We were busy enough where we were, and when we had a chance to get away, we'd go as far as possible."

"I don't think you missed much. So there's a dearth of people here who know an entry wound from an exit wound, is there?"

"There aren't many of us here who have the expertise. Some in Northern Ireland, but not so much in London. Usually if there's something interesting happening, they send for me."

"So what happened to those boys?"

"One had two slugs in the abdomen. His spleen had to come out, and he's got a shorter intestine than he did yesterday morning. One of the kidneys might pose some problems too. He'll live, but he'll remember that adventure for the rest of his life. Another one got plugged in the chest. Bullet flattened itself against the back of the rib. He'll make it too, though we'll advise him not to take up smoking. Or the triathlon. The third boy, we don't know yet. He's still alive, but the bullet went up under the chin, made a mess of his palate, and ended up in his brain. He could be back on the street in a few months, no dumber than he ever was, or he could be in a morgue tomorrow."

"Marko," Irena interrupted, "David really ought to be going. He looks as if he's about to fall over with exhaustion. I've written down my details. Put them in your wallet and don't lose them. We'll talk tomorrow evening. Come at around six; we eat early. Okay? Tomorrow evening. I've got your details from what you wrote on the records. They are correct, aren't they?"

"Harry filled in the forms, so they must be right."

"I'll see you then."

"It was nice meeting you, Marko," said David.

"The pleasure's all mine, Doctor."

34

STRUMBIĆ WOKE UP with a hangover. No, that was an understatement. It was to an ordinary hangover what the Hindenburg disaster was to a barbecue flare-up. Encyclopedia entries could be written about the state of Strumbić's head.

He rubbed his face, the bristles making a coarse brushing sound against the rough, broad palm of his hand. Small empty bottles seemed to cover the floor around the bed.

He sat up, instantly regretting moving. What he needed was seltzer water and a good, solid shot of slivovitz, followed by one of those English breakfasts that either cured or killed.

But he didn't have time for any of that. Didn't matter. He couldn't count the number of times he'd gone to work not having showered or shaved, having slept in the car after a hard night on the booze because he couldn't see the road.

Luckily the estate agents weren't far, a few streets away in Mayfair. Besides, who cared what they thought about how he looked or smelled? They worked for him. They could keep their opinions to themselves. Not to mention he'd rip their throats out if he found they were cheating him.

The Saturday morning tourists were already filling Piccadilly. Strumbić walked through them, still struggling out of the fog of the previous night. Had he been less hungover, he might have noticed the tall, blond woman standing at the curb, waving down a taxi.

A young and expensively groomed man stood up as Strumbić walked into the office. The man wore his hair slicked back and a tailored blue pinstripe suit with a fraction too much cuff showing. Strumbić noted his square gold cufflinks, as he was meant to. There was a vague scent of lavender about the man.

"How can I help you, sir?" If the man was surprised at Strumbić's appearance, the grey stubble and bloodshot eyes, the heavy smell of sweat and dissolution, he didn't show it. It didn't do to prejudge Mayfair clientele. Sometimes millionaires dressed like bums. And many bums dressed impeccably. He maintained an interested expression of solicitude, though his body tilted back a couple of centimetres.

"I want Harry," Strumbić said in his ponderous accent, the w coming out as a v and the Harry sounding more like harim without the m.

"You've only just missed her. She went out to see a client. I don't think she'll be back this morning, but she should be in Monday. Is there anything I can do for you?"

"You are agents for me. I have apartment in Hampstead."

"Are you selling, or are we your letting agents?"

"No, you do my bills and have keys when I am away."

The young man looked towards an unoccupied part of the open-plan office.

"I'm afraid there's no one around in that department. There are usually only a few of us in on Saturdays, and only when people have made appointments. Can I take a message for someone and they'll get back to you on Monday?"

"No. I have lost keys to apartment and need keys you have. You keep them here. I need to go to my apartment today."

"Ah, I see, you want the spares. What's your name and where is your apartment?" the young man said, walking towards a locked filing cabinet in a separate room at the back of the office.

"Smirnoff. My name is Smirnoff and apartment is in Hampstead, East Heath Road."

"Oh yes, of course, Mr. Smirnoff. You rang a few times asking for Harry over the past month, didn't you. She was away on holiday, and unfortunately she was the only one who knew about your circumstances. Something about work to your building. It happens all the time. Clients are always shocked by how much the management companies charge for works, and how extensive they can be."

"Yes."

"Well, your keys should be no problem. All I need is a piece of photo ID. A passport is probably the best thing."

Strumbić was stopped dead. He kept his passport with the Smirnoff name in a safety deposit box in a bank around the corner from the estate agency. It was not an ID he wanted to lose or anyone to find. It was his U.K. ID, and it had been incredibly expensive to produce. It was a genuine British passport and not obtained through official UDBA channels or the unofficial sources he had in Croatia. It had been done through friends of friends of friends. Unfortunately, the safety deposit box key was on the chain della Torre had stolen. Luckily, the estate agents had the spare.

"I haven't got ID. Not now. But you give me keys and I get you ID."

"I'm sorry, sir, it doesn't work that way. I need the ID before I can get you the keys."

"Passport is in bank. You have keys to bank safety box. Give me keys and I go to bank and get ID."

"I'm sorry, sir. Really, I can't give you the keys without some ID first."

"You take keys, you come to bank with me, and we get passport together, then you give me keys. Okay?"

"I'm sorry, sir, but I can't leave the office, and the only other people here have appointments they're waiting for, so there's no one we can spare to go to the bank."

"Okay. When your office close, you come to bank. Okay?"

"I'm sorry, sir, but we're open until twelve-thirty, and most banks shut at midday on Saturdays. If you come back on Monday, Harry will be able to vouch for you. She knows you and she won't need an ID, or she can go to the bank with you, but there's nothing I can do right now."

Strumbić was beginning to get agitated, and the young man saw it. He took a step back as Strumbić clenched and un-clenched his fist. Strumbić looked around. There were other people in the office; besides, this man knew where he lived. If he threatened him or used force to get the keys, the police would be onto him pretty quickly. This might not have both-ered him ordinarily, but he'd shot three kids the previous night. It made him a little sensitive about calling attention to himself.

"Really, sir, I would love to help. I know you've had some problems with your apartment and now with your keys, but I assure you, come in on Monday and it will all be resolved."

"Do you have Harry's address and telephone number for home?"

"I'm sorry, sir, we can't give our staff's private details to cli-ents. I know it doesn't sound very helpful, but there's nothing I can do for you today. You really will just have to wait until Monday."

Strumbić knew there was no way around the problem. Or at least not immediately. He couldn't go to the bank and ask them to open a safety deposit box for him because, for one thing, he didn't have the key. And for another, they had his ID. But he wasn't going to let this pomaded, self-certain prick win out either. He left the office without another word.

Instead, he took a stroll around the block. Halfway up the street parallel to the agency, he saw the alley. He walked along as if he were meant to be there, past the Dumpsters and chained-up motorbikes, until he found what he was looking for: the back of the estate agents' offices. He went up to the door, gave it a slight push, took note of the lock. He looked at the bars on the windows and at the alarm box higher up. He wandered up and down the alley, having a good look at all the buildings, making mental notes the whole while.

And then, when he was satisfied, he wandered off to look for a new suit. Blue pinstripe. He rather liked the effect. Maybe he'd look for some cufflinks while he was at it.

Which was how the afternoon went. A handful of shops, interwoven with stops in the local pubs. The English were mean with their whisky, measuring it out to the last exact drop with an instrument better suited to a chemistry lab. But he liked the beer. And the atmosphere.

He came back from shopping laden. And mellowed. In one set of big green M&S bags, he carried a blue pinstriped suit and a dark grey suit. And in a generic yellow plastic bag, a boiler suit. He dropped the business suits off in the hotel room and got dressed in the universal workingman's uniform, slung a bag of tools he'd picked up at a Soho hardware shop over his shoulder, and went wandering into the hotel's service areas looking for a ladder.

Fully equipped, he went out the hotel's back entrance and made his way through the Piccadilly crowds, his labourer's clothes granting him instant invisibility, to the alley behind the estate agents'. It was as empty as it had been earlier.

He propped the ladder up against the back wall and secured its feet with a heavy lump of concrete that was probably used to hold open self-closing fire doors. The back of every office building had one. The ladder wasn't quite as long as he'd hoped, but the alarm box was fixed fairly low on the wall and he could just reach it. The unit was sealed to prevent it from being disabled. But with a bit of muscle power and the aid of a crowbar, he managed to lever a small opening in the case. He sprayed the contents of a can of insulating foam into the box until it leaked out. Then, with red electrical tape, he covered the alarm light as neatly as he could. Of course, it was possible the alarm was linked to the local police station. But even if it was, they'd send a cop round and when he didn't see a flashing light or hear a deafening clanging, he'd probably just shrug it off. He would if he was like any of the cops who'd worked for Strumbić.

Strumbić got down and slid the ladder behind some rubbish bins before admiring his handiwork. Unless they looked hard, they wouldn't be able to tell there was anything funny about the alarm light. And the damage to the box was negligible.

The question now was how he was going to get in. The windows were all barred. The back door was metal with a metal frame built around it. But there was enough of a gap to get a sharp edge in where the latch was. It was crude, but a good push with a crowbar would snap the emergency lever on the inside and pop the door open. He'd be able to use the same method on the interior doors as well.

With the crowbar hidden behind a Dumpster alongside the rest of the tools, Strumbić headed off to find something to eat.

He found a steak restaurant in Soho. It looked like a bordello, furnished almost exclusively in red velvet, and was almost completely empty even though the street outside was heaving with tourists, drunks, locals, freaks. The whole world was there.

Strumbić took a window seat, from which he watched a couple of black women standing against a wall slightly apart from each other on the opposite side of the road. They were engaged in a running conversation broken frequently by comments to passing punters and the occasional thigh-slapping laugh. They were tall, built like Amazons, huge chests and bottoms stretching their tight leather skirts. The whole while they watched him watching them, giving him beaming smiles. As he finished his well-done rib-eye and baked potato, he threw them a wolfish look and they sauntered across the road. They joined him in his booth by the window. The restaurant's management didn't seem to mind.

"You looking like you could use some company, honey."

"You could get two for the price of one, tonight only, honey. Aren't you going to offer us a drink?"

"What you want to drink?" he asked in his cartoon accent.

"Oh, you foreign."

"Where you from?"

"Russia."

"Russia. We love Russia." One of them called the bored waiter over. "Three black Russians for us, honey."

"Anything else?" the waiter asked.

"Three more," said the other Amazon. "Our white Russia friend love black Russians. So long as the black don't be rushin' too much. Honey, we be nice and gentle and slow."

They threw themselves into a conversation Strumbić understood only half of, maybe less once he'd downed the cocktails. But there was no confusing the message on either side. He had time. He wouldn't go back to the estate agency until later. He had a whole evening to kill. All that was left was to negotiate a price for two hours and all the frills.

As a cop, he knew the risks of being rolled by prostitutes when the punter took on more than one. It wasn't so much the women who represented the risk but the fact that one could keep him occupied while the other opened the door for the pimp, who'd usually come in packing a gun. But he was confident the hotel would do a good job of keeping out any unsavoury characters. Other than the ones brought in by guests. Besides, he'd hidden most of his money, only keeping handy enough to have a good time.

"You one rich Russian," the taller, more buxom one said as she wandered through his bedroom suite.

The other one cracked open the bottle of champagne from

the mini-bar fridge. Strumbić sat on the sofa drinking the fizzy wine as they danced for him to music with an electronic beat piped in through the hotel system. One then pulled his shoes and socks off as the other did a striptease, exposing her pneumatic chest. The girls were down to their leather skirts, dancing, kissing each other, when he decided to join the fun. He got behind one, pulled her skirt up, and pulled down on her thong, reaching around.

He wished he hadn't. For a moment, he was confused. Very confused. He knew what it was but not why it was there. He jumped back as if it'd bit him. He'd been feeling up a man. Through his horror, all he could think of was getting hold of the Beretta, which was hanging up under his jacket in the cupboard.

He flew into a rage, but before he could do anything he regretted, the transvestite hookers did something he'd never have expected in ten lifetimes.

They apologized.

"We sorry, man. We thought you looking for our type of fun. Hanging in Soho in a boiler suit, we thought you gay. We don't be charging you. Be cool and have a good night."

They were big. Much taller than him and, he saw now, muscled. But they held their hands up and made to leave, as if it had all been a misunderstanding. He hadn't even shown them the gun.

Strumbić didn't hold grudges. And he could see the funny side of things. They were so solicitous of his feelings, blaming themselves for not making it clearer what was happening, that their regret shone through even his poor English and their West Indian accents. He'd never seen or heard anything of the sort. Normally, outraged punters get beaten up by the transvestites, who then clean him out. Or the transvestite demands the agreed-on fee and ends up getting shot or bludgeoned.

But never, ever had he heard of an amicable apology and

willingness to go without payment, or even to find someone who might suit him better so that they could all party together.

Which was what they did. One went down to the hotel bar and picked up a couple of normal, good-looking hookers. And they all had a party. They ordered more booze—much more booze. One of the real girls had some decent white powder, whatever it was. He paid for the lot. It wasn't a cheap night, though he wasn't exactly sure quite how expensive. Didn't matter. This was exactly why he wanted to move to London. To do stuff he couldn't even begin to imagine doing in Zagreb.

It all went so far beyond the realm of what he'd thought possible that he wondered whether he'd borrowed someone else's imagination. Some very strange, very perverse, very creative artist of the impossibly degenerate.

As a young cop, he'd heard stories of Weimar from a retired old detective who'd spent his own youth in Germany. He and the other rookies had laughed at the detective's improbable stories, buying the toothless old man drink after drink as a reward for his concupiscent flights of fancy. About how you could buy three generations of prostitutes from the same family. Or how there were specialized alleys in Berlin for all sorts of perversions. One for female amputees. Another for male ones. One for women who'd do it with animals. How money could buy anything. Never in Zagreb had Strumbić run into more than the smallest corner of the kind of perversity the old man described.

But it now dawned on him: the veteran hadn't made anything up.

Strumbić didn't mind that the transvestites spent much of the evening searching for his money when they thought he wasn't looking. He'd expected no less. They looked everywhere. They tried to pull up the carpet. They checked the curtain rail and the turn-ups of the curtains. They looked in the toilet cistern. They looked through every drawer and under the mattress.

He'd left the room safe open, sparing them the trouble. They took the backs off the telephone and the television. He knew because they'd put them back without tightening the screws. They checked his shaving cream to see if it was fake and they just about ripped his suitcase apart, pretending to play some game with it. All they found was the money he'd allocated for the evening. And the Beretta, which didn't seem to surprise them. It amused him how thorough they were. They showed him grudging respect.

He let them stay until he wanted to leave for the estate agency, which was probably a mistake. It amused them so much that he was putting the blue overalls back on to go out that they followed him: two black transvestites, a couple of ordinary prostitutes, and a pimp who tagged along when he saw them leaving the hotel.

Strumbić was relaxed and happy, having partied harder than he'd ever partied before. Whatever it was that had gone up his nose made him feel sharp and alive, while the endless booze gave him a warm feeling towards his companions. Encouraged by his entourage, he bought a few bottles of whisky from an off-licence that opened illegally after hours to customers willing to pay double the normal price. It was shut at the front, but round back there was a queue of punters placing their orders through a barred window.

At first, Strumbić tried to fob off his new friends with the booze, but they had marked him like lawyers latched on to a rich man's corpse. Drinking normally made him relax, and he'd compensate by being extra vigilant. But there was something else involved here, the euphoria of total freedom. It made him indiscreet. And his new friends wanted to help.

So all six of them broke into the estate agency.

35

ANZULOVIĆ WAS STILL stiff. He had a feeling his back would never properly straighten again. The hotel mattress was even less comfortable than the Merc's seat after an overnight drive. A broken fan belt en route had delayed them. It seemed the Zagreb mechanic who'd serviced their car had used second-hand spares.

They'd arrived in London late, and he and Messar had found a budget hotel well outside of central London, taken a room with twin beds, and thrown themselves into a snoring competition. Now and again one would wake up the other to tell him to shut up, but mostly they were unconscious. Neither had slept much during their marathon drive through Italy and France.

They drove back into the centre mid-morning, not quite believing how much traffic there could be on a Sunday. Anzulović was sure their trip would be wasted. Who worked Sunday mornings? But Messar insisted. And he was right.

They found a pretty young man guarding the agency door while police and various other people wandered around inside.

"We look man here — Strumbić," Anzulović struggled to say. He was hopeless with the language, constantly fishing for words with a rusty hook that had lost its bait.

"Sorry, I can't help you. We're shut. We had a break-in last night, and we've got a real mess to clear up." Anzulović nodded as if he understood. "They went for the keys, though I shouldn't be telling you that. They had a party here as well; Smirnoff bottles all over the place. I dread to think what else we might find. Very clever, they were. Disabled the alarm system before they broke in. Filled the box with foam and put tape around the light. Seemed to know what they were doing." The pomaded young man had been put on the door to keep people at bay. He seemed happy to have somebody to tell the salacious details to.

Anzulović thought he'd maybe understood one word in four. "My English, not good. Someone speak here . . . *Italiano?*"

"Italian, no, I'm afraid not. I mean, Harry does, but I haven't seen her yet. She'll probably put in an appearance. All the agents are, it's such a mess."

"*Hrvat?*"

"What's that? *Cravat*, did you say?"

"You speak Russian?"

"Nope. I've got German and French, though, if either of those work for you."

"Cherman—*Deutsche?*" Messar interjected, understanding the gist of the conversation and then latching on to one of the only words he recognized.

"Is this better?" The young man switched into a singsong Swiss German.

"Yes. Looks like you have some problems here," Messar said, taking over from a relieved Anzulović, who had only schoolboy German.

"A break-in overnight. It looked professionally done, but then they had a party in the office. They left the place a pigsty. What they did in the rubbish bins! I had to go out back and throw up. Who knows what they took, besides enough keys to unlock half of London. The rich half. We have to spend the morning calling owners. It's an absolute nightmare."

"I'm sorry to hear it. We're looking for a man who has dealings with you. His name is Strumbić."

The young man shook his head. "Nothing I recognize, but I'll ask around the office if you like."

"He might be using another name. I have a picture of him here." Messar pulled an official ID photo out of his briefcase.

"Oh yes. That's Mr. . . . the name's on the tip of my tongue . . . Mr. Smirnoff. Smirnoff, that's it," he said, his voice trailing off, looking back towards the bottles stacked on a desk, where they'd been cleared off the floor. "Like the vodka."

"Do you know anything about him?"

The young man had a faraway look and then a sense of dawning realization. "You know, if I was at all a suspicious sort, I'd say it was that bastard," he muttered in a low voice, still speaking German. And then to Messar, "Yes, he was here yesterday morning. Very rude and very insistent. I had a feeling that if there hadn't been other people in the office, he'd have had fun knocking my teeth out."

"Sounds like him. What did he want?"

"His keys. He said he'd lost them and wanted the spare set we keep for him."

"Keys for what?"

"His apartment."

"He has an apartment in London?"

"Yes, in Hampstead. A very nice one, apparently."

"And he didn't have keys?"

"No."

"Did you give them to him?"

"No. He didn't have any ID on him and said he needed the keys to get it. Some story about his passport being in a bank safety deposit box. I shouldn't really be telling you all this, but he was such a bastard. Sorry, you're not friends of his, are you?"

"No, we're not friends."

"Good. I didn't think so. You won't tell anyone I told you, will you?"

"Not at all," said Messar, showing his teeth the way a shark might. "So where exactly is his place?"

"Really, I can't tell you that. His keys seem to have disappeared with some of the others. I just can't tell you where he lives. That would be wrong. Who knows who you are? I mean, you could be some tax collectors or mafia or something." He caught Messar's smile. He held up his finger and ducked into the office, coming out with a clipboard fat with papers. After a moment's searching, he added, "Besides, we need to send someone to the Pryors on East Heath Road, apartment 4D, first, just to make sure everything is okay."

"East Heath Road, you say," Messar said, noting the address down in his little notebook.

"Oh, I didn't say that. I didn't say anything."

"Well, thank you very much for not talking to us."

"Thank you for not listening... And whatever you do to the bastard, just make sure it hurts," he added as the UDBA men left.

.   .   .

The pretty dyed-blond nurse got della Torre a newspaper in the morning because, she said, he didn't watch television and you could never tell how long it would take to be discharged. A doctor had to see him first, another urologist, and he'd fill out a prescription, and then it would take time to get that filled by the hospital pharmacy, so he could find himself waiting until the middle of the afternoon before he got to go home. So she'd taken the liberty of borrowing one of the consultant's Sundays because he was too busy to read it anyway and it's a pretty day to go for a walk on the Heath.

He thanked her for the newspaper. It helped to distract him from the cardboard-tasting breakfast and the coffee that somehow managed to be at once acrid and bland.

There was a report that Croatia and Slovenia would declare independence in the next couple of days, though it wasn't yet a certainty. The Yugoslav army had made it clear that it would respond to any such gesture. He tried to believe that he could stay out of it. Avoid it somehow.

But it was like watching a brush fire in the distance while surrounded by stands of dry eucalyptus with the wind blowing in his direction. He could smell the inevitability even though it still seemed impossibly remote. It was funny to think he was more afraid of going to America than he was of heading back into that conflagration. Or maybe that wasn't so funny.

A story about a shooting on a train in south London caught his eye. Some teenage muggers had been wounded by their intended victim. The boys Irena's man had treated, della Torre supposed. There was a pen portrait of the shooter, an anonymous face that looked familiar because it could have belonged to almost any stodgy middle-aged man in a suit. England's Bernie Goetz, the newspaper said. Good for him, della Torre thought.

36

STRUMBIĆ SHOWERED, SHAVED, and dressed. Eagerness to be getting to his place woke him early. Not so early that Mrs Strumbić wouldn't have had time to do her ironing, cook a stew, make a strudel, and still berate him over his indolence. But early for someone who'd had the sort of night he'd had.

He was thinking of Mrs. Strumbić altogether too much for his liking. But she kept popping up in his mind with her damned dustpan and brush. And she made awfully nice strudels.

But she couldn't match the English for breakfast. While he was in the shower, they'd delivered proper hangover food: eggs, bacon, fried bread and mushrooms, beans, tomatoes.

He felt the keys in his pocket and laughed. He'd had harder times getting into cigarette cartons than he had breaking into that estate agency.

He'd popped the back door, the alarm not making a peep. Once inside he'd made a beeline for the cabinet, opened it with the crowbar, found his file, and got his keys. The trannies loved that cabinet. All those keys to all those expensive houses, addresses conveniently attached.

They partied in that office. But only in a mellow way.

They didn't destroy anything wantonly. Just took some keys

and mixed the others up. Spilt a bit of booze. Made some long-distance phone calls. One of the trannies spent most of the night on the line to relations in Trinidad. They drank, sitting in those plush chairs, feet up on desks. They only switched one desk light on. Nobody passing on the street looked in. When they needed to, they pissed in a wastepaper bin. Strumbić was pretty sure that's all they had done.

There were fond farewells for the trannies, who'd seemed pleased with their haul of keys. He laughed. If there was any-thing worth finding in those houses, the trannies would find it. He'd been tempted to go straight up to Hampstead. But his money and things were back at the hotel, and by the time he got back, the evening had caught up with him.

After he'd eaten and sorted himself out the following mor-ning, he went into the hall outside his hotel room and waited, making sure no one was coming or likely to be leaving their room and that the maids weren't around. When he was con-fident, he carefully extracted the pin that held shut the glass emergency door to the cupboard holding the fire hose and pulled his money out from between its loops. *One day there'll be a fire. And then*, he reflected, *I'll be out of luck. But not this time.* He felt the fat stack of large-denomination notes, British and German, and thought about how very much more was waiting for him at his bank, even after its recent pilfering.

He looked forward to getting to the apartment. For a while it had seemed the whole world was conspiring against him, enjoying the fruits of his hard work. Messar keeping an eye on him. Those bastard Bosnians threatening to kill him. Mrs. Strumbić would have given him an infarction had he spent any more time at home. Bloody Branko for not keeping up with the mail, though he couldn't blame the poor man too much. Those prick kids on the train. The estate agents.

It made him feel like a superman, surmounting impossible odds.

He flagged down a black cab in Piccadilly Circus and enjoyed the ride through Regent's Park and then up the hill to Hampstead and from there to the Heath. They passed a car that looked uncannily like a green Zastava, but Strumbić corrected himself. Surely he was mistaken. Why would anyone in the civilized world ever want to drive one of those junk heaps?

He looked forward to his new life. But when he got to the flat, he was perplexed.

The key fit. The place was as he'd remembered it. Only it seemed to be lived in. The food in the fridge wasn't the spare essentials the estate agent was in the habit of leaving for him. It was bits and halves and some things that needed throwing out. Then there were the clothes, mostly women's, but some men's as well. He could have asked the porter, but he'd already told the man to mind his own business if he knew what was good for him.

His flat. All the stuff he'd rented off that woman agent — books, furniture, curtains, dishes, everything. And things he hadn't.

The drinks cabinet in the apartment was well stocked, at least. Whoever's booze it was. He pulled out a three-quarters-full bottle of whisky and turned on the television. He clicked off the Beretta's safety and then put the gun on the arm of the sofa and sat down. To wait.

.   .   .

Della Torre walked back to the apartment. It felt good to be alive and pain-free. In the end it had taken longer than he'd expected to get signed out. And then there was another wait while the hospital pharmacy filled his prescription for painkillers he no longer needed.

He'd been astonished at how leisurely the process of leaving the hospital had been. It was already late afternoon. He'd have to hurry if he was to get home, shower, and change, and make it up to Irena's place on time. But first he needed a real coffee, not the stewed dishrag they served at the hospital, and a cigarette. He'd take a taxi; he could afford it.

He'd dressed in what he'd been wearing the previous night. No, the night before that. Harry hadn't brought him a change of clothes. Working the silver cufflinks through the holes in his folded French cuffs, he'd thought of Harry picking them out in that shop on Bond Street. He buttoned the top button on his white shirt and knotted the blue-on-blue Italian tie. He'd had it cleaned, but it was looking tired, old. Like him. There was more white in his hair than he remembered; there were new creases in the corners of his eyes.

It was a lovely, sunny afternoon. People were being dragged onto the Heath by their dogs or their children or sometimes both, wistfully clinging to their Sunday papers, though it was too late to be reading them now. Soon they'd be on to Monday's news.

Opposite the pub with a big beer garden, the gravel parking lot was full, and the traffic was slow on narrow East Heath Road. Normally he'd go through the Heath, up a long meadow to the apartment building, or maybe take a little circuit through the woods, but this time he took a more direct route on the pavement along the road. He wanted to get back and wash away the hospital feeling that coated him.

He noticed a green Zastava further up the hill. Or he thought it was a Zastava, though it might have been another boxy imitation of an ancient, slightly less boxy Fiat. It was hard to tell with the police van right behind it obscuring his view.

A Zastava in London? Almost as bizarre as a good-looking woman choosing to drive around a 2CV that looked like a circus tent. Surely she could have afforded something else.

Still, he knew that eccentric collectors had bought East German Trabants after the Berlin Wall had fallen. Maybe they

were doing the same with other near-useless cars from the rest
of the old Communist bloc. He couldn't see it ever being anything other than a minority pursuit. Maybe Harry'd buy one.

He wondered whether he'd see her at home. The thought
that he'd frightened her away, chased her out of his life, depressed him. But it shouldn't have surprised him. The UDBA
cast an ugly black shadow, even here.

.   .   .

"How many times we going to drive up and down this road? I
knew we should have got the exact address out of him," said
Besim in the odd, snuffling way he talked these days. The
banana-shaped Bosnian next to him was pretty sure it had to
do with the car accident, what with Besim's having had his
nose smashed and losing the whole front row of his top teeth.
But it might have been a cold.

"It's that building in the middle, halfway up, I'm sure of it."

"So why we driving up and down, then?"

"Maybe we'll spot him faster than if we just walk around."

They'd arrived the previous morning. The first hour or so,
they drove up and down that hill road, and then they decided
to walk it. There were houses on one side. They looked for
names next to the buzzers, but the English didn't seem to like
people knowing where they lived.

They found a corner store and bought salami and bread
and a couple of cans of beer, ate in the park, and then went
back to their scouting. The beer helped, so they bought some
more, getting merry by late afternoon. They drove up and
down a few more times, though Besim said that he'd heard
something about how the English stopped people for driving after they'd been drinking. He knew about these things.
The banana-shaped one said he couldn't have had too much
to drink, because he could still drive. Besim agreed, but they

left the car near the bottom of the Heath anyway and bought some more beers.

They wandered around the park for a while. Growing up in the Bosnian hills, they were good at orienting themselves in woodland. They just strolled and drank until it got dark, when they found a little clearing in the middle of dense undergrowth that was canopied by big trees. Including a hollow one.

"You could fit somebody in this thing," the banana-shaped one had said, running his hand along a smooth vertical cleft in the wood, around waist-high and only wide enough to take his fingers and only a hand's-breadth long.

"Get a dolly bird in there, you could have some fun without having to look at her," Besim snuffled.

"Why wouldn't you want to look at her?"

"I don't know, if she was ugly or something."

The banana-shaped one nodded. It was certainly a big hollow, right through the middle of the ancient tree. Apart from that narrow vertical cleft and a small hole towards the bottom, the only entrance was through the top, about two metres off the ground, though the tree's protruding roots made something of a ladder.

They'd spent a good night there. They hadn't even thought of looking for a hotel. Though there were odd squealing and grunting noises throughout the night. Besim thought it might have been wild pigs. The banana-shaped one wasn't so sure.

"How long you think it'll take us to find Strumbić?" asked the banana-shaped one as Besim drove up the hill for the... he'd lost count. It must have been a couple of dozen times at least. They'd spent the morning walking around the woods before taking to the car, but had been driving around in it since.

"Till we find him. Not so bad here," said Besim.

The weather wasn't too hot during the day and not too cold at night. Food was decent, if expensive. And the park was homey. They'd even found a shelter, like an open-sided cottage, that looked like it would be comfortable if it started to rain. There were signs a tramp was living there, but the Bosnians figured he'd be easy to move along if it came to that.

"Nice-looking women in London."

"Not bad."

"Nice-looking."

They were heading up the hill when the banana-shaped one caught sight of a very familiar-looking pedestrian going in the same direction.

"Hey, slow down," he said.

"Can't. Bastard cop's on my ass," Besim said, looking in the rear-view mirror.

"Then pull into one of the side roads. I'm seeing somebody that looks like the prick who pushed me off that cliff. You know, that guy in Zagreb we were supposed to do."

"Yeah? Think he knows where to find Strumbić?"

THE SMELL OF cigarette smoke should have alerted della Torre. He unlocked the door and then back-heeled it shut, hoping to catch sight of Harry. He was in the sitting room before he noticed Strumbić sitting on the sofa, gun in hand and a bottle of whisky on the coffee table in front of him.

"Gringo? I should have known it'd be you." Strumbić raised the gun a little, as if to make clear it wasn't just for show. Otherwise he didn't move. Della Torre stood stock still, wondering whether he might be able to run before Strumbić shot him. He decided that was unlikely. So he smiled instead.

"I wondered what idiot leaves a Beretta on the middle of a bed, where it's not even good as a paperweight. Only you," Strumbić said.

"Julius, what a pleasant surprise."

"Zip it. It's not pleasant for either of us, and I'm the only one who's got a right to be surprised. Sit down." He waved his gun towards the facing sofa.

"Mind if I use the facilities first? Doctors told me to piss as much as I can."

"I'll join you," Strumbić said, standing up.

Strumbić kept the gun pointed at della Torre's back as he

used the toilet. Strumbić stood on a low footstool and relieved himself in the sink.

Back in the sitting room, della Torre sat opposite Strumbić and poured himself the remaining finger of whisky from the bottle.

"So you ran with my money, my car, and my keys and then decided to pitch up in my apartment. You and Irena, eh? Didn't know she had so many clothes. Where is she now?"

Della Torre saw Strumbić's confusion but didn't disabuse him. Irena had been clear: she wouldn't be coming to the flat. Whereas if Harry did, Strumbić might not connect her with him.

"At work. She works at the hospital."

"Nice and homey. And you're the ones who've been draining my account. How did you work that one? Kickbacks to the estate agent?"

"No, I said you were my cousin. I was staying here, and you wanted some money moved from your account to another one, but it had to be done discreetly, for tax reasons."

"And she swallowed that?"

"She got it in writing."

"From you?"

"No, from Mr. Smirnoff."

"Me?"

"Remember all those times you asked me to sign off for you on reports because you were otherwise engaged? Did you really forget I learned your signature?" Della Torre was thinking fast. "You didn't change it when you changed your name. Works with the bank, works with the estate agents. The girl had nothing to do with it except organize some friendly builders to send cost invoices. For a small fee."

"Hmm." Strumbić nodded. He appreciated well-constructed scams, though maybe not so much when he was the mark.

"You should take more care next time."

"Thanks for the advice." Strumbić didn't sound thankful.

"Hey, what are friends for?"

"So now you owe me fifteen thousand Deutschmarks and thirty thousand pounds, unless you've taken more out of the account. I haven't been able to check yet. Not to mention three months' rent on this place. What do you think? Another three thousand pounds?"

"You owed me some money out of that fifteen thousand Deutschmarks."

"Oh yeah, that's right. How much was it? Four thousand?"

"Eight."

"Liar."

"Worth trying."

"So, you going to pay up?"

"Will you take a cheque?"

"No. Cash. And blood."

"You'll make a mess of the apartment."

"I wasn't thinking of doing it in the apartment. There's a great big wood out there. People letting off fireworks all the time."

"In the daylight?"

"We'll wait. Maybe Irena can join you."

"She works through the night."

"Lucky her. She'll live a whole day longer than you. But first she'll get me my money. I don't trust you."

"Don't you think they'll trace a couple of bodies back to this place when they pop up? You can't bury anyone deep enough in that park to keep the dogs off. And some fisherman would hook any corpse dropped in the ponds."

"Yeah. You know, you're right. It'll just have to be a suicide."

"Suicide?"

"Overtaken by remorse, they'll say."

"What, for stealing from you?"

"No. You'll shoot yourself with a gun that's already been used on a couple of kids," said Strumbić.

That's why the artist's impression in the newspaper had looked so familiar. Della Torre could have kicked himself.

"Oh. I see. You mean, the guy who shot some teenage muggers on the train decides on the only honourable way out?"

"Hey, smart guy. How'd you know?"

"I read the papers. There's a nice Etch A Sketch of you in them."

"Etch A what?"

"A drawing. How about the people who'll recognize me from this building? They'll come back to this flat, and then where will you be? You look a lot more like you than I do."

"All the cops will recognize is the gun. Your face won't look so pretty as it does now. But they'll be able to match the gun and that'll make them very happy. Handy, you leaving me a replacement here."

"Think nothing of it."

"Done."

"And Irena?" Della Torre asked, grateful that she had her own place. On the other hand, he worried about Harry.

"If she gets back tonight, I'll give you short odds on murder-suicide. Otherwise, poor distraught woman will throw herself in front of a train or something. Killer husband takes his own life. What would you do if you were in her shoes? Distraught, humiliated, horrified, nothing left to live for."

"Did you read that one in a book?"

"No, death report. About five years back."

"I must have missed that one."

"Not a lot of publicity. The husband was a cop."

"And when they trace us back to this apartment? You might want to think it through again. Maybe it'd just be easier to ask for the money back and let us disappear into the night. After all, we kept the place lived in for you."

The telephone rang. Both men stared at it. Strumbić finally picked it up.

"Hello," he said with his heavy English vowels.

"Yes, is Stru... Smirnoff. Yes... No. Is fine... Yes... No one... No... We talk soon about building works... Is fine... I understand... No, is fine... Cousin told me all about... Was confusion, now is fine... I call in week."

He put the phone down, reverting back to Croat.

"The estate agent. She seemed to be surprised it was me. I guess she was looking for you, to tell you somebody had stolen their spare keys to the apartment. Very bad of that someone. The world is full of dishonest people," Strumbić said.

"I guess it is."

"She and I will have our conversation later in the week. She may not be my agent much longer. For one thing, her agency's security is too lax for my liking. And I've decided I don't like the furnishings that much either. I'll get my own."

Della Torre reached forward for one of Strumbić's Lucky Strikes on the coffee table.

"So the old man in Zagreb who hired the Bosnians left you alone."

"Your UDBA friends were so far up my ass nobody else could get a look in."

"What happened to the Bosnians?"

"Fucking Bosnians. I'm going to rip their throats out if I ever see them again. Good thing for them they're too stupid to make their way to London. Don't think they let clowns like that in the country."

"You know, you start shooting people, killing people, ripping their throats out, and pretty soon you're not going to be welcome in England. This is a pretty peaceable place," della Torre said.

"This country's a dump. But at least they know how to party."

"I'm just saying, Julius, you might not want to go spreading too much mayhem if you're really intent on becoming the English gentleman I know you are deep down inside," della

Torre said. "I mean, look at that suit of yours. What is it? Marks & Spencer?"

"Only the best will do."

"Did you get the three-for-the-price-of-two deal?"

Strumbić wasn't one to spend too much time talking about clothes. He contemplated della Torre with an appraising eye.

"You know, Gringo, I've always been fond of you. That's why I kept buying those crap files off you. Charity. So you could eat, have a few luxuries. But frankly, you took advantage. You really took advantage, and I had to get a bit of return on my investment. I'm sorry I stole those files, but what's done is done. Anyway, if you hadn't tried to screw me you could be clear by now. With the war kicking off, the UDBA aren't going to bother with you much longer. You probably don't even know the favour I did you in Venice."

"Favour?"

"Yeah, favour. You'd jumped a boat in Piran and UDBA had a reception lined up for you in Venice. Except I made sure Branko got to you first. Packed you off on a train, he said."

"Don't tell me. An ex-cop."

"He got into a slightly sticky situation in a deal we were doing with the Macedonian mob about ten years ago. Had to leave sharpish. He does a little freelance work for me still."

"How come he's in Mestre then, and you're not?"

"Well, you see, not everyone's clever."

"Send him my regards."

"He's down a leg. Not going to be much use to anyone soon. Still, he's as faithful as an old dog."

"Another legless old cop."

"That's not funny."

"And being told you're going to be shot in the face as soon as it gets dark is?"

"I'll make sure it hurts as much as my shin did," said Strumbić, rubbing his leg.

"So how'd you get out of the cellar so quickly? Did your girl-friend find you? Or was it your wife?"

"I used matches and an iron bar. You shouldn't have left me the cuff keys. Or you should have shot me in both legs. By the way, you also owe me three cartons of Luckys."

"You'll have to get one off Anzulović."

"He's not so bad," Strumbić said, rubbing his chin. "But that bastard Messar that works for him... How much does Anzulović know about what happened that night, by the way?"

"As much as I do."

"About the files, the Dispatcher?"

"Everything. Didn't he tell you?"

"Might have done. But I wondered how much he was guessing."

The buzzer sounded. There was an intercom down to the main entrance. The porter would call visitors up.

"Expecting anyone?" asked Strumbić.

Della Torre shook his head.

The buzzer went again.

"Want me to answer?" asked della Torre.

"Leave it."

"Won't the porter know we're here?"

"And? If I don't want to answer, he'll know to tell whoever it is to piss off," said Strumbić. He made as if he didn't care. But he'd sat forward on the sofa, suddenly alert.

"There's something else I meant to ask you. You didn't drive here in a green Zastava, did you?" della Torre asked.

"Never touch the stuff. Why?"

"I thought I saw one drive past."

"A green Zastava, you say? Funny, thought I saw one too," Strumbić said, frowning.

"Maybe it's fashionable."

"A Zastava, fashionable? Not even in Albania."

"You're right. Some things are never fashionable anywhere.

Like being middle-aged and fat," said della Torre, on careful consideration. "I'm hungry. There anything to eat?"

"You'd know better than me, seeing as you filled the fridge."

"Mind if I fix a sandwich?"

"Go ahead. But if you come at me with a knife or a frying pan, you're a dead man."

"You remember the frying pan story?"

"How could I not? I'm the one who had to warn off the old bag who tried to kill you with it."

"I forgot."

"Still got it?"

"Only thing I ever cook with. At home, that is. A sort of memento mori."

"Latin, never my strong subject."

"What was?"

"Making money."

"A useful talent. Wish I had it," della Torre said. "So how'd you get away?" He was in the kitchen, pouring himself a glass of beer, Strumbić standing in the doorway behind him.

"Told them I was going to Italy on an art tour. What do you think? I just buggered off. They've organized the police into battalions. Minute I came off sick leave, they were putting me in one. Fuck that. So I fixed up a hire car in Trieste and then snuck my way over. I left a note saying I needed to find myself; my karma was bad and the feng shui would be better somewhere else."

"Feng what?"

"Something my bimbo was reading in one of her magazines. All about being calm and not sleeping in a boneyard or over a shithouse. Or something."

Della Torre laughed. "I could almost see you writing it. If you were literate."

The buzzer sounded again. And again they ignored it.

"Somebody really wants to say hello," said della Torre.

"Tough. Say, there's a back exit, isn't there?"

"I thought you owned this place."

"I do, I just haven't spent any time here."

"There is a door, but you use it and the fire alarms go off."

"You mean they take the rubbish out the front?"

"No, they've got a way out through the plant room."

"Well, that's what I mean."

"Down the service elevator at the back. What are you doing?"

"I'd like to have a look to see who's wanting so badly to say hello."

"Yes? And I come with you?"

"No."

"So what happens to me, then?"

"Either I knock you out or I tie you up. Or both. I feel like knocking you out," Strumbić said, with too much relish in his voice for della Torre's liking.

"Hit me too hard and you'll kill me. Very hard to get rid of a body on your own."

"Thanks for the tip. You're right. I'll tie you up and then give you a good kicking."

"Why don't you just save the aggression for later? —I mean, when you're shooting me. It'll be a lot more satisfying then."

"You know, that's what I like about you, Gringo. Always helpful."

Strumbić wasn't gentle about how he tied della Torre up, using the tough nylon cord from the curtain pulls. He was thorough, precise, and didn't leave della Torre any opening to struggle. By the time Strumbić was finished, della Torre was trussed as expertly as if the Ancient Mariner had been tying the knots himself, wrists tied to ankles behind his back.

Della Torre tried as best he could to bear the pain like a man and hoped his hands and feet wouldn't gangrene.

"Want a gag?"

"Not really," said della Torre, trying to keep the tears out of his eyes.

"I'd love to say I trust you not to yell, but I don't. Can you breathe out your nose?"

"Yes."

"Doesn't matter anyway. I'll be back before your hands fall off. If I'm not, you'll have a new nickname. Stumpy."

"Mmmm," della Torre moaned through his gag as he struggled to find a comfortable position on the living room floor. There wasn't a hope in hell. Nor was there any chance of getting to a sharp object that he might use to saw through the cords. Strumbić was too smart for that. He'd tied him to the radiator.

Della Torre waited. He counted seconds at first. His heartbeat. His breaths. He tried thinking pleasant thoughts to get his mind off his shoulders, thighs, and back. Momentarily he was hopeful. If he couldn't walk, Strumbić wouldn't be able to get him onto the Heath to shoot him. But then his spirits sank. Strumbić would just throttle him in the flat and work out some other way of getting rid of the corpse. Besides, della Torre found it hard to be positive when he was in so much pain.

The telephone rang. It rang on and off—for how long, della Torre couldn't tell.

Strumbić's quick trip to see who was taking an interest was becoming endless. The afternoon light crawled along the floor of the flat and then up the opposite wall. At least he hadn't had the sun in his eyes, della Torre thought, reflecting on the victims of the Apaches who'd been staked out on their backs in the open desert, face up, with their eyelids cut off so they couldn't blink. *Nothing like reflecting on somebody worse off to make you feel better*, della Torre thought. Only it didn't work.

He'd developed so many cramps and his hands and feet were feeling such crushing pain from lack of blood flow, that he started looking forward to Strumbić getting back and shooting him. He was trying to remember if the kidney stone pain was as bad. Couldn't have been. Nothing could be. It felt like hours, though he knew it hadn't been that long. Thirty, forty minutes from when Strumbić had left?

He almost wept with relief when he heard the key at the door. The coffee table blocked his view and he couldn't see Strumbić come in, but he was willing the bastard to be quick. Why was he taking so goddamn long?

"Marko. I didn't see you down there." The voice he heard wasn't Strumbić's.

Harry used a kitchen knife to cut him free. For the first few minutes all he could do was suck air and try not to scream with the explosion of pain as blood recirculated through his hands and feet.

"Strumbić. Careful, he'll be back anytime."

"I don't think so."

"Why the hell not?" della Torre asked through parched lips, his jaw barely functioning better than his useless limbs.

"I was outside on a bench. I wanted to see what was happening but I didn't want to come in. I rushed home from work after I called here. Somebody had broken in. A colleague finally tracked me down at my mother's."

"Slow down."

"I came back and sat on a bench outside, watching the building. I saw Strumbić come out. A couple of guys got to him really quickly. I think they had guns. They walked him into the woods."

"Shit. What'd they look like?"

"One was pretty tall and sort of bent to one side. The other one was shorter, looked like a boxer. He didn't seem to have any front teeth."

The descriptions meant nothing to della Torre.

"Was either of them white and blond? And looked like he stepped out of a Nazi recruitment poster? I mean original Nazi, not neo-Nazi skinhead."

"No. But there were a couple of other guys, and one of them

looked like that. They followed the guys with Strumbić, I think."

"Which way did they go?"

"Down the path to the woods."

"Stay here. I mean, don't stay here. Get the hell out of here. Go back to your mother's or something. I'll get in touch. Stay the hell out of the woods, though."

Della Torre kissed her hard and fast and hobbled out of the flat as quickly as his near-crippled feet could take him. The door slammed behind him before he could hear Harry shout, "Your gun, Marko..."

STRUMBIĆ KNEW HE'D been stupid. Deeply stupid, because he thought he'd been so clever. Where'd he think they'd be, in the trees?

They'd got to him before he'd even noticed them. He'd been careful, waiting a long time by the back door before sneaking out of the building. He'd stayed hidden behind some big bushes until the stupid birds caught his attention, a squawking flock of green parakeets that belonged on the Heath about as much as the Bosnian holding a gun in the small of his back.

The other Bosnian relieved him of his Beretta.

"Nice to see you boys," he said. "Coincidence bumping into you in London."

"Heh, Besim. Say hello to Mr. Strumbić, who happens to owe us a lot of money. What a coincidence. Where's your friend from Zagreb?"

"Up in the apartment," Strumbić said. "Shall I take you up? We can have a beer and talk about the old days."

"We'll deal with him later. Right now it's Mr. Strumbić's turn," the banana-shaped Bosnian said. "We want our money."

"It's up in the apartment. Just back there. We can go up, I'll give you what I owe you, and we'll have a drink and a laugh.

What do you think?" Strumbić put on the sort of soothing, friendly tone that worked so well when he played good cop.

"How does that sound, eh, Besim? Mr. Strumbić wouldn't try to screw us, would he? He's a nice honest fellow, isn't he?" said the skinny, bent Bosnian. "Or maybe his friend will try to wrap his tie around your neck again, eh?"

Besim the driver pulled Strumbić's wallet out of his back pocket.

"Not bad. Must be about ten thousand Deutschmarks here. And about a thousand pounds," said the skinny one. Besim snuffled a laugh.

"That should make us square, boys," said Strumbić amiably. Besim was prodding him towards the woods while the talkative one walked beside him.

"We've got expenses to think about. London's not cheap. Then there's the funeral money for our dear cousin. And Besim could use some new teeth."

"Dear cousin... teeth," Besim repeated, whistling the words across his naked gums.

"Maybe we'll see what you've got back at the apartment later. Nice place, is it?" said the skinny one. "Maybe we can sort out the other guy too. Finish the contract, see what you've got up there."

"If you fellows are sore that I didn't let you in when you buzzed, it's a misunderstanding," Strumbić said.

The Bosnians stopped.

"Buzzed?" asked the talkative one.

"Yeah, just a little while ago. That was you, wasn't it?"

"No. We didn't know you lived there until we saw you prowling around."

"So you mean it's just bad luck that I bumped into you? That out of the whole of London you should find me here by chance?" Strumbić asked, incredulous. Had all the gods decided to piss on him at once?

"Naw. We had the name of the road you live on from that friend of yours in the hospital in Venice. Didn't get the address, though. We've been driving up and down the street since we got here yesterday. Long drive from Venice."

"Shit. I knew it was too much to expect Branko to keep his mouth shut. How'd you find him, by the way?"

"Pink Mercedes. Very easy to find. We had some friends keeping an eye on you in Zagreb, and then when you got on the bus, we followed you out. Almost fooled us when you got off in Rijeka, didn't he, Besim? Very sneaky of Mr. Strumbić, almost like he expected somebody to be following him. We got a bit muddled in Trieste, but there we were at a traffic light and who should pull up behind us in a pink Mercedes with no roof? You looked like you were driving a pair of lady's underpants. Fast, that car. We'd have lost you again, but we kept seeing the pink Mercedes. Saw you talking to your friend's landlady and then you disappeared again. Didn't matter." The Bosnian laughed silently. "Your friend's landlady took us to him. And he told us where you'd be."

Strumbić swore. Fucking pink Mercedes.

"You didn't do anything to the poor guy, did you?" he asked. "Though he probably deserved whatever it was."

"Not really. But he was legless when we left."

Besim laughed, a snuffling sort of laugh that sounded like a mastiff with a cold.

"So who was buzzing the flat, then?" Strumbić asked, more to himself than the Bosnians.

It was that changeover time for the Heath. Kids, young families, joggers, and dog-walkers were heading home, while men, single or in groups of two or three, made their furtive way into that pocket of wilderness.

Strumbić and the two Bosnians attracted no notice. They were in the shadows, following narrow tracks among the brambles, moving in single file. Strumbić knew he hadn't a hope in hell of making a run for it. These guys wouldn't think twice about making a sieve out of him.

Past the shrubbery and bushes they came into a beech wood, clear of undergrowth but canopied by high branches, last year's mast making a carpet for them. A woodpecker drilled away somewhere above. At one point a dog lolloped up to them, an overweight black Labrador. The talkative Bosnian turned his gun on it and for a moment Strumbić thought the dog had had it. But its owner called and it ambled off.

They crossed a broad path. There were a few people in the distance, but no one Strumbić could have begged mercy from. It was astounding how the park could absorb people and still seem empty.

"You boys seem to know where you're going," Strumbić said, a note of false bonhomie in his voice.

"So do you," said the talkative one.

"Do I?"

"Yup. Just here."

They'd gone up a little hill, all the while under the cover of the wood, except for when they'd skirted a hidden meadow the size of a country garden. They stopped at a big oak tree with a cleft in its trunk around waist height. The hole ran vertically for about half a metre, fat at the edges and widest at the middle, so that it looked like a vulva you could put your fist through.

"Okay, time to give us your keys," said the talkative one.

Strumbić raised his hands and gave a shrug as if to say *You can't be serious*.

"Keys. Or we'll have to shoot you first."

Strumbić got his keys out and handed them over.

"Isn't that nice. It's got the apartment number written down on the little tag," said the skinny, bent Bosnian. "Okay, now up the tree."

"You want me to climb the tree? Go up the tree?" Strumbić was puzzled. Did they want him to get as high as possible so they could shoot him down? Was this some strange Bosnian sport? He wouldn't put it past them. He'd heard of them planting victims head-first in the ground, feet up in the air. Alive.

"I hate to tell you boys, but this climb looks a bit challenging for a forty-a-day guy like me. It's been nearly twenty years since I got myself up a tree. And that was only to get into a girl's bedroom."

"Trunk's hollow. Get inside from the top. It opens just over your head."

"You want me in a hollow tree?"

"Sure. Easier than digging a grave."

"Oh. Thanks. A living coffin."

"Get on with it."

"And you shoot me through that hole, is that the game?"

"Yup. Besim might even let me have a few goes. What do you think, Besim?"

The toothless Bosnian shrugged.

"Up you get, or we'll have to shoot you first and then tip you in."

There really was nothing for it. Strumbić climbed the tree.

.   .   .

Anzulović couldn't quite believe his eyes. It couldn't have been anybody other than della Torre going into the building. Della Torre minus a moustache.

They'd staked it out, parking the Mercedes on a side street where they had a clear line of sight to its main entrance, and were waiting for Strumbić when della Torre showed up. He was inside before they could react.

"Looks like I was right: our friends are in this together. What do you think? Is Strumbić already in there? Do we say hello?" Messar smiled ironically. It irritated Anzulović.

"Give it a little while. See if they come out together. Or maybe Gringo's waiting for him," Anzulović replied curtly.

"It's nice that we'll be able to sew up all the loose threads in one go," Messar said.

"We'll wait to see what happens. We know Strumbić is in town. With just the two of us, we'll have to think about how to get them back."

"I was thinking in the trunk, in a couple of body bags, if they don't want to go in cuffs."

"Maybe that's a little drastic. I'm still not so sure they're the bosom buddies you think they are." Anzulović whistled a little tune that Messar didn't recognize. It was from *The Odd Couple*.

"I might check on them." Messar was impatient. It was unlikely that if they went back to Croatia they'd be able to send a team to pick up della Torre and Strumbić. They weren't even sure whether the UDBA would exist after Croatia declared independence, which, together with Slovenia, it threatened to do the following day.

Messar left the car and went into the building. He'd wanted to go up but the porter stopped him, so he buzzed the apartment instead. He came back to the car but didn't stay long before trying the apartment again.

"He's not answering. Think he knows it's us?" Messar asked.

"Maybe he's worried it's somebody else."

They waited. How long had it been since della Torre showed up? Almost two hours? It was getting on for early evening; they'd have to think of something soon.

A dish of a blond who got out of a taxi by the building and then went to sit on a park bench under a tree offered Anzulović a distraction. *You're never too old or dull to look and imagine what might have been*, he told himself. He felt a pang of regret. If only he were twenty years younger, and richer. And better-looking . . .

He shrugged it off. Goli Otok was real life. Not beautiful blonds. Still, his mind wandered to happier subjects. He pictured himself in the Cary Grant role in *To Catch a Thief*. If anything, this one was even better-looking than Grace Kelly. He

tried not to look at her too much, to keep his eyes on the building. It was hard to exercise discipline. He hadn't done a proper
stakeout in years; he didn't really count the wasted wait for the
Dispatcher. But he'd spent a lot of time watching Grace Kelly
movies.

And then, there was Strumbić.

"Eyes sharp," said Messar, the moment Anzulović spotted
him.

Strumbić had come from around the back of the building
looking up, something catching his attention. He wasn't alone
long. A couple of guys joined him. One went right up against
his back while the other frisked him.

They seemed to know each other. Talking and walking towards the woods. No rush. No sudden moves. Like they were
old friends standing very close to each other, except Anzulović
would have bet good money that the one at the back, dressed
in a farmer's navy suit, was holding a gun.

"What do you think?" Messar asked.

"I think we follow those guys," Anzulović said, getting out
of the car.

"What about della Torre?" Messar asked.

"Forget about della Torre for now. Strumbić and his friends
are the people we need to talk to. We'll look for Gringo later."
Maybe he'll get away, Anzulović thought.

Anzulović was across the road, Messar right behind him.

"Recognize those two?" Anzulović asked.

"No. But if I were a betting man, I'd lay good money on their
being Bosnian. Or Macedonian."

"Or from any very small village that hasn't discovered television or indoor plumbing."

"Bosnian, then. Macedonians have TV."

They followed behind, keeping just at the limits of sight, as
quietly as possible, into the gloaming of the Hampstead woods.

Everything hurt. His hands hurt and his feet hurt and it hurt to run. Della Torre loosened his tie with fingers that were swollen like cooked sausages. He'd put it on when he left the hospital but had regretted it every second he spent on the floor. Christ, how much pain could life inflict on a person?

Della Torre got to the edge of the woods and then didn't know what to do. Three hundred hectares of park, and half of them forest. What day was it? Sunday? If he started looking now and Strumbić and his companions stood still, he might bump into them sometime before the end of the week.

London summer evenings seemed to last forever. The sun had dropped below a long, flat layer of clouds, turning their undersides a livid purple and black. But in the woods it was already twilight. Della Torre wished he'd brought a flashlight. His trousers kept catching in brambles.

And then, there it was. The sound of big branches breaking under sudden, heavy weight, three times in rapid succession. Except they weren't branches. It reminded him he didn't have a gun.

At the sound of the first gunshot, Strumbić thought that Besim had missed. How could he have missed from thirty centimetres? Then he thought that somehow he'd been shot but just hadn't felt it. No, he'd been shot before. And he'd felt that. Maybe he was dead. Maybe this was what being dead was like. The next two shots came close together, and he realized they had been fired away from the tree.

"Who was that?" Strumbić knew from the old-lady lisp that it was Besim asking.

"Don't know. You hurt?" asked the other Bosnian.

"Didn't hit me."

"Me neither. Got him, though."

"Who is it?"

"Don't know."

"Is he dead?"

"Don't know. I think I winged him with the first one. The second one took him down."

"What's he doing walking around the woods with a gun?"

"Don't know."

"Well, see if he's still alive."

Strumbić could hear the one who curved like a banana walking away, then shouting back: "He's breathing, but he's very sleepy. Got him in under the jaw."

"In the neck?"

"Naw, under the jaw and up. At least I think that's what happened. Bleeding a bit. You'd have thought it'd be more, though." The talkative one sounded disappointed.

"It's that crap gun you use. Couldn't put a hole in a turd. How many times did you have to shoot that guy in Karlovac?"

"Got him four times."

"And he lived."

"Well, I nailed that woman of his with just the one."

"Heart attack," Strumbić muttered.

"What?" asked Besim.

"She died of a heart attack," Strumbić said a little louder, regretting calling attention to himself.

"See? What'd I tell you?"

"You going to talk to that tree or are you going to shoot it? Time we were leaving."

"Heart attack. Should have guessed. That crap gun of yours."

"My lucky gun. Anyway, let's get on."

"Hands up. Put your hands up." The order came from behind a holly bush.

"What now?" asked Besim.

"I think it's the cops," said the talkative one.

"London cops talk Croat?"

"Hands up or I shoot."

"Hey, I recognize that voice."

"Last time. Hands up."

"Okay. Shoot then," said the talkative Bosnian.

That had della Torre stumped.

•   •   •

The shooting made Anzulović hurry. Whatever had happened, it wasn't likely to be good. He told Messar to stay put and keep his head down while he went round through the shrubbery to cover the little knoll from the opposite end, bottling up the Bosnians in that patch of open wood. How was he to know he'd have to go through a bog to get there? And now that the shooting had started, there was a solid wall of brambles and holly between him and them. Anzulović hauled himself through the squelching mud as quickly as he could, breathing hard, stumbling in the deepening gloom. Twigs scratched at him. Cattle would have made less noise.

By the time he got there, all he could see was one Bosnian at the big tree in the middle and the other one a little further down the slope. Where the hell was Strumbić? And then he heard someone shouting from one of the bushes to the right for the others to get their hands up. If he didn't know better, he'd have said it was della Torre.

In unison, the Bosnians fired into the shrubbery, their gunshots echoed by the sound of their bullets rending foliage. Anzulović rose from his crouch, holding the gun in regulation two-handed stance—unlike the Bosnians, who fired like cowboys in a third-rate western—and squeezed off one, two, three shots. The Bosnian in front of him spun and dropped to his knees, taking cover behind the tree. At exactly the same time there were two muzzle flashes directly opposite, on the path where Messar was hiding. Anzulović heard branches parting twenty metres above his head.

"Besim, what the hell happened?" asked the thin Bosnian.

"Get down. There's somebody back that way."

"There's somebody this way too. You okay?"

"Bastard got me in the wrist. Hurts like hell," Besim said in his odd, snuffling voice.

"Can you hold a gun?"

"Shooting hand's fine."

"Somebody's shooting this end too."

"How many of them are there?"

"Three at least," said the skinny one.

"That's two too many. Come on, we can get out back this way, that way's the swamp."

"What about Strumbić?"

"Oh yeah," said Besim.

He stuck his gun into the tree and pulled the trigger twice. Anzulović could see enough of him to fire again, then the Bosnians made themselves scarce.

Carefully Anzulović crept forward, but the Bosnians had gone.

A flashlight shone in his face.

"Stop. Put the gun down. Put your hands up." It was a woman, speaking English.

He left the gun on the ground and raised his hands, motioning her to lower the light. It was blinding him.

"Jesus," he said once he could see her. It was Grace Kelly. Pointing a gun. Straight at him.

The bushes to his right moved. She half turned.

"Marko."

Della Torre had been winging it, and then suddenly there was cavalry on both sides.

"That you, Gringo?" asked Anzulović.

"Anzulović? Where's Strumbić?"

"No idea."

"Who's that?" Harry asked.

"Harry, what the hell are you doing here?" della Torre demanded.

"I brought your gun."

"Hey, give me a hand with Messar. He's been hit," said Anzulović to della Torre, though he kept his eyes on the English blond.

"Dead?"

"No. He's got a hole in his chin. But he's breathing. He's out, though."

"Shit. Where's Strumbić?"

"Think those Bosnians took him with them?"

Della Torre looked at Anzulović and then at Harry, and made up his mind. He switched to Italian.

"Harry, give me the gun and the flashlight. You two, see if you can get Messar back to the flat. You speak a bit of Italian, don't you, Anzulović? Harry does too. I'll see you back there."

Della Torre went charging after the Bosnians.

. . .

Anzulović had just shifted Messar into a position where he could lift him when he heard a noise. A sort of grunt coming from the tree. He let Harry take Messar's sitting weight, put his fingers to his lips, and did a squat run towards the tree. There was definitely a rustling, scraping noise coming from it. With some difficulty, Anzulović hauled himself up the trunk to where he could see into it. He half-expected some wild animal. No, he wasn't sure what he expected. Certainly not what he found.

"What the —"

"Here, give me a hand."

"Strumbić."

"Yeah. Who's that?"

"Anzulović."

"Who?"

"Anzulović."

"Fucking Anzulović. I owe you one. Well, give me a hand out of this fucking tree."

"What are you doing in there?"

"Sightseeing. What do you think? Getting shot at by a couple of fucking Bosnian jokers."

Anzulović hauled him up. Strumbić slithered out over the edge of the trunk and down heavily, so that the two men fell in a heap.

"Bloody hell, you're heavy. You okay?"

"I'll live. Took a chunk out of my leg, though, bastard. Hurts like hell. I think I'm deaf in one ear. And I can't hear out of the other one."

"Can you help me carry Messar back to that apartment?"

"He dead?"

"No, though I don't know how badly hurt."

"Where's della Torre?"

"He's gone after the Bosnians. Thought they'd taken you."

"Has he? Crazy bastard. Here, give me your gun. Wait, who's that there?"

"Grace Kelly, I think."

The woman looked familiar to Strumbić. It was too dark to tell, but he could have sworn it was that estate agent woman. "Well, you and Grace Kelly are going to have to deal with Messar on your own. I'm going to hobble after della Torre."

"Can you manage? You've just been shot."

"Flesh wound. Took a slice out of me, but that's all. Give me your gun and I'll make hamburger out of that Bosnian prick."

.   .   .

Della Torre kept the flashlight aiming down in front of him. They had a lead on him but no light. He thought he heard them somewhere ahead. But when he got there, nothing. The woods had an earthy smell of rotting wood and leaves, a verdant and mossy maze. Now and again he could make out velvety sky. Overhead a songbird chirped bursts of sweet, high rhythm.

There was just enough remaining dusk to move at a cautious speed. He used the flashlight as little as possible, not wanting to draw attention to himself. This bit of the woods was mostly open, with not much undergrowth, though there was the occasional fallen tree to negotiate. He moved carefully across the soft, springy ground as it sloped gently downward. There were hardly any low branches to walk into. He took care not to stumble over protruding roots.

There. It sounded like somebody falling into a pile of kindling off to the right. Della Torre flipped on the flashlight and swung it round. He wasn't sure. Yes. It looked like one of them. He kept the beam on the Bosnian, who was struggling through a barrier of heaped dead branches. *Got you now,* he thought to himself. Only then did he wonder where the other one was. Maybe the thought was prompted by the sound of a fat length of wood whistling through the air just before it hit him on the side of the head.

.   .   .

Strumbić's leg hurt like hell. He didn't get a good look at the woman, but it sure wasn't Irena. The more he thought about it, the more she reminded him of the estate agent. Grace something-or-other, Anzulović had said. No, that wasn't the name of the estate agent woman. It was... He couldn't remember.

Had Gringo given them his key? If they were going to the flat, one of them must have it. Didn't matter; Strumbić was going to get his own back from those bloody Bosnians.

Bloody, bloody Bosnians. Fancy them wanting to shoot him inside the tree. He'd straddled the hole as best he could, pressing his legs against the sides, lifting himself up out of range, but not high enough that a bullet didn't put a furrow in his calf. It felt like a line of hornet stings, but at least he could walk. Problem was, he didn't know where to go.

A couple of times he thought he saw a flash ahead. Little staccato spikes of light and then lengths of darkness. He couldn't hear much beyond the constant motorway sound in his head. It was unbelievable, the concussive sound of the explosions concentrated in the hollow of that tree. So he kept his eyes as focused as possible inside the constricting darkness of that wood.

The light shone again, further to his right but now fixed on, bouncing slightly. *Della Torre?* he wondered. *The Bosnians? Somebody walking a dog?*

·   ·   ·

The wood was soft, mostly rotted through, which was why it splintered when it hit della Torre. Had it been fresh, the force of the blow would have fractured his skull. As it was, he figured on being left with an ugly headache. Which, under the circumstances, would probably last for the rest of his life.

"Who is it, Besim?"

"You got the flashlight?"

"Recognize him?"

"Maybe." Besim bent down and tugged on della Torre's tie. "This thing sure smells familiar."

"I do think it's our old friend. The one who didn't like your driving."

"I think we owe him something."

"Shame we haven't got time to pay him back fully. I'd like to peel his skin off and salt him first, like the Turks do."

They were distracted by a noise behind them. The skinny Bosnian swung della Torre's flashlight in the general direction, raising his gun at the same time. A couple of men, naked below the waist, ran off into the undergrowth.

"You see what I see, Besim?"

"I see it. But I'm not understanding it."

"I think that's what we heard last night. I told you it wasn't wild boars."

The skinny Bosnian fired.

"Shit. Oh my god. Shit, oh my god, I've been shot." The men raced into the woods screaming with fear and pain as the Bosnians doubled over with laughter.

"He shouldn't have looked back. Think he'll remember to wear trousers next time?"

"Uh-uh," said Besim through bouts of snuffling-dog laughter.

"Your turn," the banana-shaped one said, his attention shifting back to della Torre.

Besim raised the gun in his good right hand while the skinny Bosnian kept the light on della Torre.

"I'd rather throw you out of a moving car. But this will have to do," said the banana-shaped one.

The two gunshots came so close together that della Torre could have sworn they were one.

39

BETWEEN THEM, THEY managed to drag Messar through the woods and up to the building. He was a big man, tall and muscular, and it wasn't an easy job. They didn't talk much, just enough for Anzulović to tell Grace Kelly that he worked with della Torre. She said, "I know."

She went through the front door on her own, for once not passing the time of day with the porter, and then opened the back door by the garbage bins so they could take the service elevator up and avoid bumping into any people. Messar wasn't bleeding too heavily, but his neck and chest were a mess. They got him to the apartment and laid him down on the bed in the spare room.

"He needs a doctor," said Harry.

Anzulović shrugged. A doctor, once he'd seen the bullet holes, would mean police. Police would mean an inquest. And that would mean jail time for them all. Yugoslavia barely existed. There was little chance of the embassy's bailing them out, getting them off the hook. The Croats wouldn't do it for a bunch of UDBA people. And neither would Belgrade for a bunch of Department VI Croats. Besides, who knew how the UDBA would react?

On the other hand, if there was a friendly doctor, one who could keep things quiet, maybe keep Messar alive long enough to be got back to Yugoslavia, or what was left of it, maybe they'd be able to work something out. They'd driven to London in less than a day. He was sure that with Strumbić's and della Torre's help they could do the trip back even faster.

Anzulović knew he was clutching at straws.

"We need doctor, yes, but quiet doctor. Not talk about this to police," he said.

"Do you think Marko's wife, Irena, would help?"

That was it. He'd known she was in London. Only problem was, where? And did she care enough about della Torre to help?

"Yes, but how find her?" he asked.

"She works at the hospital down the hill. I'll try her." Anzulović had too much on his mind to think about how Grace Kelly and della Torre and Irena and Strumbić were tied together. But he made a mental note to find out. Some other time.

Harry spent a quarter of an hour on the phone, at first not getting through to the switchboard and then not getting through to the X-ray department. When she did, they told her Irena wasn't working that night. And they wouldn't give Harry her home number.

"I'm sorry," she said to Anzulović.

But he had a thought. "Wait. I get."

He'd taken the Department VI job so he'd never have to run stairs again. But the lift was busy and he didn't have time to wait. He was out of breath by the time he got back to the flat, a folder in his hands.

"I have number for Irena home," he said. It was from the time she'd called della Torre's father. He gave it to Harry.

"Yes?"

"Irena? Irena della Torre?"

"Yes. Who is this?" Her English was accented but clear.

"My name is Harry. I'm Marko's friend."

"Ah, yes, Marko. Don't tell me, you're calling because he wants to apologize for not bothering to show up tonight, but he's too much of a coward to do it himself. I called the hospital; he was discharged this afternoon."

"I don't know about any appointment he had with you. But he couldn't. He was tied up. I mean really tied up. With rope. Strumbić did it. And now I need your help." Harry was talking too fast, maybe too loudly, the pitch a little too high. She wasn't one to panic. Never had been. But the stress of the situation was palpable down the phone line.

"What is it?" Irena's voice echoed Harry's edge.

"There's a man here. He's a colleague of Marko's who's been shot in the jaw. We need a doctor, but it has to be discreet."

"Let me speak to Marko."

"He's not here. He's gone after the men who shot his colleague. We need help."

"I'll be there in ten minutes. You're just up the hill, aren't you? Give me the address."

Irena was as good as her word. She came with a doctor's emergency bag and didn't stand on any ceremony, just asked where the patient was.

"Irena."

"Anzulović, fancy seeing you here."

"Funny circumstances."

"Aren't they. Where's Marko?"

"He's chasing a couple of Bosnians."

"And Strumbić?"

"He's chasing Marko."

She nodded, not looking very happy about any of it.

Carefully, she tilted Messar's head. She opened his mouth and a wash of blood and saliva flowed out. More came out of his nose.

"Lucky he's not choking on the blood. There isn't a huge amount of flow."

She looked carefully at the wound in his mouth, inspected

his tongue and his palate. She took his pulse and then his blood pressure with a cuff.

"There's not a lot I can do here. I need to see what happened inside his head. I'll set up a drip for him. There's the hole in his shoulder as well, but that's not important. The bullet might still be in there, but it doesn't seem to have done any damage to any significant blood vessels. As far as I can tell, the one in his jaw skimmed the bone, mostly missed his tongue, but made a mess of his palate. I don't know what it's done to his brain, other than the fact that he's unconscious and still has reflexes. That's a good sign. But I need to get him to the hospital."

"No police," said Anzulović.

"I'll see what I can do."

Once she'd got the drip into Messar and had Anzulović standing over him holding it, she asked Harry for the phone.

Irena got through to whomever it was she was calling much more quickly than Harry had, and then she talked for a long time in quiet tones. Harry didn't listen in — tried not to listen in — but kept hearing bits like "autopsy" and "dentist," none of which made any sense.

"Do you have a car?" Irena asked, when she'd finally hung up.

"Yes."

"We'll need to drive Messar down to the hospital. We'll go through the emergency room entrance. There will be a wheelchair waiting for him there. But we won't check him in. We'll take him to the autopsy room. It's quiet there this time of night, and it's well equipped. It's also clean. Even better, the old dental surgery rooms are on that floor. They've got X-ray machines, so we'll be able to take a picture of his head without going into the main X-ray suites. To do that, he'd have to be admitted. Even so, we may have no choice. We'll see. How quickly can you get the car out front?"

"Five minutes, max," Harry said.

"Okay, then get it. Anzulović and I will bring him down."

"If you go out by the service entrance, I can pull up right out-side the back doors. Go down the service elevator. Anzulović knows where it is."

"Good. Let's go."

.   .   .

Della Torre was looking up at the Bosnians, though one of his eyes seemed to have lost focus. They were laughing uproar-iously about something, and even though his head felt like a dropped watermelon, he smiled reflexively. And then realized they were probably laughing about how they were going to double his weight with lead. Once he'd recovered sufficiently from his laughing fit, Besim edged closer and pointed the gun down at him.

Funny to think they'd come to a wood in the middle of London to do what they'd intended to do in a wood outside of Zagreb.

Della Torre couldn't tell what happened first. The explosion, the searing pain, the muzzle flash, or the explosion. That didn't make sense. Two explosions? And then he realized that Besim was no longer standing up and that the banana-shaped one was crouching, little bolts of white light flaring from the end of his gun, one after the other, aiming into the trees. And when he stopped, he pulled another gun out from his trousers, and that one also sent strobes of light across della Torre's retina. And then the tall, thin, banana-shaped Bosnia was also down.

The whole while, every last nerve cell in his body felt like it had lodged itself somewhere between his shoulder and his wrist, sending explosive signals of violence into della Torre's brain until the deafening rattle of pain was overwhelming. At the same time, his ears were drumming with the sound of his heartbeat overtop of a woollen dullness as thick as felt boots.

In the fragment of light that remained, della Torre could see a dark form standing, pointing a gun down at him. His thoughts pushed themselves elsewhere, anywhere, to forget the impending end. He couldn't see clearly, his eyes blurred. Was it Strumbić? Maybe it was Svjet...

In his mind's ear the A minor third movement was playing, just as he'd listened to it with Svjet. Svjet had introduced him to the unutterable beauty of late Beethoven. He forced himself to listen to the remembered music as words came silently to his lips, a prayer for the hard road to heaven.

Hail Mary, full of grace, the Lord is with thee, blessed art thou among women now that the evening is spread out against the sky like the fruit of thy womb upon a table, let us go, Holy Mary, Mother of God, pray for us sinners, wer, wenn ich schriee, hörte mich denn aus der Engel Ordnungen, because this is the way the world ends, Hail Mary, full of grace, now and now and vides ut alta stet nive candidum Mother of God, les neiges d'antan now and now and yesteryear at the hour of our death, full of grace...

It was Strumbić. He was bending over him, shouting, though for some reason the sound of his voice was far away.

"What?"

Strumbić knelt by della Torre and pulled him up.

"Come on." He'd finally made himself heard. "We've got to go. Now."

"Go where? Aren't you taking turns with the Bosnians? You're going to shoot me next. Then one of them's going to shoot me. Then you're going to shoot me. Then the other one's going to —"

"Shut up. Can you stand?"

The miracle was that, with a bit of help from Strumbić, not only could della Torre stand, he could even walk, with his left arm flopped down beside him.

"Come on," Strumbić said. "We've got to get the hell out of here. There'll be cops everywhere soon, and I thought I heard a helicopter. Let's go."

"Aren't you going to shoot me?" Della Torre sounded almost disappointed, though it was the pain in his arm speaking.

"No, I'm not going to shoot you."

"Why?"

"I'm sentimental. And because you're more useful to me alive now that your UDBA friends know where I am."

"What about the Bosnians?"

"What the hell do I care about the Bosnians? I got my wallet and keys back, and now I don't give a fuck about the Bosnians as long as they can't shoot me. And they don't seem in much of a shooting mood anymore."

They stumbled and staggered through the wood, using della Torre's flashlight, which Strumbić had found by the glow of his lighter. They tried not to use it. Already they could see other lights being flashed elsewhere in the wood. And there was that helicopter somewhere overhead. Unable to walk straight, the brambles tore at them. A branch caught the corner of della Torre's eye. Walking while trying to keep his arm from moving too much was harder than he thought possible, and no less excruciating.

They got to the edge of the woods and they could see blue lights flashing up and down East Heath Road, wailing sirens everywhere, though thankfully no police had stopped at the building yet.

"So how the fuck do we get in? That bastard porter will get the cops onto us before we press the button for the lift," Strumbić said.

Della Torre jerked his head forward.

"Back door. Somebody seems to have propped it open."

"So they did," said Strumbić. "What are you waiting for?"

·   ·   ·

They got Messar to the hospital in the 2cv, an old blanket wrapped around him. Anzulović and Irena shifted him from the front seat onto the wheelchair that had been left for them. Irena told Harry where to find them once she'd parked the car.

Harry made her way to the autopsy room without having to ask anyone. It was in a quiet part of the hospital, sheltered from the pandemonium brewing on the streets around it. She'd only just parked the car when she started hearing sirens coming and going from every direction, police cars flashing past in one direction while others headed in the other. The whole fringe of the Heath was a wasp's dance.

No one was in the room, so Harry hovered outside until she spotted Anzulović further down the corridor.

"What's happening?"

"They're taking pictures of his head. X-rays in there."

"Who's they?"

"Irena and some doctor. Didn't introduce to me."

They waited, pacing nervously like anxious relatives. They were there maybe half an hour before Irena came out.

"The bullet shattered his palate and then dented his skull but didn't make it into the brain. It doesn't look like there's any swelling of the brain, though you can never tell with these things. The doctor is patching him up a bit. He wouldn't really be able to operate for another day or two, so we don't need the autopsy room, but Messar needs to stay under close observation."

"You mean in the hospital?" Anzulović asked.

Harry stood back, not understanding what they were saying but not imposing herself either.

"I'm afraid so."

"Is there any way I can drive him back to Zagreb?"

"You'd need somebody with training, a doctor or nurse. He's going to need morphine and a drip and constant vigilance that there's no pressure building up in his skull."

"Can you come, Irena?"

"No."

"Do it for Gringo."

"No."

"If we stay here, we're all fucked. You know that, don't you? I'm not even thinking about having to spend time in jail here. How long do you think the UDBA would give us? Renegades, they'd call us."

Irena nodded; she knew the truth of what Anzulović was saying. Della Torre had told her how the UDBA's assassination squads hunted down dissidents and defectors. How they killed whole families. How they'd operated in Britain before.

"Messar's not staying here," Anzulović said. "Not alive. And if he's going to die, he might as well die on the way back to Zagreb. If you don't come, Messar will just have to take his chances. But he's not staying here. Neither is Gringo. He's been gone long enough. We're going to need him back in Zagreb. Unless the Bosnians or Strumbić get to him first."

Harry's ears perked up every time she heard the name Gringo, though she didn't understand anything else.

"Are you asking after Marko?"

"Yes," said Irena testily, her worried expression mirroring Harry's feelings.

"Is there a telephone I can use? Maybe he's made it back to the apartment," Harry said.

"Or maybe all those sirens are for him," said Irena in a low, worried voice.

Harry had to phone three times before someone picked up.

"What?" It wasn't della Torre.

"Mr. Strumbić? This is important. I'm a friend of Marko's, Marko della Torre. I know that you want to kill him. If you have him with you, put him on the phone. Otherwise I will call the police and tell them who you are and what you've done. Do you understand? It's important that you understand."

"Yes, yes. He not dead. He here. Wait," he said.

"Marko?"

"Who's that?" he sounded groggy, thick-headed.

"It's Harry, Marko. It's Harry. Thank god you're alive. Are you okay? Something sounds wrong."

"What is it?" Irena hovered impatiently over Harry's shoulder.

"It's Marko. He's alive, but there seems to be something wrong."

"Who's that you're talking to?" della Torre asked.

"Irena. Your wife. I'm at the hospital with Messar."

"Tell her my tennis-playing days are over."

"He said something about not playing tennis anymore."

"Tennis? He doesn't play tennis."

"Marko, what's going on?" Irena asked, taking the phone from Harry.

"Irena. Sorry about dinner. I was tied up. We'll get divorced some other time."

"Never mind. Tell me, what's the matter?"

"Somebody tried to rearrange my elbow to look more like my asshole. And it hurts. I might need another one of your suppositories."

"You were shot?"

"Yes. And clubbed. I'm a little hard of hearing."

"Wait there. We'll get you to hospital."

"No hospital. I don't want the police. It's a hell of a mess up on the Heath."

"No police. We'll have a look at you without police. It'll be as if you aren't even here."

"Will you have a look at Strumbić too? He's looking a bit peaky as well."

Irena turned to Harry.

"Can you do another ambulance run for us?"

Harry nodded.

By the time she and Anzulović had got della Torre and Strumbić down the hill, there were police everywhere on the roads and circulating around the hospital. Harry dropped them off at the emergency room entrance, and Anzulović took the other two to Irena.

Thankfully no one took an interest in three men who looked as if they knew where they were going. Strumbić had bandaged della Torre as gingerly as he could and put a torn bit of sheet around his own leg, which had been steadily leaking blood. They'd put on some fresh clothes, which helped. Anzulović wondered how long it would be before the police traced them to the apartment building.

Della Torre was lying on a blanket on the autopsy table. Irena had rigged a drip and had given him some morphine, and Strumbić was in a chair, also with a dose of painkiller, when the doctor came in.

He seemed familiar, though della Torre's senses were crackling in all directions. He heard everything from down a long tunnel. Most of him felt not numb, but a couple of centimetres out of focus. Except for the pain in his arm, which he was conscious of, though it didn't hurt. He knew the man. Tall, slightly stooped. Receding black hair. Roman nose, small glasses. Just couldn't place him.

"Ah, Mr. della Torre. I see we can't keep you out of hospital. You've made it a regular pilgrimage. Let's take a look at that arm. I'm David Cohen, if you remember me."

It came back to him, snapped into sudden focus. Irena's new man.

"Can you follow my fingers with your eyes? Can you hear?"

"Yes, Dr. Cohen. How could I forget?"

"How's the pain?"

"Better than kidney stones. Worse than being tied up."

"Oh."

"How are those boys of yours, the ones in south London?"

"They'll live. At least until they get shot or stabbed again."

"What about the one with the bullet in his brain?"

"He woke up this morning. If there's brain damage, they haven't found it yet. I suspect it's a similar injury to that of your friend with the bullet in his head. In the boy's case, the bullet bounced off his jawbone and up." Cohen examined della Torre's arm while he talked. "The bounce took some of the momentum off the bullet, so it didn't penetrate the skull. Whereas with your friend in the other room, the bullet just went straight up. Which is very curious. I'd say it was a nine-millimetre shell, more or less the same as the one that hit the boys in south London, but either this one was shot from a very great distance or something took the momentum out of the bullet."

"How is he doing?" asked della Torre.

"Well, he's got a new hole in his head, and blowing his nose might be uncomfortable in the future. But the bullet, which cracked his skull, stopped short of his brain. Doesn't mean he's in the clear, but he's not in critical danger," Cohen said as he tidied della Torre's elbow and applied stitches. "Nor are you, though you're going to have to withdraw from Wimbledon this year if you're left-handed."

"Right-handed."

"Oh, so you'll be fine, then. I've done a bit of temporary patching, but you're going to need surgery to put the bone together. That doesn't need to happen straight away, but you can't leave it too long. I'm afraid you're going to have to modify your golf swing, though."

"Doctor, we can't go to the police."

"So I understand. I don't know if I can help you. I'm going to have to leave you people shortly — my pager's been on overdrive. I've been told there are three men with bullet wounds coming in. I mean, other than you three. My colleagues are already dealing with one downstairs — he's got a superficial but very painful graze of his penis. I'll be very curious to know how that happened. The other two are more serious. Possibly life threatening."

"They're a couple of Bosnian criminals who like firing their guns. We got in the way. I think you may find they prove to be suspects in the shooting of your young men."

"I see."

"We are Yugoslav police. All of us here, except for Irena. We've been tracking them for a few months, but we're not officially in this country. It would be very embarrassing for all concerned if we were connected with the shootings here. It would put everyone in a difficult position. Including Irena."

Della Torre tried to think straight. Tried to guess how close this Dr. Cohen was to Irena. Tried to appeal to him by raising the threat to her as subtly as possible. Under normal circumstances he could do these things, relying on his smile and conspiratorial friendliness to get a witness on his side. He wasn't sure how successful he'd be from a prone position on an autopsy table.

The doctor left the room to look at Messar again. Irena returned with Anzulović.

"Pilgrim." Della Torre was muttering to himself, the morphine taking the edge off his pain and returning his thoughts to the source of his present difficulties.

"Has this near-death experience given you religion?" Irena asked.

"No. It's a word that got me shot."

"I thought that was the Bosnians."

"Them too."

"John Wayne," said Anzulović.

"What?"

"It's a famous line from one of John Wayne's movies. 'Pilgrim, you caused a lot of trouble this morning; might have got somebody killed; and somebody oughta belt you in the mouth.'"

"Thanks, Anzulović. That really makes my head ache less," della Torre said.

Dr. Cohen wheeled Messar into the room. His head had

been stabilized by a frame that sat on his shoulders and was bound to his forehead. Irena stitched the wound on Strumbić's calf. Dr. Cohen waited for her to finish and then spoke generally to the room.

"I have three patients to see downstairs as a matter of urgency, which will prevent me from talking to the police for a couple of hours. But when I've finished, I will have to tell the police that earlier I saw some other suspected shooting victims in the autopsy room. When the time comes, I will tell the police all I know, though that isn't very much. Two hours."

"I don't know how to thank you, David," Irena said.

"I hope this doesn't come back to bite us, Irena. Both of us. I fear it will. I don't think I'd do this for anyone else."

"I know," she said, walking over to kiss him. Anzulović didn't know where to look. Even Strumbić raised an eyebrow. "I'll have to go with them," she continued. "If it's okay here, if the police don't want me, I'll be back. Soon."

He gave a scant nod of the head. "I hope so. I really do. Maybe we can talk a little more then."

"Yes," she said. "I owe you that at least."

Dr. Cohen left them. Irena went soon after to collect some of her belongings and whatever medicines and dressings she could assemble from the hospital for the trip. Strumbić sat, his trouser leg rolled up above the wound. Messar was silent and bandaged. Della Torre looked over at them through a fog, the pain in his arm dulled.

"Marko, how are you?" Harry knelt down beside him. He hadn't seen her come into the room.

"A little better than kidney stones. Worse than being tied up. But a new kind of pain. The drugs help," he said, less groggy than he'd expected to be.

Pieces of a story were assembling in Strumbić's mind. When the estate agent had spoken to him on the phone, demanding to talk to Gringo, he'd known. He didn't know how or whether

Irena figured in the scam, but he knew he'd been set up by the estate agent. Obvious, really.

She was a dish, he thought to himself. It softened the blow slightly, being stitched up by a beautiful woman. He didn't know why, because the money was still gone. Until he found some way of getting it back. But it was better than getting robbed by an ugly Bosnian.

"I think we need to go now," Anzulović said.

"What is it?" They could hear the stress of the evening in Harry's voice, her fear that the men were talking about something even worse.

"I've got to say goodbye for a little while," della Torre said.

Irena took them through the hospital's back corridors, where no one stopped them or even paid them any attention. They got down to the loading bay for the hospital's plant and equipment.

"I've packed a few things: some morphine, some penicillin, a couple of bags of saline solution. Some dressings. But we need to be fast. We need to get Messar to a hospital as quickly as possible. No more than twenty-four hours. Maximum."

"Everyone have their passports?"

It was a foolish question. Their passports, whether legitimate or fake, would have been stapled to them from the moment they'd left Yugoslav soil. East Europeans clung to their documents the way the British clung to their accents. Della Torre still had his Italian passport in his suit. He would have to leave his other things with Harry, including his precious American documents. He'd rely on the UDBA ID to get him back into the country.

Anzulović went with Harry back up the hill to fetch his car. The rest of them waited by the service entrance, listening to the screaming sirens tearing along the local roads and the helicopter overhead.

The Merc was a mid-sized saloon. They'd be cosy on the

trip down. But the car was fast, and should be reliable now that the fanbelt had been replaced. If anything could get them to Zagreb in a day, it would. They assembled themselves in it, Messar and Strumbić in the back, Messar's drip tied to the hanger strap overhead, Irena between them, and della Torre in the passenger seat, his injured arm strapped against him.

"When will you be back?" Harry asked.

"I don't know." He paused. "Listen, Harry, I'm sorry. I'm sorry for not being honest with you. For not telling you. But some things..."

She brushed the corner of her eye with the back of her hand.

"Will you be okay?" she asked.

"I don't know."

"Will they do anything to you when you get there?"

"I don't know. Just that my chances will be better with the help of the folks in this car. We all kind of need each other right now. The people the UDBA send out to fix problems like us are good at what they do."

Tears ran down her face. She kissed him tenderly through the open window, and again Anzulović looked away, not really knowing what to think. Other than that he needed a cigarette. Many cigarettes. It was going to be a long drive. And he suspected he'd be doing most of it.

40

"**N**ICE OF YOU to stop in, Gringo."

"Least I could do."

"How's the arm?"

"So long as I don't move it much and I eat painkillers like they're sweets, I'm fine. How's Messar?"

"He'll live. They've got him bandaged up and on drugs, and no damage to the brain. For which we have to thank Irena and her friend. How is she?"

"She's gone back to London. Picking up her car and my stuff. Mind if I sit?"

Anzulović waved his hand towards a chair. There were packing boxes stacked up in the corner of the room. And there were fewer people in the building. It had become a veritable *Mary Celeste*.

"So what's happening?" della Torre asked.

"What's happening about what?"

"Anything."

The Croatian government had declared independence, as had the Slovenes. So far there was just a state of nervous tension in Zagreb. A few air-raid warnings had sounded. People had been puzzled by the noise at first but now knew to run to shelters. But those had just been drills.

It wasn't so quiet in Slovenia, though. Yugoslav army tanks had driven into the new republic to retake crossings the Slovene police had captured from the federal border police. The little band of London's wounded had only just crossed before the Slovenes took over.

It would have been a different story had they arrived at the border a day later. By then the Slovenes were shooting at army units who haphazardly returned fire, and nothing much was getting into or out of Slovenia across the Italian border.

The Yugoslav army conscripts didn't know what was going on and didn't want to shoot at what they saw as their own people. For the Slovenes, though, the Yugoslav army and state were now enemies. Croatia, meanwhile, just watched, biting its nails.

"Well, the UDBA in Croatia is officially disbanded. So we're out of a job. But that's okay, because we weren't being paid anyway. We are, however, being absorbed into the Zagreb police. Which means we'll finally be drawing a salary again."

"Croatian intelligence?"

"Military intelligence, run by the police. God knows they could use a little. The Croatian secret service wouldn't take us. They only wanted what they call real UDBA people, not fakers like us who just try to make sure everyone stays honest." There was a hint of irritation in Anzulović's voice.

"Military intelligence. Oxymoron."

"With special emphasis on the *moron*. You know Colonel Kakav, yes? Well, he's our new boss, unfortunately."

"Probably not good news for me."

"Probably not. He has a bee in his bonnet about Zagreb cops being shot by UDBA agents."

"So what happens to me, then?"

"Nothing. Everyone's too tied up with the small matter of civil war to be worried about you just now. Don't worry about it too much. Strumbić wrote an affidavit about how you didn't shoot him, though he's neglected to sign it so far. And once Messar is whole again, he'll be writing about how you saved him from the Bosnian assassins we were all hunting down. But I'd keep my head down for a while, if I were you. And I wouldn't be tempted to skip the country. That's official, by the way."

"Right."

"Croatia may not be recognized by anybody out there just yet, but one day, if we're accepted as something more than just some place for the Yugoslav army to piss all over, the government here will have extradition treaties. And if I know Kakav, he'll be itching to use them."

"What if the Yugoslav army wins?"

"Then we've all got problems, haven't we."

"At least the Bosnians won't be bothering us."

"That's true."

"Irena called. She said the Bosnians are still at the hospital. Apparently they're not telling anyone much of anything. They'll be spending some time in jail on weapons and attempted murder charges. One of their guns was linked to a shooting of a group of teenage hooligans."

"She got back okay? I was a bit worried about whether she'd make it out when they started shutting the borders," Anzulović said.

"She made it out. Took a flight from Vienna. Only ended up missing a day's work in the end."

"She's superhuman," Anzulović said.

"She is."

"She's best out of here. It's going to be a shitshow before long."

"She's coming back."

"What?" It was the most animated della Torre had ever seen his boss. "She's what?"

"She's coming back. Seems to think that she'll do more

good as a doctor here than as a kidney-stone photographer in London."

"Crazy girl." Anzulović shook his head.

"What about the Pilgrim thing?"

"What about it?"

"The file has to do with a bunch of nuclear centrifuges the Swedes were selling us in the mid-1980s and we were selling on. Somebody doesn't want people to know about it."

"That sounds like a good idea, not knowing. I think we'll forget all about that stuff and hope it goes away, that's what I think," Anzulović said.

"I was never interested in the first place."

"I wish I believed you. Anyway, I don't think the Dispatcher will be bothering you. The orders came from Belgrade, and if he's still an agent of Belgrade's and living in Zagreb, now that the bang-bang has started he won't last too long. But I can't guarantee it," Anzulović said. "Why don't you make yourself scarce? Go to your father's and enjoy the sun while you can. You're on disability right now. I'll square it with Kakav. I'll see what I can do about keeping you out of Goli Otok once people turn their attention back onto you."

"Gee, thanks."

"Listen, Gringo. There's a short supply of good people. Of good intelligence people. You're going to be needed a lot more out here than in some prison cell. Even Kakav will realize that. Get better and then we'll see."

"Thanks, Anzulović." Della Torre got up to leave. "Where are they moving us to? Police headquarters?"

"Think they tell me top secret stuff like that? I have no idea. I have no idea when we're vacating this place. Can I make a suggestion to you?"

"What?"

"I've got those hobby files of yours. You can have them back, but I think, quite frankly, you ought to make a nice bonfire out of them before they get you into any more trouble."

"Sure thing."

"And Gringo..."

Della Torre had just opened the door. "What?"

"She was a peach, that one in London. Much as I love Irena, that Grace Kelly of yours was a real peach. You're a lucky man."

"Funny. I don't feel it," he said, and closed the door behind him.

COMING SOON

FROM HOUSE OF ANANSI PRESS
IN OCTOBER 2013

Read on for a preview of the next thrilling Marko della Torre novel, *Killing Pilgrim*.

STOCKHOLM, FEBRUARY 1986

THE MONTENEGRIN HAD been smoking, fiddling with the car's tuner, searching out something other than inane pop music or indecipherable talk radio, when Pilgrim and his wife walked past, unaccompanied.

He hadn't seen them leave the building because, he shamefully realized, he hadn't been looking. Every time before, Pilgrim's chauffeured car had drawn up outside. But that night there was no car.

The Montenegrin reached under the seat and brushed the smooth metal of the Smith & Wesson revolver with his finger. It had become a talisman.

He would have preferred a smaller-calibre pistol with an efficient silencer, one of the official standard issues. But this was the gun the boy had found for him, and so this was the gun he would use.

The boy had guided him to an isolated spot in a forest nearly two hours west of the city, where he was certain of privacy, and there he tested it at various distances. He hadn't dared risk smuggling a weapon across Europe and had worried about the quality of equipment he'd be able to get his hands on in Sweden, but the boy had done well.

The Montenegrin slipped the gun into his coat pocket and got out of the stolen Opel. He followed the couple on foot, discreetly, as he'd learned to do over long years of practice.

Pilgrim and his wife walked to the nearest metro station, where they waited for a train in the direction of the city's shopping district. People recognized him but left him alone, though one youth made signs behind Pilgrim's back. The man's face was unmistakeable: round, with a beak nose and hooded eyes, like a vulture's. The wife was unexceptional. Small, dowdy, utterly forgettable, though by now the Montenegrin was familiar with her too, having watched her do her shopping at the local supermarket like any other middle-aged Swedish housewife, filling a basket with milk, vegetables, a roll of aluminum foil, toilet paper.

The Montenegrin bought a ticket and waited at the other end of the platform. The train was full but not crowded. He stood well away from the couple but within sight. Pilgrim seemed agitated, glancing frequently at his watch. His wife patted his arm, a gesture that spoke of long familiarity with her husband's impatience. They went three stops on the green line from the old town on its island of narrow cobbled streets, its mustard-coloured stone buildings with gas lamps on wrought-iron brackets, its palace's flat, unimaginative grandeur. They got off in a nondescript part of Stockholm: nineteenth-century apartment blocks with restaurants and shops on their ground floors fronted a long, straight avenue. Except for the cold, it reminded the Montenegrin of Belgrade.

He joined the flow of passengers leaving the station, keeping Pilgrim and his wife in sight as they and a handful of others hurried to a cinema a block away.

Pilgrim walked to the front of the queue, as was only natural, but then his wife gently upbraided him for his rudeness, making him take his place at the back. Pilgrim looked both irritated and chastened, but when he got to the ticket window he paid like everybody else and disappeared into the theatre.

The Montenegrin checked the running time to see when the show would be ending. It was something frivolous about Mozart, a summer comedy for the dead of winter, according to the poster. Popular. Maybe because there wasn't much else to do in Stockholm. It was an expensive town in which to drink, eat, smoke.

He took the metro back to the car. It was a short drive, but it took him a while to find somewhere to park that was out of sight but easy to access. His sense of direction had failed him in this unfamiliar town; he ended up on the wrong side of the cinema from the metro stop, on a parallel street farther away than he'd intended.

He walked back towards the movie house and stood silent sentry at a shop window diagonally opposite, in clear sight of its entrance. He was early, but he wanted to be ready if Pilgrim walked out before the end. So he waited, half staring at the darkened display, illuminated solely by streetlight, struggling not to shiver despite the new blue overcoat and cheap knitted cap he'd bought a couple of weeks before in Copenhagen, where he'd briefly stopped to find a car with Swedish plates.

Several times he glanced around the intersection, but the streets were mostly empty. There wasn't much snow on the ground, but it was cold enough for him to feel the fine hairs in his nose start to freeze.

He stamped his feet, the dance cold people do when they're waiting, but resisted the temptation to walk some warmth back into his legs. The film would be ending soon.

He pressed his fingers to his neck, feeling for his pulse, using the psychological tools he'd been taught to force himself to relax. Nerves were inevitable, expected, even for a professional. They kept him sharp, alert. But unfettered, they caused mistakes.

It worried him that he hadn't had time to plan properly, to get a clear idea of each subsequent move. Normally he'd have been directing a team from a safe distance. He'd have had people doing fieldwork for weeks in advance, with a whole intelligence portfolio at his disposal. Then there would have been a separate squad, given exact instructions down to the colours of their ties. They wouldn't know why, but they'd know when and where, to the minute and the metre. And if they got it wrong...they were deniable. All with criminal backgrounds and a good reason to keep their mouths shut.

Not now. This time he was standing at the front, with no one behind him. The intelligence, the fieldwork, and the execution were all down to him. No safety net. No support. Just an unwritten promise in return for success.

No, he wasn't quite alone. But he didn't count the boy, whom providence had somehow sent him. Despite his youth, the boy was capable and smart, even if he smoked dope most evenings or went out to sell it.

Professionals also get lucky, the Montenegrin reminded himself.

It was lucky Pilgrim and his wife had decided to take the metro to the cinema that evening. And that they'd gone unaccompanied by a bodyguard.

Every day since he'd arrived in Stockholm, the Montenegrin had driven to Pilgrim's apartment building well before dawn, waiting and watching. Then he would shadow the man and his two uniformed bodyguards, tracing the short route to his nearby offices. Once Pilgrim had returned home, unaccompanied, in the mid-afternoon. A missed opportunity.

Most evenings, the Montenegrin would sit in his car, engine running, smoking cigarettes, watching. Pilgrim would return home flanked by a pair of uniformed men, different ones from the morning team. Usually he'd go out again, collected by a chauffeured car, mostly alone, though his wife had gone with him once or twice. He'd come back the same way, the driver getting out and opening Pilgrim's door and then escorting him to his building.

At first the Montenegrin worried he'd draw attention to himself, sitting in a parked car in this affluent neighbourhood for hours on end. But then he noticed others doing the same, from similar cars, cheap Opels, rusty Volvos, Fords. It puzzled him at first, but then he realized it was husbands dropping off their wives for night-cleaning jobs. Some worked for only a couple of hours, and the husbands would wait. Or they'd come back early in the morning. He was just another waiting husband, another poor immigrant.

It was the third week of this slow, methodical surveillance. He had another month to work out how to get the job done in a way that got him out of the country safe and anonymous.

Maybe if he spoke Swedish as well as the boy did. He got by on his English and German but ... No, it didn't matter what language he spoke. Even if he succeeded, he'd never escape Pilgrim's security.

Except that evening there was no security.

It was after eleven o'clock when the film ended. His feet were numb. He ought to have bought felt-lined boots, like the Korean-made pairs he'd seen the Kurdish immigrants wearing in the suburb where he was staying. The cinema doors opened and people spread into the deserted street like oil from a ruptured pipe. The crowd broke up into couples and small groups, some of whom passed the Montenegrin, talking animatedly before dispersing into the night.

He felt a sudden panic when he saw people emerging from around the corner. There must be a second exit. He swore under his breath but restrained himself from racing round to see whether Pilgrim had used it. If Pilgrim was going to the same metro station he'd arrived at, he would have to pass this way.

Pilgrim. The Montenegrin didn't understand why he'd been

given that code name. Or who chose it. The man seemed nei-ther religious nor holy.

But where was he? The Montenegrin grew anxious. Maybe he'd been absorbed into the parting crowd. He'd worn a non-descript overcoat and hat, was of average height and build. Bundled up against the cold, he could have been any middle-aged man.

The Montenegrin's thoughts adjusted to failure, returning to what he needed to do over the coming days, weeks, willing patience in himself. But he couldn't suppress the ripple of re-gret. He grimaced at the acres of time he would have to spend on dull surveillance, the mountain of work ahead. He'd wait until the cinema crowd had disappeared and then drive back to the suburbs. Sleep and then start again early tomorrow.

The Montenegrin was cold. Even the short walk back to the car would be a chore. But his discomfort, his gloom, evapor-ated in an instant, his focus narrowing sharply again when he saw, from across the light flow of traffic, Pilgrim exit the cin-ema. The man and his wife were among the last to leave.

They and another couple stopped under the cinema's rigid awning, talking in a huddle, as people did in these cold places. There was a lack of formality in the encounter, though it wasn't overly animated, suggesting they saw each other frequently. The couples exchanged kisses and broke off.

The younger couple walked towards the Montenegrin, but Pilgrim and his wife turned in the opposite direction. Whatever they were doing, they weren't taking the route they'd come by.

It could be that they were going to walk home. Or perhaps they were walking to the other metro station, just beyond the stairs he'd parked by. One stop less for them to travel.

The Montenegrin crossed two roads—he resisted taking the shorter diagonal route for fear of drawing attention to himself—keeping an eye on Pilgrim and his wife as they am-bled down the long main avenue, which was lined with young trees, their bare, dark trunks made stark by the street lights. His gloveless hand was in his pocket, securing the revolver's heft against his thigh.

The couple was fifty metres ahead of him. A plan coalesced as he drew closer.

His shirt was clammy with sweat. White fluorescent street lamps cast a hard-steel light on the night. The couple came to a white church set in an open space; it looked almost Orthodox, except for its tall, domed tower. They crossed the main road and stopped to look at a window display. The Montenegrin had narrowed the gap enough to slow down, carrying along on his side of the road, walking the length of the church. When he reached the end of the block, he crossed over, waiting at the traffic light as he'd seen Swedes do.

He took a few strides along a smaller perpendicular street so that he could see when the couple came to the intersection. It was risky. It meant they'd be out of sight. But it also meant they wouldn't notice him when they resumed their walk.

He stood in front of a lit stationer's window, wishing his daughter could hold the expensive colouring pencils on display, which he would dearly love to buy for her. He tried to push her out of his thoughts. To focus. Solo surveillance was hard. Teams of three or four, or better yet, two teams of three were ideal. How he wished he had the people to do this job properly. Professionally.

He mocked himself for wishing the impossible. Why not just wish his wife back to life?

A young man brushed past him, absorbed in the headphones of his Sony Walkman, a miracle of Japanese engineering. Maybe he should buy one for his daughter. That was something she might enjoy more than pencils. He breathed steadily, consciously, the crisp air making him cough.

He looked up and saw Pilgrim and his wife at the intersection, only metres away from him, continuing along the main avenue, walking a little more briskly now.

The Montenegrin looked around to make sure no one else was following. The street was nearly empty. He turned the corner, lengthening his stride so that he caught up with them before they'd made it halfway along the block.

He was directly behind the couple, though they didn't seem to have noticed him. He put his arm over the man's shoulder and said *"Hej"* in a hearty tone. Pilgrim looked up at him, startled, as did his wife.

They smiled as if they felt they ought to know him, yet doubt creased their foreheads. It happened to famous people frequently. People recognizing them but not knowing quite why, thinking perhaps they were old acquaintances. The woman said something to him in Swedish. The Montenegrin exhaled a little sigh of relief. He'd confirmed the target to certainty. There was no mistake.

The couple kept glancing nervously at the silent stranger in the cheap coat. He stepped away from them, almost apologetically, and they kept walking, perhaps slightly faster, though it was hard to tell.

They hadn't gone more than a couple of metres before the Montenegrin started following again, hand deep in the overcoat pocket, gripping the butt of the gun, index finger straight beside the trigger. With a practised thumb he cocked the gun as he drew it out of his pocket, and in a smooth move he slid his finger between the trigger and its guard.

The red and white muzzle flame was brief and bright against the city's hollow artificial light.

The first bullet took Pilgrim down. The second, fired immediately after, was wasted.

Pilgrim fell hard, in the way the Montenegrin had seen other men fall, not even twitching once he'd hit the ground.

He was at the bottom of an alley that led up to a set of stairs, near the top of which he'd parked his car. He jogged away from the dead man, along the alley and then up the stairs, which he took two at a time, keeping his right hand in his pocket to prevent the still-warm gun from falling out and gripping the rail with the other.

Halfway up, he stopped, thinking he could hear footsteps behind him.

But from below there rose only the echo of a woman's scream, a howl of horror and agony.

He counted as he climbed. Eighty-nine steps.

Soon people would be coming. Very soon.

The car wasn't far now. He knew this was only the start of a very long night. But it had been a good beginning. A lucky one.

Behind him Pilgrim lay prone, his wife kneeling, keening, by his side.

Olof Palme, prime minister of Sweden, was dead.

ALEN MATTICH was born in Zagreb, Croatia, and grew up in Libya, Italy, Canada, and the United States. He went to McGill University for his undergraduate degree and then did post-graduate work at the London School of Economics. A financial journalist and columnist, he's now based in London and writes for *Dow Jones* and the *Wall Street Journal*. The second Marko della Torre novel, *Killing Pilgrim*, will be published in fall of 2013.

ACKNOWLEDGEMENTS

It should go without saying, but all the characters and situations in this story are works of fiction. There is no political subtext, only a desire to entertain.

I owe thanks to many people. The ones who had the most direct input into the creation and publication of this story are, in their order of appearance, Lucy Vinten Mattich, Andrew Steinmetz, Luke Vinten, Hilary McMahon, Gren Manuel, and Janie Yoon. To them, my boundless gratitude.

But above all I'd like to thank my children, Pippa, Tilly, Kit, and Bee. Their wit, joyfulness, hard work, and perseverance taught me that much can be achieved on the strength of discipline, effort, and revelling in what you do.